ALSO BY JAC JEMC

False Bingo

The Grip of It

My Only Wife

A Different Bed Every Time

EMPTY THEATRE

MCD  FARRAR, STRAUS AND GIROUX NEW YORK

EMPTY THEATRE

Or, The Lives of King Ludwig II of Bavaria and Empress Sisi of Austria (Queen of Hungary), Cousins, in Their Pursuit of Connection and Beauty Despite the Expectations Placed on Them Because of the Exceptional Good Fortune of Their Status as Beloved National Figures. With Speculation into the Mysterious Nature of Their Deaths.

JAC JEMC

MCD
Farrar, Straus and Giroux
120 Broadway, New York 10271

Title-page banner art, display type, and chapter opener ornaments
by June Park.

Library of Congress Cataloging-in-Publication Data
Names: Jemc, Jac, 1983– author.
Title: Empty theatre: or, the lives of King Ludwig II of Bavaria and
   Empress Sisi of Austria (Queen of Hungary), cousins, in their
   pursuit of connection and beauty despite the expectations placed
   on them because of the exceptional good fortune of their status as
   beloved national figures. With speculation into the mysterious
   nature of their deaths / Jac Jemc.
Description: First edition. | New York : MCD/Farrar, Straus and
   Giroux, 2023.
Identifiers: LCCN 2022044447 | ISBN 9780374277925 (hardcover)
Subjects: LCSH: Ludwig II, King of Bavaria, 1845–1886—Fiction. |
   Elisabeth, Empress, consort of Franz Joseph I, Emperor of
   Austria, 1837–1898—Fiction. | LCGFT: Biographical fiction. |
   Satirical literature. | Novels.
Classification: LCC PS3610.E45 E47 2023 | DDC 813/.6—dc23/
   eng/20220919
LC record available at https://lccn.loc.gov/2022044447

Designed by Abby Kagan

Our books may be purchased in bulk for promotional, educational,
or business use. Please contact your local bookseller or the Macmillan
Corporate and Premium Sales Department at 1-800-221-7945, extension
5442, or by email at MacmillanSpecialMarkets@macmillan.com.

www.mcdbooks.com • www.fsgbooks.com
Follow us on Twitter, Facebook, and Instagram at @mcdbooks

1 3 5 7 9 10 8 6 4 2

For Judy

The Sehnsucht motif, a lonely wandering voice in the night, softly uttered its tremulous question. Silence followed, a silence of waiting. And then the answer: the same hesitant, lonely strain, but higher in pitch, more radiant and tender. Silence again.

—THOMAS MANN, "Tristan"

As long as I have a want, I have a reason for living. Satisfaction is death.

—GEORGE BERNARD SHAW, *Overruled*

EMPTY THEATRE

Prologue: An Omen

✳ ✳

FORTY YEARS FROM NOW, Ludwig II will be murdered: by himself; or by the doctor who had declared his mind unsound; or by an assassin hired by disgruntled statesmen; or by fear and ambition—his own or that of others; or by the gentle, nudging tide of the Würmsee; or by some symphony of these; or by none of them.

His body will be found, drowned in the shallow of the reeds, his doctor floating a few feet away; his jacket turned inside out on dry land missing a bullet hole's worth of fabric, or not.

His cousin, Empress Sisi of Austria, waiting across the lake, will think she hears a cry and pace the shores, wondering if her kindred could possibly be strong enough to swim all that way.

But before that—because the story will unfold no differently if you learn the outcome now or later, because the ending will confound you no matter where it finds you, because if you combine enough answers they don't look much different than a question—it is best if you know

now: before Ludwig II is found dead, he will *live* with such a violence of feeling that his body will shake when he witnesses extreme beauty; when, onstage, Elsa makes the mistake of asking the Knight of the Swan his true nature and learns that he is, in fact, Lohengrin, protector of the Grail, Ludwig's sensitivity will force him from his box seat to throw up in a bucket positioned just out of view of the audience. Ludwig will invert his fortune by paying for operas he cannot afford. He will call for castle after castle to be built, never finishing a single one, his vision always outpacing the material world.

Ludwig will row out to a small, secluded island and snag his way through rosebushes—Alpenfees and Eurydices and Gretels, the names of which he prefers cupping in his mouth to lacing their sweet perfumes through his nose—tucking himself into their sturdy leaves and buxom blossoms, trying to escape bad news, but it will find him, again and again.

After all of this, Ludwig's cabinet of ministers, frustrated, maybe even convinced they are in the right, will declare him mad. They'll make a list of his indiscretions and read it so many times, they'll lose track of which items are bolstered by evidence and which will crumple under the slightest stress, like a plaster model never replaced by its marble heir. Rightfully. Wrongfully. They will pay a doctor to guarantee Ludwig's lack of sanity without having met him and they will depose him and lock him away in a castle-cum-asylum.

———

This is after Ludwig has been named King at eighteen, a young man forced to rule too young, a romantic hero to the Bavarian people, crowned with a job he was not designed for.

Born seven years before her cousin, Sisi will always treat Ludwig like a little brother, sharing her own experiences on this parallel path of royal obligation, but her powers of empathy will repeatedly be pushed to their modest limit. The demands placed on an empress are different than those exacted from a king. Sisi will lose an infant, resent a daughter to the point of neglect, suffer the suicide of her son, and suffocate a fourth child with all of the devotion she denied the others. She will flaunt her loyalty to the Kingdom of Hungary, even to the point of snubbing the Austrian Empire. Deemed the most beautiful woman in Europe in her youth, she will stop sitting for portraits at age thirty-two; in fact she will stop sitting almost entirely, filling her days with walking and riding to keep her figure trim, shrinking herself to hide from all those prying eyes. Sisi will wander as far away as she can—to the countryside of England, Madeira, Corfu—in an attempt to gain control of the life she feels has been stolen from her. Thirteen years after Ludwig's passing, Sisi will meet her own dramatic end: on a stretcher in a Swiss hotel, bleeding out from an Italian anarchist's stab wound, the ambivalent martyr of Austria's last grasp at remaining a major European power.

But first, before all of this can happen, Otto Friedrich Wilhelm must be born.

In Tribute

※　※

ONE HUNDRED ONE CANNON SHOTS pummel the air to announce the good news. On this, the 25th day of August, 1845, a prince has been born.

Crown Princess Marie Frederike—whose son Otto Friedrich Wilhelm has just emerged from her, like the pit pulled from a cherry—glances at him for only a moment, nodding once—like she is agreeing that a bottle of wine is fit to drink—before he's passed to the wet nurse.

King Ludwig I, the child's grandfather, receives the good news while riding on horseback in a parade through the streets of Munich celebrating his own birthday, a national holiday. "What marvelous luck!" he exclaims, for the child has been born at the same hour, even, as he, on the feast of the patron saint of Bavaria, St. Louis, his namesake. King Ludwig I pulls on the reins to turn back to the palace, so he might request, in the way only kings can *request*, that the child's name be changed to match his own.

———

Prince Maximilian, never even having laid eyes on his firstborn son, agrees easily to the name change. "If it matters so much to the old man, so be it."

His wife, the Crown Princess—a straight arrow all the way, fond of errands of exertion and sharp air, a trait to be inherited by her son in the form of midnight rides through the snowy mountains—is unable to hide her displeasure. "The newspapers have already been notified," she says.

"But have they been printed?" Prince Max asks. "And even if they have, how great an expense could it be to have them *re*printed? It is a remarkable coincidence, you must admit."

"Fine, then." The Princess rakes her resignation over her vocal cords. "Perhaps if our son shares the name of his grandfather, he will inherit, too, his backbone, for that has obviously skipped *your* generation."

When Ludwig I meets Ludwig II, he tells the infant loudly—the grandfather's hearing being rough and deaf to nuance—the tale of their hallowed patron. "We are named after Louis IX of France, sponsor of the arts and architecture. Fair and just above all, a man of frugality, and you are destined for such a life of vision and advocacy."

But Grandfather Ludwig has not yet met the greatest calamity of his own life, a woman who will put pressure on every angle of his virtue, who will collapse his good intentions. Ludwig I does not yet know to warn Ludwig II that he might suffer the same strain of crisis. He does not mention that the Crusades, in which Louis IX fought, marked one of the darkest moments of human history, a pure and unveiled campaign of extermination, erasure, intolerance. Ludwig I tells Ludwig II only of the beauty and grandeur that await him, and sings him an old lullaby as the baby gambles against sleep:

> We proud children's men
> Are poor and vain;
> We do not know much,
> but spin spirits of the air
> We look for many arts,
> but come further from our goal.

The child bursts into tears.

Crown Princess Marie Frederike visits her son daily. Even if he's feeding at the time she arrives, the Queen asks that the wet nurse leave them alone. Interrupted and hungry, Ludwig cries—rooting, rebuffed.

More than once, Crown Prince Maximilian hears the wails of his son in the courtyard below and looks out, ready to send a servant to insist the Prince be brought inside, ready to reprimand the nurse for not better tending his son's needs. More than once, he sees his wife holding the screaming child and shuts the window instead.

In Which Devotion Is Born

✳　✳

SOME SIX MILES AWAY at the summer palace Possen-hofen, on the banks of the Würmsee, Elisabeth, affectionately known to her family as Sisi, learns of the birth of her cousin Ludwig.

At seven years old, with two older siblings and three younger, it's not as though Sisi has any shortage of playmates, but she does love a reason to show off. Her home is an idyllic place where her father, Duke Max—not to be confused with Prince Max of Bavaria—plays the zither and her mother, Princess Ludovika of Bavaria, complains about his lack of skill.

Sisi is allowed to ride her favorite pony the thirty miles around the lake in a loop with a chaperone, and the only thing that brings her greater joy is when her father invites over members of the circus to teach her riding tricks.

A new cousin to whom Sisi can show off her formidable skills? A dream come true. Sisi knows it will be years before the baby is old enough to register awe, but she can be patient. "Can we send my cousin a gift?"

"Your father has already composed a song for little Ludwig," Ludovika tells her.

"But *I'd* like to send something," Sisi says. "A bouquet of jasmine from the garden?"

"Of course, darling," her mother says.

"Every day until I am allowed to meet him?"

Ludovika, despite the extravagance of such a request, agrees. "As long as you pick the flowers, I will have them delivered." Ludovika assumes Sisi will tire of this task, but her determination is as tenacious as the delicate white buds that pepper the arbors.

For the rest of his life, Ludwig will love the herbal stir of jasmine and never wonder why.

A Matter of Taste

✳ ✳

WHEN LUDWIG IS SEVEN MONTHS OLD, his wet nurse dies of typhoid fever. The picky child won't accept any other's milk for days. The doctor urges Princess Marie Frederike to offer her son her help, but she can't bring herself to make this sacrifice. Ludwig's body weight halves itself, and the women charged with his care worry they might lose the child if a solution isn't found soon. Another beautiful young nurse runs to the kitchen and returns with a bottle of arrack. She rubs a little of the coconut-flower liqueur on her nipple and Ludwig finally latches with fervor.

"The Prince knows what he likes," the nurse says with a smile, and her companions laugh for the first time since losing their friend the week before.

An Interruption, with Insight into Matters of Legacy

✳   ✳

A DANCER ARRIVES TO MUNICH in time for Oktober-fest. A festival created to commemorate the wedding of Grandfather Ludwig I's marriage to his wife, Queen Therese, in 1810, now marks a celebration of Bavarian nationhood—both matters to be challenged by the nimble visitor.

Born Marie Dolores Eliza Rosanna Gilbert, this dancer has made a different name for herself. Posing not as Irish, as her origins allow, or even Indian, as her upbringing might lend credence to, but Spanish, she has come to be known by the world as Lola Montez, the woman who gets what she wants.

Accepting all variety of favors from her wealthy fans, it is possible even she might privately define herself as more a courtesan than a dancer, though of course she'd never admit this to anyone. Arriving in Munich armed with a vitae of lovers including piano it-boy Franz Liszt and epic novelist Alexandre Dumas, Lola won't stop short of the highest conquest: a king. At the police station, registering for the Strangers List, Lola is unable to produce any of the official paperwork she's required to submit, and in the field labeled "Accompanied by," she smiles to herself as she writes, "un chien," referring to her sole companion, her dog, Zampa. Already, the wake of trouble forms behind Señorita Montez. Her influence spins its skirts.

Ludwig I puts down the Cervantes he's reading to receive a letter from the director of the Royal Court Theater: "The well-known Spanish dancer, Lola Montez, has arrived and requests to dance on this stage during the intermission of our play, *The Enchanted Prince*. In past visits to other theaters, police intervention was necessary due to the public offense prompted by said dancer, but she tends to deliver considerable profit with her appearances. Your Majesty's most obedient and devoted servant requests your counsel . . ." Ludwig I pauses here and replies, asking that Lola pay him a visit to explain her transgressions in person.

On a foggy October morning, Lola arrives to the Residenz in a fiacre, despite the short distance between the Promenadeplatz where she is staying to the Max-Josephplatz. To make money, one must have money, and renting a carriage so that she might convince the palace of her good breeding and ample means seems well worth the investment.

A military adjutant greets her at the wide doors and takes her up the grand staircase to the royal apartments.

———

The King finds himself immediately caught in the net of Lola's beauty. He sees first her luminously pale bosom, the fine features of her face, and then allows his eyes to wander over the form of her black velvet dress and matching crown of hair, the dark setting off the light so beautifully, a chiaroscuro of the flesh. He pauses and remembers to speak. "Hola, bella dama!" he says. Lola curtsies deeply, and on her rise, he kisses her hand.

Lola tells the King of her desire to perform on the stage. She pantomimes a short but not half-hearted version of her "Spider Dance." She lifts her skirt just above the ankle to show her delicate foot stomping the invisible pest. With a spinning flourish, she strikes a tableau, and breathes deeply.

The King can't help but eye her neckline. "Nature or art?" he asks.

Lola, never blind to an opportunity, corsetless because of the athleticism of her performances, tears off her bodice, revealing the answer to the King.

"I see," he says, hard of hearing, his sight, though, fully intact. He knows his power in this position, but restrains himself. He is a married man, leery of spies and the rumor mill. He must ensure that Lola can be trusted. He steps out of the room and asks that the court seamstress be called to his chamber.

When the dressmaker arrives, she struggles to hide her shock, and Ludwig attempts to ease her concern. "A pity that ladies must be elbowed into dresses so tightly that the threat of their bursting might occasionally come to fruition," the King says, knowing she will not press the issue. The seamstress stitches an extra panel of fabric into the gown, hurrying her needle along the seams and then herself out of the room.

When Ludwig I bids Lola adieu, he tells her how happy he is to have met her.

Lola quotes her friend George Sand: "There is only one happiness in this life, to love and be loved." She smiles sweetly and curtsies again, backing her way out of the room with such steady grace that Ludwig imagines a spider descending its silk.

"I will see you on the stage," he says.

The orchestra strikes into "Los Boleros de Cadix" and Lola holds her pose, looking for the King in the center of the ring of boxes, but she doesn't see him. She begins the cachucha, tapping her castanets together, languidly weaving her arms above her head, jutting her small foot into the light. The tempo picks up and her movements become more passionate. She dashes around the stage as if chased by a spider and then reverses roles and pretends she is the predator, pursuing her prey. When the orchestra sounds its final note, she smashes the arachnid and freezes in place. She finds Ludwig with friends in one of the side boxes and holds his gaze for the entire round of applause.

What follows can be told like any number of myths read to little Ludwig II: A King falls hard for a con artist. The King believes every lie she tells: about her origins, about her unwavering desire for him, about her innocence.

And in the meantime, Ludwig I has her painted so he might add her to his Gallery of Beauties. He awards her a seat in the Court Theater that she has reupholstered in red velvet, so that even when she is not in attendance, the King

will be reminded of her love. He waits patiently to consummate their feelings, claiming to be her first and only
love, unaware of her still living husband and the string of
affairs she's conducted through the capitals of Europe; believing her to be younger than she actually is; completely
convinced that she's as Spanish as she claims to be. She is a
master of her disguise, keeping all of her former versions
neatly out of sight. Meanwhile, the rest of Munich witnesses, through the numerous wide-open windows of the
house the King has purchased for Lola on the Barerstrasse,
Lola cycle through a series of escorts: the young Lieu-
tenant Nussbammer, who comes to her defense when she's
accused of being a *Goldgräber* on the street; Fritz Peissner,
the head of the student union protesting and then flipping
to protect Lola's increasing influence; the majority of the
other students in the Alemannen Fraternity, too.

Lola presses Ludwig to increase her allowance and then
the wages of teachers, and this is where real damage is done.
It is here, where she pushes into politics, that the people
begin to object. She spits on people and pulls guns on them
in the street and challenges them to duels, and Ludwig dismisses these behaviors, calling them "passion." The police
plant a spy in Lola's house to confirm her affairs, and Ludwig vows to break with her, but she wins him back by denying everything that she has been accused of.

Ludwig's family expresses their concern. His sister
writes, "The world forgives this type of thing in young
men, but in old men . . . Release her hand from you, fill it,
give her money, lots of it if necessary, as long as she leaves.
Use your mind, use your will! I pray to God to help you."
Ludwig doesn't offer her money to go, but multiple members of court do. Lola knows, though, that the King has

the deepest pockets. Ludwig sees her persistence as proof, only, of her love. He orders another portrait of Lola, but the painter adds funereal flowers to her hair and a belt of snakes. Behind her a headsman's block and axe wait menacingly and a newspaper proclaiming her former lover Dujarier's death by duel sits open before her. Ludwig demands the portrait be painted again and, at the next session, Lola sics her dog, Zampa, on the painter's white pet peacocks. Lola gives Ludwig an alabaster model of her foot as a thank-you gift for his devotion to her. In exchange he naturalizes Lola without the approval of the Council of State. Mobs form in protest outside her apartment and she toasts them from her balcony, spilling the champagne onto their heads.

The Pictorial Times of London publishes a long list of facts about Lola, revealing her true age, origin, marital history. Lola panics at the thought of Ludwig believing a word of the list, and sends off a batch of corrections—all lies, but Ludwig accepts them. It's possible he no longer cares about the truth.

Finally, Lola and the King have sex, but Lola warns him that they mustn't make a habit of it. Lola, after all, is young and fertile, and every union is a risk. Ludwig, showing the flexibility of his understanding of her, asks if she's borne any children before, but Lola insists that she has just lost her virginity to the King. Ludwig discards this curiosity to revel in his virility. "I am Vesuvius, which seemed burned out, until it suddenly erupted once again!"

Lola clips pieces of flannel from a blanket and wears them under her corset, then sends them with notes to the King on the days they don't see each other. The letters also contain complaints. "If you loved me, I would be a countess by now."

Lola tells a servant to load her empty suitcases onto a carriage and to let it be known she's leaving Bavaria altogether.

Ludwig rushes to her home to stop her.

Lola, having been poised at the entrance to her carriage for over an hour to create the perfect tableau, delivers her speech when Ludwig arrives: "I cannot stay amid spies and enemies. If I stay, you must promise me that we will make quick work of establishing my position in the court."

Ludwig agrees readily and Lola steps down from the carriage, making a show of lugging one of her suitcases.

"You shouldn't carry your own luggage," Ludwig says, pulling the case from her hand to pass it to a servant, but the case is light because it is empty. The servant fails to make eye contact and Lola, too, has already turned away, daring the King to demand an explanation. Ludwig considers his options and lets it go.

"Come for a ride with me. It has been too long since I've driven myself." Ludwig helps Lola into the seat beside him. The two ride through the countryside until the sun begins to set, reveling in their anonymity. They strategize: Ludwig advocating for patience and tact, and Lola recommending brute force. Back at Lola's apartment, the King lays kisses on every inch of her, from her mouth to the tips of her fingers and down each leg to the soles of her feet.

"Have you always loved feet?" Lola asks, hiding her revulsion.

"Only yours, mi amore. Yours are so delicate, but

strong. There is only one part of you I like more," he says, inching his hand up her leg, but she brushes him away.

Ludwig celebrates the consummation of their love by awarding Lola the title of Countess of Landsfeld and writing her into his will. October 8th is Ludwig and Lola's anniversary. She's been running this circus act for a solid year. Ludwig surprises Lola the night before. He enjoys their time together so much that, in the morning, he requests that her yearly salary be doubled. When the minister of finance recoils, Ludwig explains that maybe Lola will keep within her budget if it's a bit larger. The minister has a feeling this will not be the case, but he has learned better than to voice his opinions.

Lola is happy to hear the news, but there is always more to ask for. She asks when she might have a formal presentation at court, and Ludwig says he will broach the subject with Queen Therese.

Before the topic can even be avoided, though, the King receives a formal note from his wife, whom he sees every day. He wonders if the walls have ears. She writes, "I owe it to my honor as a woman—which is dearer to me than life itself—to never, under any circumstances, see face-to-face she whom you have raised in rank; should she seek to gain admittance at court, you can tell her, you know it for a fact—yes, from my mouth: the Queen, the mother of your children, would never receive her. And now, not one word more, either written or spoken, of this difficult matter. You will find me, as before, cheerful, grateful for every joy you give me, and ever watchfully endeavoring to maintain for you, my Ludwig, the untroubled tranquility of our home." The King sets down the note and resolves to be more secretive about his visits to Lola, finally having to face the fact that his wife knows what he's up to, but wishing he could protect her from the symptoms of that truth.

On New Year's Eve, the Alemannen line up to give Lola a kiss on the cheek at the party she throws for her devoted student guard. She promises her favorite, Peissner, that the King is nothing more than a father figure to her and dons his sash as he strips down to his underclothes in triumph. The other fraternity brothers do the same, unaware of the reason for their celebration, and hoist Lola onto their shoulders and parade her about the room until the Countess is run into the chandelier and knocked unconscious.

Two Alemannen settle her on the floor and press a napkin to the gash in her forehead, while others run to fetch a doctor. The men are so drunk they don't think to put their pants on before the doctor arrives, and everyone knows the best doctor is always the one with the best gossip.

The King fawns over Lola and her bandaged head, but can't resist asking what happened.

"You wouldn't believe me if I told you," Lola says.

But he would, and that's the trouble.

The armed forces request that they pledge their allegiance to the constitution rather than to the King, so damaged is their faith in Ludwig.

The students revolt. The King closes the university. Riots. Lola is forced to leave Munich, but she sneaks back in, over and over again, until Ludwig revokes her citizenship and exiles her. At this news, Lola writes, "Oh Louis, Louis, how you have betrayed me! After all I've suffered for you, chased from Munich for my devotion to you, your conduct appears strange and heartless. You are *truly weak*; now it is clear. Farewell. Later you will see your error. My conscience is clear and pure. I am forever, in the midst of your total abandonment of me, Your faithful and once beloved Lolitta."

All hail Lola, Queen of the gaslight, Countess of nothing.

Ludwig receives this note and makes his decision. He tells Lola before he tells anyone else. "Very dear Lolitta, to whom I am so, so devoted, within this hour *I have abdicated the crown*, freely. The choice was my own. My plan is to come to you in the month of April at Vevey, and to live there by your side. God knows when I would be able to see my Lolitta again without this. I put down the crown, but I cannot leave Lola."

King Maximilian takes the throne, but even this does not satisfy the people when they hear that Ludwig plans to visit Lola in Switzerland. They demand his allowance be cut off if he carries on with her.

"Isn't this why I gave up my power? So that I could do as I please?" Ludwig asks his son.

Max has sympathy for his father, but he cares more for Bavaria. "The rest of the world believes you abdicated for the good of the country, not for your mistress."

Ludwig delays his visit to Lola.

Her belongings arrive in Geneva: all fifty-six crates, all eight tons. Lola, though, does not have the cash to pay the freight bill. In fact, already, the collection letters have found her: from the jewelers, from the bread-crumb trail of hotels, from the florist supplying fresh arrangements to her every day. Finally, Lola must suffer the consequences of her own debts.

Lola begs Ludwig and blackmails him from afar, but the King is exhausted and knows he can't have what he wants and so why should Lola? There is no rehabilitating his reputation, and Ludwig can now see himself the way the people see him: a sucker, a dupe, one more spider crushed under Lola's heel.

Rights and Privileges

✳   ✳

A MONTH AFTER KING MAX INHERITS the throne from his father, in April of 1848, another Otto is born, brother to Ludwig II. This time, their grandfather has no opinion about the child's name and so Otto he remains.

The sight of his brother surprises Ludwig. He has not seen a baby before. This helpless nugget is not as worthy of his company as he had hoped. At the constant mewling of the infant, three-year-old Ludwig, accustomed to his nurse-maid's lullabies, shouts, "Otto, that is not singing!" and doubles his brother's screams with his own until the child is taken away.

Ludwig I visits and reads to his namesake. He draws out the story of the Holy Grail, the boy's attention rapt. He reminds Ludwig II, "You will be a king someday, too, like Arthur was and like I was." It stings Ludwig I to use the past tense, but his thoughts are quickly diverted as he watches the boy's vision cloud.

"I'd rather be Parsifal."

"You want to fight."

"No, I'd rather quest for the pretty things, for the things that give life meaning."

"Ludwig, you will be in charge of all of the people in this land. All that is theirs will be yours. Every cow in every barn, every cake in every kitchen, every home and every swimming hole: all of that will belong to you. Nothing is beyond limit. You needn't seek it, only protect it, nurture it."

Ludwig I can see Ludwig II's dreams transform behind his eyes.

Queen Marie Frederike walks the children through the mural-coated hallways out to the garden. She allows Ludwig to wander the hedges while she gazes at the infant Otto and feels . . . profound boredom. She worries her hands will tan in the bright June heat and calls to a servant for a pair of gloves. She stands to relieve the pressure of her corset pulling all that had previously been stretched to its limit into an internal mash, and Otto, lying on the edge of her skirt, falls off the bench. He screeches. She picks up the child quickly and traces him for bruises. The wet nurse emerges to take the baby and Ludwig's governess also appears.

"Where's my boy?" Fräulein Meilhaus asks.

The Queen doesn't like it when the governess refers to Ludwig this way. "Nearby. I heard his humming only a moment ago."

Fräulein Meilhaus calls, "Ludwig! It's time for your lesson!"

They hear a splash and a giggle, and there is the Prince, fully clothed, wading up to his waist in the fountain.

Once he is dry, Fräulein Meilhaus walks Ludwig through town. When he wants candy, she asks him to pick out the correct number of coins he needs to give to the clerk. The clerk bows to the Prince, thanking him for his business.

Back at the castle, the governess pulls books from the shelf for their afternoon lesson. When she turns, she sees Ludwig hide something behind his back. She holds out her hand and he turns over a cheap-looking blue-and-silver purse. "Did you steal this?" she asks.

Ludwig shrugs. "One day I shall be King and all that belongs to my people will belong to me."

Fräulein Meilhaus hauls him up by the arm. "Well, at that point you'll be able to do whatever you like, but for now you're under my watch. Come. You're going to return this to the shopkeeper."

Ludwig howls. His wrist aches as Fräulein yanks him along the winding road of Füssen. By the time they arrive at the shop, Ludwig's tears have stopped, but their crimson bloat remains.

The shopkeeper says, "Look at that face!"

"He's only sorry he's been caught," the governess says. "Come now, Ludwig. Apologize to the merchant."

He resists several moments longer before mumbling, "Entschuldigen Sie."

The shopkeeper wishes he didn't need to take part in this display. He'd seen the Prince pocket the purse earlier, but saw it as another tax nickeled and dimed.

———

Ludwig dreams of having a second self, one that could do all the nasty chores of his life, math and history lessons and physical drills, so that his true self might go about his day untroubled. Or his doppelgänger might be a playmate, a companion, someone who would surely go along with whatever Ludwig wanted because he would have the same wants and needs. Ludwig stares into his mirror, hoping to see the image in the glass make a move slightly different from his own, but he is not so lucky.

Christmas is spent making a feast for the residents of a children's home. Ludwig helps ladle out the liver dumpling soup and rotkraut. He suppresses his gags as he watches the children eat what he sees as slop. But his disgust at the food cannot sour him on the joy of doing something charitable.

In fact, he begs King Max and Queen Marie to allow him to return on New Year's Day to hold a lottery, giving out random presents to each child. Ludwig sees one girl particularly disappointed in the wooden doll that's been chosen for her and he hands her a delicate perfume bottle instead. The girl's eyes shine back at him, pledging gratitude and allegiance. Ludwig, too, would prefer a curio to a silly old toy.

This time Ludwig insists they serve the children the veal and wurst that he prefers. The orphans return to the counter again and again for seconds and thirds until they run out. For dessert, they have only plain vanillekipferl to offer. "Couldn't we have made a plum cake?" asks Ludwig.

Fräulein Meilhaus tells him that while they have enough to feed the two Princes, there are not enough plums in the kingdom to feed all these children. "And besides," she says, "look at how happy they are."

Ludwig takes a seat with some of them. "Do you like these cookies?" he asks.

A little boy looks deep into Ludwig's eyes and says, "They are the most delicious things I have ever tasted."

Fräulein Meilhaus feeds one of the cookies to Otto. He grins, still young enough to be indiscriminate. Ludwig sees the satisfaction on his brother's face as he gums the sweet and feels jealousy without understanding why.

Former King Ludwig I, smarting from the way all honor and duty have been stripped from him, distracts himself by pointing out the columns around the summer palace to his grandson. He names each one. He traces the shapes of windows and asks little Ludwig for answers. He speaks of exotic locales the boy might visit one day, and of the responsibility of a king to sustain his subjects with beauty and majesty, but little Ludwig stops paying attention when his grandfather mentions the necessary political and military duties that constitute the bulk of a king's work.

On the Origin of Discontent

ON THE OTHER SIDE OF MUNICH, Sisi breaks off from a game of tag to sit alone beneath a tree on the great lawn of Possenhofen. Her mother, perched on the terrace, notices her daughter sitting silently by herself, idly pulling out handfuls of grass and rolling them between her palms. Sisi doesn't watch the other children. She stares off into the distance and her mother wonders what it is she's thinking about. She worries about Sisi—the way she will not hold still for lessons. The tutor who tied Sisi to her chair has been fired, but Ludovika worries that damage has been done. When her sister's family had visited recently with her youngest children, Sisi hadn't said a word. She'd barely even looked up from her lap for the entire week, let alone play with her cousins. The other children have had similar spells over the years, but they have passed more quickly. It is possible, Ludovika thinks, that the Wittelsbach blood courses through Sisi more insistently than it does the others.

For all her life, Ludovika has been warned about the eccentricity that runs through the family line. That is the word that everyone uses—"eccentricity"—though the tone with which the word is spoken always lines the word with an omen. When Duke Max proposed to Ludovika everyone warned about the danger of doubling the Wittelsbach heritage. It had a history of filling aunts with delusions and uncles with obsessions, but she had loved Max then, and besides, as was often the case with these matters, their marriage would prevent the family's power from becoming diluted. The only reason to marry outside the family would be to gain a bit of ground somewhere, and the foreign liaisons available then would have provided no real advantage. Unlike her sisters, who had all married up, Ludovika was granted, as husband, her odd though charismatic cousin Max, who wished for nothing more than to run away with the circus. Understanding that she was being dealt an inferior hand, Ludovika vowed to raise her daughters in such a way that they would be granted the most beneficial unions available to them, even if their destinies were determined by the dreaded duplication of Wittelsbach blood.

Ludovika worried something might be wrong with Sisi from the start. From the moment she was born, Sisi had shown signs of this melancholy strain. If she had been colicky, that would have been one thing, but the infant Sisi fussed silently—often refusing to eat, sleeping far less than her brothers and sisters did, never wanting to be held. In fact, Ludovika had been astonished by the strength Sisi exhibited as a newborn and even a bit put off by the intuitive way in which Sisi could writhe her ten pounds around, insisting she be put back down in her bassinet. Still, people cooed over the contrast of Sisi's deep brown eyes to the bright blond of her hair. Hadn't the previous children tested the boundaries of Ludovika's love with their neediness?

With this baby demanding less of her time and attention these days, who was she to complain?

Indeed, Sisi has remained willful, getting more and more independent as the years pass. Ludovika is mostly proud of her daughter's refusal to rely on others. She hopes it will serve Sisi in the difficulties and trials that present themselves as she surges toward adolescence. It has been a joy to raise her children out of arms' reach of court life, but Ludovika wonders what complications this might cause for the girls, specifically. Boys are allowed their idiosyncrasies. Girls are supposed to be polite, blank slates onto which the rules and traditions of their family by marriage might be written. Ludovika promises herself to ask the new tutor about etiquette lessons. Such lessons might be a bit premature for Sisi, but they are overdue for Nene, and why not let them learn together? Perhaps her sister's company will help Sisi stay focused.

Now, watching Sisi holding up a single blade of grass against the sun, squinting, the duchess calls out to her. "Sisi!" Ludovika says, and her daughter looks over. "Come here! Papa needs a companion to go gather the fallen apples from the neighbor's yard." Sisi is up on her feet in no time, running to join her father in his petty theft, and Ludovika imagines herself as having saved the day. She has diverted another of Sisi's storm clouds from the clear sky of this otherwise perfect day.

A Survey of the Kingdom's Holdings

✳ ✳

A T FIVE, LUDWIG WEEPS HIMSELF TO SLEEP. He clings
to his governess when it's time for her to leave him for
the day. In the company of his parents for dinner, he dashes
his plate to the floor after he's eaten to get them to notice
him at all. Every morning, he delays getting out of bed for
as long as possible. It's not as though a boy this small can
know why he's doing such things, but we can: every day is
the same, and even when he finds ways to entertain himself, he is discouraged from those activities and told to do
something else instead. He is the freest he will ever be in
his life and he feels utterly restrained.

When he sneaks off to the buildings that pepper the
grounds, he can pretend himself away. He can distract himself with his imagined circumstances. He can talk to
himself as though he's a different playmate entirely.

Until at dinner, he is chided for his murmuring.

When no one is looking, Ludwig sneaks out to wander the
grounds of the Nymphenburg on his own.

In the Pagodenburg, he climbs to the second story and

looks out on his surroundings, imagining he is a noble-
man, not a ruler, but the romantic subject of some story far
enough from his daily life that he can yearn for something
else—not more than he currently has, just different.

In the Badenburg, he splashes around the room-sized
bath, thinking of his aunt Marie's obsession with cleanli-
ness. Her insistence on wearing the whitest whites so that
she might spot any fleck of dirt and change into a fresh set
of clothes. Still, she is not the most eccentric among his
family. His aunt Alexandra believes she once swallowed a
glass piano. When Ludwig visited her, he asked how it
might be, allowing his aunt to pull his hand to her belly so
he could feel . . . nothing at all. Aunt Alexandra had done
away with the whalebones the other women wear, convinced the corset would not fit around the piano caged inside her ribs. "Ludwig," his mother had said, snatching his
hand away, "we must be going. We will keep you in our
prayers, of course, Alexandra." As the door shut behind
them, Ludwig had sworn he heard the muffled smash of a
fist on keys.

"Mother, how could she fit a piano inside of herself?"
Ludwig had asked her as they boarded their carriage home
that day.

"Of course she hasn't, child. She is deluded. The Wittelsbach blood has turned in her. It happens sometimes,
and if you are not diligent, it might turn in you, too. You
must be careful never to fall too deeply into your imagination, for where most people's feet will find the sandy bottom, we tread our water farther out in the vast sea, and if
we lose our tread, we are certain to go under."

Always these metaphors to explain what needed to be
covered up and veiled and hidden, lest rumors spread. But

Ludwig can't help but trust Aunt Alexandra. If she feels a piano inside of her, how could she be wrong?

In the bath, Ludwig imagines all the things he might swallow whole if he is not careful: a rocking horse, a throne, a swan, the whole sun, his own self. He touches his belly and dreams of ways to both grow and disappear.

A groundskeeper shoos Ludwig away from the Magdalenenklause, but not before he can ask why they don't fix up the old building.

"It's supposed to look like that, I guess." The groundskeeper laughs. "I'm with you, kid. The whole place reminds me of a pile of bones, all those stones and seashells."

Ludwig wrinkles his brow. He tries to twist his mind to find the beauty in this place, and if he blurs his eyes just right he can see a hazy sort of aura around the mosaic. He thinks of the grottoes where Apollo's oracles lived—Delphi, Corinth, Clarus—and wonders who he will be.

Ludwig loves the Amalienburg the best. No one uses the small pleasure palace anymore, but the riot of rococo stucco and woodwork adorning the walls is kept polished just in case. In the blue-and-white tile of the kitchen, Ludwig pretends to be a beautiful young cook, unaware of her royal heritage, separated from her family on a hunting trip and raised by peasants who worked their way up into palace service. She stirs imaginary pots, and when invisible boiling oil splashes her hands, the smooth skin remains unmarred, so exquisite are her genes that it will not accept the offense of a burn. The family the Princess-cum-cook serves punishes her all the more for her beauty: the way her face doesn't dim with fatigue and hard work, and her spirits don't falter even when she is made to do the meanest tasks. A visiting Prince takes notice. Ludwig imagines him: broad, ruddy, noble. Despite her common dress, the Prince knows immediately that this servant must be of royal blood. No common person could be so flawless. He insists on marrying her, but his parents refuse. He would lose his spot in the royal line, and for what? But a series of coincidences reveal that the cook is indeed the long-lost Princess, the rightful heir to a throne, and the Regent has known all along, but kept it a secret to ensure his reign. Overnight the Princess has left her apron behind and is now a Queen, betrothed to the man who loved her when the world told him not to. Little Ludwig lies on the daybed in the bright light of the bedroom, regarding the pastoral scenes stacked on every wall, imagining the walks and rides the couple will go on together, feeling the Prince's strong embrace, until he hears the call of Fräulein Meilhaus, sitting outside, telling him it is time to work on his studies.

The King and Queen suggest Ludwig return to the orphanage to serve the children their dinner again the following Christmas, but Ludwig has lost interest. Instead he makes lists of what he desires: a song that can be heard only in the heart, a tropical bird that might sit on his shoulder, a tree big enough to live inside, something that is only special when he is around but changes back to normal when others are in the room.

But under the three-story Tannenbaum, he finds a

model train, a new set of blocks, a knife with a dozen blades flexing out, a portrait of Jesus praying on the Mount of Olives, a watch. He knows better than to be disappointed. He admires the book of prayers inlaid with ivory and a lapis lazuli cross, but when his mother opens it to suggest a prayer of thanks, he tells her to put it down or she'll get it dirty.

He uses his new blocks to model himself a castle, a mountain lodge, a sepulchre. He knows he must fashion happiness for himself.

At Berchtesgaden one afternoon, the family enjoys the view of the Watzmann mountain as they sting themselves into relaxation with sharp, fresh air.

Playing outside the hunting lodge, seven-year-old Ludwig hog-ties Otto and gags him. He knots a handkerchief around his thrashing brother's neck and, turn by turn, twists it tighter with a stick he's inserted into the binding. "I will behead you for your impudence!" he whispers as Fräulein Meilhaus shows up to separate them. Ludwig protests, "This is my vassal and he dared to resist my will! He must be executed!"

The Fräulein tells Ludwig, "The knife's edge between your reality and play could stand to be dulled!"

Ludwig whines while Otto, gasping for breath, scurries into the lodge.

Fräulein Meilhaus approaches the King's bedchamber, where he spends most of his day working at a desk too small for his tasks.

The King reacts to the news by stomping into the parlor. "Where is he?" he barks. The Fräulein informs him that Ludwig is in his room, but the King doesn't count the whereabouts of his children as essential knowledge. "And which room is that?"

If there is embarrassment in his voice, she doesn't hear it. She steps ahead of him, refusing to charge forward with his same urgency, forcing him to walk more slowly. "It's right here, Your Majesty." She sweeps her hand into the next open room and catches Ludwig's eye for only a moment before the King shuts the door behind him. She hears what sounds like a swift slap followed by a cry, and then a paddle hitting something both hard and soft: flesh-covered bone.

For days, Ludwig carries himself tenderly, and Fräulein Meilhaus hopes the Prince has learned his lesson.

Freedom

✹ ✹

SISI AND NENE RUN WILD in the forests around Possen-hofen. They explore every inch, learning all the best hiding spots, where it's cool and dry even on the most humid summer days. They mark their spots by leaving their hair ribbons tied to branches of trees and arranging stones in tidy cairns. They are free.

Even on days in Munich, the girls wander the streets without chaperones, trusted not to cause too much trouble while their father goes to accomplish whatever errand or recreation he's searching out that day. The girls spend some time quietly wandering the halls of the Alte Pinakothek, dreaming themselves into each artwork, but they can never stay focused for long, and eventually go back outside to chase one another through the parks and gaze in wonder at the rising structure of the new art museum being built nearby that former King Ludwig commissioned before stepping down from the throne. By the time their father finds them again, the girls are stuffed with pretzels and small beer, and ready to sleep through the carriage ride home.

Some nights, after a long day on the trails around the

lake, after she has brushed and watered him, Sisi sleeps in the pile of hay in the corner of her horse Hedwig's stall. The earthy smell of the stable is a comfort to her, and waking with the sun means a fuller day of riding to follow. The wind blows the straw from her hair and the wrinkles from her dress, but the scent of the stable imprints Sisi with a musk that is rare in a girl her age. When she arrives home in the afternoon, no one notices that her bed has not been slept in and that her breakfast has gone untouched, and that is precisely the way Sisi likes it.

The Collection of Beautiful Heads

❋ ❋

IN THE GALLERY OF BEAUTIES, Ludwig stares at the bright portraits of the women his grandfather admired. He can feel, even young as he is, that it is a shame that a prince should wish to be anyone else, but here, laid before him, are several dozen beautiful women—all with less power than him—even his mother and his grandfather's mistress Lola—and he would rather be any one of them: the shoemaker's daughter, the butcher's daughter, the bookkeeper's illegitimate daughter, the tailor's daughter, the cabinetmaker's daughter, all of those princesses and countesses and baronesses. In any of those roles he could disappear. He could keep on pretending, protected by the guise of his parentage or his spouse. He stares at each one and invents their inner lives: interests and dreams and petty inconveniences and pleasant daily routines that involve baths and salves and one hundred strokes of the brush before bed. He can imagine a different life for each of the women every day, and no future of his own.

"Your Highness, mightn't you like to go out and play?" Fräulein Meilhaus asks him.

"The play I'm doing here in the company of these beau-ties is all the more worthy, for it is happening purely in my mind," he replies, irked at the governess's ordinary way of governing.

A servant enters young Ludwig's chamber. The Prince catches sight of the man and turns to the wall.

"Master, your morning tea and biscuit," he says, wait-ing to be dismissed, but Ludwig refuses to address the ser-vant. The steward backs out of the room and reports the incident to the majordomo. "Prince Ludwig wouldn't re-lease me. He wouldn't even look at me."

The butler nods and sends a different servant to fetch the tea service later that morning. Ludwig catches sight of this young woman and, again, turns to the wall. The ser-vant can't take the tray away without permission, and so she, too, leaves without having completed her task.

The butler calls over the first servant to join the second and looks them both up and down. The first servant is pale, his chin crumpled back into his neck, his ears un-even. The second servant's eyes are heavy-lidded and small, her nose wide and her hairline low. The butler won-ders if it could be that Ludwig's tolerance has narrowed to exclude the more asymmetrical individuals on staff. Maybe all those hours in the Gallery of Beauties have tainted his acceptance of ordinary people. He dismisses the servants to their chores and hatches a plan.

The butler sends a pretty young maid, unsullied and vibrant, to retrieve the tea service next. She returns with the dirty dishes and reports a pleasant exchange with the

Prince. Later that evening the butler deploys a plainer servant to help Ludwig ready himself for bed, and this servant says that the Prince turned to the wall and failed to acknowledge his presence. The butler sends a handsome, tidy man to the Prince's chamber and he completes the task with ease.

The King does not thrash the child when the butler tells him about this newest development. Instead King Max asks his son, "What is the meaning of this? You're tolerating only the most handsome servants?"

Ludwig is surprised he's been caught at his game. Rather than trying to make excuses for himself or deny the accusations, he sits taller. "If I'm to promote peace and beauty in the kingdom, then I must surround myself with the same. It doesn't serve me to gawk at the unseemly."

The King scoffs. "On the contrary! You should encounter people of all types and never allow them to see the difference reflected in your face. As punishment, we'll ensure that only the servants you dismissed will wait on you moving forward until your behavior improves. May I remind you that you are *six* years old? *Six*. Not a king yet."

Ludwig cries out with frustration and the King excuses himself. "You heard all that, I assume," he says to the butler. The butler shakes his head. It is punishable by law to eavesdrop on the King's conversations. "Don't be foolish," the King says as he struts back to his chamber. "Only the repugnant monsters can serve the boy now. Find the most deformed and beastly staff and send them his way." The butler shudders and replies in the affirmative.

Back in the servants' quarters, he tells the three stewards refused by the Prince that they've been named Ludwig's caregivers. The servants know better than to cast glances at each other.

For the next week, the Prince transforms, but not in the direction they hope or expect. He goes from looking at the wall to crying out upon sight of the servants, rubbing his eyes as if they've been jabbed. He weeps and writhes about, resisting as they try to dress him, recoiling as if their touch scalds his delicate skin. He dashes his dinners to the ground and flees the room when a maid enters to conduct her quiet duties. When he sees one of the comelier servants in the hall or out on the green, he begs them to help him, to bring him something to eat, but they refuse, aware of the orders that have been given.

Eventually, the King relents, furious that he has to reverse his decision. He tells the butler to allow the child to pick who he'd like to wait on him, but Ludwig refuses the task of choosing. He insists this be done for him, so that he doesn't have to spend even a moment looking at the less attractive. The butler makes his best guess, and lines up the finalists, pretty as can be. The Prince still looks away. "Pick the stunning ones. Don't pretend you don't know who qualifies!" The butler resents that he's being forced to do this. The servants will hold it against him and not their Prince. For days, weeks even, they'll cast sideways glances at him for his insults.

The servants curl each other's hair with a heated knife sharpener. The cooks complain that the ceramic rods are covered with burnt strands. The ladies talk the men into letting them dust their cheeks with powder and rouge. Everyone is afraid of being dismissed. Servants faint in the halls from their restricted diets. Men pilfer razor blades from the King's barber to be sure their skin remains un-marred by the facial hair the Prince finds so grotesque. It is uncertain whether it's Ludwig's behavior that has im-proved or the beautifying efforts of the servants that have removed the need for his resistance.

When the King is informed that Ludwig's favorite type of play is dress-up—black curtains wrapped around him like a nun—Ludwig's father gives him lead soldiers, which Lud-wig immediately passes on to Otto. The King wonders if the wrong son was born first.

Ludwig reads *Stories for Little Boys: An Amusing Book for the Moral Improvement of Children*. He reads about a sailor and a baker and a woodcutter, imagining himself in each profession, but the book ends too quickly. "Is there another such volume?" he asks Fräulein.

"No," she apologizes, "I'm afraid there's only a version intended for little girls."

Ludwig pauses and says, "Well, that must be better than nothing."

When it arrives, Ludwig prefers it to the boys' volume. The little girls in this book do not have jobs so much as attributes. There is a slovenly girl and a sulky girl, a glut-tonous child and a cruel one. Ludwig notes their bad be-haviors with pleasure, building his store of possibilities.

Queen Marie asks Fräulein Meilhaus to take Ludwig's pet tortoise away. "He's grown too attached to it. He mothers the thing all day, swaddling it and feeding it with an eyedropper. He should be trying to set it on fire or something."

Fräulein Meilhaus waits for Ludwig to leave his room

before she can vacate the reptile. When he returns, she acts as if nothing has changed. "Where is Clever Hans?" Ludwig cries, lifting the bed skirts and peeking behind the couch.

"Who?" Fräulein Meilhaus asks, with a tilt of her head.

"My turtle! What have you done with him?"

"Is this another of your imaginary friends?" The governess feels a pang, wondering why this is the tack she's taken, but Ludwig rushes from the room, on the hunt.

That night, at dinner, Ludwig asks after the unusual texture of the meat in his soup.

"Chicken," his mother answers before a servant can say a word.

But the King sees this as a moment to bolster the boy's nerves. "Don't lie to the boy. It's turtle meat. A delicacy," he says.

Ludwig vomits his supper onto the floor. He doesn't cry, but excuses himself, his feet tracking through the puddle of sick. The disgusting trail should serve as a lesson to his parents, but it's the servants who will have to clean it up, so no one learns a thing from this cruel attempt at discipline.

Why Franzl Always Wears His Uniform

I N FEBRUARY 1853, Ludwig's cousin the young Emperor Franz Joseph goes out for a walk with an aide-de-camp on the ramparts. A man with a long, thin knife runs at them, the knife slicing off a corner of the Emperor's high uniform collar, leaving a gouge in his neck, but missing the artery. The aide wrestles the attacker to the ground and knocks him out.

The man's first words upon waking in the company of the police are "Long live Kossuth!," invoking the name of a Hungarian nationalist. Ludwig's cousin recovers, but the words of protest echo in the young Prince's mind: a threat and a warning that will haunt his expectations for his own future rule.

The attempt on Franz's life has made it all the more clear that he must marry immediately and produce an heir, in the event that some future attack proves successful, and his mother, the Archduchess Sophie, has just the candidate in mind. She calls up her sister Ludovika in Munich to ask her to pay a visit with her eldest daughter, Nene.

The Challenge of Empathy
✦ ✦

A T EIGHT YEARS OLD, Ludwig is separated from his governess and confidante, Fräulein Meilhaus.

The Queen introduces a new tutor to the Princes on a morning hike, and while attempting to win favor by scrambling up a steep rock to pluck some edelweiss, the tutor loses his footing and knocks his head bluntly on a stone. As his body pulses with a rigid tremor, the Queen tells Ludwig to get help, but Ludwig asks, "Can't someone else do it?" He struggles to tear his eyes away from the spectacle.

The following day Major General La Rosée takes the tutor's place. His first rule of order is that the boys will fraternize with only nobility. Ludwig tells the major general about his weekly trips to the countryside to pass out gifts to the peasants, and La Rosée tells Ludwig such outings will no longer be possible. Ludwig grabs a rug beater and gets in one good smack before the weapon is wrestled away.

At the end of the day, La Rosée pays a visit to the Queen

and releases an armful of blunt objects on the table before her. "I'll need a plain classroom: just a desk for myself and a table for the boys if I'm to get out alive. No decoration."

The Queen understands.

When Ludwig's behavior doesn't improve, the tutor recommends ice baths to calm the Prince's hyperactivity. Ludwig screams and struggles through the entire ordeal, but La Rosée keeps pushing him back in. "Why can't you behave like your brother? Be a good little frog!"

Ludwig writes letters to Fräulein Meilhaus begging her to return. The governess responds only with recommendations of things the Prince might enjoy: fairy tales, games, the opera she has just seen—*Lohengrin*.

When Ludwig asks to go see the performance, his parents refuse. "Wagner?" the Queen asks. "He's a revolutionary—and a bit maudlin, if you ask me. You're too young."

Ludwig wails and the Queen forbids the governess from corresponding with the boy again.

On a walk into town with Leinfelder, the court archivist, a beggar asks Ludwig for his charity, and Ludwig turns his pockets inside out to discover he's spent all he has. He asks Leinfelder if he might *borrow* a coin or two: Ludwig's first loan. Leinfelder complies, though the change he pulls from his pocket is the difference between his having chicken with his dumplings or not. Leinfelder knows he will never see the money again, but he is touched by the boy's benevolent soul and he does not know how to refuse him. Plain dumplings today in the hopes of the Prince's good graces for all the tomorrows to follow.

Yearning Love's Blessed Glow

✳ ✳

SISI WATCHES as her mother and Nene oversee the packing of their bags for the trip to the Austrian summer palace of Ischl to meet Emperor Franz Joseph. Sisi admires her beautiful older sister and imagines how perfectly Nene will inhabit the role of Empress. The girls have taken etiquette lessons together, to buff and polish their rustic upbringing, but Nene has absorbed the new skills more fully. Sisi is always forgetting some little propriety or another. Nene, however, is a master mimic. She is taller than Sisi and so all the more striking when she stands up straight and glides through her gestures with the new grace she's internalized by always looking straight ahead instead of down; she steps delicately on the balls of her feet, allowing a controlled bounce that never clunks like Sisi's forceful stride. It is all very proper and impressive, and it's sure to fit right into the formality of the Austrian court.

At Ischl, though, it's Sisi's natural energy that attracts Franzl's eye. He knows his mother doesn't like complications. He begs the Archduchess to marry the younger Bavarian princess instead. A cousin, after all, is a cousin, in terms of alliances. Despite Sisi's youth, the Archduchess must agree that there is something about Sisi's features that she can imagine handsomely combining with Franzl's in what she hopes will be a bevy of heirs. Any chance should be taken to override the reiterations of genes caused by so much inbreeding.

Sisi's portrait is painted as an engagement gift: clad in a black velvet habit, lace lining her throat and wrists, a plume of feathers tucked into her hat. On the day she presents the painting to Franzl, he suggests they go for a sleigh ride through the newly fallen snow, but the Archduchess stops the couple in their tracks. Sisi has one purpose alone as future Empress, and catching a chill or rattling her insides might endanger that purpose.

When Sisi returns home, she pens a letter to her aunt and future mother-in-law, thanking her for her hospitality and using the familiar form as she has for her whole life up until this point. The letter Sisi receives back is signed by Franz, warning Sisi to adhere to formalities. Sisi cries, already overwhelmed by the way her life is changing.

Sisi's first task to prepare for the wedding is to build her trousseau. She takes pleasure only in choosing her riding habits. Her mother picks everything else: seven formal gowns, fourteen high-necked silk dresses for everyday wear in winter and nineteen thin frocks for the summer— all with their accompanying petticoats, corsets, sleeve puffs, and crinolines, sixteen hats and fourteen dozen lace-trimmed sets of chemises, chemisettes, and pantalettes. Every day for months, Sisi and her mother trek to one convent or another to tailor a muslin mock-up of each dress to

Sisi's shape. They choose fabrics and make sketches of the embroidery patterns. Sisi feels guilty asking this work of the modest sisters, their own clothing so simple and unadorned.

"Do you wish you could wear such things?" she asks a young postulant.

"God is our husband and he doesn't care what we wear," the girl responds.

"I don't know that the Emperor gives a damn about all of this, either," Sisi snorts. "His mother does, though."

Ludovika replies, "She will also expect you to cease cursing and making your pig noises."

Sisi's ego bruises easily. Before, her mother had been charmed by her daughter's disregard for airs, but now she seems concerned only with Sisi's fitting into the role in which she's been cast.

In Munich for the official court ceremonies, Sisi invites Franzl to a performance of *William Tell*.

"Perhaps I am not being received as warmly as I thought," Franz responds.

"What do you mean?" she asks.

"Have you any idea what the play is about?" he asks. "The hero murders an Austrian ruler."

Sisi flushes and runs off to tell her father.

"That was no mistake, my dear. It is a reminder that our pride in Bavaria is still superior to any new allegiance to Austria."

Franzl, ever the good sport, though, attends. Sisi's stomach tumbles throughout the performance with nerves.

Afterward, Franzl shakes Duke Max's hand and says, "It is not one of my favorite plays, but the production was outstanding nonetheless."

"You are smart to have come. My daughter deserves a man who will face the challenges presented to him. I see you are just that," Duke Max replies.

Sisi watches on as she is passed from hand to hand.

A steady stream of doctors, priests, and lawyers descend to examine and assess Sisi.

Each prodding Sisi endures prompts a gift from Franz as an apology for the trouble. She threads a portrait of him onto a bracelet that rests just above her tepid pulse. A servant presents a bouquet that Sisi nearly drops, but when she focuses her eyes, she realizes it is so heavy because it is not plucked flowers but a cluster of carefully arranged diamonds. She wears her new sable-lined coat, even inside, and she trains her parrot to say, "Ich bin kaputt." *I am broken, I am broken, I am broken.* When people ask her why the parrot can't say more, she giggles and says, "He's already given you his answer."

As the wedding day approaches, Sisi sits alone in her room and cries. Despite her love for Franzl, she can't manage to expel a mantra from her head: "If only he weren't Emperor."

Husbandry

✦ ✦

In vienna, a new bridge is built across the river for Sisi's entry. Palms are planted all along the banks. Every dome in the city shines with a new coat of polish. Horses are freshly groomed and shod. The city attempts to match the beauty of its new Empress.

The Archduchess opens a case to survey what will be Franzl's wedding gift to Sisi, an intricate diamond crown. Her lace mantilla snags one of the prongs, and the crown crashes to the floor. The Archduchess scrambles to pick it up and sends it out to be repaired. The servants are sworn to keep the accident a secret, but one omen as serious as this is enough to cause everyone's eyes to begin hunting for more minor indications that the marriage will not end well. And indeed the warnings are everywhere: the auriculas, usually hearty by this time of year, haven't bloomed yet; the giraffe in the Schönbrunn Tiergarten escapes and somehow goes missing for an entire week; Cardinal Rauscher comes down with a case of influenza so bad that the Archduchess considers postponing the wedding. If people are looking for reasons these two should not be wed, there are plenty of anomalies to be interpreted as such.

But still, all pushes on. On April 22nd, the Viennese set out to picnic on the side of the grassy Leopoldsberg to watch Sisi enter the city.

She can't believe the number of people trying to sneak their eyes into her carriage. She can't imagine anyone could care so much about her.

The coach is shooed on to Schönbrunn, where she is greeted by a tiny woman. Countess Esterházy, with her sour mouth and puckered brow, curtsies. "I'm your lady-in-waiting. I'm to help you learn the manners of the Hapsburg court," she says.

The next morning, they set to work memorizing her lines for the many ceremonies she'll participate in. Sisi trips over her words as a team of people primp and polish her. They pile her hair artfully within the ring of a diamond crown. When she emerges from the Augarten Palace, she is nudged on before she can examine the Rubens paintings decorating the sides of her coach.

At the Hofburg, Sisi pushes a single delicate foot through the carriage door. She gathers her skirts and the crown catches on the doorframe. Her hand goes to it and the crowd gasps. The Archduchess, standing steps away from her son, recognizes the echo of her own mistake. Franzl offers Sisi his hand. Her dress takes so long to emerge from the coach that the crowd believes it might be some magic trick. Those standing near the front of the mass of people see that her skin is palest pink rose and her cheeks just a shade past that, like tight peony buds. Her complexion contrasts beautifully with her chestnut hair and her dark, warm eyes. Every feature of her face is architecturally arranged, delicate but strong, to stunning effect. She is tall and slender, with a swiftness to her step. To the people standing farther back, she is a blur of energetic grace. This is her formal introduction to Vienna. Tomorrow she and Franz will be married.

On the 24th morning of April, 1854, Sisi and Franzl leave the Hofburg for the Church of the Augustinians, a few hundred meters away. The procession inches along for an hour.

Sisi's white-and-silver dress, covered in fresh myrtle blossoms, grows tighter around her in the heat. When she finally passes through the doors of the church, the atmosphere inside is all the more stifling because of the thousands of attendees contending for the little bit of oxygen left. Sisi blinks her way up the aisle to Franzl, who leads her to the high altar to kneel on the prie-dieu.

The ceremony alternates between the Emperor's commanding pledges and Sisi's breathless replies. The audience angles farther and farther forward, searching the air for her answers until the shock of guns and church bells jolts them back into place as Sisi slides the ring onto Franzl's finger.

Sisi wishes she could run from the church, but the couple must kneel again, to listen to the clichés the Cardinal has to share about the strength of the empire. The sun withers to nothing in the sky before Sisi and Franzl are allowed to struggle back down the aisle. Sisi wants to clap her hands to her ears against the roll of kettledrums and the caw of trumpets. The fake privacy of the stuffy glass carriage provides only a small amount of respite in the hour it takes them to return to the palace.

In the throne room, Sisi and Franzl collapse in their seats. The stays of Sisi's corset dig into her hips. Her neck aches from the weight of her long hair wrapped around the heavy crown. When Sisi's hand grows tired from holding it up for kisses of congratulations, she is brought a small cushion on which it might rest. Noble after noble coats her hand in cottony spittle. The couple moves to the dining room with only their immediate family, but Sisi can't think of eating, nauseous at the thought of what else the evening holds. While the others finish their meals, her mother shows Sisi to a back hallway, where a dozen pages light her way with candelabra.

The Countess Esterházy and four maids undress the bride and tuck her in. Sleep pulls at Sisi right away, but a knock at the door awakens her. It is the Archduchess silhouetted in the light of the hall. "May you be fruitful," she says, before stepping aside to reveal Franzl.

The door closes, and Franzl undresses, crawling into bed. Sisi tries to will herself to turn to him, but his snores sound first.

The following night the couple sits at a table perched above a hundred guests. Sisi talks to every single one, and afterward, again, they welcome sleep before any other milestones can be achieved.

But on the third night, Franzl finds her beneath the sheet. He is exceedingly gentle, even apologetic, which does little to calm Sisi's nerves. When he climbs atop her, he has trouble finding the way they fit together. He asks for guidance, but Sisi hasn't the slightest idea how this is supposed to work. Franzl has at least dallied. Sisi squints through the act. She finds the ordeal mostly unpleasant, except for the comfort of wrapping her legs around him. She imagines she is being allowed to ride a horse like a man does, not sidesaddle, but astride, feeling the power of the animal more closely. Before Franzl finishes, Sisi finds the perfect metaphor to describe his breath: a belching steam pipe.

On the morning of the fourth day, Sisi and Franzl eat breakfast with the Archduchess, and Sisi wonders if this is how it will always be, their marriage lived under motherly surveillance.

The Archduchess is in a giddy mood, and Sisi realizes it is because of the mark left on the bedsheet. Sisi can't bring herself to respond to a single question.

Later that day Sisi steps out of the Hofburg, to the protest of her ladies-in-waiting, but she doesn't get past the front step. The crowds of people who chant her name alert the Archduchess to Sisi's departure. "What on earth do you think you're doing?" she asks.

"Going for a walk," Sisi says.

"An Empress cannot go for a *walk on the street*. You're welcome to visit the palace garden in the company of a guard."

Sisi returns to her room. Who would choose this limited life? After being raised with such liberty, it is impossible for her to see any of the luxuries she is now allowed as an improvement. She is required to give up too much in exchange. Sisi is alone in a house full of strangers, unable to do as she pleases, her business known to all. She wonders how everyone in the court could be so cruel and unfeeling. She vows to behave with more kindness and compassion if—*when*, she must say *when*—she has a daughter-in-law of her own.

When Franzl arrives to bed that night, Sisi cuddles into him and tells him how happy she will be when all of these obligations are over and they can enjoy each other's company on their honeymoon.

"My darling, you know I'll have to work when we're at Laxenburg. The world will not wait for me to finish my holiday."

"What sort of holiday is that at all, then?" Sisi says.

"A holiday for you." He turns away, shy of asking her for a favor two nights in a row.

Franzl, in the glow of his new marriage, grants Hungary general amnesty, freeing close to four hundred political prisoners and allowing many exiles back into the country. When the Hungarian noblemen arrive to deliver their gifts to the Emperor and Empress, they are surprised by what they see. Sisi has talked Franzl into dressing as a hussar, and Sisi has fitted herself into the velvet bodice and embroidered skirt of a Hungarian noblewoman. Countess Esterházy has taught Sisi a few words in their visitors' language, which she stutters out shyly, and the Magyars are touched.

To close out the wedding festivities, the Archduchess grants Sisi's one request. On April 29th, Herr Renz's circus, the highlight of Sisi's childhood, comes to town.

Her father, Duke Max, sits in the front row with his daughter. A carousel of beautifully clad horses prances in choreographed formations. Sisi relishes the risk and joy that powers the show, but she is not allowed to greet the ringleader, let alone try out a riding trick or two. Everything she loved about the visits from Herr Renz in her youth has been drained from this experience. Here is one more thing that Sisi is allowed to look at, but not to touch, one more thing she used to hold close that is now at arm's length.

After the performance, Sisi goes for a walk with her mother and father beneath the freshly green chestnut trees of the Prater. "Do you like it here?" Ludovika asks her daughter.

Sisi is afraid to answer honestly. What, after all, is there to like about the last week? She decides not to respond.

Her mother presses. "You know, it might feel as though you *don't* like it at first, because no matter how wonderful, it will be different from the way our life is at Possi. But I do hope you'll eventually be able to see what a magnificent fortune has been granted you in this position. You know Nene—"

Sisi cuts her off. "Yes, I know Nene would have died to be Empress. I am well aware. You needn't make me feel guiltier than I already am."

"That's hardly my point. I just hope you'll try to do as you're told and find some form of joy in that."

Sisi's eyes wag. Do they think she does not understand that she is to do as she is told? Does her mother think that it has somehow escaped Sisi's attention, when every day she is physically pushed from task to task and denied even a moment to herself? "Tell me, have either of you derived your greatest joys in life from doing what you're told?" She looks at her father.

Duke Max clears his throat. They are circling back to

their carriages: the one that will return Max and Ludovika to Possi and the golden wedding carriage that will take Sisi back to the Hofburg. Max kisses his daughter's hand and bows, as is required of him now. He leans in to whisper, "Speaking of, Sisi, you'll have to come to Possenhofen for visits, as often as you like, of course, but all of this etiquette stuff is not for me. I don't belong here, so best if I keep away so I don't embarrass you." When he pulls back, he sees the look of hurt on her face, and musters an apologetic, but uncompromising smile.

Sisi's mother hugs her and tells her she's perfect, but perfect is not what Sisi has ever wanted to be.

In the carriage on the way to their honeymoon, Sisi and Franzl spy the destroyed banks of the Danube. "What could have happened?" he asks.

"I heard the gardeners saying that people are digging up the palms as souvenirs," Sisi says.

"My God, they love you. They'd never do such a thing for me." Franzl laughs.

Sisi feels a quiet pride, but underneath it: a threat. Dedication like this is a burden, especially when the people see you as a trinket, a symbol, something pretty to keep and fondle. If the trinket breaks, if it loses its shine, it no longer has value.

Laxenberg, too, bores Sisi.

Every day, even if there are no planned visitors, she is led through hours of ablutions, until she is a mannequin: stiff, buffed and polished, wound and pinned and posed.

She isn't allowed to row out onto the man-made lake herself. She can only sit passively and stare around at the exotic trees—the clammy locusts and the sugar maples and the Turkish filberts, all somehow thriving despite their being imported—while a servant pulls the oars alone.

Franzl hasn't the time to play blindman's buff with her, so he orders the chambermaids to join her, causing Sisi to feel pathetic and desperate. She leaves her housekeeper wandering the grounds blindfolded and returns inside for some tea.

Sisi suffers through her "vacation" for two weeks before she holes up in her room with the curtains drawn and writes a poem:

> Now in a prison cell I wake
> The hands are bound that once were free
> The longing grows that naught can slake
> And freedom, thou hast turned from me.

If Sisi wants these feelings kept secret, then she shouldn't leave them out for anyone to find. The ladies-in-waiting, worried for their mistress, or simply well trained, hand the poem over to the Countess Esterházy, who reprimands the indifferent Sisi. "We should put you in the House of Moods," the Countess says.

"I'm sorry?" Sisi asks, thinking she is being threatened with an asylum when she hasn't even been married a month.

But the Countess explains, providing only the smallest amount of reassurance. "It's the upside-down house on the grounds Franz the First built for his wife, so she could go there when she felt logic no longer applied to her."

Sisi strangles her scream of frustration. "Is it so illogical that I expected to spend my honeymoon with my *husband*?"

The Countess replies coolly, "If you understood all that your husband is responsible for, yes."

Franzl, who has been returning to Vienna for longer and longer stretches of each day, arrives to Laxenburg at 8:00 p.m. that evening and Sisi hands him the poem herself.

"Are you so unhappy? Do you not have everything you've asked for? It's not as though we've locked you in the dungeon."

"I don't have *you*," she says.

He hugs her to him and says that this is the balance they will have to get used to: most of the day apart and, if they're lucky, dinners together, before he must finish his work for the day. Sisi dreams of another life.

Back at the Hofburg, her days are filled with court women whom she slyly wanders away from. The ladies are, for the most part, middle-aged. It's true their dresses were all made in Paris, but they appear as though they've been chosen by a blind servant who has asked for the fabrics that are least popular. They try to reel her back in, explaining the complexities of their gossip, but she can't muster interest.

When Sisi stands to excuse herself, the Archduchess insists she stay. Sisi replies, "If I'm to remain here in the company of these empty-headed women, then I'd like a beer."

The Archduchess clears her throat and says, "I will

have the servants bring you some tea. Beer is fine and good
at Possenhofen, but not in a royal palace."

"I'll get it myself, if I must," Sisi says.

"Sit," the Archduchess whispers. "I will get you some
flat beer in a teacup and you're to complete the illusion by
sipping it daintily. Understand?"

"Bring a whole pot," Sisi says with a smile, and sparkles
her eyes back at the group, who have quieted themselves
to listen in. "And who will make sure this story makes it to
the grapevine?" Sisi asks.

"Beg your pardon?" one of the women says.

"Yes, best you should," Sisi coos.

Franzl invites Sisi along on a state visit to Bohemia and
Moravia. They visit hospitals and institutions that bring
tears to Sisi's eyes. She has not, to this point, been exposed
to suffering of this kind. She holds the hands of even the
contagious. She strokes the faces of children and soldiers
and speaks softly to the agitated.

One evening the Archduchess asks Sisi and Franzl to stay
for a moment after the plates have been cleared. "I have
good news! You are expecting a child."

Sisi asks what she means. She doesn't understand how
the Archduchess could know this before her, but then it
clicks into place. The court physician has informed the
Archduchess first. Why would this be different than anything else?

Franzl claps his hands with pleasure.

The Archduchess smirks at Sisi. "Sisi, you'll need to stop spending so much time with your parrot. The child will resemble what you gaze upon. I'd suggest you look at Franzl instead. He is so handsome, isn't he?"

Sisi's brain batters the inside of her skull with the inanity of this suggestion, but she nods.

"Franzl, you'll have to be gentle with Sisi," the Archduchess says with a tilt of her head.

Sisi's vision goes dark with disgust and she retreats to her room. She does not want Franzl to see her cry.

A Swan's Song

✴ ✴

QUEEN MARIE ENJOYS THE RITUAL of telling nine-year-old Ludwig the same story each night before bed. "Zeus created Venus from the foam of the sea, but the other waves were jealous. They, too, wanted to be transformed, and so Zeus scooped up another handful of the foam and made a swan: fluffy and white as the roiling water, proud and strong on the pitch of the waves. Mute for most of its life until its death, when it releases its story in a series of long runs of notes."

"Why must the swan be silent for most of its life?" Ludwig nuzzles into his pillow. The question is not new.

The Queen's answer is a little different every night, and perhaps that is why Ludwig loves the story so much. Tonight, she answers, "It is only when death threatens that the swan feels itself safe to reveal its secrets." She touches Ludwig's brow and sees that he is already asleep.

The Most Beautiful Woman in Europe

✳   ✳

THE MONTHS OF PREGNANCY do not suit Sisi. She insists on hiding herself away.

"Let the people rejoice in the imminent heir!" the Archduchess says, wishing to show off how well her daughter-in-law is fulfilling her purpose.

"I'm disfigured," Sisi says. She refuses to dress, to have her hair done, even to let Franzl sleep in the same bed as her.

The Archduchess opens the gardens of Laxenburg, so that people might stroll about, glancing into the leaded windows to try to find the lump of the Empress inside. On days when Sisi admits her health is not impossibly bad, the Archduchess urges her to go for a ride in an open carriage, cradled by pillows and blankets to absorb the jolts of the pitted roads.

At their country house, the Kaiservilla, Sisi is slightly happier. Franzl can spend a morning off shooting chamois in the woods while Sisi is most bogged down in her nausea. Her mother and siblings visit to keep her company and distract her from her misery. By the time Franzl returns home from the hunt, Sisi has often recovered enough to go for an afternoon walk.

But for anything more intimate than this with Franzl, Sisi has been indisposed. He can't help but think back to the time before he married, when he snuck small whims into his daily routines. The court ladies never refused him, and he imagines it would be no different now. He tells himself that he need only make it through the healthy birth of his heir and then life will return to normal. He convinces himself he can wait as long as that.

Pregnancy has been causing Sisi's hair to shed with increasing rapidity, and she panics at the thought of going bald. She asks her hairdresser to show her the lost strands after styling her hair each day. "This child is making a monster of me in every way!"

The hairdresser washes Sisi's hair in a slurry of eggs and brandy. As the pregnancy progresses, a silver bowl fills with a new tangle of stray hairs each day. Sisi plucks a strand out of the bowl and stretches it between her fingertips, nearly straightening her arms, and crumples over the bulb of the child inside her.

Fearing that she might be assigned a different, less desirable role—emptying bedpans or washing underclothes—the hairdresser smears a line of glue beneath her apron, and when she finds a strand in her comb, she hides it out of sight. The silver bowl holds fewer and fewer hairs each day, until the Empress expresses her relief that the worst must have passed.

———

In March 1855, Sisi gives birth to a daughter. As soon as the girl emerges, she is whisked away to a wet nurse, and the Archduchess names the baby Sophie, after herself.

Sisi hears all of this from the other side of the room, and rather than the initial bliss of motherhood, she feels relief that the Archduchess's eagle eye might now be trained on the infant instead of her.

Sisi immediately asks for her hair to be arranged and her face to be made up. She requests a clean nightgown be slipped over her shoulders. She hides her muddled midsection beneath a great quilt, trying to sit up as much as she can before Franzl is allowed in.

He perches on the edge of the bed. "Sophie is perfect."

"But she is a girl. I've failed you," Sisi says, meaning she has failed herself. She'll have to go through this ordeal again. "Where is she now?" she asks.

"She's been moved to the nursery beside my mother's apartment." Franzl holds his smile in place.

"On a different floor?" Sisi asks.

"Yes, you've done your part. Mother can take over the technicalities now. You must rest and recover." He smiles reassuringly, but Sisi cannot bring herself to mirror him.

On May Day, Sisi is made to ride in a carriage through the Prater, but she hides her face behind a fan. "Their gaze won't wear out your loveliness, you know," the Archduchess says, but Sisi shivers at how corpulent she finds herself compared to her former collection of angles. Even though she hasn't been nursing the child, she must stuff rags into her corset to soak up the leaking milk and towels into her bloomers to collect all the blood and pus and urine. She wants to show these rags to each person who insists she is beautiful.

With time, though, the leaking subsides and the corporeal wounds heal. Sisi takes up riding again. She stretches and pliés at the barre. She hangs from a metal pipe until she can pull her chin over it. She lifts weights in every direction, pausing every so often to swallow a raw egg to reinforce her stamina.

The Archduchess tells her to take it easy.

"Oh?" Sisi asks. "You'd prefer I don't return to my prior *exertions*?"

The Archduchess knows precisely what Sisi implies. "You might limit yourself to the most *essential* activities."

Sisi cracks another egg.

Franzl enters the room to bid Sisi adieu on his way to a military inspection in Galicia. "Why don't you visit Possenhofen while I'm gone?" he says, hoping this will cheer her.

The Archduchess interjects. "An Empress must hold the place of the Emperor while he is away. You'll stay here, Sisi."

"Oh, there's nothing for her to do here," Franzl says. "Let her go see her family."

"The baby is far too young to travel," the Archduchess counters. "I'm sure you don't want to be apart from Sophie, do you?"

Sisi replies insouciantly. "It's not as though I'm allowed much time with her."

The Archduchess is shocked. Even Franzl is surprised at Sisi's willingness to be separated from their daughter, but he opts not to contradict himself.

When Sisi arrives at Possenhofen, her mother's and sisters' eyes look everywhere for the baby. "Where have you hidden her?"

"The Archduchess has kept Sophie behind. It's as though I gave her up for adoption to the empire. It's miserable."

"You don't *look* miserable. You look to be in perfect health. I daresay you're thinner now than you were before you gave birth."

"Yes, well, that's because I can't eat anything they make. I miss Cook's food. I will eat while I'm here—stock up for the months ahead. Nene, would you like to go for a hike with me? I'm so excited to be able to roam freely."

They hear another carriage in the distance. Sisi sighs. "The ladies-in-waiting. It seems I will never shake them. If we leave now, I might have a few more hours of peace."

Sisi and Nene set out into the hills behind Possenhofen, but the ladies-in-waiting run to catch up. It's a struggle to keep pace with the athletic sisters. The ladies know if they ask how much longer they'll be walking, Sisi will only venture farther out to punish them. When they arrive back to the castle, the sun is close to setting, and the ladies-in-waiting doze over their dinner plates. Sisi suggests they retire early, and then sneaks to Nene's room so they can gossip, unsurveilled.

"You would have made a better Empress than me," Sisi tells her sister. "It's a mistake that Franzl picked me over you. You are so proper and I daresay you'd enjoy court life, though it makes me feel dead inside."

"But you love him."

Sisi falters. "Love is really nothing in the face of circumstances so ill-fitted as this."

"Sisi, it's done. Why dwell? You mustn't tell Mother, but I've been researching convents. It's time. My opportunities have dried up."

"You are twenty-two and beautiful."

"I am past marrying age, and the King won't approve of the only man who appears willing to entertain the idea."

"You've a suitor then."

"A Thurn und Taxis brute. But I'd be taken care of for life. They have gobs of money, you know. *And* he's kind."

"I will ask Franzl to talk to the King."

"I can't see it making a difference."

"Are you that set on putting on a habit?" Sisi asks, trying to make light of the situation.

Nene wipes her tears away and agrees it's worth a shot.

The next day, Sisi finds her father having breakfast at the dining room table. She doesn't ask where he's been—in the bed of some village woman, no doubt.

"My Sisi," Duke Max says, putting down his porridge spoon to envelop his daughter in a hug. "I'm about to head out to watch your brothers practice their jumps. Do you want to come along?"

"I'd prefer to do a few of my own."

"That's my girl," the Duke replies.

Sisi goes to put on her riding habit, and Countess Esterházy steps forward to tell Sisi she might think better of this idea. "You do have an empire to rule over now," she says.

"Enough. I see the Archduchess has fettered your brain."

Out in the dressage ring, Sisi jumps the highest hurdles, bouncing from the saddle with each landing, feeling her stomach drop, like the sensation of falling in her sleep. When she dismounts, her hair is mussed, but her cheeks glow with cheer and vigor. Her mother's fluffy spitz dogs run up to her and she kneels down, letting them lick her face.

The dogs follow them to lunch and one sits on her mother's lap. While they wait for the soup to be brought out, the Duchess lists all that is beginning to bloom on the grounds this time of year as her fingers comb through the dog's fur. "Your beloved jasmine that you sent to Ludwig when he was born, the poppies, the mock sweet orange. It smells incredible out there, doesn't it?" She pinches the dog occasionally and deposits her findings on her bread plate. The ladies-in-waiting lean over covertly, trying to see what it is. A servant swaps in a new dish each time he enters the room, but still, there are full minutes when fleas, some wriggling with life, some crushed, their egg sacs like flecks of dandruff, sit on the gleaming china.

When Sisi goes to baby Sophie on her return home, the infant screams. "She's not used to me," Sisi says. "I'd like to spend two hours a day with her instead of one." The Archduchess can't think of a reason to refuse. When nothing changes, Sisi visits for three hours a day. Still the child resists her, crying until she is returned to her grandmother.

At breakfast, soon after the return of the Emperor, the Archduchess congratulates Franzl on the fact that he will become a father again. Sisi sits, detached, at the table, feeling a dismal déjà vu.

Winter comes on quickly, and Sisi laps the halls of the Hofburg with a blanket caped around her shoulders. None of her coats fit over her growing belly. It's almost as cold inside the drafty corridors as it is out. She imagines herself an airship, floating high above the sky, a dirigible that would be easy enough to pop, the relief she'd feel whizzing through the air, settling at the top of a tree where the breeze is fresh. The atmosphere of the apartment where she is stabled like livestock grows staler by the day, sharpest when she returns after time outside the room.

In the summer, Sisi pushes another girl into the world. This time, Franzl fails to cover his disappointment. "We'll try again," he says. Sisi sees no reason to hide *her* dismay at another round of this misery.

Franzl must make a state visit to Venice and Milan, the Italian states still smarting at their failure to achieve independence from Austria six years before, ready to boil over from a simmer to a second attempt at revolution if not tended to. He knows, as with Hungary, Sisi's beauty will be an asset in this tense situation.

"I'll bring the girls," Sisi tells the Archduchess.

"Gisela is far too small, and Sophie has barely recovered from her cough."

"She'll benefit from the warmer climate."

"Lombardy and Venetia, dear girl, is an armed camp, not a health resort."

"There is no safer place for her to be than in the company of the Emperor. I don't think you realize that I'm not asking for permission. While we're away, Franzl and I have agreed that the children's nurseries will be moved downstairs nearer to our own apartment."

"Impossible. Sophie will be utterly confused and Gisela is in need of round-the-clock care."

"I will take charge of them. It is Franzl's desire. You have done an excellent job, but the children must bond with their mother." It is true that Sisi wants the children to love her—and wants to love the children more, too—but it is also true that she wants to take something away from the Archduchess in the same way the Archduchess has taken so much from her.

The Archduchess sneers. "I won't oversee such a transition."

"Fine. Your responsibility is only to keep yourself out of the way of those who will."

The Archduchess shakes her head. "Maybe you'd like to move your horses to the third floor, as well?"

Sisi chooses not to say a word.

"I wish you safe passage, *Your Majesty*," the Archduchess says. Only a mother-in-law can mock an Empress in this way.

Left to His Own Devices

✳ ✳

LUDWIG, ELEVEN, IN HIS IDLE HOURS free of his tutor, models the Holy Sepulchre with clay. He reads Heine poems copied in his mother's hand, each instance of the word "love" replaced with "friendship":

> So, little, youthful maiden, come
> Into my ample, feverish heart
> For heaven and earth and sea and sky
> Do melt as friendship has melted my heart.

The Queen tells her husband to take Ludwig along on his daily walk, but Max can't see a reason for it. "What am I supposed to talk to the young man about? We don't share a single interest."

The King goes out alone, and when he approaches the cascade at the end of one of the Nymphenburg canals, he spies his son in the distance and turns back toward the trees, hoping Ludwig did not see him.

Mother Knows Best

❈　❈

SOPHIE AND GISELA ARE VIOLENTLY ILL for the entirety of the journey around the corner of the Adriatic. Sisi, hearty as ever, tends to them with little rest. She wonders if she has made a mistake, if it's too late to charter another boat to take her home with the babies, but when the yacht enters the lagoons, Sisi is overcome with the magic she's heard about only in stories. The babies are finally calm. It is good she is there to stand beside Franzl.

The Venetians who line the canals ogle the young couple. But it's schadenfreude rather than admiration that drives their interest. No cheers are rallied, no banners waved. Sisi's stomach clenches in fear. She clutches Gisela to her tightly as they disembark, and the Countess Esterházy follows close behind with Sophie. Sisi believes they are protecting the girls, but she also knows that the people are less likely to spit on a woman carrying a small child, so, in that way, the babies act as armor for the women.

At dinner that night, Alexander of Hesse has to keep clearing Sisi's skirt from his lap. She is accustomed to the spacious tables of the Hofburg, but here, the guests are packed tightly into a small dining room, no doubt to try to make up for the fact that very few people have deigned to attend. Sisi waits as course after course is served, declining to eat more than a bite of each, offending everyone. Sisi can offer only her halting French and the few mangled phrases of Italian she's prepared. She mutters the same words over and over again so many times that Alexander can't help but take advantage of the girl he sees as a twerpy accessory to the Emperor. He resents that, because he married for love, he has been forced to constantly relocate to remote and rustic stations, never landing in the comforts of Vienna. This little girl, though, has been allowed a life of perfect luxury, when, from what he's heard, the Emperor also chose her over her sister for love. The double standards and the froof of her skirt in his lap push him to the edge. He checks to be sure he is out of earshot of Franz and turns to Sisi. "Do you like the taste of shit?" he asks.

Sisi hears only the word "gusto" and assumes they must be talking about their meals. "Delizioso!"

Alexander asks her, "Would you give up all of Austria for one night with an Italian cock?" He smiles to encourage her.

Sisi assumes she is being complimented, and so she repeats, "Grazie, grazie. Il piacere e tutto mio."

Everyone in earshot hides their faces, knowing that if they reprimand the Prince, the Empress will catch on. If they laugh, they will only egg on Alexander. They try their best not to react at all.

The next day, the couple holds court, but only 30 of the 130 invited attend. "Well, this continues to be absolutely mortifying," Sisi says. The women who do present themselves are, at best, the second class. The heat used to press their best dresses has only helped to release the trapped body odors, causing Sisi's head to ache. She excuses herself to tend to the babies, although they have more than enough care, but just as she is about to abandon him, Franzl decides on a drastic measure. He gathers everyone's attention to announce a pardon for those condemned for high treason since the War of Independence. The room gasps and the conversations fizz.

That night, before the Emperor and Empress go out, Sisi kisses her daughters' sleeping heads, wondering if there's any use in even trying to appeal to the people.

But every box in the theater is filled. Bodies stand and cheer as Franzl and Sisi take their seats. Sisi strains against her corset, pride filling her in a way that food seldom does.

"Let's stay here for Christmas," Sisi suggests.

"Mother won't be happy," the Emperor says.

"If we stay a little longer, our dedication will be proven to the people," she replies. "We can't give up now." Sisi does not mention that a Christmas alone with the children, away from the Archduchess and her rules and regulations and surveillance, sounds like a precious rarity to relish while they can.

Franzl can't deny that Sisi's instincts have proven themselves astute in the past and agrees to stay.

Word spreads of the warmth following the imperial family through the provinces. Verona revives the Feast of the Gnocchi and Franzl breaks the record for the speed with which he eats his plate of dumplings, but Sophie is the one who steals the show, grinning broadly when one of the doughy nuggets is fed to her.

Their luck is short-lived, though, and in Milan, protesters have pushed the town to boycott the Emperor's visit. The government pays country people one lira each to line up and welcome the couple. In the theater, servants fill the seats, wearing purple mourning gloves. Not even the little girls win a wink from the Milanese. Here, the people are wise to them as a symbol of past and future subjugation.

When the couple returns to Vienna, the Archduchess's face falls. Sisi relishes her mother-in-law's obvious disappointment that Sisi is not swollen with another child.

On the top of Sisi's stack of mail she finds a brittle yellow pamphlet dated 1784. She reads: "The destiny of a Queen is to give an heir to the throne, not advice. If the Queen is so fortunate as to provide the state with a Crown Prince this should be the end of her ambition. If the Queen has no sons she is merely a foreigner in the state and a dangerous foreigner at that—for fearing to be sent back from whence she came she will always be seeking to win back the King by other than natural means. She will struggle for power and position by sowing discord."

Sisi stalks up to the apartments of the Archduchess. "Is this your work? An old libel against Marie Antoinette?"

The Archduchess feigns a squint. "Whoever left it has a point, at least."

Sisi goes to Franzl's office. "Tell your mother that it is neither her place nor her privilege to draw such comparisons. Anonymous threats have no effect on me. Insult me to my face or I feel no insult at all."

Franzl picks up the pamphlet, fury growing in his brow. "I'll show this to the police."

"Please. The police will only spread rumors. If I'm to conceive another child, then I can't have my character attacked. The nerves will make me indisposed."

"Don't spend another thought on it. Go out to the stables and see your darlings. Your correspondence can wait until tomorrow."

Sisi accepts the dispensation from her duties. While out walking she hatches a plan.

The next morning, she asks for a moment on the Emperor's schedule. Franz, surprised to see his wife during the day, says, "Sisi, I haven't the time to pal around."

"I'd like to make an appointment to go for a ride this weekend. I have a proposal to make." Franzl is skeptical, but his secretary pencils her in.

Visiting the new nursery to see round, pink Gisela, Sisi finds Sophie huddled with her grandmother, telling her all sorts of made-up adventures from their time apart. Sisi had hoped the distance would cure her daughter of her preference for the Archduchess. Frustrated, she claps her hands, like she would at one of her hounds. "Sophie, come. Sophie, sit here by me." Sophie casts her eyes up at her grandmother, but follows her mother's commands. "Franzl says we'll need to go to Hungary in May, and we'll be taking both of the girls with us."

"But Sophie is even weaker than when you left for Italy," the Archduchess argues.

"The Emperor has decided."

———

Sure that Sisi must be endangering her beloved granddaughter, the Archduchess goes to the doctor herself. "Didn't you say that travel would not be good for Sophie?"

But Sisi has beaten the Archduchess to the punch. The doctor says what his Empress has commanded him to say. "The journey to Budapest is little more than a pleasure cruise. The children will be fine."

The Archduchess can see through him immediately. "We should all be so lucky as to get a clean bill of health just because we demand it," she says. "If the children fall ill, we'll know who to blame."

When Saturday arrives, Franzl dresses in civilian clothes.

At the stables, Sisi jokes, "What a relief. I thought the military jacket might have become glued to your body. You look like a cobbler in a Sunday suit. Loosen up. Your bones will hold together, I guarantee it."

His shoulders fall; his knees unlock. "You like imagining me as one of your beloved townspeople." This is the Emperor's brand of flirting.

"What I'd like is a hospital," Sisi says.

Franzl stiffens again. "You and the children have the best possible care here in the palace."

"No, no. Not for us! I'd like to accomplish something, and I've decided what I want most is to open a hospital. I'd like to feel as though I've done some good. Can you help me? Can you free up the funds?"

"My darling, there are far more pressing issues at play.

If you are looking to be helpful, you could attend more of the state functions. I fear I'm often found flailing alone— all business and no congeniality. Your charm and beauty make all the difference."

"I can try to be better about that, too, but believe it or not, behind all my glamour, I also have intellect." Sisi mounts her steed.

Franzl knows a bargaining chip when he sees it. "It may take me some time, but yes, you're right. A project of your own would do you good. Need we go on this ride if this is settled?"

Sisi coughs. "I wouldn't want you to spend unnecessary time with me." Sisi giddyups her horse to avoid the feeling of having been done a favor. Franzl knows if he doesn't follow it will be as though he's done nothing for her at all, but there is so much work to be done. He lets her ride on ahead and turns back to his desk.

On their first evening in Budapest, the imperial family processes across the chain bridge over the Danube that connects the two sides of the city. Sisi marvels at the thousand thin tapers lit along the way, careful to keep her wide lace sleeves hugged in tight. Fireworks pop open the sky for what seems like forever, but when the display finally ends, Sisi can see that all of the windows of the city have been blacked out.

When they approach the palace for the state ball in their honor, a minister intercepts, loading them into a carriage to take them to a different location. "What's the matter?" the Emperor inquires.

"There's been a boycott. The people aren't ready to acknowledge that German is the official language now. We'll go to the national theater instead."

When the carriage arrives, the theater is abuzz with merrymakers. If they hadn't been turned away from an empty ballroom, they'd have never known there was an issue.

"I'm sorry that we must put on such a show," the Emperor tells Sisi in bed that night.

"It's nothing we haven't been through before," she replies. "If we arrived and they were already convinced of us, what would be the purpose of the visit? We're here to win them over, right?"

Franzl rolls Sisi to him. "You've already won me over, and yet I still appreciate your visits."

"Yes, I'm aware," Sisi says.

The Emperor kisses her neck and Sisi, distracted, comments on how much she enjoyed the day. "Buda is so perfectly reflective of the old world, and Pest of the new—such a happy marriage."

"Not unlike ours," the Emperor says, lifting the Empress's nightgown.

"I even sort of like that they don't fawn over us."

"I can take that note," the Emperor says.

"All the sycophants of Vienna wear on me. And so many handsome people here."

Franzl pulls away to get a look at Sisi's face. "Oh?"

Sisi, who often forgets she is only nineteen, hasn't allowed herself to admire anyone except Franzl in the entirety of her life, but something about the different smells and styles of Hungary have awakened a dormant sensuality in her. She can even entertain, if briefly, a thought of how she might wield her power over her subjects, but imagination is scandal enough. She pulls Franzl to her with her new ideas in mind and Franzl does not object.

At the racecourse on Margit Island Sisi delights at the twang of the Gypsy music. She begs Franzl to dance a czardas with her, but dancing is not a dignified act for an Emperor, and so Sisi is forced, instead, to watch as the dancers move slowly at first, picking up speed until they are just a whir of spinning skirts before her. "How do you say 'fast' in Hungarian?" she asks.

Franzl smiles. "I believe you're looking for the word specific to tempo, and that is 'friss.'"

The accordion pulls itself dramatically together and apart. Keys chirp. A violin bends in and out, waffling in place and then jumping high then low. More strings join and a languid melody snakes in. Sisi's breath disappears, even though she is standing still.

The schedule of engagements proceeds at such a frenetic pace that the Empress is only apprised of the children's well-being once in the morning and once in the evening.

"You could have left them with my mother, you know," Franzl tells her.

"I could not have, and you know why," Sisi replies flatly.

"Why haven't you told me Gisela is ill?" he asks.

"It's nothing. A cold," she says. She keeps from him the red bumps lining Gisela's hairline, not wanting to bear the brunt of Franzl's ire. "We'll just delay our tour of the countryside a day or two."

Mistakes and Resentments

✴   ✴

BY THE TIME GISELA IS WELL, though, Sophie has taken a turn.

Sisi wants to blame Sophie's tears on the fever alone, but she knows that the girl misses her grandmother. "Of course, I'd hate to turn back. We're finally beginning to gain some ground here. Do you think it's as serious as all that?"

In Sisi's presence, the doctor has trouble ignoring his desire to tell her what she wants to hear. "It's possible it's just that late tooth coming in."

Sisi runs her tongue over the messy scrabble in her own mouth, and accepts his answer. Sisi and Franzl leave the children to rest in Buda while they depart to the country.

In the small towns, the peasants are not mired in the same politics as city people, and they cheer as Emperor and Empress promenade through their stone streets.

Upon being introduced to the oldest man in the town of Tiszacsege, Franz asks what he might do to please the people of the village. The old man replies, "The people are all right, sir. It's only that wretched priest who is black and yellow up to the ears."

"You mean he supports the Hapsburgs?" the Emperor asks.

"What's that?" the old man says.

"The priest is loyal to the Emperor, you mean," Franz says, raising his voice.

"That's right," the old man says, oblivious.

"You know that I am a Hapsburg myself," the Emperor pushes.

"Come again?" the old man says.

"I *am* the Emperor," Franzl shouts, trying to get the words deep enough into the man's ear that he'll hear them.

"Well, then, get on with you," the old man says, turning away.

Sisi lets out a high-pitched squeal, entertained by the old man's indifference. Franzl can't help but smile himself.

The mayor, though, is mortified. "I assure you that old man is not representative of our people," he insists. "My sincerest apologies."

Franzl tries to show his good humor. "I appreciate honesty, all told." The mayor lowers his head deferentially.

In the southern city of Debreczin a telegram from Dr. Seeburger waits for Sisi. "Return to Buda. Sophie's condition worse."

Sisi and Franzl return to the palace, but the only news the doctor has to share is that there is no hope for the girl. The measles that passed through Gisela so briefly took firmer hold of Sophie, graduating first into pneumonia and then encephalitis.

Sisi crouches by the side of Sophie's bed for twelve hours straight. She clutches the fussing child's hand, as its grip weakens in her own.

Later that evening, Franzl sends a telegram to the Archduchess and his father: "Our little one is now an angel in heaven. We are utterly crushed."

When the Archduchess is woken with this message, she cries out. "Damn her!" she screams into her pillow. It's an hour before she asks the telegram to be read again, and realizes she must confirm. "Sophie? It must be Sophie, right? Ask them which one!"

Sisi can't stop pacing the room where her daughter lies. She batters herself with her fists and bites her hands. The doctors suggest sedating her, but Sisi lies on the bed beside her daughter's body weeping. After the twentieth hour, dehydrated and exhausted, Sisi faints, and the orderlies move her to her own room.

When Sisi's eyes open again, she sees Dr. Seeburger before she sees Franzl, and her body, despite its fatigue, throws itself forward to pummel the man. "You! You told me she would be fine! You said it was just her teeth," Sisi hollers. "You'll be exiled! Your license will be revoked!"

"Sisi," Franzl says, "he did everything he could."

"Our child is dead! How can that be everything?" she pushes. "You are no longer my doctor and you are not to touch Gisela."

———

Several days later, as they lower the small coffin into the Hapsburg crypt at the Capuchin church, the Archduchess holds tight to Sisi's waist as she tries to throw herself in after the box. The Archduchess doesn't say a word when, day after day, rather than attending her royal duties, Sisi asks for a carriage to take her from Laxenburg back to Vienna, so she might open the crypt and cry alone in the dark. Sisi can't stand the Archduchess's kindness.

The Archduchess delivers Gisela to Sisi each day, certain the mother will want to spend more time with her remaining baby, but Sisi refuses the girl. "She's the one who gave Sophie the measles," she says. "I can't bear to look at her."

In August, Franzl resumes the interrupted tour of Hungary alone.

Sisi is tempted to go with him, eager to get away from the prying eyes of the Hofburg again, but she is too stiff with grief.

In the words of the people who greet him, asking about her, Franzl hears both their admiration for her and their pity for her loss. It is *Sisi's* daughter they console him over, not *his*, so they are surprised to see the Emperor's eyes water. Conversations come to a halt and Franzl feels increasingly lonely in his loss. He resents his wife for bringing the girls along with them when she had been advised against it, but more, he is angry at her for not fighting harder for Sophie before she was sick. He is aware of the way his mother and his wife use the children as bargaining chips, but even when they get what they want, they are never contented. He should side with his wife in these arguments, but he owes so much to the Archduchess, first of all his emperor-ship. Without his mother's advocacy, he might still be waiting out his father's term and Austria would have surely already fallen. But he is the one with the power, and slowly, carefully, over the last decade he has been establishing his own primacy with her. He has made choices that go against her advice. He has proven that sometimes he does indeed know better.

He only wishes that that had been the case with his firstborn child. If he had paid closer attention to the girls, perhaps he could have saved Sophie. He recommits himself to his fatherly diligence and dashes the tears from his eyes.

Back in Vienna, Sisi drafts suicide notes and leaves them out for anyone to find. The servants clear the cupboards of anything poisonous. They remove all belts, rope, and ribbons from her apartment. They cut the Empress's meals up for her so she might not be tempted with a sharp edge.

But none of these interventions changes the root of her depression. Winter comes on and Franzl returns, and Sisi is still not herself.

She has grown manic with the desire to produce a legitimate heir. The doctor tells the Archduchess that Sisi is with child again and the Archduchess tells only Franzl the news.

The doctor recommends they find a way to calm Sisi if she's to carry the pregnancy to term; they must unstick her from this rut of guilt and grief.

Franzl invites Sisi's mother to visit so that she might provide Sisi comfort. When she arrives, she embraces her daughter. "You're pregnant!" she cries.

Sisi sighs. "I wish I was."

"You are," she says. "I can tell by your skin, your smell."

Sisi looks to Franzl, and he smiles, nodding once. She weeps at the ways in which her body is no longer her own before that feeling gives way to relief.

The Archduchess can't help herself. "The doctor says you must take care of yourself. You can't worry. You have to eat. No horseback riding."

Sisi knows the routine.

The news is announced in Vienna and the palace is flooded with tokens of the country's well-wishes: prayers and notes and advice for how to ensure it's a boy. In a fit of superstition, Sisi spends the following months reading and responding to every single letter.

On August 21st, 1858, the rumor buzzes around court that the Empress has gone into labor.

In her room, delirious with a pain she had not felt with the birth of either of her daughters, Sisi rolls her eyes white as she tenses with a contraction. "This child won't inherit the throne, either."

The midwife and the doctors reassure her. This is the Prince they've been waiting for, but the Archduchess is superstitious. She watched the diamond crown falter twice in the days leading up to the wedding. Even if Sisi is spouting fevered nonsense, an omen is an omen.

At midnight, Dr. Seeburger finds Franzl at his desk to tell him his son has been born.

Franzl goes to Sisi and kneels beside her to pray. Sisi won't believe even Franzl that she has birthed a boy. When she finally sees the proof, she rattles inside her skin. At twenty-one, Sisi has now completed her primary function in life: she has produced an heir.

Sisi's hand searches her deflated abdomen. She is essentially a door, a portal to be passed through, an entryway for the next generation.

He Said, He Said

✳   ✳

AT THIRTEEN, THE STRESS of Ludwig's schedule of courses begins to take its toll. Otto reports to the Queen that, while playing billiards, Ludwig kept telling loud voices behind him to quiet down, but Otto heard no one aside from his brother.

When the Queen confronts him, Ludwig claims it was Otto who was talking to ghosts. Each brother apparently haunts the other. The Queen calls in the royal doctor, who chalks the behavior up to ordinary play. "Just two brothers trying to get the other in trouble."

But the doctor tells his wife, who is a certified gossip, and soon rumors have spread that the boys might be held together by the Wittelsbachs' loose screws.

Ludwig receives an allowance, and learns to keep his own accounts, but, like his grandfather's mistress, when he's spent his cache, he just sends his additional expenses to the court financier. He makes charitable donations to those he believes deserve his mercy. He buys knickknacks for his mother—glass figurines and silver boxes with red velvet

secrets. He buys flowers and arranges them into sweet bouquets for his mother's ladies-in-waiting and sends whole
armfuls of jasmine to his cousin Sisi when he hears she has
given birth to an heir. He buys yo-yos and rackets for Otto
and then takes them away. Ludwig buys chocolate that he
eats too quickly; bread to crumble up and feed to the deer
and swans and fish when he goes out into the forest; ivory-
handled toothbrushes. He tries to limit himself to only
two pairs of gloves a month, but sometimes he splurges on
as many as six or seven.

He shakes hands with the peasants he visits on his rides
in the countryside on the days when La Rosée is indisposed, but after the gloves have touched a commoner's
hands, he throws them into the grass. The peasants hunt
the countryside for these discarded treasures and tuck them
away in hope chests or sell them to pad their daughters'
dowries.

Hours and Days—Eternal Biding

✳ ✳

SISI, DEEP IN A HOLE that no one has yet named post-partum depression, is denied all access to her newest-born and tries to find a way out of her feelings. Maybe she no longer loves Franzl. Maybe she never did. Maybe he feels the same and always has. She tries to work out an equation in her head that explains how much each of these loves relies on the other, but she has never been taught math, so it's a lost cause.

Her only hope is to test him. Sisi writes Franzl a note. "Do you have any interest in seeing me? Maybe I've done my job in giving you a son, so now you have no need for me? You'd rather spend your time worrying about the plots of Plon-Plon over in France. If you don't respond, I'll have my answer. Your loving wife, Empress Elisabeth of Austria." Sisi knows that mentioning Plon-Plon—Napoleon III's distant cousin, a corpulent playboy who pretends he has any governmental say whatsoever—will only insult Franzl's hard work. Sisi recalls the single dinner she and Franzl had with Plon-Plon and the pathetic way he kept starting sentences, "My cousin, Napoleon the *First* . . ." as though the two had ever been alive at the same time.

But Franzl doesn't take the bait. "My poor darling Sisi—how I would love to spend just one hour in your company. But here I am tied to my desk, snowed under with papers."

Sisi pouts at not even having managed to annoy him.

Even the news that Nene will finally marry her Thurn und Taxis prince fails to lift Sisi's spirits, and she sends her well-wishes from afar.

Sisi goes for long horseback rides alone, and when the Archduchess complains of the Empress's isolation, Sisi invites along her groom, with whom she can practice her English.

The Archduchess, frustrated that this looks even worse, asks Franzl to intervene.

Franzl hasn't the time, but, ever the eager-to-please son, he writes a note to his wife. "I cannot allow you to ride alone with Holmes, for it is not correct. I would see it more fit that you ride with the Controller of the Imperial Hunts. He is of a rank and class suitable to accompany and protect an Empress."

"The Archduchess doesn't want me to hang out with you," Sisi tells Holmes in perfect English, with a roll of her eyes, and the pair laugh in every language.

On Christmas Eve 1859—her birthday—Sisi arrives to the family party in her new blush moire dress and a mood.

The Archduchess gasps, "You look as delicious as a zuckerl!"

Sisi, embarrassed at being compared to a sweet, retreats from the room until Franzl cajoles her back in, her eyes as pink as the rippled silk of her skirt. Twenty-two, a mother thrice over, still stuck in a grief that will never end for her lost firstborn, if she was a candy once, she is no longer. She believes her once pristine, glossy container has been chewed up and spit out. Sisi sits in her chair, despondent and distant. The children link hands and make a circle around her, singing carols. "Silence!" Sisi shouts, and the children burst into tears and then Sisi cries again, and, across the room, even Franzl's eyes grow wet at the thought that his wife will never be happy.

With Austria's defeat to Napoleon III in the Second Italian War of Independence, the nation hits a low point, and at that bottom bodies are stacking up. The economy has tanked and Franzl can't help but feel responsible for the record number of deaths by suicide. Everyone that Sisi passes in court or on the street has recently attended a funeral. Sisi knows from experience how empty condolences feel.

The Polish Disease
✳ ✳

RUMORS WORM INTO SISI'S EARS confirming her worst suspicions. The Emperor has become reacquainted with a Polish woman he knew before their marriage. Sisi presses her ladies-in-waiting, threatening to release their secrets if they don't tell her everything they know. One woman ventures that she has heard that the affair was the Archduchess's suggestion.

But the ladies beg ignorance when Sisi asks who the woman is.

At the dinner table Sisi pretends nothing is wrong. She doesn't bother to put a single morsel of food in her mouth. "I visited the infirm soldiers again today," she says. "And I hear there is a cholera epidemic in Vienna. The hospitals need to be much more advanced and they must accommodate more people."

"I know," Franzl says.

Sisi scowls. "You act as though I'm asking for a dollhouse."

Franzl, usually so pragmatic, resists giving Sisi what

she wants, despite its being something Austria also desperately needs. If pressed, he would say he's too busy, but underneath that answer are a host of reasons her request is not a priority to him. Denying Sisi is a punishment for her not serving as a more consistent figurehead by his side. "Once you've proven you can handle the basic duties of an Empress, I will consider your request."

"Franzl, this isn't a hobby. There are suffering people who need help. I am not concerned with impressing your royal cronies."

"I don't think you understand that impressing my *cronies* also ultimately helps the people in averting wars and preventing the country from falling into a deeper depression."

"Fine, but people need hospitals *now*. I will do everything else you want me to do, but we need to start building hospitals now. Forgive me, but the people love me, do they not?"

"Being that you almost never go out in public, it is a mystery as to why, but yes."

Sisi's jaw sets. Franzl is rarely as indelicate as this, and when he is, it stings.

"They don't need to see me all the time to know I love them. I want this hospital so they know we care if they live or die."

Franzl struggles to argue with this point, and makes a jab. "They love you because you are beautiful and you are the mother of their next Emperor. If they knew you—"

"Yes, if they knew me like you do," Sisi says. "I see. Fine then. We'll just wait for more people to die. Emperor knows best." Sisi excuses herself from the table and Franzl feels the pangs of having gone too far.

In October, Sisi's wrists and knees swell, and the doctors can't find a cure.

Incognita, the Empress goes to a physician outside the palace. She dresses plainly, hiding her hair in a bonnet, smudging coal on her face.

The doctor tells her the truth: syphilis. Sisi knows there is only one way it might have been passed to her: Franzl's liaisons.

Numb, Sisi returns to the court doctor. "I am ill and I need time to recover in privacy." She coughs and glares. "We both know what it is I have, but you will give it a decorous name."

The doctor diagnoses a lung infection. "Consumption," Sisi calls it, because the word feels appropriately dramatic.

"There are any number of health resorts nearby that might allow you to recuperate. Do you have a preference?" Dr. Skoda asks by way of apology.

"Did you say Madeira is the only logical option?" she asks, sending herself far away.

The doctor redeems himself.

When Sisi informs her mother-in-law of her planned journey, the Archduchess rolls her eyes. "It's a mistake. Ce voyage malencontreux." Sisi's French is so bad that the Archduchess has taken to saying everything in both German and French.

Sisi scoffs. "Who asked you? Qui vous a demandé?"

Apparently Sisi has been studying. "Pas mal," the Archduchess responds.

It's possible that all of the fake coughing has truly irritated Sisi's lungs. "I must go away," she tells Franzl. "Perhaps you already know why."

The couple play a game of chicken. Sisi won't say she has syphilis and Franzl won't ask. Or it's possible that Franzl is missing the point and believes Sisi is still wounded by his excuses for not granting her a hospital.

"All the way to Madeira, though?" he asks. "I'm sure we could arrange a villa for you in Meran or Abbazia."

"It must be far away, in a place where I'll have no obligations. I need privacy."

"Would you like me to go with you? I think I could go for only a few days, but—"

"No, I would not like that."

"None of the royal yachts are outfitted to make such a trip in winter."

"You could ask Queen Victoria if I might borrow one of hers then."

Franzl, guilty, stops questioning her. "Yes, of course."

The waters prove rocky as the winds shift with a particularly blustery autumn, and Sisi's ladies-in-waiting prove ill-suited for the voyage. Sisi, though, paces the bow of the ship even as snow falls, letting the wind whip her hair like a sail. Unlike when she is at home, she eats boiled potatoes and salted meat, and even clinks her beer mug with the sailors, as they listen to the rest of the passengers groan and whimper their holy rosaries.

As the days turn themselves over, the black basalt cliffs

come into view. The docks of Madeira are decorated in flowers, proof that the secret of the Empress's visit is out.

Sisi seems vibrant. She strolls through the winter streets and chats with everyone. Occasionally she lets out a little cough. She compliments a fluff of a sheepdog and asks the owners if she can have him. The people don't know how to turn her down.

An Introduction

✴ ✴

LUDWIG BUYS A PORCELAIN FIGURE of William Tell after seeing Schiller's play. He admires the figure's muscular legs, sliding a finger into the space between the knees. He strokes the rosy cheeks and cleft chin so much that the glaze starts to dull. He dreams of grand gestures, steadfast allegiance to both family and country.

Ludwig writes the King and Queen a formal letter requesting he be allowed to attend a performance of *Lohengrin*. He's been begging for years, since Fräulein Meilhaus wrote him about it, and finally, now that he is fifteen, they have been worn down and relent.

Ludwig sits in the royal box with the court archivist, Leinfelder, and allows himself to be carried away by what unfolds onstage.

The Knight of the Swan appears from the ether to save Elsa from the accusations posed against her, with one condition: that she never ask who he is or where he is from. But fear and doubt creep in and Elsa begs the Knight to reveal to her his origin. Bereft at her lack of faith, he reveals that he is the Knight of the Grail and son of King Parsifal. Now that Elsa knows the truth, he must go home. Elsa dies of grief at losing her beloved.

Ludwig is overcome. He knows that he, as a future King, is also a messenger from God, and there are always more people *against* saviors than there are *for* them.

At breakfast the next morning, Ludwig cannot stop raving over the performance. His mother, seeking not to encourage the young man, performs her indifference.

King Max arrives to the table jubilant—an anomaly. Sullen Ludwig is skeptical. Little Otto absorbs his father's good humor readily. Queen Marie goes on eating. "Are you all right?" Ludwig asks.

"We have cause for celebration! Das flittchen is *dead*."

Ludwig looks to his mother, who doesn't react at all.

Otto recoils. "What is a flittchen?"

Ludwig asks, "Which flittchen?"

"Your grandfather's mistress, Lola. No longer a concern of ours."

Ludwig understands now, but he had thought her threat had been long neutralized.

"The bösewicht had a stroke. She tore our family apart, left the kingdom in tatters, made a fortune selling tickets so she could tell her lies, and *now* she is dead."

Ludwig realizes he would like to know more. He has been offered only the most sanitized version of events. He has never seen his father so happy, and he is both horrified and intrigued at the joy Max takes in this news.

He seeks out his grandfather in his apartment. The shades are drawn. Ludwig I holds an alabaster mold of a tiny foot.

"Grossvater, I've come to check on you."

"What a sweet young man you are. I suppose your father told you the news of my Lola."

"How is it that you can still think of her so fondly?" The Prince takes a seat.

"You are too young to understand wanting something that the world denies you."

"But I do understand. I'm sure of it."

"I know that I am the only one who believes it, but she loved me. And I loved her. It is possible to love a person without agreeing with them. Lola knew what she wanted and she stopped at nothing to get it, and *then—then!*—she would change her mind and want something else, and she never questioned herself. We are expected to be consistent, to set our sights on one goal and never waver, but Lola was malleable. She changed when she saw fit to change; she let the world alter her."

Ludwig II doesn't understand fully, but he cannot deny his grandfather's sincerity. He stands. "I am sorry for your loss, Grossvater."

"You are the only one," Ludwig I replies, and clasps his grandson's hand with gratitude.

In fact, Lola is not dead. She is in a coma that she will recover from to survive another year, but when the news announcing her death arrives again, no one will pay attention. Her rumors have always trumped her truths.

Ahem.

❋   ❋

As CHRISTMAS APPROACHES, Franzl sends a court member to Madeira to deliver him an honest account of Sisi's well-being, hoping he reports that she can come home soon. The spy returns bearing news to the contrary, though. "I am terribly sorry to say that I think she is still very ill. Her cough seems in no way better. Mentally she is terribly depressed, almost to the point of melancholia. During my visit she shut herself up in her room and cried all day."

When the messenger departs, though, cheery life as usual resumes. The ladies-in-waiting know better than to point out these sharp fluctuations in the Empress's weather. They endure the tempests with patience, knowing that the next day they will be treated to a bright sky, and write home rumors that the Emperor doesn't know what to do with when they inevitably reach his ears.

Letters arrive from Gisela, but Sisi can hear the voice of the Archduchess behind the notes.

A statue of St. George appears in her room. Her lady-in-waiting comments that it's kind of the Archduchess to send an icon of the patron saint of England while the Empress is there, but Sisi knows better. St. George is also the patron saint of syphilis.

Sisi stays away for six months—an eternity with children as small as hers. Her first month away is heaven, but then the five that follow increasingly disappoint her. She misses Gisela and baby Rudolf, but knows that the children would not be hers even if she were home with them. She knows that Franzl has far greater responsibilities than attending to his wife. She knows that the women at court feel greater allegiance to gossip than to keeping her company. At home, she has nothing at all. At least alone in a spa town she is not reminded of the nothing. She can pretend that her days are intentionally leisurely, that the leisure isn't a rebellion against all of the responsibilities forced on her.

But Franzl has been experiencing one of the most difficult periods of his rule. His letters grow increasingly desperate for her return. By April, Austria has already cycled through two constitutions in her absence, and Sisi can tell that Franzl's distress and regret are genuine and urgent. Sisi goes home.

In Vienna, the crowds gather to celebrate the return of their Empress.

The Archduchess has trained the children to perform their excitement at seeing their mother again, and Sisi believes their joy. She lifts both Gisela and Rudolf as though they are trophies for the recovery she has supposedly made.

The Archduchess has arranged both a court ball and a state dinner, hoping that she might minimize the individual meetings required of her mercurial daughter-in-law. Sisi doesn't see this for the act of generosity it is, though. Instead she accuses the Archduchess of having planned more obligations for her than she can tolerate. "I'm ready to move on to Laxenburg," Sisi tells Franzl. "The Hofburg has already tired me out." Franzl knows that when Sisi says "the Hofburg," she means his mother. Desperate to keep her happy *and* at home, he tries to cancel some of her appointments, but Sisi's habit of nervous coughing returns, threatening to take her even farther away.

Audience

✻ ✻

A T SIXTEEN, Ludwig's music teacher declares him talentless. "He can't distinguish a waltz from a sonata," he tells the Queen. "He wants only to let the music *wash over him*. He cares nothing at all for technique. It's not worth my time."

The Queen can't help but agree. She has overheard Ludwig battling with the teacher. If he doesn't like a lyric, he asks why it was so poorly written. If he doesn't like a musical phrase, he changes it or skips over it altogether. The Queen wonders if it's possible this is a sign of genius—or lunacy.

With his time no longer taken up by piano lessons, Ludwig can focus on his new interest. For close to an hour each day, the court hairdresser uses heated tongs to curl waves into Ludwig's straight, dark mane.

"At least with the piano, you were learning a skill," his father tells him. "You should be spending that hour each day with me, as my apprentice."

Ludwig pouts. "If I didn't have my hair curled each

day, I couldn't enjoy my food." The Queen decides it must be lunacy.

When Ludwig hears that another of Wagner's operas, *Tannhäuser*, is being performed at the Court Theater, he asks Leinfelder to accompany him again.

Tannhäuser, another knight, must choose between a princess and the goddess Venus, who lives in a grotto beneath the castle.

Ludwig's reactions are so overblown that Leinfelder worries he might be having a seizure, but then the Prince turns to him, alert, if overcome. Ludwig clutches Leinfelder's arm and whispers, "Have you ever seen anything so magnificent?"

In Absentia

❋ ❋

IN JUNE, HOME ONLY FOR TWO MONTHS, Sisi asks Dr.
Skoda if he might send her to Corfu.

"I worry people might question my decision to send
you there, as malaria has been an issue—" he starts.

"I'm glad you would recommend Corfu," she replies.

Corfu is a dream. Sisi bathes in the sea and sails the opal-
escent waters and goes for walks under the bright moon.

Sisi says she will go to Venice—much closer at least—if
Franzl brings the children to her there, but she claims she
is not well enough to return to Vienna.

"Fine," the Emperor says, accepting her statement
without necessarily agreeing with it.

Upon being reunited with their mother, the children snif-
fle for days. They miss their grandmother and don't understand why they've been parted from her. The Countess
Esterházy, who's been sent to look after them in the Archduchess's stead, hawk-eyes Sisi's every move. Sisi begs

Franzl to take the Countess with him when he leaves. "If she is dismissed as Mistress of the Household, I'd feel more bonded to the children, blessed to have their company all to myself. The children are beholden to the Archduchess first, the Countess second, and me a distant third. I have no power at all."

"If it will keep you here in Venice, then I see no other option," he says.

Sisi tries to teach the children Marokko, the Hungarian game of pickup sticks, but the children insist the Archduchess has taught them different rules. She takes them on long walks along the quays by the canals, but the children tire quickly and beg to be carried. At home, she reads to the children in Magyar about how Emese, the pregnant wife of Ügyek, the descendant of Attila the Hun, dreamed a Turul bird appeared to protect her as a great river flowed from her. She saw the dream as a prophecy of the line of powerful rulers she would birth, and how her grandson founded Hungary.

"Grandmother reads to us in German and points to the words I can sound out on my own," Gisela says to her mother at the end of the story

"I understand. It is also important for you to read and speak Magyar, too, though, because, as the imperial family, we are responsible for the Hungarian people, as well."

"Yes, but *we* are not Hungarian," Gisela argues.

The Archduchess has trained the children well.

"Very well, then. No more stories today," Sisi replies, removing Rudolf from her lap.

"What will we do now?" Gisela asks.

"I have business to attend to. Your governess will find something to occupy you," Sisi says, glancing at the young lady who is always standing by.

Sisi goes to her dressing table and regards the photographs she has tucked into the frame of her mirror. Comparing herself to other stunning women, planning new beauty regimens, making a strict schedule of the small amount of food she'll eat that day—all of these things do well to distract and occupy her.

Dr. Skoda pushes back, refusing to prescribe another spa trip. Sisi tells Dr. Skoda she can no longer trust his care. He is fired, as he expected he would be.

Sisi's childhood doctor, Dr. Fischer, examines her. Immediately, he identifies her ailment, but there is no paper trail of a prior diagnosis.

"Doctor, I am in a most delicate position, so I hope you'll see fit to comply with whatever it is I request so I might maintain what little health I have left, as well as my *privacy*."

The doctor breathes a sigh of relief. She knows. "What is it you need, Your Majesty?"

"Maybe if I were to take a hydropathic cure in Kissingen," she suggests. "And you might give me a new diagnosis. I fear I've become *anemic*."

Sisi has tired of the constant hacking. She has dug through the medical texts and found another disease that might explain the way her joints balloon.

"Yes, I think that is a diagnosis," he replies.

"Thank you, Dr. Fischer. I see, in all this time, you haven't lost a bit of your skill."

"Would you say a month in Kissingen would suffice?" he asks, getting out his pad.

"A year, I think," Sisi says.

Dr. Fischer clamps his eyebrows in place to keep his reaction in check. "I'll have to recommend that you eat a bit more, as well."

"I can compromise," Sisi says with a smile.

But Sisi tires of Kissingen after only four months and returns home. In isolation, even luxury can grow old.

Seeing and Being Seen

✳ ✳

AT SEVENTEEN, LUDWIG IS RARELY SEEN without a book. He imagines himself into the position of d'Artagnan and the Three Musketeers. He admires the pluck of upstart Becky Sharp in *Vanity Fair*. He tries to read Gustav Freytag's *Debit and Credit*, a six-volume social novel exploring the interactions between three different classes and families (bourgeois, nobility, Jew), but the dry realism causes him to drowse. He is a solitary young man; he continues to prefer the company of stories.

Ludwig buys golden chains, quill pens made of peacock feathers, and a medallion with a diamond cross. When he receives a brooch for his birthday bearing a picture of his mother, he complains, asking what he is supposed to do with such a thing.

But then a realization lights up a new corner of his imagination. "Did you have this custom-made for me?" he asks her.

Queen Marie is too sturdy to be hurt by his disappointment. "Yes. If you hate it so much, you can give it to your father. He won't wear it, but at least he won't insult me when he receives it."

"And how did you go about doing that—having it made?"

The Queen explains, makes it all sound so easy, and indeed it *is* easy for the royal family.

Ludwig asks for special buttons to be molded for his suits and cuff links that bear designs from the ornaments on his wallpaper. He replaces his peacock pens with swan quills. He doodles floral motifs and has them embroidered onto new robes, always underwhelmed by the final product because he has no talent for design, but happy, nonetheless, that his every whim has been satisfied.

He deserves it. He is to be King, after all. Sooner, too, than he expects.

"The Urning, too, is a person."

✳ ✳

SISI ATTENDS THE COURT BALL to welcome in the new year in a bare crinoline with camellias strewn through her hair, her diamonds left behind in the safe. When the Archduchess sees her enter, she turns to Countess Esterházy. "She is perfection, even when she wears glorified undergarments."

Franzl's brother Ludwig Victor loops his arm through Sisi's, and she oozes with anticipation. Only Ludwig Victor's brand of gossip titillates her. He knows every lie the people have spread about Sisi: affairs, frigidity, neglect of her duties and children, abuse of her mother-in-law. Sisi fills her tank of resentments. Finally, Ludwig Victor points at Sisi herself. "And this woman, she *says* she is sick, but that is just to escape her bore of a husband and her tiresome children."

"That's quite enough, LV." Sisi frees her arm. "You can go play your game with someone else. I know we're all the same to you. No confidence too sacred. No truth that can't be improved."

Ludwig Victor feigns ignorance and apologizes. "I'm sorry, love. You know Mother hasn't given up. If I wouldn't marry your sister, why on earth bother trying to marry me off to the Brazilian Emperor's daughter? It has me feeling nasty. I think we all know I have as much interest in marrying as your cousin, Prince Ludwig."

Sisi replies, "Oh, Ludwig's so young; we don't know what he'll get up to yet."

"Up to my spleen, I expect."

Sisi swats him. "He might be the perfect match for Sophie."

LV gapes. "Why would you put your sister through the same rigmarole twice? I've spent more time with Prince Ludwig than you, and a lady knows," LV replies, clutching imaginary pearls.

"*How* do you know?"

"In the same way you know your Franz desires you."

"I'm nothing to desire after birthing three children. I'm used up in Franzl's eyes." She stops herself from telling LV about the syphilis. She knows the temptation to share such information would be far too great for him—it is so perfectly disgusting and human, something the Emperor and Empress should never be.

"Nonsense," LV replies. "You know very well he would have you every night if you'd allow it. And you're so much prettier than he is. If only I liked women—"

"You are lucky I believe in a forgiving God," she says.

"Oh, God has nothing to do with it. We both know that. Money and politics. Family lines and legacies. If you don't reproduce, you're no use. If there *is* a God, he's good enough not to have made me a woman. I'll give him that."

"Too generous," Sisi replies. "In any case, Franzl knows better than to send you away."

"Does he? He's sending Max to the other side of the

world," LV says, referring to one of the brothers between them, the one the Archduchess loves best, the one they've been using as a scapegoat in Italy for years now.

"Yes, but the Emperor can tolerate you," Sisi says.

"Still, even if Max annoys him, shipping him off to Mexico? It's a death sentence. Franz will be happy only when Max's head is on a stake."

"I draw the line there, LV," the Empress replies.

"The lady falters!" Ludwig Victor laughs. "What fun to find a new rule in the game!"

Too Little, Too Late

✳ ✳

A T POSSENHOFEN, SISI'S MOTHER IS TRYING to find a suitable husband for Sisi's sister Sophie. "You have done the family no favors with your theatrics," her mother says.

"'Most Beautiful Woman in the World' is no currency, I guess," Sisi replies.

"It's not only you. Your father hangs around with circus people. Your sisters and brothers are no help. Mathilde's got her bastard baby. Ludwig Wilhelm married an actress and Gackl has his quackery. We could start our own sideshow."

Sisi thinks they might be better off, but she gets her mother's point. "Don't be so dramatic," Sisi says. "Sophie's lovely. It will be no trouble to find her a husband of the highest order."

"It has already been trouble," her mother clarifies.

Sisi thinks of LV's supposition about her cousin, the Bavarian prince, and has an instinct to prove him wrong. Certainly, if any male thought he would prefer the love of another man, Sophie would be the one to prove him wrong. "What about Cousin Ludwig, the Bavarian prince? I have been meaning to pay him a visit now that he is older. I will go and vet him for you."

Sisi's mother replies, "I'd be careful. You know how testy Marie and Max can be if an appointment isn't on the calendar weeks in advance."

Sisi opts to write a letter instead, hoping to be invited for a visit. She doesn't mention Sophie. No need to get ahead of herself. She knows her cousin is young and assumes he will appreciate a more casual note, rather than a formal letter. She begins with flattery, reminding him of her devotion since his birth. She calls out how it would be a shame not to visit together while she is just across the lake from Berg, his family palace. She mentions LV, taking a chance that association with him won't eliminate her as fit company. She has heard he likes *Lohengrin* and closes her letter with a lyric.

> Nothing can bring me calm,
> Nothing can banish my fancies
> Save—though it cost my life—
> To know who you are!

Sisi hopes her tone is clear—a joke writ large, hyperbole to show common ground—but no answer arrives before she must return to Vienna.

On one of her regular visits to the asylums, patients are paraded past Sisi to bow and wave.

Sisi handpicks whom she'd like to talk to, and an

orderly stands by. One patient says he believes that a man plays a saxophone inside his head at all hours. He has asked to have the man removed, or at least to have his saxophone taken away, but the doctors refuse. Sisi is able to offer sympathy in the form of her own familial history of family members invaded by instruments.

One man complains of being held in solitary confinement, of the way not seeing other humans for weeks at a time empties him of hope. He watches the slot in the door for a glimpse of the guards bringing him his mush at mealtime. He shows Sisi the bruises on his elbows, his knees, his head, from where he knocks himself about in frustration. Sisi wonders why these men, who have done nothing that they can blame themselves for, aren't allowed a bit of softness: a bed with a mattress and pillow, cushions on the walls to stop them from trying to replace the mental anguish with physical pain.

One man believes he is the Emperor and so Sisi must be his wife. When he leans in to kiss her, the orderly pulls him away to his cell.

Sisi, startled, says she'll see only one more after this. Her final visitor seems calm and composed. "What's your name?" she asks.

"Oscar," the man replies, with a nod of deference.

"And how are you, Oscar?" she asks.

"I'm well. I don't like this place, but I survive."

"How do you pass the days?"

"I have some sheet music. I've drawn myself a set of piano keys on a rag. I move my fingers through the motions and if I concentrate hard enough, I can hear what I play. At night, I make memory palaces. I imagine rooms one by one, as if I am taking a journey. In each room, there is an object and that object reminds me of something that has happened in my life."

"What do you remember?"

"Swinging from a tree when I was a child, running to jump on the back of the ice carriage, making grass whistle between my thumbs, holding my friend Friedrich's hand, the texture of the spaetzle he would make between my teeth, so chewy."

"And why are you here? What is your condition?" Sisi asks.

"I am here because I loved Friedrich," he replies.

Sisi grasps his hand and wishes him a different fate.

She finds the head doctor before leaving. "There are certain improvements for which I'd like to provide additional support. I know you are doing the best you can with the budget you've been given." She's granted him this assumption, but it is wrong. When budgets are cut, only the prisoners' privileges are narrowed. The doctor says nothing of this, and thanks Sisi for her offer, already thinking of how he might spend his raise.

One summer afternoon, Rudolf climbs high enough into the heart of a linden tree that he can see only leaves below him. In his fumble to descend, his hands slip. He falls and hits his head on a stone. A gardener rushes him inside, where a doctor attends him and calls for his grandmother to return from her holiday and his father to return from a conference. He does not call for Sisi, who is in Kissingen taking the waters.

By the time Sisi is notified, Rudolf is mostly recovered. Sisi comes home immediately with carriages full of expensive gifts. The boy, bored even with the new toys, asks his mother for stories, and she complies, making up trolls and ogres and princesses. One afternoon the Empress tells her son a story of an enchanted horse that wants to roam freely, but his masters keep him contained in his stall in the stable. At night the horse escapes and runs so fast his feet don't even touch the ground. At the first light of day, the horse returns to the stable to avoid punishment. He does this every night until one evening the horse runs faster and farther than he ever has before, and as he approaches the shore of the bay, he doesn't stop. He is certain that he can leap over the water and land on the island barely visible at the horizon.

Rudolf's eyes glow with attention.

Just as the Empress leans in to finish the tale, the door opens. The Archduchess says, "How's my boy?"

"Mother is telling me the most marvelous tale!" Rudolf exclaims, but Sisi is already out of her seat, discarding the horse figurine she was prancing through the air before her son. Sisi cannot bear to compete with the Archduchess, and so the horse in the story remains forever suspended over the sea.

The Archduchess tells Sisi that her commitment to studying Magyar three days a week sends the wrong message to the Hungarian people, who are supposed to be speaking German now.

Sisi waves this rebuke off. "I want to understand the people I rule, and to do that I must understand how they think, and how do you think but with language?"

It is not long before she surprises Rudolf's nurse by

greeting her in her native tongue. The Archduchess bristles when she hears them chatting, unable to determine what sort of misinformation Sisi is passing on in regard to her grandson.

Sisi writes Rudolf notes in Magyar—a secret code he can understand because of his Hungarian nurse—and the Archduchess confiscates them, taking them to the Countess Esterházy for translation. To her relief and disappointment, she finds they usually relay some foolishness, a joke or a rhyme, but she keeps them from the boy all the same.

Franzl finally opens the hospital Sisi has requested, informing her with a brief telegram to bring her home from wherever she's wandered off to this time.

She visits the wards where the Hungarian soldiers have been signed in as the first patients and tells them clunky jokes. They thank her for her dedication to them, while the Austrian orderlies scowl at having to care for people they believe should either be shipped home or allowed to die.

Two Princes

✳ ✳

PRINCE PAUL VON THURN UND TAXIS, a brother of the prince who married Nene, is assigned as aide-de-camp to Ludwig. At first, Ludwig is put off by the handsome young man, jealous of the ease with which he carries himself, but soon Paul and Ludwig become inseparable. Ludwig looks to Paul for cues on what is fashionable, how to behave, and who to associate with, but tries to play it off like it's Paul who's copying *him*.

On vacation in Berchtesgaden, Paul and Ludwig go out for a hike. On the mountain, they happen upon a woodsman, clad only in leather lederhosen, fit as a fiddle. The Princes invite the young man to join them in their picnic. Ludwig boils with admiration. The man's physique is so strong, his skin so ruddy—he seems more alive than any of the people Ludwig encounters at the palace.

Once they've returned from their hike, Ludwig calls in a metalworker to talk to him about a work of art he'd like to commission: a statue of a young, strapping lad, axe in hand, chopping firewood.

When the craftsman allows some confusion into his

brow, Ludwig clarifies. "As tribute to the value of hard work."

The metalworker mocks up a sketch. Ludwig asks that the chest be broader, the hair longer. His calves need more definition and his hips should be narrower above his muscular thighs. The Prince relishes the opportunity to indulge his fantasy, even if the only way he can safely do so is behind the veil of art.

On his eighteenth birthday, Ludwig wakes before the sun. He rows out onto the Alpensee and casts his line, pulling up a nine-and-a-half-pound trout, which he delivers to the kitchen and asks to be served for breakfast. That evening, fireworks jolt from the parapets of Hohenschwangau, causing the family's convivial singing to crescendo.

Ludwig unveils the finished lumberjack statue to Paul at the party and Paul commends the Prince's good taste.

The Queen finds this friendship sweet but potentially suspect. Rumors about the boys have made it to her ears. When Paul departs for the evening, the Queen can't help but address her concerns with the birthday boy. "Paul lives a life of frivolity. As heir apparent, you need to think carefully about who you choose to consort with."

Ludwig hisses, "Must you try to take everything remotely good away from me?"

"And speaking of legacies, you mustn't burn any bridges that might improve the possibilities of your creating an heir of your own. I know you never wrote back to your cousin Sisi. A shame she's already married off, but she has what seems to be countless sisters who are equally fit to be a royal consort. If you offend one, you offend them all."

"Sisi *is* incredibly beautiful, and I cannot deny that such exquisiteness does deserve my attention. I will write her back from my dungeon."

"Oh, yes, Lieber Drachen. Spit your fire in your dungeon."

Though the Queen has ordered that Paul not be allowed an audience with the Prince at the Residenz, Ludwig attempts to work around this limitation by walking to Paul's house in the Türkenstrasse, but Paul does not answer. Ludwig notices an envelope under a flowerpot, though. It is addressed only to "L." "Don't press the fulfillment of your wishes too much. My present position is at stake. One must be enough of a man not to show every disappointment in one's heart. God—if it pleases him—will bring us together sooner or later. I wear your chain and consider it a symbol of the faith with which our friendship is bound together." The letter is signed "PauLudwig"—a mixed message of union and division.

Ludwig hides his heartbreak behind offense that Paul has given up on him so easily.

Common Courtesy Dictates

✳   ✳

BISMARCK VISITS NYMPHENBURG in August when King Max is away in Frankfurt. He notices that the Queen never addresses Ludwig. When talk turns to the political situation, he notices the Prince downing glass after glass of champagne. At one point, Ludwig interrupts the serious talk to ask Bismarck if he's seen *Tannhäuser*.

The Queen breaks in. "Ludwig, I said we are not to talk about the theatre at the dinner table. Please!" She signals to the waiter to stop refilling Ludwig's glass, but Ludwig picks up the empty flute and holds it over his shoulder.

Bismarck defends Ludwig, knowing a diplomatic kindness to the boy now will pay dividends later. "I have seen others of Wagner's works, but not yet *Tannhäuser*. I am curious to hear about it."

Ludwig's spirits perk as he launches into a synopsis. "First of all it is a stunning production, and the lakes they've painted for the Venusberg are the most perfect shade of turquoise, despite the darkness of the cave. Naiads and sirens float through the water and lounge about the banks. Dancing nymphs and bacchantes disport themselves about the stage for the ballet. Then Tannhäuser sings a love song to Venus, but he's also begging her to let him go. Of course she gets quite angry, but eventually breaks the spell, releasing him, but predicting he will be back in time. The stage transforms and Tannhäuser finds himself in a beautiful valley, where he kneels before a shrine—you see, he is battling personally between a sacred and profane love . . ."

The Queen tries to catch Bismarck's eye to imply, *Perhaps now you understand why I tried to avoid this*, but Bismarck prefers this to the Queen's dry small talk, and he pays the Prince his utmost attention.

In January of 1864, King Max comes down with a flu that goes ignored for too long.

By March, Ludwig has avoided seeing his father for weeks when the Queen finally tracks him down in his bedroom. "Can it wait?" he asks, not lifting his eyes from his book.

"I'm afraid it can't." If the Prince would turn his eyes from the page, he might see his mother's sadness. "Ludwig," she says, almost as though punishing him with her harshness, "your father is dying. We must prepare you to become King."

Ludwig looks up with the sting of this news. Only days ago his father had been declared surely curable with some hot tea and rest.

"It's moved to his lungs, and it's only a matter of time." The Queen excuses herself to weep privately.

Still, Ludwig does not go to his father's side. He calls for a horse to be saddled. In the cool, gray light of the mountains, he stops at a peasant's house and knocks on the door.

A woman answers, stunned to see the Prince before her. She invites him in and asks her daughter to make coffee while she and the Prince take a seat near the hearth.

"Within days I am to be your new King." Ludwig is surprised to hear himself say it.

The woman and her daughter share a look of shock. "Of course, it will be our honor to serve you, Your Highness, but is it true? Is the King . . . ?"

Ludwig dashes his mug upon the ground with a cry of agony. "I've only now just heard the news myself."

The women wince, suddenly aware that they know nothing of the future King's personality. If he has a violent streak, then they have invited trouble. The mother proceeds cautiously. "This is a very heavy burden for such a young man to bear," she says, and the daughter nods sympathetically. She is only thirteen, but already she has borne more responsibility in her life than the Prince.

"The problem is that I have no interest in it. I believed I had a whole lifetime to do something else before the mantle fell to me."

The woman sits up straight, like her back is strapped to a board. The girl averts her eyes. The woman searches her mind for a solution. "Your Highness, please, join us for supper. We have only dumplings and some tripe, but the lion's share is yours if you'll do us the honor."

Ludwig thanks the woman through his sniffles.

When the woman's husband arrives home, soaked in sweat and melted snow, he bows nervously upon seeing the Prince. After dinner, they teach Ludwig to play skat. He imagines himself a part of the family, and begins to cry again for all he's been deprived of, forgetting all his privilege.

The castle bustles with questions about where the Prince has gone. At midnight a search party bundles up and sets out. It won't be the last time he needs finding.

The peasant family buries its yawns. The woman takes a chance. "Your Highness, we'd be honored if you'd stay with us. You can have our bed and we will sleep by the fire."

Ludwig has not been trained to refuse things out of politeness or to know when he has overstayed his welcome, and so he accepts.

In the early hours of morning, a quick, heavy knock bounds through the cottage.

The man of the house opens the door and is immediately pushed down by two soldiers. He watches as the Prince is towed out of bed. The soldiers strap his boots onto his feet and place hands under each of his arms, his heels dragging in protest. Ludwig is too distressed to thank the family for their hospitality.

Letters arrive to the Queen, offering princesses. The Queen shows each bid to Ludwig, but he refuses to read them. He can't countenance the idea of marriage right now along with all of the other imminent changes.

Kings and queens delay promising their daughters to anyone else in the hopes that the Bavarian Prince might choose them. As the weeks go by, a nickname forms for Ludwig—the spinstermaker—as though the young princesses are growing haggard in a fortnight.

Ludwig hides in the theater, watching a performance of *Lohengrin*, trying to make the most of his endangered freedom, until it is insisted that he join the family in the bedroom of the King at the Munich Residenz. Max holds Ludwig's arm in his weak grip and says, "My son, when your time comes, may you die as peacefully as your father." Ludwig doesn't find anything peaceful about this scene.

He kisses his father's head and then Max gasps, and Ludwig knows he is gone. He stands and takes a step back, at a loss for how to announce such news.

"Is the King alive?" asks Queen Marie.

Ludwig replies in the affirmative, "He is alive in heaven."

The room should cry, but first there is a buzz of misunderstood relief before they comprehend what Ludwig has actually said.

Otto says, "Your Majesty King Ludwig," and bows to his brother for the first time.

Ludwig cannot suppress a great nervous laugh, as the others in the room genuflect to him. Everyone waits for him to say something—to acknowledge his position or to order them into action—but Ludwig is absolutely frozen.

The cabinet secretary, Franz von Pfistermeister, always prepared, knows the proper procedure, though. "If you'll excuse my interruption, Your Majesty, we will call an Accession Council together so you might take your oath and we can begin the transition."

Ludwig can do little more than nod, as the rest of the room springs into motion.

Priorities

✻　✻

HIS FATHER'S FUNERAL PROCESSION is an odd moment to fully inhabit his new power, but Ludwig
strides with import down the street behind the coffin in
the early spring light, clouded but bright. The people of
Munich shout, "The King is dead! Long live King Ludwig!" He deigns to reach out his hand and the people grab
hold. The women swoon at his tall, athletic frame, his
ivory skin and dark curls.

The Queen watches her son trying on his new title, and
says to her lady-in-waiting, "Max died too soon."

Ludwig has only one idea of his own. "Is Wagner on the
Munich Strangers List?" he asks Pfistermeister. With Max,
Pfistermeister had mostly to execute the King's sound decisions. With this fledgling, he has a sense that he might
need to do much more. Pfistermeister asks Ludwig which
Wagner he might be referring to, and Ludwig bangs down
his fist. "Richard, of course! The composer! Who else?"

———

Wagner is visiting friends when a servant delivers him a calling card reading, "Secretary of the King of Bavaria," and Wagner laughs it off. "The creditors are getting very creative," he says, pouring himself another glass of wine.

The next morning, though, Pfistermeister calls again, this time at Wagner's hotel. He hands over a ruby ring and a note: "As this stone burns, so do I burn with ardor to behold the creator of the words and music of *Lohengrin.*" The secretary tells Wagner the King intends to become his dedicated patron. Wagner is surprised, skeptical even, but accepts the invitation.

Deep in debt, Wagner pays his hotel bill with an expensive snuffbox, and says a prayer that this will be the last time he needs to forfeit his treasures for his debts. He checks himself into the finest hotel in all of Munich.

When Wagner reports to the King's chambers, he is overcome by the woody smell of chypre. He looks around for the source of the scent, but as he approaches Ludwig, he realizes the young King is doused in the perfume. He breathes through his mouth, well aware the sacrifice will be worth it.

He and the King exchange effusive compliments for an hour and a half. Ludwig asks about the status of Wagner's current projects. Wagner tells Ludwig that work on *Das Rheingold*, the first component of a four-part project called *Der Ring des Nibelungen*, is nearly complete and work on the second part, *Die Walküre*, is well underway.

"When do you think the first installment might be performed?" Ludwig asks.

Wagner laughs. "It will take me some time. I intend for all four operas to be performed only when the cycle is complete."

Ludwig fakes a smile, cocks his head. "And in the meantime?" he asks. Surely his status as King and his clear devotion can hurry Wagner along in the process. If nothing else, he needs something to tide him over.

Wagner can see the King is displeased, but there is no rushing his composition. "We'll remount old productions."

Ludwig frowns. He doesn't know how to negotiate. He has only ever wielded tantrums to get what he wants in the past. He has never assembled a battery of tactics that he might manipulate as necessary. If he had paid attention to any of his military lessons, he might at least find a metaphorical equivalent within this conversation, but Ludwig is at a loss. He is uncomfortable in his newly awarded power. He has such admiration for the composer that he must summon every bit of his courage to try to intimidate him. "That will not be good enough." He feels a rash break out on his neck.

Wagner hates compromising, but he knows he must. "I'll take some time to work on something new that's a bit less ambitious. Give myself a break from the Gesamtkunstwerk."

"Good, good," Ludwig says. "Keep me apprised of your progress. I would like to approve your ideas before you pursue them."

Ludwig sees the grimace stretch across Wagner's face and self-corrects. He fears going so far as to offend the composer. He doesn't understand that Wagner needs Ludwig as much as Ludwig needs Wagner. "Rather I'd like to know about them right away so I might support you in any way I can."

Wagner bows his head. Both men can feel the significance of this connection. Neither can summon the words to name this meeting, but each can tell that the other will change the future of their life entirely.

Before he can say anything else that might damage this budding friendship, Ludwig concludes their meeting then and there.

At the hotel, Cosima asks what that smell is. "It is the scent of my trouble turning on its heel, my love," Wagner replies.

Beyond a knowledge of Wagner, Ludwig's lack of expertise is quickly made clear. He asks his councillors what his father might have done in such a situation, and follows that advice to a fault. The councillors realize they hold great sway, and take full advantage.

The secretaries visit every morning from eight thirty to ten. Ludwig eats his second breakfast and then each day of the week, Ludwig invites a minister to come instruct him on a different area of the country's government at eleven. At noon he grants audiences for several hours and then goes for a walk or a ride. Dinner at four. More reports from the secretaries at six. And then Leinfelder reads the newspapers aloud to the King until it's time for bed.

Ludwig tries to focus, but feels his imagination's strong pull. When things go wrong, he blames his cabinet.

The cabinet secretary asks Ludwig, "Should we have done the opposite then, Your Majesty?"

Ludwig says, "Well, clearly."

Pfistermeister dares to ask, "And what would that be?"

Ludwig, panicking inside, maintains his airs. "If I need to tell you, then we are in serious trouble."

Pfistermeister recognizes this as misdirection: the King hasn't the slightest idea of what is happening, and Pfistermeister realizes this means he needn't consult the King at all. He begins forging Ludwig's signature. He steps away from cabinet meetings to "take counsel with the King" and returns quickly with only his own decision.

Despite this lack of skill in governing, the people are thrilled with their new King.

Crowds clamor outside the Residenz hoping for a glimpse of the brooding young man. As long as the people are distracted and happy, Pfistermeister sees fit to keep the politics of King Max moving forward in Ludwig's name.

Ludwig rents Wagner a chalet on the shore of the Würmsee, near his own family retreat, but they seldom see one another. In person, Ludwig finds himself tripping over his words. He writes Wagner long letters instead, calling him "Great Friend." He tells himself that if he doesn't disturb Wagner, the *Ring* cycle might be completed more quickly.

Statesmen take notice of this relationship and wonder, aloud, if Wagner is not Ludwig's Lola Montez. "'Lolus,' we'll call him," jokes one member of the cabinet to another.

"Or 'Lolotte'!" the other responds, and they laugh until they discover that Wagner's salary is higher than that of a senior civil servant with nearly two decades of service.

Wagner moves to a mansion in the Briennerstrasse. Pfistermeister recommends against this move, sure the people will object to Wagner living in such an opulent neighborhood on the King's dime, but Ludwig says, "He's free to live wherever he likes. I'm sure he's chosen something within his means."

Pfistermeister is not sure why the King might assume such a thing, considering Wagner's history of debts. "He's decorated it like a gaudy brothel!"

"Haha, Wagner's tastes do run a bit purple. I daresay it's why I like him."

Wagner can sense the outside forces desiring to pull them apart, and pens an essay with Ludwig in mind, naming it "On State and Religion." He stresses the importance of a King continuing to explore his contemplative and artistic interests alongside the demands of ruling a kingdom. Wagner writes, "An irrecusable urge to turn his back completely on this world must necessarily surge up within his breast, were there not for him—as for the common man . . . a certain distraction, a periodical turning-aside from the world's earnestness which else is ever present in his thoughts."

Ludwig thanks Wagner for putting his feelings into such eloquent words, and the people go wild with adoration for the new definition added to Ludwig's identity as a ruler; they call him their Dream King.

An Exchange of Gifts

✳ ✳

SISI REQUESTS A COMPANION with whom she might practice her Hungarian. The list given to her is full of countesses and baronesses, but Sisi chooses the one without a title, the Hungarian daughter of a friend of a friend who has been put on the list as a favor. *Of course*, the Archduchess thinks, *she* is the one that Sisi chooses.

Ida Ferenczy, twenty-four years old, arrives at Schönbrunn with a secret. No one knows that the girl is acquainted with two of the leading Hungarian politicians: Ferenc Deák and Count Gyula Andrássy.

Despite her ulterior motives, Ida enjoys the Empress's company even in their first meeting. Sisi poses questions, with genuine interest, about the girl's family and home, and Ida manages to make the Empress smile, proving her wit with some informed jokes about court life.

"I must go, but I will say: I'm very pleased with you. We shall be much together," Sisi promises Ida.

Alone, Ida looks at the portraits that decorate the walls of the salon. Each of the horses is labeled with the name the Empress has awarded it: Dayrunner, Silver Moon, Pansy, Penelope, Archie. She thinks about penning a letter home, but she knows these names are not the information Deák and Andrássy seek.

The next morning, Sisi hands Ida the first text she'd like to study. Ida takes a seat, but the Empress stops her. "No, no, not here. You'll read to me as we walk," Sisi says.

"But how will I see where I'm going?" Ida asks.

"I'll guide you," Sisi says.

In that first month, Ida must wrap her ankles each morning to prevent them from turning. She knew there was risk involved in her attempts to deepen Sisi's investment in Hungary, but she had never imagined *physical* danger. Still, Ida dismisses her selfishness; an ankle is a small price to pay. Sisi leads them through the low meandering path of hedges in the Grand Parterre, and through the radial array of animal pens at the Tiergarten, up the hill to the Gloriette, and then through the winding gardens back to the palace. Ida sees none of it, but as she stumbles through a volume of Eötvös, her steps slowly grow assured.

On her next visit to Possenhofen, Sisi and Ludwig finally make a time to meet one another. Ludwig, newly crowned, should be busier than ever, but he seems to have limitless time to chat with Sisi. She is surprised to see him rowing up to the shore of Possi alone. Sisi asks a servant to bring a picnic out to the water's edge for them.

She has seen photos of the young King. She knows the way every girl in the kingdom pines after him. He has the reputation of being a bad boy, with locks so dark they shine almost blue. He is her Wittelsbach inverse: the people revel in her flawless light, and long to take shade in his brooding shadow. His reputation, though, is unfounded; it is only that he is an almost blank slate onto which the people might project their fantasies and hopes, for he has not yet proven what type of ruler he will be.

Sisi quickly judges Ludwig to be naive, romantic, nervous. He hounds her for advice, but changes the subject constantly, making it seem as though he's not listening. But he is. If he's failing to internalize the lessons with the different ministers, his ability to take in every pearl of Sisi's wisdom proves that he's capable of learning if he cares about his subject. In Sisi he sees a role model: a beautiful enigma, an elegant iconoclast. He has much to learn.

They commiserate about their obligations. They exchange favorite lines of verse. They share beauty secrets and Ludwig vows to wash his hair in eggs and brandy, too. When Ludwig complains about the time it takes to wave his locks, Sisi counters him with the fact that her hair takes an entire day to dry and a good three hours to be set.

"You must tell me the rest of your beauty secrets, for, already, I can feel myself aging," Ludwig begs.

"You're nineteen, silly," she says.

"Yes, but you are my senior and you look younger than me." His eyes show genuine fear. "I notice you don't move your mouth very much when you talk, and that you withhold your smile almost without exception. Your looks shine with a serenity that doesn't require joy. Is it to avoid wrinkles?"

Sisi pauses. "I will share a secret with you, dear cousin, but you mustn't tell a soul."

Ludwig crosses his heart, thrilling at what Sisi might reveal.

Sisi smiles broadly, allowing her mouth to reveal yellow, crooked tombstones of teeth jutting out every which way.

Ludwig, never good at hiding his reactions, recoils.

"Then they're as bad as I feared," Sisi says, shutting her lips.

"But no one need know," Ludwig says, trying to shake the image from his mind.

Sisi tells Ludwig about the bars and rings she's had installed in the palace so that she might do her exercises. Ludwig plots to request the same.

"My only other secret is that I travel with my favorite cow, Hildegarde. I've become absolutely unable to drink the milk from any other animal."

Ludwig finds permission in hearing of these eccentricities. "In our positions, we can really do anything at all," Ludwig replies.

"How I wish that were true, cousin," Sisi says with a sigh. "I do all of these absurd things *because* I'm forbidden from doing what I truly want to do."

"And what is that?" Ludwig asks.

Sisi poses behind her fan. "It is necessary to have some secrets one keeps for oneself." In fact, if Sisi were able to name what she wants, she might tell her cousin after all they've shared this afternoon, but for now she can only identify that there is *something* that is either out of her reach or consistently being snatched from her grasp. She feels a lack, but for now it is a secret even from herself.

Ludwig scoffs and changes the subject. "Do you sing? You know you would make the most magnificent Elsa."

"If I sing even a single note, it's somehow out of tune."

"Shame. If I could do anything, I would live out the plot of *Lohengrin*."

Sisi gasps. "Ludwig! That would be an absolute tragedy! You wish for your love to die when she finds out your true identity?"

Ludwig turns away. He has no tolerance for differing opinions. "You said, only a breath ago, that everyone must have a few secrets just for themselves. How is this different?"

Sisi pauses. It may be they are even more similar than she thought: this cynicism about never being truly seen. If they are kindreds, though, she knows she will not need to explain herself. She wonders, instead, what it is that Ludwig is so sure he can never reveal to another, if LV had been right about her cousin and his preference for the love of men. Sisi kisses her cousin on the cheek. "My wish for you is that you can set every secret free, and if you figure out how, you will tell me immediately."

Ludwig looks back at his sweet cousin. "You are a gift."

Sisi takes his hand. "If I am a gift to you, it is one given in return."

Threats

✻   ✻

FRANZL IS CONFUSED by Sisi's newfound attachment to Ludwig. Since her visit with Ludwig, she has not stopped talking about him. Considering the way Sisi rebuffs Franzl's advances each night, he wonders if something more might have occurred between them than simple friendship. Of course, Sisi's response (or lack thereof) to Franzl is nothing new, but he has yet to determine what weather it is that directs her winds, and he is a man of reason and science, and so he sets out hypotheses and tests them. He asks Sisi not to invite Ludwig to her birthday party on Christmas Eve. This year they will keep the party small and invite only local family.

Sisi is disappointed not to show off the Hofburg to her new confidant, but, surprisingly, for once, she is able to enjoy the day. She loves the rich smell of the pine logs burning and the sweet waft of the pot of stewing apples. Her ears perk to the hiss of the moisture seeping out of the ceramic ovens and the pop of the chestnuts. She doesn't let anyone fill her crystal mug for her with the hot punch because she loves the feeling of standing over the pot and letting the steam open up her face while she fills her own.

Gisela and Rudolf, eight and six, are old enough to coax their way into staying up late and making the adults join them in their games. Rudolf hides and the rest of the family count to twenty—a dangerously high number considering how large the Hofburg is and how far a little boy can run in such a span of time. Sisi is the first to find him, and they crouch together behind a coffer for what feels like forever, trading whispered secrets and squeezing each other into silence when they hear footsteps approach.

"Who is your favorite?" she asks him. She cannot help herself.

The boy is young. He can respond only in the present tense. "You!" He showers her with kisses and Sisi accepts his answer as permanent, the greatest gift she could ask for.

It is then that the Archduchess finds them, but Rudolf is so distracted by Sisi's undivided attention that the spell remains unbroken. For one perfect moment, they form a friction-free trio, their laughter at their inability to conceal themselves behind the wooden chest multiplying until they are found by the others and the game ends.

Now that Rudolf is of schooling age, the Archduchess begins to take the child's daily routine more seriously. As Sisi had lost interest in the children's education, the Archduchess had gradually taken back control. She puts out calls to the best professors in the country to see if they might spare some time to design the Prince's lessons. All are too proud to turn down the crown, but many struggle to simplify their university courses into something appropriate for a young boy. Rudolf can barely follow the content and the

Emperor calls for a change. "Count Gondrecourt will take over."

"Why? He doesn't even strike me as particularly intelligent," the Archduchess replies. "I should think Rudolf deserves more than a standard military tutor."

"He needs to learn discipline above all else, and the tutors you've hired haven't the slightest idea how to keep him under control. Once the Count has taught him some restraint, we can bring in more learned men."

Before long, Rudolf is showing up to dinner shock-eyed and twitchy. "What's wrong with him?" the Emperor asks the Archduchess.

"Don't you hear the shots in the afternoons? The Count fires pistols to get him to focus," she says.

The Emperor, ruled by pride in this moment, pretends this sounds like a reasonable idea. Sisi sits miserably silent, but no one notices her lack of opinion. She has been denied any agency in relation to the children, and she has taken to abstaining completely from voicing her thoughts when the subject of their care and keeping arises. This silent treatment, though, has little effect, as Franz and the Archduchess do so well to fill the air with their own theories and methods. Sisi chews her tongue to keep quiet, but nothing could compare to the pain of the fear she has for her little boy.

As the weeks go by, Rudolf spends more mornings in bed than at his lessons. He breathes into his hands and clamps them to his forehead before the Archduchess enters his room. He spits on his palms. He keeps a pepper shaker under his pillow so he might summon a sneeze as he hears the click of her heels down the hallway.

When the doctor examines him, he tells the Archduchess that Rudolf suffers only from nerves, a word that the Archduchess hushes from the doctor's mouth, leery of the Wittelsbach legacy.

She calls off the lessons for that afternoon and approaches Franzl in her study. "Son, I know you think that Gondrecourt is helping bolster the child's focus and bravery, but yesterday, as I understand it, the Count locked Rudolf in the Lainzer Tiergarten and told him that if he didn't answer his homework questions quickly enough the wild boars would eat him."

The Emperor stifles a laugh. "Well, there are very few boars in the forest and I've never seen one near the gate, have you? It sounds harmless enough."

"He is the heir to the throne, so no risk is worth it, but even if the child *is* safe, he's scared half to death. He pretends to be sick to avoid his lessons."

"Well, he gets that from his mother," the Emperor says. "I don't have any interest in rewarding such behavior."

"You must ask the Count to be a bit gentler," the Archduchess bids, and Franzl agrees.

Two mornings later, before the sun has risen, the Empress wakes to screams. She opens her shutters to see little Rudolf standing in a foot of snow clad only in his pajamas. Gondrecourt shouts questions to the boy. When Rudolf gets one right, he is asked another. When he gets one wrong, he is made to lie down in the snow until he answers correctly.

Sisi rushes to Franzl's study, where he's been awake for hours, and breaks her silence. "This must be stopped. He'll catch his death."

"I was put through similar trials," Franzl says, which is true.

"I have lost one child, Franz," Sisi replies. "I will not lose another."

"If he begins to complete his studies to the Count's satisfaction, this stage will not last long," Franzl says.

That morning, Rudolf shivers over his oatmeal, and Sisi sprinkles extra raisins and brown sugar into the bowl as an apology.

Later that afternoon she drafts a formal letter to Franz, the only way she believes she might be heard. "It is my wish that full and unlimited powers should be reserved to me in all things concerning the children. Either Gondrecourt goes, or I do."

Franzl receives the note and fires Gondrecourt. He *knows* better than to think this will keep Sisi in the country, but that doesn't mean he can't *hope* now is the time that she will change.

Sisi appoints Colonel von Thurnburg, who strikes a more measured balance between discipline and knowledge. Rudolf behaves himself for fear that they'll reverse their decision. The Emperor, the Archduchess, and the Empress are all, finally, surprisingly, content.

Charge the Palace

✳ ✳

LUDWIG COMMISSIONS AN OIL PORTRAIT of himself and presents it to Wagner as a gift. He hints that he'd like a portrait of Wagner in return.

Wagner arranges for an artist friend to paint him.

Ludwig marvels at the likeness. "Well, it is lovely, my Great Friend! I thank you for this gift."

Wagner bows, but he is thinking that the King has misunderstood. On his way out, he tells Pfistermeister he'll have the artist send the palace an invoice.

"An invoice?" Pfistermeister asks.

"The King requested the portrait. It is more commission than gift."

Pfistermeister, goggle-eyed, responds, "If you can't afford a gift for your patron, maybe we should find you a home more within your budget, outside the Briennerstrasse."

Wagner huffs and pays the artist himself. All his money comes from Ludwig anyway.

The painting is exceptionally ugly, but then so is Wagner. This is one instance in which the King will make exceptions to his standards of pulchritude. Pfistermeister can't resist telling the King that Wagner tried to bill the palace for the gift. Ludwig, knowing Pfistermeister is already fed up with his Friend, pretends Wagner is in the right, but he skips the performance of *The Flying Dutchman* the following weekend and the newspapers fly off the presses in a tizzy. "The King and His Great Friend Fight!"

Wagner requests an audience with Ludwig and is denied.

One evening, Wagner receives a knock at his door. His servant reports that it's an old woman in tattered robes saying she has an important message. Wagner chastises the servant for bothering him with such an inquiry, and the servant dismisses her. When Wagner returns later that night from a stroll, the woman is still waiting in front of his home. "Herr Wagner," she says in a throaty voice, "I beseech you: you will only benefit from what it is I have to share."

Wagner, vain, curious, and slightly disturbed, invites the woman in.

In the parlor, she sits across from him at the table. Her cloak hides much of her face from him, and he leans forward trying to look into her eyes. She grasps his palm. "Do you believe in the stars?" she asks.

Wagner, skeptical but intrigued, responds, "Must I?"

This answer proves enough for the old woman. "I tried to provide the wisdom of the stars to King Maximilian and Ludwig I before him, but they did not heed my warnings. My record, though, has proven that the stars hold all the answers."

Wagner, getting impatient, says, "Go on then."

The woman's voice raises to that of an incantation. "In

the stars it is written that this young King is called to greater deeds. I want my King to have peace, and you, Herr Wagner, must guard him against the misfortunes through which evil men seek to ruin him as they ruined his father and grandfather."

Wagner is pleased to be given this responsibility. "Have you any advice on how it is I go about helping the King to avoid his ruin?" he asks the soothsayer.

Her eyes roll back in their sockets. "You will know."

The already self-important Wagner feels an added gravity invade his intentions: all he need do is follow his instincts. For some time now, he has been thinking his horrible thoughts about the idea of a "Horde," or a supremely powerful master race, descended from an "Ur-vater." Such an egotistical idea—to imagine a new way in which not only his country but the entire world should be organized—is run-of-the-mill for Wagner. The mystic's vision affirms his suspicion that Ludwig might be the King to lead this Horde. While the Civil War rages on in America, Wagner is forming his own opinions of supremacy, and Ludwig's dedication to him and his ideas suggests that there is a way to further their plans and ideals.

The old woman stands to leave, taller, Wagner thinks, than when he ushered her in. He bids her adieu, and now the voice that responds sounds familiar, though he cannot place it.

On the day of the premiere of *Tristan und Isolde*, debt collectors arrive to Wagner's home. Cosima—daughter of Franz Liszt, mother of Wagner's child, wife to Wagner's conductor Hans von Bülow—runs to the court secretary to beg for the amount requested. Once the bailiffs have been paid off, Wagner sits at his desk with his head in his hands. The day has already been ruined. He refuses to go to the theater.

But the show goes on. The crowd is moved. Ludwig is rapturous despite not being able to congratulate Wagner personally on the new show. He is accompanied by his old friend Paul von Thurn und Taxis. Now that he's King, Ludwig's mother can no longer adjudicate his friendships. Paul does not care for opera. He dozes through the performance, but Ludwig is so dazzled by the stage, he doesn't notice.

After the show, Ludwig and Paul go for a night ride in a carriage into the woods. Ludwig shakes Paul, asleep again, to go for a walk with him, but Paul just nestles more cozily into his seat. Ludwig wanders away, unaccompanied, to weep. Would that Ludwig might be granted such a potion to ensure that his beloved would love him back. Until then, like the doomed lovers of the show, he, too, will meet with his beloved only in the cover of night via his dreams until the eternal night of death.

Cross Your Heart, Hope to Die

✻ ✻

SISI RETURNS TO BAD KISSINGEN for her summer rejuve-
nation. Letters arrive every day from Ludwig. She loves
the way he writes—always hyperbolic, whether exalted or
diminished. His drama is addictive. Dozens of pages of
effusive praise for *Tristan und Isolde*. Verbose apologies
for not visiting, blaming the doctors for saying his lungs
get worse in Kissingen's humidity. Detailed accounts of
his rides through the Bavarian countryside she misses so
much. What he writes of best, though, is the overwhelm-
ing beauty of other people. Rarely going deeper than mus-
culature or bone structure. Ludwig is a person who sees
beauty in flesh, and it feeds her own obsessions. After
reading his description of an actress he admires, she stays
in the sauna until she feels emptied of herself. She pulls
herself up on the bar an extra set. She declines to eat a single meal.

But even on the days she feels like she is advancing
toward some nebulous, vanishing goal, she is lonely. She
writes to Ida, "Life is so gloomy. I go for a great many
walks, which occupy almost the whole day, and I read a

great deal, but it's not nearly as efficient as when you read to me. God be with you and don't get married while I am away."

Ida wonders why Sisi can't try to read to herself while she walks as Ida does for her, but then she thinks of Sisi tripping, of her delicate, fleshless bones, of the way her crinolines might leave her stranded upon the ground, rolling in a wide circle. Any injury could mean that Sisi loses what little interest she seems to have already in the Hungarian cause. A distraction might dissolve any dedication, and then Ida would be stuck in Vienna with no purpose at all.

Ida has not written to the boy she loved back home since arriving to the Hofburg. The Empress has impressed on her that she shouldn't encourage his affections. Now that she has been established as a noblewoman, more attractive options are sure to present themselves, but Ida gets the feeling that Sisi would prefer she become a spinster so she might remain in Sisi's service indefinitely. Maybe, Ida thinks, slyly advancing the agenda of Hungarian demands could be enough to fill a life.

Ida writes, "When you return to the Hofburg, it is essential you visit with Gyula Andrássy. I understand your husband once sentenced him to death, but so much has changed. I've told him of your investment in the Hungarian language and culture, and he is very eager to meet you."

Sisi, skeptical of any obligations, hems and haws at first, but then: "Such a meeting will surely upset the Archduchess, so please set it up."

When Sisi returns, Ida mentions what she knows of Ferenc Deák's plans for Hungarian-Austrian relations. Sisi thinks the plan seems more than sound and she ventures to share a summary of the plan with Franzl for his consideration.

"*You* know who Ferenc Deák is?" Franzl asks.

"Of course," Sisi says. "What do you take me for?"

Franzl pauses. "I'd think he'd be too boring a character for you."

Sisi smiles. "I am only disinterested in things that matter little to me."

The Emperor hires Winterhalter to paint a portrait of Sisi. She hates sitting for the sessions and asks that for every ten minutes of posing, she be allowed to walk for five.

On the day that the portrait is unveiled, Sisi gasps. The white ball gown hovers around her like a mist. Diamond stars chart a constellation down her braids. "It's divine," Sisi says.

Winterhalter says, "When I showed the sketches to Empress Eugénie in France, she said, 'Finally I can cede my status as the loveliest crowned head of Europe.'"

"You'll have to do another," Sisi says. "I'd like you to paint something more intimate that Franzl might hang in his office."

Winterhalter commences the second painting the following week. He is surprised to find the Empress awaiting him in a simple white dressing gown, her hair plaited loosely on either side of her head. He tells her to take position, but Sisi asks him to wait a moment. She turns, folding the two hanks of hair over each other in a knot across her chest, and sets her face with a dignified smirk.

"You know what it is you want for this one, I see," Winterhalter says.

"I want to appear as Franzl sees me in the morning. My hair tied in this way shows that my love for Franzl is protected."

Winterhalter dips his palette knife into a shimmering white to begin mixing the colors of the Empress's skin.

If Only

LUDWIG CLAIMS HE'S SICK, weak, not fit for travel. But only when he is scheduled to attend an army maneuver. The generals get catty in their daily logs: "If the King is able to row the Alpsee for hours at a time he should be able to devote a few days to the army."

Sisi hears of Ludwig's illness and pays a visit to see what the matter is. In his room, she has to peel back cover after cover to find her cousin deep inside. "Is it contagious?" she asks, her handkerchief guarding her mouth and all those teeth.

Ludwig glances behind her. "Are you alone?"

"Yes, of course."

He throws back the covers, fine. "I can't bear to attend those tedious drills. The helmet spoils my hair and all I can think of while I'm there is the progress I'm losing on my other work."

"Your work."

"In bed, at least, I can daydream uninterrupted. I can think an idea and then think it again more deeply. Out at the barracks, I'm constantly being called upon to voice some good word about something or other I don't under-stand at all."

Sisi identifies with this dismal sense of obligation, but it is easier to tease in someone else. "You poor, overworked King."

Ludwig grumps. "Do you love the Emperor?"

Sisi halts her proverbial horse and turns to Ludwig. "Where did that question come from?" she asks, and real-izes she must answer, "Of course."

"I'm not sure I can put Mother off any longer in her quest to find me a wife."

"You should marry Sophie. She's such a dear, and you're interested in many of the same things. Besides, it will mean I can visit you both at once. Do it for me!"

"I worry I could never be happy no matter who she is," Ludwig says.

"Ah, like your grandfather," Sisi replies. "I've heard about the dancer."

"Tell me how you and the Emperor fell in love. Enter-tain me."

"The Emperor and I are hardly what you should base your fantasy upon. Our passion has faded."

"But tell me about the beginnings. Tell me about when it was new."

"Franzl invited my family to Ischl. Mother thought it best Father stay home so he didn't ruin Nene's chances with his hijinks. I came along only to keep Nene company. Ischl is a casual summerhouse. Like Berg is for you. It was more formal there than the way I grew up, but joyful and free compared to what I know now of life in the Hofburg.

"When we arrived Franzl was out on a hunt. I should

have known then what a trial the Archduchess would be the moment we arrived. We were dressed in black, mourning a great-aunt who had passed away, and I heard the Archduchess pull Mother aside and comment that black did not suit Nene. My mother laughed and said that mourning wasn't meant to suit anyone. She promised we'd dress with more color the following day. She chided the Archduchess for not wearing black herself, and it was then I remembered they were sisters. At the time, I saw the Archduchess so rarely, I had to remind myself she was my aunt.

"Just then, Franzl rode up on his horse. He dismounted and addressed Nene first. He greeted us all, and I curtsied deeply. He said, 'And this must be wee Sisi, along for the ride, playing princess, eh?' When he lifted my hand to kiss it, I looked at him and we both blushed, but I must admit, the engine of my heat was anger. How dare he call me, a fifteen-year-old woman, 'wee'! It was an insult.

"I could tell he had startled himself, looking into my eyes, though I was too young to understand what he was afraid of. Just then, a cart pulled up with the carcasses of a capercailzie and a chamois, both of which he'd killed. I was impressed until we went inside and I saw how commonplace this was for his family. The stairway was lined in hundreds of sets of horns, all adorned with plaques saying who had killed what animal and when.

"Our trunks were brought in and we were shown our rooms. I heard a military band strike up in the garden below as Mother was trying to pep Nene up by pinching her cheeks and repinning her curls. I asked Mother if I could go down to the garden, but she told me I had to wait until

Nene was ready. Perhaps she'd seen the look Franz had given me.

"The Emperor waited for Nene outside, and he asked if she'd like to go for a walk. She obliged, though he cast a glance my way. I realize now he probably wished he could walk with me instead. I sat beside my mother and the Archduchess, listening to their boring chitchat.

"The dinner we ate with them was simple, but abundant: rindfleisch, Salzburger nockerln, Kaiserschmarrn. It made us feel welcome. It disarmed us into thinking we were not so different from the Emperor. The men drank tankards of beer in a go, and let out belches at the end to show their satisfaction, and all I could think to myself was, *If an Emperor is allowed such a gaffe, then why do we give Father such a hard time?* I didn't realize that the rules were different at Ischl—that in Vienna, Franzl drank wine if he drank at all and insisted on keeping his head about him.

"That night, or so I'm told, Franzl admitted to his mother that he admired me. The Archduchess refused to believe he preferred a little monkey like me, but in a line of stout Bavarian women, I'd been told my long limbs were something to be admired. Franzl says he thought me 'as fresh and unspoilt as a half-opened almond.' It was then I understood I was just an ornament. Up until this visit I had cared little about how I'd looked. Yes, I'd receive compliments, but more emphasis was placed on what we *did* as children, not how we *looked*. I was flattered, but I also felt a deep discomfort to be prized for my beauty above all.

"At dinner on the second night, the Archduchess seated me beside her, nowhere near Franzl. Nene was seated between the Emperor and his father. The Archduchess brought up topics I hadn't a clue about. Nene had been groomed for such an encounter, but in the course of my life so far I'd scarcely talked to anyone but my family. I was too nervous to eat.

"Franzl invited me to attend the ball the following night despite his mother's protests. Nene wore a white satin gown that might as well have been her wedding dress. I had on a plain voile dress, in a pale pinkish orange, the color of the sky when the sun is already deep below the horizon—a child's dress, but still, Franzl barely glanced at Nene. He leaned down to me and said, 'If we're not careful, that diamond barrette will pierce my heart as surely as Cupid's arrow.' I smiled. What else might I have done? I didn't want to steal him from Nene, but is it stealing if he was never, in fact, hers? When the cotillion began, he left Nene's side to invite *me* onto the floor and then we danced the entire sequence together. At the end he asked that all of his bouquets be laid before me.

"The next morning, when my governess—I still had a governess—asked if I was pleased, I could only admit that I felt extremely embarrassed, for I knew how Nene would feel passed over and I hated the idea of being the cause of her disappointment. I tried to talk to her, to tell her that all of this mattered little to me and that I would return home at once so she could get on according to plan, but Nene has always been so gentle. She told me that it didn't matter to her, either. She would find another husband, and better to figure out Franzl's preferences now rather than later.

"That morning was the Emperor's birthday. The Archduchess allowed that I might sit next to him, but she informed me of this kindness as if it were an insult. That afternoon, we all went for a ride: the Archduchess, Nene,

Franzl, and myself. Franzl and I had trouble finding words for each other, though we certainly looked for them in each other's eyes the whole way out to St. Wolfgang and back. Nene talked nonstop to make up for it, and the Archduchess didn't try to quiet her.

"Back at Ischl, Franzl and his mother disappeared behind a door for a long while. Franzl kept smiling at me after that, like he had something to say, but he never said it.

"I found out we were engaged once I'd arrived back home at Possi. I burst into tears and my mother asked why I was crying at such good news. Didn't I love him? I said, of course I loved him. How could I help but love him?

"Every day I received a note from him saying how much he longed to be with me again, but all I could do was look at everything I had known up until that point and think about how it would soon be taken from me. At Possi I could pick flowers in the woods, and cover my hands in blotted ink writing poems, but in Vienna I'd have to wear gloves every day, and I worried what it would do to me not to feel the world beneath my fingertips.

"Franzl had more titles than I was able to remember, and I was supposed to know what each one signified. 'His Imperial Majesty Emperor of Austria and King of Jerusalem, heir to the Iron Crown of the Lombard Kings, the Apostolic Crown of St. Stephen; King of Bohemia and Margrave of Moravia; Duke of Parma, Piacenza, Modena, and Guastalla, of Cracow and Lorraine; Grand Prince of Transylvania and Voivode of the Serbian Banat; Lord of Dalmatia and of the Bucovine.'" Sisi recites the list like a prayer she's spoken every night, like a pledge voiced with her hand to her heart.

"To me, it was one long nonsense word meaning only

responsibility and obligation. I had to bribe my tutor to tell me why the Magyars hated Franzl so, and it was then I learned of the bodies swinging from the gallows, the men taking their lives in their prison cells, complications that were being kept from me, as though I couldn't understand, or, worse, wouldn't care." Sisi takes a breath and slips her hand into her cousin Ludwig's. "All of this is to say: Yes, I loved him, but enough to give up my life as I lived it? If it had been my choice, no. Maybe you feel the same about being King?"

"You understand me, cousin."

"You need to get out of bed."

"I will think of you and be strong."

Peer Pressure

❉ ❉

COSIMA, WORRIED the King and Wagner are growing distant, takes it upon herself to copy some of Wagner's writing to send to Ludwig. Grateful for the gift, Ludwig reconnects with his Great Friend, who has a long list of ideas, at the top of which is a festival theater in Munich in which the *Ring* cycle—still years from completion—might eventually be performed. Ludwig's cabinet refuses to support another cent of Wagner's work. "If you build a theater here, he will soon run the city and then the country, too," they tell Ludwig, who is insulted at the way they malign his ability to rule.

The King writes the Great Friend to suggest, instead, Bayreuth, a small mountain town a day's journey from Munich, for the festival house: a destination instead of a convenience. A large sum of cash waits for Wagner at the castle.

Wagner can tell the cabinet has been advising Ludwig to keep him at arm's length. He thinks of the fortune-teller's recommendation that Wagner protect Ludwig from the unworthy advisers, but he has just had a burst of inspiration he dares not interrupt. Wagner knows that cash instead of credit is a sign that Ludwig is acting on his own. "Cosima, I can't possibly stop my work right now. You'll need to pick it up for me," he tells her.

She knows this is not what Ludwig thinks he is buying with his forty thousand gulden, but she shows up to face Ludwig's disappointment and collect the money all the same. "He's writing for you," Cosima explains, and Ludwig's wounds are licked.

In November, Ludwig invites Wagner to spend a week at Hohenschwangau. "Parsifal," Wagner writes in response to the invitation, "how could I possibly refuse?"

Once there, Wagner posts oboists on each of the castle's turrets. The King wakes to the music. As the sun stretches over the mountains, he hears the parts of Lohengrin and Elsa, calling back and forth above him. *Bliss*, Ludwig thinks. *I will do anything for this genius's salvation.*

In December 1865, a series of articles comes out pitting Wagner against Pfistermeister, and the cabinet secretary threatens to quit if Ludwig doesn't take Wagner out of the equation. "I can only support your work if you leave Bavaria," Ludwig tells his Great Friend.

"How is it that ordinary men are telling the King what to do?" Wagner asks, and Ludwig is nearly shaken by this sentiment. He can see, though, the trouble that would be caused if he lost Pfistermeister. It would become immediately apparent that Ludwig doesn't know a thing, and he fears he'd be forced to learn. Pfistermeister does everything for him and makes no issue of it. He tells Ludwig when he really must step up and comply and perform his role—*perform* being the opportune word, for Ludwig is truly acting out his part, rather than taking action.

Wagner holds his ground, refusing to go. A letter arrives to the Briennerstrasse from Ludwig setting a twenty-four-hour deadline: "I know you feel with me. I know you can measure the whole depth of my sorrow. *Never* doubt the fidelity of your Best Friend."

Wagner asks Cosima to pack his bags. She pouts. "What am I to do without you? You know I must stay here with Hans."

Wagner replies, "I'm sure this will blow over. I'll be back soon enough." He spends the afternoon stitching a small book together for the King. When Ludwig bids him farewell later that afternoon, Wagner tells him: "Carry this with you always. What you have here are my general opinions on most matters of importance, a personal ethics if you will. With a greater distance between us, I hope it might be of use." Ludwig throws his arms around Wagner and Wagner thumps Ludwig's back vigorously before pulling away. "Enough."

Instead of the Great Friend's absence forcing Ludwig to work, though, it sinks him into a depression that allows even less to be accomplished. The servants bring trays to the King's bedroom and take them away untouched. Ludwig allows in only Paul with his nightly bottles of arrack. He writes long, rambling letters to Sisi to vent his feelings, but half of them are illegible with drink and the servants throw them in the fire.

In Mutual Pursuit

✳ ✳

FRANZL AND SISI RETURN TO BUDAPEST the following winter. Sisi is credited for every one of Franzl's successes; his mother is blamed for every setback.

Franzl sits down with Deák, and finds many of the man's suggestions reasonable. The generals and aides-de-camp at Franzl's side try to tell him that Sisi has gotten in his ear and he is not thinking straight. Franzl ignores them and shakes Deák's hand. "We are on a path to an Ausgleich, but we have a farther distance to travel than can be accomplished on this visit alone. I thank you for beginning this discussion with me," Franzl says.

At every event the same man hooks his eyes into Sisi's. She has only seen this man in effigy at the gallows: Gyula Andrássy. When they are introduced, he whispers, "Éljen Erzsebet!"

Though she usually takes such a salute in stride, she can't help but blush this time.

Franzl witnesses this but isn't the least intimidated. He

sees only that Sisi has won over a former revolutionary with her beauty.

After that, Sisi spends every minute offered her with Count Andrássy. His ideas are bold, but he shares them with a conviction that Sisi watches with the attention she usually only brings to circus performances. Ida had been right in assuming the two would get along. Andrássy knows how to turn on his charm to get what he wants, but, having witnessed him in many diplomatic relationships, Ida can tell that Andrássy is going beyond his usual niceties. He must be able to tell that Sisi is genuine in her interest, and it's possible that the lure of an Empress, willing to prioritize her devotion to his country above her own, is enough to make him feel something more himself. Ida hopes that this affinity will not disrupt the goals of the nation.

They speak intimately about the state of Hungary, and Sisi agrees with Andrássy that there's no real reason Austria couldn't allow Hungary its own rulers, constitution, diet. Andrássy, with his rakishly parted curls and brow that gives the impression that every glance is clandestine, can see the effect he has on the Queen, but all of Hungary relies on his behaving with decorum. One afternoon, listening to Sisi speak in her lilting Magyar, Andrássy loses himself thinking of something Ida has recently revealed to him: the Emperor and Empress sleep in different rooms. Perhaps the Emperor is not as virile as people make him out to be. Perhaps the Empress is left with unsatisfied desires.

He imagines running his hand along her jawline, his thumb levering her chin, opening that mouth she keeps pursed so tightly. He has never seen her eat. He has never seen her lick her lips. He imagines slipping his finger in and seeing if she accepts it. He would plant his hand in that luxurious hair, pulling her toward him, leaning in to kiss her and let his palm wander to the edge of her bodice. He imagines unlacing her, the layers of her that would fall off like snakeskins, until he reaches the soft warmth held securely inside.

"What do you think?" Sisi asks.

Andrássy crosses his legs and asks if she might repeat the question.

"A monument to Jókai: It seems a writer of his caliber is due for some recognition, don't you think?"

"An excellent idea," he says, but the Empress can sense his distraction.

"What are you thinking about?" she asks.

"Hungary, Hungary, always about Hungary," he says. "I wish I might let myself free of it sometimes, but it is my blessing and my burden to be so consumed."

"If the Emperor's cause goes badly in Italy it pains me," she replies, "but if it goes badly in Hungary it will be my death."

"I am pleased to hear that, but I fear you're showing us too much preference. Stay neutral. You needn't bear the burden of Hungarian advancement alone."

Sisi had hoped her enthusiasm would please Andrássy, but she romanticizes his rejection, thinking his contrarian heart knows only how to resist, making him all the more intriguing to her.

Ida, pretending not to hear on the other side of the room, doesn't dare turn around when the room goes quiet and stays that way for a long time. Ida's heart beats faster and faster. She does not want any part in this. She wishes herself somewhere else. But she wants Hungary to be awarded its list of demands. Her mind whirls with confusion as to whether whatever is happening in the silence will help or hurt those goals. Finally she hears a loud clatter, and turns without thinking. Sisi and Andrássy are backing away from one another in their seats, Sisi dabbing at a stain on her skirt; a teacup that had been balanced on the table between them has irreversibly shattered on the rug below. "I'll call the maid," Ida cries, relieved to have a purpose again.

Sisi writes to Ludwig about the handsome revolutionary who has further convinced her of his cause. She tries on Ludwig's style of flowery description, hoping he appreciates the artfulness of her response and will not read too much desire into it. Her cousin, she has come to understand, values the concept of chaste, aesthetic devotion. Passion needn't play a part.

Franzl visits alone the room where Sophie died. Sisi can't bear to join him. He finds it stuffed full of flowers brought by the wives and widows of men who fought in the Hungarian uprising. All this time and still dozens of bouquets show up each day.

Standing on the platform, bidding Hungary adieu after six long weeks, Sisi speaks in her stilted Magyar to those gathered: "I hope soon to return to my dear, dear Hungary." The Empress remains standing before the crowd, hoping that some of those closest to her might see the tears in her eyes and spread their rumor, for if she had her way, she would have done much more to fulfill the requests of the people. Andrássy bows to her, wishing it was he who could offer his hand to help her onto the train.

In Vienna, the future is bleak. It has become increasingly clear that Bismarck is dead set on taking the first opportunity to declare war in an effort to destroy Austrian hegemony. Bismarck has told everyone *except* Franz that this is the only way Prussia can thrive, but Franz is no fool. The writing is on the wall. Even Sisi can see it plainly. "Maybe I won't go home to Possenhofen this year," she offers.

Franzl's relief is plain.

"I have LV at least to keep me company," she replies.

But this doesn't last long. Ludwig Victor is caught making a pass at a count in the bathhouse, and Franzl recommends he go to Salzburg and stay there.

"I'm sure he's learned his lesson," Sisi argues. "Let him stay. He is my only friend."

"I'm sure he has *not*. In Salzburg he can do as he pleases and no one will know. I'll assign him a ballerina as adjutant to keep him in line."

"Franzl, no need to be nasty." Sisi has not seen this side of her husband.

"Since when do you dislike ballerinas?" Franzl plays dumb.

"Someday we will have to stop hiding away everything that is unfamiliar to us," Sisi replies.

"I know LV all too well," Franzl replies.

Sisi writes LV a long note, pledging her devotion and apologizing for his unfair treatment.

Ludwig Victor writes back: "And you said Franzl

would never send me away. At least admit I was right and promise you'll visit."

And Sisi does.

No rain falls in the spring. A foehn blows off the Alps, kicking up dust, and causing Sisi to develop a real cough in place of her usually fake *het-het*. Sisi remains at Schönbrunn, her ghostly wheeze proof of her dedication.

When Franzl finishes his work for the day, he retrieves Sisi and they walk together in the garden. "Everyone who supports Bismarck is making a big mistake. We appeal to the noble sentiments: patriotism, honor, principles of law, energy, courage, decision, sense of independence. Bismarck reckons on the lower motivations of human nature: avarice, cowardice, confusion, indolence, indecision, and narrow-mindedness. I suspect even the people allied with him are not sure why it is he's doing what he's doing."

"Yes, I know," Sisi replies. Franzl, usually mum on political affairs with Sisi because of how clearly she does not care, has not been able to talk about anything else for the past few weeks, and Sisi, for once, has taken to patiently listening and agreeing with him on all points in an attempt to soothe him.

"And your cousin is doing nothing to help us," Franzl says.

"I know. I hear Ludwig's doing nothing to help Bavaria, either, though."

"Prussia is about to devour all of us whole," Franzl says. "I worry about his sense. It's not as though there's rhyme or reason to any of the choices he makes, but he might choose the nonsense that benefits us just this once."

Sisi hears her husband.

When Ludwig writes back with his compliments on the poetry of her letter describing Andrássy, she responds reminding him of their family ties, of the way Bavaria and Austria have always fought on each other's behalf. Previously, Sisi has limited her political dealings to the Hungarian question, but if there is any way in which she can help Austria's cause, it is to put a little pressure on her devoted cousin.

A Personal Battle

✳   ✳

A DECISION RESTS ON LUDWIG'S SHOULDERS: his mother is a Prussian Princess, his dear Sisi an Austrian Empress. No matter the decision he makes, war approaches.

Ludwig tells Paul, "I am sick of this eternal Schleswig-Holstein business. It's insufferable, and it really couldn't matter less to me."

Paul could strangle the King, knowing Ludwig will shape the future of Europe with his decision. "But you understand it's not about Schleswig-Holstein. It's about Prussia and Austria."

"Yes, but why? No one can seem to explain it me!" Ludwig moans.

Paul knows the King does not actually want to understand and that he's so far behind on foreign relations that it would take all afternoon to catch him up, and even then, none of it would stick. "Ally yourself with Austria," Paul tells Ludwig, and the King does as he is told. Württemberg does the same, as do many of the southern states and smaller middle states, mostly in the hopes of keeping their thrones. But nearly all of the North German states ally with Prussia, and Bismarck also talks the Kingdom of Italy onto his side, promising to make the Austrian surrender of Venetia a condition of peace to assist in Italy's unification.

Officials tell Ludwig it is time to mobilize the army, but Ludwig resists. "I *won't* have a war," he says. The Hapsburgs have ruled for so long, he reasons, is there really any need to challenge them now? Why can't everyone be happy with what they have?

Instead Ludwig writes an announcement declaring that he will step down from the throne, handing the crown over to Otto, and runs away. "I'm not fit to deal with situations like this. It's best if I remove myself." By the time the cabinet receives Ludwig's decree, the King has escaped the Residenz and rowed a small boat out to the tiny Roseninsel in the Würmsee. On the land sits a small house built for his mother. He hides from the aftermath of his decision and writes Wagner: "Increasingly, the horizon darkens, the bright sun of peace is in terrible torment. I implore the Friend to send me a speedy answer to the following question: if it is the wish of the Dear One I will gladly renounce the throne and its barren splendor, come to him and never part from him." The King is looking for anyone he can pass the blame to. Ludwig knows that, if the outcome is bad, he will be blamed, but how can he be blamed for something he doesn't understand? All this fighting caused by some dispute all the way up in Denmark, and now the Italians are involved, too. Ludwig hasn't anything against the Italians. Ludwig hasn't anything against anyone, only those who are trying to fill his precious days with the minutiae of borders and who is in charge of whom. If everyone took a moment to think about what mattered to them—surely beauty and art and fine living—they'd settle down and appreciate the peace they were so set on destroying. Ludwig will opt out, and that is that. He will remove himself from the position and go on living his life. Let Otto deal with it.

Wagner's servant is used to his hollering. "What is the King thinking? This will be our downfall! Does he not realize that without the crown, he will have no more operas?" He writes, feverishly, in a hand barely legible, that the fantasy world will be stunted if the King doesn't pay the least bit of attention to the real world. "Renounce, I beseech you, during this half year, all concern with art and our plans . . . turn your attention with the greatest energy to affairs of state; remain in your Residenz, stay with your people, show yourself to them. Remember the great regret your grandfather had for relinquishing his post, and remember that his action delivered him nothing of what he hoped it would. If you love me, as I have earnestly hoped, then hear my pleas. I will continue our work, and the reward of my industry will wait for you on the other side."

The King rescinds his resignation. On May 10th, 1866, Ludwig issues the orders for mobilization. But on May 22nd, he doesn't open Parliament as planned, claiming to be sick. The statesmen aren't able to locate the King to insist he keep his promise. At Wagner's home, a man shows up at the gate wearing a black coat and wide-brimmed hat. "A Walter Stolzing is here to see you, sir," a servant relays.

"Good God!" Wagner shouts. "Let him in!"

"Happy birthday!" Ludwig cries, embracing Wagner. "Did you like that bit? Walter Stolzing from *Der Meistersinger*?"

"Yes, I understood. You've lost your mind. They'll hang you for this!"

"I couldn't miss your day, my Great Friend!"

The two sit down to lunch, Wagner on edge, waiting for a soldier's knock on the door. It takes him five days to convince Ludwig to go home.

The Bavarian newspapers blare incensed headlines. They blame Wagner for the carelessness of the King and they go low in their attacks on the composer. The *Volksbote* publishes an article revealing the true nature of the relationship between Cosima and Wagner, and Cosima's husband, forced to face the situation, challenges the reporter to a duel if he doesn't post an apology.

Wagner, suddenly wanting to protect Cosima from the shame of infidelity, writes to Ludwig, asking him to right the situation. "I've made, here, an affidavit, confirming there is absolutely no truth to the allegations and it would be of the greatest service to us if you would sign the letter yourself, so that the newspaper will issue a retraction."

Ludwig believes his friend and signs readily.

The newspaper prints an insincere apology.

In June, Ludwig tells his guards to block the entrances to Berg. A messenger arrives to tell the King that Prussia has declared war on Austria, but the guards refuse to deliver the news.

"You must be kidding," the messenger says.

The guards shrug, following orders.

The messenger returns to his dispatcher with the news that the King will not accept the announcement of war.

The prime minister, Pfordten, goes to Berg himself to confront the King. He insists on entering, breaking past the guards and running through the halls, hunting for Ludwig. In the King's bedroom, he finds Ludwig and Paul von Thurn und Taxis dressed as Barbarossa and Lohengrin, reciting poetry to one another, Paul in canary-yellow tights and Ludwig in apricot.

"This is what's more important than the fact that your countrymen are giving their lives?"

Ludwig points to the door. "If we're at war, I don't know what it is I'm supposed to do about it." He is telling the truth.

Pfistermeister and Pfordten—Pfi and Pfo—marvel over their bad luck. A Schattenkoenig such as this should make their jobs easier, allowing them to rule discreetly without interference. Ludwig, though, is so inaccessible it's impossible to get his signature on *their* decisions.

Ludwig declines even a visit to the troops for morale's sake. "I can't bear to gaze upon those clipped hedgehogs." He passes off the task of leading the troops to his uncle.

———

Searching for new places to escape to, Ludwig rides to the top of the Jugend Mountain, near Hohenschwangau. A wooden bridge his father had built stretches over a waterfall in a steep, narrow gorge. He considers jumping, but looks out around him at the land stretching in every direction and imagines another way.

And in Exchange

✻   ✻

FRANZL FRAYS UNDER THE PRESSURE.

"The hospitals are full," Franzl admits to Sisi, without meeting her eyes.

She resists chastising him.

"I know you wanted to build more, but while we could have built hospitals, we couldn't have produced, from thin air, the doctors and nurses to staff them," Franzl says defensively.

Each morning Sisi visits a ward. She brings around a jug of water to fill the glasses of the soldiers. She ignores the stench of the oozing wounds and the dead spaces where limbs should be, and instead looks into the soldiers' confused faces.

"Empress?" the men ask, and when Sisi curtsies to them as a thank-you for their service, they think maybe they have died.

Deák and Andrássy greet Sisi at the Budapest platform, alongside thousands of Hungarian people cheering her

name. Sisi, often shy of attention, must admit that this re-
ception is better than the spit that has flown her way in
Vienna for the last week.

She writes Franzl to recommend they relocate the
whole family. "I think it would inspire even more confidence if you named Andrássy as Minister of Foreign Affairs, too. If not Minister of Foreign Affairs, then at least
Minister for Hungary. The great necessity at the moment
is for the country to be kept calm and for it to place all of
its strength at the Emperor's disposal. Do it for Rudolf,"
she begs. "If all of these efforts fail, he will have nothing to
rule over. I am convinced that if you trust Andrássy im-
plicitly, the monarchy may be saved."

Franzl has heard the rumors that his wife has fallen
under the spell of Andrássy's brooding good looks. He replies, "I cannot give up that degree of power to Andrássy
at this point, but I will send the children to Buda."

The Prussian camps advance closer every day. A lookout
perched on the Kahlenberg Hill at the edge of Vienna
sees the campfires in the countryside, and Franzl understands the urgent need to take action.

He writes back to Sisi to make a concession, though not
the one she wants. "I have summoned Deák in secret, so do
not make any promises to Andrássy. The Prussians may
attack any day. God protect us. God protect Austria."

You've forgotten something, Sisi thinks. *God protect
Hungary, too.*

Franz Deák turns down the Emperor's offer, though.
"You don't want me. You want Andrássy," Deák insists,
and Franz, rather than feeling frustrated at having sum-

moned the wrong man, feels relief that Sisi's recommendations are indeed not driven—at least not solely—by a crush.

After a mere seven weeks and a bloodbath at the Battle
of Königgrätz, Prussia wins the war. Its summoning of
the powers of democracy against the nationally divided
Austria, the greater number of Prussian troops and their
positioning around railroads, with quicker-loading needle
guns—all of this has given Prussia a distinct advantage.
The terms of the peace negotiations are held up by Prussian King Wilhelm I's insistence that Austria surrender
territory, but Bismarck finally convinces Wilhelm that
Prussia mustn't fatally wound those with whom later they
will have to live. The resulting treaty establishes the with-
drawal of Austria from the federation of North German
states being formed under Prussian leadership, the future
of the relations between South German states among one
another and with the North German Confederation to
be decided independently at a later date, the alteration of
possessions in North Germany, and a reparation of forty
million thaler paid by Austria to Prussia for the damages
of war. All of these conditions force Franzl to face what
he has been fighting for so long: the loss of the dominant
position Austria and the Hapsburg line have held for
centuries.

He writes to Sisi: "I do not know what the Prussians
are doing to the rest of Germany, but that is no further
concern of ours. We shall focus on Hungary for the time
being. Now that we have survived this ordeal, I should like
to ask a favor. If only you would pay me a visit it would
make me endlessly happy. I long for you so."

Sisi pities her husband and his neediness and shows Andrássy the telegram.

Andrássy doesn't want to cut their visit short. He finds himself most at ease in her company, but if there is a way in which he is similar to the Emperor, it is his implacable practicality in prioritizing his political goals. "You should go. Perhaps in person, you can convince him to finally give me my post."

"I cannot stay away from *Hungary* for long," she says. This is the closest she's come to voicing her feelings.

He breathes. "Make it short then," he says. "A woman of your persuasive powers surely won't take long to accomplish her goal."

Sisi wishes he'd told her to stay, but she follows his suggestion and goes to Vienna for a long weekend, speaking of Hungary the entire time.

When she returns without a title for Andrássy, he lets his frustration get the best of him only momentarily before thanking Sisi for making her best attempt. There is no question as to whether Sisi would have done everything in her power to try to help him, and if that wasn't enough, then he can move on to his next *priority* with her.

Andrássy writes to Franzl: "I hope Your Majesty will not take it amiss and think me lacking in modesty if I voice the conviction that at the present moment, I alone can be of use."

Franzl takes it amiss and appoints the German Baron von Beust as Austrian foreign minister. He is only the more surprised when Baron von Beust makes the same recommendations that Andrássy has been making: a contented Hungary will mean a stronger Austria.

Still, Franzl uses the conciliation to Hungary as a bargaining chip with Sisi. If he restores the Hungarian constitution, she must bear him one more child to ensure their family line. A second son would be a wise investment.

Sisi can't believe Franzl would suggest such a trade. Lately, she has been weighing what the repercussions might be if she took her relationship with Andrássy one step further. She has been so good up until now; she believes none of her actions have put Austria at risk. If anything, she justifies her choices as being for the *good* of the empire. But now, this ultimatum from Franzl would stop any advancements with Andrássy in their tracks. It has been a decade since Rudolf was born. Sisi hopes that maybe another pregnancy is not even possible, and she doesn't look forward to the perfunctory efforts it will take to find out. There is no way of ensuring it will be a male, and she can't bear the idea of the Archduchess stealing another child from her or the abuse another boy would endure. Franzl assures Sisi that this one will be hers, though. He will see to it that Sisi takes charge of the child's rearing, boy or girl. Sisi sees no option but to agree.

> **"One cannot prevent people from thinking
> what they please."**
>
> ✳ ✳

THOUGH LUDWIG DIDN'T CARE about the Austro-Prussian War, he smarts at having associated with the wrong side. He wishes that Bavaria could exist on its own, allied with no one. He has no desire to join the North German Confederation, and it is a shock to see the way Austria has been cut down to size. If the cabinet had never gotten to him, his reputation wouldn't be tarnished in this way. He withdraws further.

Ludwig attends a production of Schiller's *Mary Stuart*, where he is introduced to the lead actress, Lilla von Bulyowsky. Afterward, moved by the tale of murder and intrigue, he orders that the Church of the Holy Trinity be opened so that he might pray for Mary Stuart's soul.

Ludwig invites Lilla to visit him at Hohenschwangau. They walk in the rain-soaked gardens, and Lilla worries that it is improper to lift her skirts in the company of the King. The layers of her petticoats grow heavy with dirty puddle water. Ludwig plucks some flowers from a bush and hands them to Lilla. She hesitates to accept them, for the rain will surely ruin her satin gloves, but she decides such a loss must result in eventual gain. At the palace, he tells her he adores her. When she extends a hand to brush the curls off his forehead, he recoils. It seems she has misinterpreted.

Lilla continues to be the only personal visitor allowed into the Residenz. She takes this as a good sign, performing her confidence in the face of Ludwig's mixed messages.

On one visit, he leads her to his bedroom, where erotic pictures are laid out on the bed and pinned to the wall. Lilla chooses not to be offended. She points to one photo of a woman who resembles herself. "Is this the type of woman you like?" she asks, leaning over to display her décolletage.

Ludwig winces. "I'd prefer not to talk about them."

Lilla can't understand.

He pauses before saying, "You know, I've never been with a woman."

Lilla moves to him to take his hand. "I can't believe it. You're the object of every woman's desire."

Ludwig blushes. "I think of you often at night and cover my pillow in kisses."

Lilla is charmed. "You can kiss me now, if you'd like." She moves in closer.

Ludwig, though, pulls away. "I couldn't defile you so." He leads her to the other side of the room, where he's displayed a picture of her on a small altar.

"Your Majesty, I'm honored, but I'm no deity. I'm right here beside you." She places his hand on her bosom, but he snatches it away.

"Would you recite your part from *Egmont* with me? I've memorized the scenes."

Lilla, thinking that maybe they just need to move more slowly, agrees.

The King sits on the edge of the bed and Lilla guesses that she's to join him there. They trade lines up until the moment when the two characters are to kiss. Lilla looks deep into Ludwig's· eyes, but he moves on, finishing the scene. Near tears with frustration, Lilla excuses herself.

When a castmate inquires about her visit, Lilla replies, "The King is a cold-blooded fish."

Sisi, though, has finally convinced the King to meet her sister Sophie, who she promises is sweet and innocent and beautiful. She will not prove him any trouble; in fact, he will likely feel relief to be over and done with the business of marriage and the hounds that push it on him.

"But then they'll want an heir," he moans.

"I guarantee that Sophie will be the one to bear the brunt of that burden. You need do very little to ensure such a legacy."

Ludwig shudders at the thought.

The Lady Sculptor
❋   ❋

To celebrate this victory, and to pay tribute to the Minister President who survived an attempt on his life during the war, the Prussian King orders Bismarck a gift.

When Bismarck arrives to his salon, he's sure the promise of a commissioned bust must be some sort of joke. He licks his lips when he sees fresh-faced Elisabet Ney. Her hair hovers in a ringleted halo around her head. Her figure is obscured by a blousy smock unbelted over men's pantaloons, but Bismarck can guess at her form from the way she moves, fluid and strong at the same time.

"Is that some sort of massage table?" he asks of an oversized wooden case beside her.

"I'm sorry?"

"We can do away with the ruse of your being here to make a portrait, and *get to work*, as it were, young lady." He begins to take off his jacket.

Ney realizes his assumption and plays dumb. She has gotten this far by knowing more than she says. "I take it you are familiar with the busts I've made of Garibaldi and Schopenhauer, then? It is true I do think people appear in their highest form when undecorated with the silly costumes we put on our bodies. All that needs to be known about us is plain on our faces and in the set of our shoulders."

Bismarck pauses, examining Ney. "You have really sculpted those men?" he asks. He is still convinced there must be some element of pleasure built into this transaction, even if Ney is indeed there to turn him to stone.

"I realize you must be unaccustomed to such a sight, but you are looking at the first female graduate of the Munich Art Academy. I'm sure you're clever enough to realize that a woman set on accomplishing such a goal would not stop there."

"You must be very persuasive," Bismarck prods.

"I assume you know the work of Meister Rauch."

Bismarck does not even nod. If a person knows the name of only a single German sculptor in this moment it is Rauch. To confirm her assumption is unnecessary.

"Meister Rauch awarded me the studio immediately beside his own in Berlin. I am grateful for his introducing me to a class of people who it is my privilege to immortalize, but he would not have done so if he did not see in me a skill that superseded all of his other apprentices."

Bismarck laughs. "You have built up a supreme confidence in yourself."

"Humility would be a waste of our time." Ney begins to unfold her easel and Bismarck unbuttons his shirt, having lost most, but not all, of his hope.

Bismarck can spare only an hour or so every day for the coming week, but in that time his form takes shape, and the skeleton of Ney's story is slowly made flesh. He does not usually make a habit of talking to portraitists, but this one intrigues him. It is clear her ability to tell stories and her brazen confidence must contribute to the doors that open before her. She is a queen of bold statements and obfuscation. He thinks of the con woman who toppled the first King Ludwig of Bavaria and wonders if Ney might be the answer to the larger question looming before him.

Ney can tell she is slowly captivating the Minister President, but what initially seemed like a sort of pandering bemusement has transformed. She can't help but feel the questions he asks slowly shift. But in what way? Like the inquiries parents might receive when deciding whether their daughter is fit for marriage? No, that's not quite it. It feels like she's being evaluated for possible apprenticeship.

He asks if she can provide an example of her commitment and willfulness, more specific than her plain accomplishment. Ney argues that her résumé should be more than enough, but Bismarck jokes that her feminine wiles are hard to account for. He has yet to experience any such benefits to their sittings, but that's not to say some other teacher or subject hasn't made that type of demand.

"I went on a hunger strike for three weeks to convince my parents to send me to art school. They were convinced Berlin was not safe for young women. They didn't think Rauch would work with a girl. I insisted that I didn't need them to believe in me. I believed in myself and that would be enough. I continued to refuse food. I told them if they did not believe I could make a life for myself then I chose not to continue living. They knew I meant it. They agreed to allow me to go to school in Munich if I was admitted.

They were not happy when they were held to their promise."

Bismarck challenges her. "But they did not let you go to Berlin. You showed your weakness with your compromise."

"No, because I did eventually get to Berlin, as you know. I believed if I could get out of their grasp, I would make my way to Berlin, but I needed to go to Munich first. That was not a compromise. That was a tactic toward a goal."

Bismarck is quiet for a while. Ney is pleased by his silence. Finally: "And Rauch? Every young artist wants to study under him. How did you convince him to take you on?"

"I knocked on his door," Ney states plainly.

"And?"

"He turned me away three days in a row. And then, because he could tell I would not stop appearing on his doorstep, he allowed me to submit a single composition. He was sure he would reject me the same way my parents were sure I would not be accepted to the Academy."

"What would you have done if he turned you away?"

"I knew he would not refuse me if he saw my work."

"How could you know?"

"Minister President, how do you know that Germany must be unified?"

"There is no other option."

"And how will you ensure that Germany is unified?"

Bismarck laughs, as though such a plan could be laid out in casual conversation, as though he would reveal such a plan to a young artist at all. "Very carefully," he says.

Ney smirks and lifts her eyebrows.

———

On the final day of their work together, Bismarck reveals his hand. "I've heard that you want to add King Ludwig of Bavaria to your Gallery of Great Men."

"Of course."

"I've learned a lot this week. For one, you have a talent for bending the ear of your subject."

"If I recall, you were the one asking the questions."

"I'm not complaining. Just observing. You've proven yourself to possess both conviction and the power of persuasion."

"I am flattered at your observation, and I cannot disagree."

"If I were to gain you access to Ludwig, do you think you might be able to convince him of our cause?"

"You assume your cause is my cause." Ney refuses Bismarck eye contact.

"You've done an artful job of hiding your opinion if it isn't. But that's no matter, provided you feel motivated to accomplish the goal. You clearly have a Machiavellian streak."

"What sort of motivation?"

"If you succeed, the sky is the limit."

Ney does not tell Bismarck she has done covert work like this before, transporting letters for Garibaldi across the Tyrol. What sort of spy would she be if she were to share such information, even if it proved her pedigree? "Passage to America and an endowment to begin my life there?"

Bismarck has an account outside of the Prussian

treasury for exactly this purpose. Anyone who needs a financial push to do something—or stop doing something—can get an undocumented deposit from his Reptile Fund. "For such a favor, anything is possible."

"Consider it done."

Quite the Bargain

❋ ❋

IN FEBRUARY, FRANZL RESTORES the Hungarian constitution of 1848 and gives Andrássy the appointment he
has been waiting for: Minister of Hungarian Affairs. Plans
for the coronation of the King and Queen of Hungary begin to come together.

Tradition dictates that Sisi darn the mantle of St.
Stephen herself, and the Archduchess commends Sisi's
stitches, the first she's sewn since childhood.

Sisi does not feel the same trepidation for this ceremony that she did for her wedding. She knows the people of Hungary already see her as their Queen. To her the
coronation only makes this fact official, with the added
benefit of showing that the Magyars are ready to embrace
Franzl, too.

Similar to the evenings after their wedding, though,
Franzl begins to call on Sisi in the night again, and Sisi
keeps up her end of the deal.

Is This a Joke?

✳   ✳

JUST AFTER THE NEW YEAR, Sisi arranges a meeting between Ludwig and her sister. The King greets Sophie cordially, but she has nothing to say. Ludwig excuses himself to have a word with Sisi alone. "I'm far too busy to get married," Ludwig says. "Otto can carry on the family line."

"When you hear Sophie play the piano, I believe you will change your mind."

Sophie settles her hands on the keys to play "Song of the Evening Star," from *Tannhäuser*. Sophie's voice is soft, but pure, and her beauty is *nearly* that of her sister. Ludwig looks at Sisi with a hint of hope in his eyes, and Sisi tilts her head. She told him so.

Sophie finishes playing, and Ludwig stutters out his compliments. Sophie is charmed by his ineptitude, especially knowing that behind it lies an entire kingdom of confidence. Ludwig manages to say he hopes he'll see Sophie again soon, and Sophie understands that she has been told to go home.

Alone, that night in bed, staring up at the stars burning just for him—holes punched into the ceiling letting in the light from the emptied room above him—Ludwig knows that he does not love Sophie. In the moment when she was playing and singing, he felt the quiver of pleasure, but when he imagines Sophie anywhere but on the piano bench, he feels nothing. Over the years, his mother has insisted that love grows over time. Those first pangs of attraction aren't anything but red herrings. A good man, a proper ruler, should ignore such feelings and marry for more practical purposes. With time, and familiarity, an affinity and appreciation will form.

But Ludwig has never waited for a thing. He has always acted with his gut, and if something doesn't strike his gut then it bears little interest to him. He knows—from the sheer volume of emotion that Wagner's work elicits from him, from the way his senses are overwhelmed by the words Byron arranged on the page, from the way he can float out of himself to revel in the sublimity of the natural world around him while riding—that to find a human who might make you feel so much and so acutely every day is a goal worthy of pursuit, and in Sophie he does not experience this effect. It is, in fact, difficult for him to imagine any woman posing as worthy competition for the ecstasy he experiences in the presence of great nature or art. But perhaps therein lies the answer for him, he reasons. Perhaps he need only find someone who can deliver him a steady feed of such transcendence. Perhaps the experience of love is more aesthetic and intellectual than he had previously thought.

With this in mind, Ludwig pays Sophie an unannounced visit at Possenhofen. The family is startled to see their cousin's carriage and they rush around to heat the kettle and rustle up some cake. Still visiting, Sisi is the only one comfortable enough to chide her cousin. "You have to give people some notice, Ludwig. Send a messenger ahead of you."

"I couldn't wait," Ludwig says, and Sisi, as well as the rest of the family, chooses to take this as a good sign.

The servants bring them tea, but as Sophie is settling in, ready to ask the King the host of questions she's prepared, Ludwig asks, "Would you perform for me again?"

Sophie blushes, glad she's pleased him. "I'm sure I could prepare something for our next visit, yes."

Ludwig shakes his head. "No, no. Haven't you anything you could play now?

Sophie says, "Maybe after tea, Your Majesty?"

The King smiles. "I simply cannot wait."

Ludwig's sustained eye contact is enough to push Sophie into action. "Very well. I might have something else that would please you." Sophie balances herself delicately on the piano bench.

She tries her hand at "Elsa's Dream" from *Lohengrin*. The music transports Ludwig until about halfway through, when it becomes clear that Sophie does not know this piece as well. She hits a wrong note and hums an approximation of a verse. "Stop, stop." Ludwig holds his head in his palms. "I'll return when you've learnt it better." He does not thank her family before fleeing the premises.

Sophie doesn't move for the rest of the afternoon, until she has "Elsa's Dream" down perfectly. When she plays the song without error, she asks herself why she doesn't feel satisfied, and knows the answer: her desire is not to perform for the King, but to be his wife. Being Queen will mean performing her role for the rest of the world, and she had hoped that a husband might be the one person with whom she would be allowed to drop such an act.

Ludwig writes Sophie to reveal he wants the opposite: "You know the nature of my destiny. I do not have many years to live. I shall leave this earth when the unthinkable happens, when my star no longer shines, when he has gone, the truly beloved Friend; yes, then my time will also be up, for then I shall no longer be able to live. You have taken such a true, sincere, and heartfelt interest in my fate, dear Sophie, that I shall be deeply thankful to you for the rest of my life. The main basis of our interchange, as you will confirm, has been the remarkable, sweeping destiny of R. Wagner."

Sophie is smart enough to have recognized failure, but she is disappointed at this confirmation and even a little frightened at Ludwig saying that he does not have long to live. She wonders if there is someone with whom she should share this letter. Is the letter a threat? A warning? Why is the King so casual in the way he talks about the end of his life? It's not even that she cares about losing Ludwig. It's more that she hoped all of this would come together more easily. Her optimism dwindles.

The next evening, Ludwig shares a glass of wine with Count von Holnstein and Paul. His friends discuss the fact that they're not getting any younger. "It seems it must be time for us to settle down," Paul says.

Count Holnstein laughs and agrees, "Perhaps a dual ceremony!"

The King feels left out and chimes in, "Make it a triple!"

"It's a pact, then!" All three gentlemen clink their glasses.

Ludwig goes home that night already regretting his pledge.

At the Officers' Ball a week later, Sophie is awarded a prize for her beauty. She accepts graciously, insisting they must have drawn out of a hat. This accolade, though, means a lot to Ludwig, who applauds enthusiastically. When he congratulates her, she turns away from him, still smarting from his rejection.

The orchestra strikes up a waltz, and Ludwig approaches Sophie again. "Please forgive me. I've acted rashly, and I'd like nothing more than to dance with you." Sophie assents, and the crowd's volume multiplies.

That night, despite a dusting of snow on the ground, Ludwig goes to the shore of the Alpsee and asks the stars if it's Sophie they've destined him to marry. At dawn, frozen to the bone, Ludwig rushes inside to tell his mother he's decided he'll propose to Sophie after all.

The pair dress and arrive at Possenhofen as Sophie and her family are sitting down to breakfast. When Ludwig proposes, Sophie nods, aware that she has no say in the matter.

———

A week later the palace officially announces the engagement. The King and his betrothed take a hasty engagement photo. Ludwig looks distracted, Sophie obligated. "Perfect on the first try," Ludwig exclaims, running off to the theater.

Ludwig I writes his grandson a note congratulating him: "I have, for some time, read in the looks of the beautiful Sophie, that you are deep-rooted in her heart . . . Happiness at home is the greatest blessing on earth." Ludwig II casts the note aside, unwilling to take the advice of a hypocrite.

At the engagement ball, people marvel at the striking couple. The betrothed make the rounds, visiting and receiving congratulations. Sophie has replaced her reticence with continuous chatter, but Ludwig preferred her silence.

As they approach an army commander, Ludwig excuses himself. Sophie assumes he'll return shortly, but for the rest of the evening she struggles to explain his absence to their guests.

The Queen waits up for Ludwig. "Half of the people at the party never spoke a word to you. Where have you been?"

Ludwig collapses in a chair by his mother's side. "I couldn't bear it. All the niceties, all the pretense. I ran off to catch the last act of the play."

The Queen sighs. "You stranded poor Sophie."

Ludwig slumps, growls, exits.

All around town, stalls pop up selling engravings and medallions of Ludwig and Sophie. Mothers buy one for each daughter, hoping to give them a bit of luck.

Receptions and deputations and festivities of all sorts are prepared to honor the couple, but Ludwig protests every one. "I didn't realize we were in such a hurry."

Ludwig invites Lilla to Hohenschwangau again. "I worry I'm making the wrong choice," he tells her, and Lilla's heart soars.

"You must follow your instincts. If there is someone else with whom your affections lie, it is your duty to yourself and to Sophie that you not build your union on a falsity."

Ludwig lays his head on her bosom, and Lilla, taking another tack, delicately slides away. Perhaps she can earn the King's affections by playing hard to get.

Finally, the new production of *Lohengrin* is ready for the King's eyes. Wagner has placed a longtime collaborator in the lead role. Ludwig attends a final dress rehearsal and recoils: A sixty-year-old lumpy oaf playing the Knight of the Swan? Who can believe that? Ludwig focuses his opera glasses and sees wrinkles and folds of flesh caked in makeup. As the man sails across the stage in his swan boat, he can barely keep his balance.

Afterward, Wagner defends his choice in Ludwig's box. "He is the man who could best sing the part, Your Majesty," Wagner says.

Ludwig shakes his head. "No, no, no. That wasn't acting. He just took himself through the paces of grimace
after grimace. He has no grace, no strength. And the
woman playing Ortrud? I'm supposed to believe a hag like
her would convince Elsa to reveal her secrets?" Ludwig
shivers.

Wagner goes backstage to fire the leads. Conductor
Bülow has already left for the night without any idea that
he must recast his show. Wagner sits in the empty house of
the darkened theater and resents the fact that he must satisfy the King's whims. He is grateful for Ludwig's backing, but he wishes that the King had more of a spine. He
needs his patron to stand up for him and champion his
ideas, not just pay for bespoke opera performances. Wagner's ambitions are larger than the page on which he composes, the stage of the Court Theater, the Festspielhaus he
dreams of. He has a vision for humanity, and he worries
that Ludwig is the closest he'll come to gaining the support he needs, and it will never be enough. He packs his
bags and departs for Switzerland that night, leaving the
fallout of Ludwig's dissatisfaction to Bülow to figure out.

Ludwig orders a Baroque wedding coach. He orders eight
of a special breed of black horse to pull the heavy gold carriage. He provides instructions to his servants of how he'd
like rooms of the Residenz redecorated in preparation for
Sophie's arrival. "She can be on the floor below mine, with
a staircase connecting. Isn't that romantic? A passage just
for the two of us. Her King always reigning above her!" He
has dreamt up a narrative to justify their separation.

Progress
✳ ✳

SISI BLINDS HERSELF to any trouble between her sister and her cousin, admiring the handsome couple in their engagement photo. Besides, she has more important things to accomplish before their wedding: the time for the coronation has finally arrived.

As Sisi and Franzl disembark from the boat in Budapest, they must wait for the flowers thrown at the Empress to be cleared out of their way. Once she is in their carriage, bouquets are thrust in after her, and the weight of the bundles makes her feel safe and secure.

The Hungarians have prepared a special gift for their Queen: the castle of Gödöllő for her summer residence. The gardens are scented with lilac and acacia trees, and the ground is sandy and soft, making for the gentlest of rides.

Franzl feels joy at seeing Sisi so happy. They go to the races, and Sisi waves her tickets in the air. The country people who've traveled in from every region to ride unbroken horses enthrall her. She picks winners every time.

On June 8th, 1867, the official coronation is to take place.

Sisi's robes, custom-made by Worth, are modeled after the Hungarian national dress. The white and silver brocade of the skirt twinkles with jewels, and pearls pock the black velvet bodice. White lace ruffles create curves where the Queen has none, and broad bows accentuate the thinness of her arms.

When Franzl sees Sisi, he abandons his usual reserve to embrace her. Sisi limply places her hands on her husband's back, completing the illusion of requited affection.

The music that ushers the King and Queen into and out of the church has been composed especially for this day by Franz Liszt. When the former opposition leader József Eötvös takes the pulpit, he responds to the words spoken in the Gospel: "For three centuries we have tried faith. Time and again, we have tried hope, till only one possibility remained, that the nation should be able to love some member of the reigning house from the depths of our heart. Now that we have succeeded, I have no more fears for the future."

Everyone in the audience can't help but feel as though they are at a wedding: the King and his lovely young bride, marrying into the country of Hungary.

The mantle and crown are placed on Franzl. Sisi is anointed with sacred oil that mixes with her joyful tears.

Franzl is so used to Sisi begging off obligations that he almost doesn't know what to do with himself now that she's sticking around at the ball. She jabbers on in her excellent Magyar and he watches admiration flicker in the guests' eyes.

Franzl must steel himself for what comes next. Sisi has asked that the widows and orphans of the Honvéd revolutionaries be brought out before the court and a silver casket of five thousand ducats placed before them as tribute to their loss. Franzl glances at Andrássy, knowing he must have had some hand in designing this display. But he doesn't think to look at Ida, who was first to broach the idea with her mistress.

More than one of the widows faints. The children instinctively reach into the coffin, filling their hands with the coins. Franzl feels weakened by acknowledging the debt owed to these women and children. The people, though, feel as though they've received the first deposit of their reparations.

A Perfect Pair

✳   ✳

IN JULY, LUDWIG WRITES WAGNER: "It is possible that in about eight days I shall go to Paris for the Exposition, although it goes against every fiber of my being to visit this modern-day Babylon. I hate Paris, which I hold to be the throne of materialism, of vulgar sensuality and godless frivolity. I recognize more and more the urgent necessity of erecting, as a counterbalance to this modern Sodom and Gomorrah, a seat of spiritual rulership; and you, my warmly beloved Friend, I venerate as the priest of this pure cult, the King of the ideal realm that we wish to found in this world of malice and hate."

Wagner writes back to Ludwig, telling him to try to enjoy himself.

Napoleon III invites Ludwig to stay with him, but Ludwig chooses, instead, to travel undercover. He asks his new Stallmeister, Richard Hornig, to accompany him. Ludwig has begun to look forward to the interactions he has with the man in charge of choosing his horses. Ludwig finds

Hornig young and handsome, magnetic and dignified. Hornig, having inherited this role from his father, and wanting to do right by the family legacy, does every little thing Ludwig asks. When Ludwig tells him he wants to use the name "Count von Berg" as they travel, Hornig replies, hiding any judgment, "Very well," and marks the name down in his notebook.

On the train to Paris, Ludwig keeps casting his eyes on Hornig. He has been bothered by why Hornig looks so familiar to him, until he realizes that he is the very twin of the William Tell figurine from his childhood, the one he had used to soothe himself until he had rubbed the painted features clean off the porcelain. He smiles when he realizes this, and Hornig smiles back congenially.

Upon arriving in Paris, Ludwig catches sight of the two of them together in a mirror. "Look at us!" he says. "We couldn't be more different. You, so strapping and fair. Me, so statuesque and dark. But we make a perfect pair, wouldn't you say?"

Hornig nods. "It is a privilege to accompany you on this journey, Your Majesty."

Ludwig turns to Hornig again and again at the Exposition. "Do you think Sophie might like this?" Hornig always confirms, because he hasn't any insight into Sophie's tastes, and affirming the King's opinions seems the surest way to ensure his position remains secure. The King buys Sophie a clock and linens and paper and statuettes.

Ludwig inquires about purchasing a Moorish kiosk, with elaborate stained glass and gold filigree, but he's informed that a rich industrialist has already claimed it. "Very well. I can always have one custom-made."

In the Arts Pavilion, Ludwig can't help but admire the strength and virility of the bust of Bismarck. The artist, he's told, is a woman named Elisabet Ney. "I'd like to meet her," he says, but the clerk informs him she's currently with Napoleon III. "Maybe we'll pay him a visit after all," Ludwig says to Hornig.

In the work, Ludwig identifies a gentleness that he remembers from when he met Bismarck as a teen. The hollow at the base of Bismarck's throat is such that Ludwig would like to place his fingers on it, to run them up and wait for a pulse to knock back. "It's as if Bismarck is here, covered in chalk," Ludwig jokes. Hornig laughs.

The King and Hornig ride out to Versailles to meet with Napoleon III. Gilt edges every surface. Cascades of crystal billow from the ceiling. The salons feature circle upon circle of tripled chairs, so that people might sit and pivot and never miss a conversation on any side. Ludwig remains silent for most of the tour, unwilling to let on that the palace is superior to any of his homes. He withholds his compliments, and asks after the sculptress Ney.

Napoleon waves off the inquiry. "She's an unconventional woman," he tells Ludwig. "If you're interested in courting her, I must say, she doesn't seem your type."

Ludwig scoffs. What would Napoleon guess *is* his type? And besides, Ludwig is looking to be immortalized in stone, not with flesh. "I ask because I was impressed by the Bismarck at the Exposition."

Napoleon pauses. Is it possible Ludwig is breaking down, coming around to the idea of a united Germany? He knows better than to ask. "She is indeed hungry to work with powerful men. I can connect you."

"I don't need any favors," Ludwig replies. He is no conversationalist, and he certainly hasn't brushed up on French politics before the visit. He can think only to ask more about Ney.

"She wears a tunic and pants. She's married to a doctor, but refuses to admit it."

"Then how do you know?" Ludwig asks, worried that he might be accidentally revealing his own secrets, too.

"Certainly Your Majesty has his way of vetting people before meeting them?"

Ludwig is not sure he does. Hornig speaks up to confirm, trying to save face for the King, and Ludwig shines his admiration onto the young man.

"I'd have thought you might have met her. I hear she gets on with Cosima von Bülow."

Ludwig feigns recognition. "Oh yes, it's possible the name Ney does sound familiar, now that you mention it."

The tour complete, the gossip dished out, their visit comes to a close.

Ludwig interrogates Hornig on the train ride back to Munich about his tastes. Hornig is not a complete bumpkin. His father and grandfathers have served the royal family for generations and he has always paid close attention to those willing to share information and knowledge with him. At the Exposition, he read every placard and tag. He listened when Ludwig preferred one work over another and attended to his reasoning. He knows the way such insights can be the difference between keeping his position and being replaced.

When Ludwig asks Hornig about what he admired at the Exposition and why, Hornig knows to allow his opinions to diverge from the King's just enough that Ludwig will not think that he is kowtowing to him. He strikes the perfect balance and Ludwig praises his excellent eye. He keeps smiling at Hornig and shaking his head. "Has anyone ever told you you look like William Tell?" Ludwig asks the question as though William Tell is a live human being and not a mythic figure.

"You are too kind to me, Your Majesty," Hornig replies. The King is an odd bird, to be sure, but Hornig knows that being in his good graces is a rarity. There are far worse jobs. And Ludwig amuses him like no one else. Hornig can never quite tell if the King is in on his own jokes or not, but he seems to enjoy Hornig's laughter and joins in as though it were his intention to make him laugh.

Upon returning home from the Exposition, Ludwig receives a letter from Elisabet Ney, apologizing for their not having made contact while he was in Paris. Ney tells the King how greatly she admires him, and hopes he might sit for her.

Ludwig mentions Ney in a note to Cosima, who writes back: "She was a bridesmaid in my wedding, but I don't talk to her anymore. She disagrees with Richard's politics."

Any opposition to Wagner is enough reason for Ludwig to ignore the artist.

No Punch Line

✸ ✸

LUDWIG PAYS SOPHIE A SHORT visit to deliver the gifts he chose for her. She can tell they are growing apart. She bids Sisi to write to Ludwig, to help him come to his senses. "Of course, I will," Sisi promises, "but I fear Ludwig thinks I am a one-trick parrot, repeating the same thing over and over. If I haven't convinced him by now, I don't know what would change with another note. There is only one person whom he respects more than me. You should go to him. The Meister might prove helpful."

The Great Friend is immediately taken with Sophie: her soulful eyes, her creamy skin, her regal carriage. Wagner stops short of making a pass at the young woman himself. "Certainly Ludwig's not fool enough to let someone as lovely as you go, but I'll lend my support, all the same."

Wagner writes: "I was profoundly stirred by your dear chosen one! For the first time since your fate was joined to mine, I looked into a human eye from which love for Your Majesty spoke deeply and eloquently to my soul. Oh if only you could be united soon, soon."

Ludwig wonders why Wagner's letter stirs up more feeling in him than Sophie ever has.

But still: Ludwig and Sophie set a date. On August 25th Ludwig will turn twenty-two and gain a wife.

A week before the wedding, Ludwig delivers a crown to Possi. Sophie tries it on, but it sags sadly. Her skull is too petite. Ludwig snickers. "You look like a pathetic child!"

Sophie crumples in tears, hurling the crown onto the table before her.

Rather than consoling Sophie, Ludwig excuses himself.

Ludwig asks his doctor, "What characteristics does a person need to get married, would you say?"

The doctor furrows his brow. "Nothing more than a desire to, really. It is best if a person is of sound mind, I suppose."

Ludwig nods. "And would you say I am of sound mind?"

The doctor responds enthusiastically. "Of course, Your Majesty!"

Ludwig grimaces. "But I worry I am not of the mind to marry. Perhaps there is some condition under which it's best for one's health not to join with another?"

The doctor pauses. "Your Majesty, I believe you have a case of kalte füsse as the date grows near, eh? You'll make an excellent husband, and a King deserves a Queen. Do you have questions as to what should happen on your wedding night?"

Ludwig, madly embarrassed, insists, "Absolutely not!"

The doctor apologizes, but Ludwig later regrets not taking the doctor up on his offer to clarify.

Just days before the ceremony, Ludwig postpones the wedding, setting the date for October 12th.

Sophie asks, "Must we?"

The King ignores her plea. "I don't know why we didn't plan on that day to begin with. It is both my parents' and my grandparents' anniversary. There's no reason not to continue the tradition."

All through September, Ludwig avoids Sophie. He writes to Fräulein Meilhaus, whom he has reconnected with, that every day apart from Sophie improves his mood. "The happy feeling which inspires me now can only be compared with the rapture of a convalescent who at last breathes again the fresh air after a dangerous illness. Sophie was dear and precious to me as a friend and darling sister, but she will not do for my wife; the nearer the date of the wedding came, the more I dreaded it. I felt very, very unhappy and so resolved to free myself from the self-imposed bonds and chains . . . I am still young and marriage would have been premature."

His teacher is confused at the letter. "I didn't realize the wedding had been called off."

And that is because the wedding has *not* been called off. Ludwig proceeds as if the event no longer holds a place on the calendar, but it does, and as that October date approaches, Ludwig panics and delays once more, to November 29th.

Sophie's father, furious, writes to Ludwig himself. "Set a firm date or be done with it. My daughter won't be subjected to the ridicule of the kingdom because you can't make up your mind. If it's not your intention to marry her, then set her free."

Ludwig can't believe the gall. "Isn't a King worth waiting for?" He pitches the marble bust of Sophie out the window, shattering it on the ground below, and pens her a note: "Beloved Elsa, Your parents desire to break our engagement. I accept their proposal."

When the messenger takes the letter, Ludwig slams the door, and pulls out his diary. "Sophie got rid of. The gloomy picture fades. I longed for freedom, thirsted for freedom, to awake from this terrible nightmare! Thanks be to God, the fearful thing was not realized."

Sophie reads the letter with a lack of surprise, but still grief settles over her. How is it possible that two of her suitors have done this to her? First LV and now Ludwig. She worries people will see her as defective.

Much-Plagued Spirits
❋ ❋

SISI IS FURIOUS with her cousin. If Sophie was not the woman he wanted to marry, there were far more gracious ways of ending their affair. If he doesn't want to marry at all, it's even more ridiculous that an innocent girl should bear the black mark of such a rare preference. Letters arrive from her cousin begging her not to be angry. He professes his deepest regret in the same breath as his protestation that there could be no other way. He insists that Sophie will be better off without him. He sends request after request for Sisi to visit him so that he might be sure the dissolution of their friendship has not been a by-product of this misfortune. Sisi, though, is angry. She cannot see the reason in Ludwig's choices or his actions.

Sisi asks Sophie to come to Vienna for a while. "You have nothing to be ashamed of. Only the King benefits from your hiding away. If I were in your place, I would accept every invitation, and, in general, live exactly as before, but if you want to be out of the eye of people who care about any of this, come here. You will be reminded of what a true prize you are in Austria, even if the Bavarians are blinded by their allegiances to their fairy King."

Sophie writes back, thanking Sisi for her invitation. "Not to worry. Indeed I am already tempting the affections of Prince Ferdinand, Duke of Alençon. I feel no need to make a splash here and no desire to seek comfort there with you, for, in a short while, I believe all will be righted."

Napoleon requests an audience with Emperor Franz so that he might express his condolences for his brother Max, executed while serving as Emperor of Mexico. Convinced that Napoleon is at least partially to blame for Max's death, Franzl forces him to come to Salzburg.

Franzl insists Sisi accompany him, despite her claim she's too ill to travel the short distance. He makes light of her excuse as being more of the same, but Sisi has been sick every morning for a month. Not ready to share her condition with him, Sisi takes it as a challenge to outshow the beautiful Empress Eugénie. She limits her diet to only broth for the week before, hoping to whittle her waistline and, with it, the child she fears is rooting itself there.

Crowds flood the streets of Salzburg to see the two famously beautiful Empresses meet. They couldn't care less about which Emperor is apologizing to which.

Empress Eugénie emerges from her carriage dressed in white out of respect for Franzl and Sisi's mourning. When Sisi moves to embrace her—a point for diplomacy on the part of Austria—their skirts bounce off one another and they must pause at arm's length. Eugénie lifts her veil to reveal that her face has begun to blur, ever so slightly, with age.

Sisi is a dozen years younger, and, even with her fourth

child determined inside her, clearly the fairest Empress this afternoon.

Sisi flees to Munich afterward to "visit her sisters." Ida accompanies her and helps to make the secret appointment with a doctor who will be able to confirm that the trade with Franz for the Hungarian constitution has been balanced.

Sisi frets before the appointment, and Ida tries to comfort her. She is convinced they both know the answer the doctor will give them, and it's out of their hands, so there's no use in worrying.

Sisi, though, is not certain which answer she wants. If she is not pregnant, Franzl will keep attempting to accomplish his task. If she is, her body will be wrecked anew. Yes, she would look forward to having a child all her own, but she also does not trust that this part of the promise will be honored. Why should this time be any different?

Ida understands. When the deal had been struck, there was no question in Ida's mind that the trade was more than fair: greater autonomy for Hungary in exchange for the Empress performing the duty to which every wife is bound. But Ida has seen the way the children are kept from their mother, and Ida can see now what Sisi has risked in the name of Hungary. She does her best to remind Sisi of the worthiness of her cause.

The doctor knows who Sisi is, despite her pseudonym, but this doctor is discreet. "May God bless you with another prince," he says, when he confirms Sisi and Ida's suspicions.

On her return, Sisi tells Franzl that she is pregnant, and

he cries tears of joy. When they inform the Archduchess the next morning, before Sisi has had a chance to be inspected by the court doctor, the Archduchess hides her confusion that she was not, as usual, the first to know and congratulates only Franzl.

A Crisis of Friendship

✴ ✴

Ludwig opens only mail bearing the seals of his friends. Anything with Pfistermeister's mark is put aside. He identifies the stamp of Elisabet Ney and reads: "Your Majesty, I would be most privileged if you'd allow me to sculpt your likeness. You are a singular and powerful figure, to whom I could never do justice with even the finest materials, but I do believe I am the artist who could come closest."

Since the Exposition, Ludwig has noticed many letters with Ney's stamp come across his desk, but Ludwig holds a grudge. Ney was not available to him when he asked back in Paris, so why should he make himself available to her now?

For every one letter to Ludwig, Ney writes two to Bismarck asking when she can expect his assistance in gaining access to the King, but Bismarck realizes it was foolish to ask Ney's help. He has turned his efforts to more surefire methods, gathering up the Northern German states to show the Southern German states they have no choice but to join them.

In November, Ludwig sends Wagner a note from Hohen-schwangau. "I write these lines in my cozy Gothic bow-window, by the light of my lonely lamp, while outside the blizzard rages. It is so peaceful here, this silence so stimu-lating, whereas in the clamor of the world I feel so abso-lutely miserable: all that wearing oneself out to no purpose, I simply cannot endure . . . Thank God I am alone here at last. Before me there stands the bust of the one Friend whom I shall love until death, for whom I would be ready to suffer and die. Oh, if only the opportunity were given me!"

Their friendship is a safe romance. Ludwig's ardor for Wagner has nothing to do with the material existence of the composer, and little importance is placed on being together in person. Instead, Ludwig can write carefully composed letters, pledging his allegiance and offering his own life for the sake of the art Wagner is capable of creat-ing. There is a forbidden quality to it in the way his states-men resent Wagner's say, but it feels as justifiable as his attraction to Paul has felt irrational.

It is not as though Ludwig and Wagner agree on much outside of their aesthetic tastes. Without frequent visits, they are able to mute the other's objectionable qualities. They are allowed to remain blindly committed to the idea of each other, rather than each other's actuality. Both Ludwig and Wagner have a talent for ignoring truth: they tally debts to attain what they cannot afford, they count on salvations that will not cushion their falls. Their pessi-mistic outlooks publicly curtain their private, clueless optimism. Of course, neither of them understands this about himself, but it's not difficult for those around them to see.

Wagner takes Ludwig's pledge as permission to publish what he wants without consulting the King: a series of articles impressing upon the public the superiority of the German people and the need for a bolstering of national spirit, before taking a turn toward the critical by tearing down the political regimes that forced him to leave Munich. He itemizes his grievances against church and state, and charges the monarchy with righting these wrongs.

Ludwig, his faith bruised, writes to the *Süddeutsche Presse* that it must suspend the articles' publication. He vows to Pfistermeister that he will not contact Wagner. But Ludwig suffers. He could bear, with little effect, the dissolution of his marriage prospects. He knew that any mutual feeling between himself and his past infatuations was near impossible. But the loss of Wagner's correspondence takes its toll. Ludwig can tolerate only the small enclave of Berg, where he is allowed the least bit of privacy. Tucked away as he is in his tower room, the heat rising to him, he orders that fewer fires be lit, and the far-flung corners of the first floor frost. He feels safer the fewer people are around, but to any visitors, Berg seems a haunted house, a dark, chilled cabinet of ghosts.

Less than a year after Ludwig called off his engagement, Sophie brings her husband, Prince Ferdinand d'Orléans, to visit Ludwig at Berg.

No porter greets them at the gate. A lone policeman wanders the grounds, and stops the couple on their stroll up the path. "Isn't Ludwig expecting us?"

The policeman shakes his head and lets them into the house. They rouse an adjutant, fast asleep on a bench near the kitchen, and he shows them to a freezing-cold ante-room, where two other ministers shiver in wait.

"Perhaps you can find the King and tell him he has several visitors," Sophie says.

The adjutant mopes into action.

Sophie and Prince Ferdinand are eventually led into the King's study on the second floor. They greet Ludwig warmly, but they can't hide their shock at the condition of the room. The windows bear no curtains and the paper has been peeled from the walls. The settee they perch on is missing several of its upholstery buttons, and a gash at the front edge spills stuffing. A housemaid enters with a tray of tea and sweets, but what Sophie sips from her cup is cold and the cake is stale. "What is that smell?" Sophie asks.

"I've taken up photography," the King says. "It's the chemicals."

Sophie nods. In her husband's eyes, she catches alarm. Clearly this is not what he expected—nor did Sophie. Only months before, the palace had been in prime condition: bustling with servants and ministers, everything polished and gleaming. Sophie says only, "Maybe it's best we see ourselves home."

A look of relief flashes in Ludwig's eyes. Sophie kisses his cheek. Prince Ferdinand wraps the King's hand in a shake from which Ludwig immediately tries to free himself.

After their departure, Ludwig complains to the minister who is allowed in next. "Bored to DEATH! I couldn't bear a single afternoon. It's clear now the narrow escape I made from a lifetime of such tedium!" The minister gets right to the business he must pretend to ask for the King's guidance on. Not everyone knows such formalities are no longer necessary.

In the bitter cold, Ludwig goes for midnight rides. He sits in his sleigh, while Hornig rides on horseback behind. Ludwig halts the sleigh occasionally so Hornig might dismount to adjust the King's hat or rearrange his ermine throw or peel him an orange or reposition the hot water bottles used to keep him warm.

Hornig learns to fill his canteen with spirits to keep his own warmth up, but his fingers are blue when he arrives home, and "throat inflammations" regularly prevent him from joining Ludwig at all.

Period of Infirmity

✻ ✻

IN THE EARLY DAYS of Sisi's pregnancy, it was easy enough for Andrássy to forget the terms of the Ausgleich and his appointment as prime minister, and the friendship between the two could remain largely unchanged. But as the evidence has begun to reveal itself, Sisi has been indisposed to visits, and Andrássy, now able to accomplish much on his own because of his role, seeks fewer reasons to insist on the Empress's help. What escalated their attraction—their mutual passion for the future of Hungary—has found a natural plateau in the satisfaction of their primary goal and the clear evidence that the Empress's romantic efforts are still with the Emperor. It is not that Andrássy no longer desires Sisi so much as that he has been forced to confront the reality of the power that opposes his desire.

Sisi hides herself away, hoping that the less Andrássy sees her in this state, the easier it might be for them to resume their flirtations as though uninterrupted after she has given birth, but she is so *bored* without even her normal activities because of her current condition.

———

Now that Sophie is married off successfully, having read her report on Ludwig's dismal environs, Sisi allows herself concern for her cousin. He stopped writing her months ago, but she can't imagine what could have gone so wrong in the time between. Certainly, he has a flair for the dramatic, but what Sophie tells Sisi she saw in his home sounds worse than that—real trouble, not a performance to get attention.

She writes Ludwig to ask if she might come for a visit. She tells him she is pregnant again. "I hope it will be a boy as handsome as you," she says, knowing how far flattery goes with him. "If it's the failure of your betrothal last year that has you down, not to worry; I have other sisters!" She laughs at her own joke. "But really, we will find you another wife if that's what you want. And if not, tell me what it is you do want, and we will get you that. My only desire is to see you happy, and I will do whatever is within my power to make it so. Your Elsa, Sisi." She does not know that Ludwig had taken to calling Sophie Elsa, too, or that the reference to *Lohengrin* will salt Ludwig's Wagnerian wounds.

Rudolf kills his first stag at age nine. The Emperor marvels at what a natural shot his son has turned out to be.

Soon after, Rudolf brings Sisi a stack of his drawings, and Sisi pats the cushion beside her. Her lap has grown small as her belly fills with her fourth child.

Rudolf's artwork has taken a decided turn. The pages are a veritable Audubon collection of birds that have met violent ends: a mute swan splashed with red, a hazel grouse separated from its own head, a pygmy cormorant in the mouth of a dog, a green sandpiper with a gunshot blotching its breast, diving from flight.

"These are beautiful, if a bit scary, darling," Sisi says. "You could draw some birds while they're alive instead?"

"The live ones won't hold still," he explains.

Sisi can't argue with that.

Ida has remained preoccupied by her effort to do all she can to ensure that Sisi's next child is allowed to remain under the Empress's control as promised. She suggests that Sisi give birth to the baby in Budapest. She doesn't mention that if the child is indeed a boy, his being born in the castle might allow for the full separation of Hungary from Austria in the future, but she also doesn't think that Sisi would mind such a possibility.

Sisi tells Franzl her plan. "We'll name him Stephen, after the patron saint of Hungary." Franzl knows this will cause a stir, and recognizes the play that Ida is setting up for the future of the two nations, but it's the first time he's seen Sisi smile in weeks and everything is currently a gamble.

The court gossips that the name makes perfect sense for a child fathered by a Hungarian revolutionary like Andrássy. Sisi hears these rumors and wishes they were true.

On April 22nd, 1868, Valerie is born in Budapest, and Sisi finds herself smitten. "The little divinity," the doctors call the child for the way Sisi praises her.

The Emperor does not receive his extra son, the insurance policy he had wished for.

Hallowed and Unapproachable

✳   ✳

AFTER THREE MONTHS OF HEARTBREAK, Ludwig's will crumples and he writes to Wagner. "How is your work? Plans for the Festspielhaus? Progress on *Die Nibelungen*? I await it with direst anticipation. Come to Hohenschwangau so that we might relive those glorious days we had there together. Return to me, Friend. I can't even remember what drew us apart."

Wagner receives the letter, and responds in kind. "I'm sorry to hear that you can't remember what caused our rift, as it is something that pains me greatly. Of course, I will always be thankful for the ways you've supported me, but I must refuse this support if it's to be countered with censorship. You are caught in a whirlpool of self-destruction, and it's too painful to stand by and watch. So why do you disturb the silence and wake the old hopeful echoes in me?"

Ludwig writes again: "Oh my Friend, once the world seemed rosy to me and men seemed noble; since then I have suffered unspeakably. My feelings of hate and misanthropy are fully justified. I find comfort only in thoughts of the pursuit of our ideal. I did what I needed to do to undergo purification: I shut myself away. Now, I am strengthened, and I will throw myself bravely into life and my solemn duties."

This letter satisfies Wagner. He writes back, "I believe you will be seen as the most astonishing revelation of the divine in the history of the world! Perhaps it is time for me to return to Munich."

Ludwig, though, knows the situation is not so simple. "If you return to Munich, there will surely be a revolt. Come to the Roseninsel for your birthday instead."

Wagner agrees, eager to see the island the King normally keeps entirely to himself. When the boat lands, he's startled to find only five acres of land. It takes them less than ten minutes to walk around the entire perimeter. Ludwig makes a show of hastily lighting the fireworks he's gathered for the night and they flash open the blackened sky. Ludwig tells the Great Friend, "Blow out the candles, old boy! Wish on every star! The world is yours!"

Former King Ludwig I passes away, and Ludwig II immediately realizes that, without his grandfather on the payroll, his own allowance has doubled. Dreams of how to spend the extra cash quickly erase his grief. After his visit to Versailles, Ludwig has not stopped thinking about building a palace of his own perched on the mountain over Hohenschwangau. If Wagner is a threat, if he must hold his Great Friend at a distance, then he will build a place where he can hold himself away from the rest of world more easily. The Roseninsel is too small. They can get to him there. He needs a place where he can truly hide.

Ludwig continues to entertain the admiration of his actress friend Lilla. He invites her to visit Hohenschwangau, and she fasts all week. That morning she overpaints her face. Ludwig can say only, "You look . . . changed."

Lilla blushes, though he can't see it beneath all the powder. "It must be the longing for your company."

Ludwig points up at the Jugend peak. "I'm starting work on a castle up there. The surveyors are doing their assessments. I've chosen Christian Jank to do the preliminary drawings."

Lilla is surprised. "The set designer?"

"He will bring to light what it is I have in mind. He knows this castle is to be the stage for the rest of my reign. There's no one else for the job."

Lilla nods at his brilliance.

Ludwig cocks an ear and tells Lilla he hears himself being called away, but Lilla hears nothing.

Left alone, she strolls down to the Alpensee. It is not long before the Queen is beside her at the shore. "Lilla, dear, we must discuss your visits. I fear that as long as you are in contact with Ludwig, he will not marry. We both know it is not possible for him to take you as his wife."

Lilla would love to believe what the Queen is telling her. She is flattered to be considered a threat, but the truth speaks loudly in her mind. "He has no intention to marry, neither me nor anyone else."

The Queen does not bat an eye. She continues quickly. "When your contract expires at the theater, I trust you will not renew. There is nothing here for you." Lilla's eyes become glassy.

Lilla has years left in her contract, but she doesn't mention this. She is gambling on winning Ludwig over in the meantime. "I shan't do so happily, but when my contract is up, I will leave."

The Queen squeezes Lilla's hand. "Good girl you are! What a beautiful day, isn't it?"

Lilla can't agree.

When the architect Riedel unrolls the blueprint of a three-story fortress in late-Gothic style modeled after Jank's drawing, Ludwig loses his breath. "This is perfect, exactly what I had imagined. I wonder if we might also add another wing so that Mother and I might not cross paths. And we should raise the ceilings of the throne room."

Riedel is relieved the requests are not more extensive than this and jots down the notes.

Ludwig goes on to describe different shapes for the windows and towers. Riedel flips the page. By the time they are through, it is clear the structure will need to be at least two more stories and a hundred more rooms, the style changed from Gothic to Romanesque. Riedel replies that he'll need to talk to the engineers to confirm the mountain can hold such a structure.

"They'll just need a bigger stick of dynamite, I expect!" Ludwig laughs. "Three years should be sufficient? If you get to work at once, I won't have to wait even that long." The King excuses himself to avoid any protest. He knows when to disappear.

Villains

✳ ✳

SISI COULD LOOK BACK on her years so far as Empress and mother and see every way in which she had been wronged despite all she'd done right. It was in her nature to chart her trajectory by the obstacles she'd overcome and not the challenges she had posed others.

Sisi dotes on Valerie. She cradles the baby and sings to her and even nurses her occasionally for the first few months. She goes for walks in the public gardens with Valerie in a pram, and the people of Vienna coo over the unusual sight of their Empress with the precious infant. She allows herself to forget everything else in her life. She allows her correspondence with Andrássy to fall off. She stops traveling. She pays little to no attention to Franzl or the other children, but having her around more regularly seems a marked improvement to them. She keeps meticulous charts of Valerie's sleep schedule and eating and bowel movements and baths—or rather she gathers this data from the nurses and nannies.

She keeps Valerie from the Archduchess's care at all costs. She barely even allows her mother-in-law to see the child, let alone hold her or have any say in her custody. The

Archduchess has aged quickly in recent years and hasn't the energy for child-rearing. And besides, she knows the agreement that has resulted in Valerie's birth. She knows that there is no arguing that this one belongs to Sisi. All the Archduchess would like is to visit with her newest grandchild, but she sees that Sisi holds a grudge from the way in which the Archduchess has dictated the upbringing of the others. She asks Franzl to appeal to his wife. It is cruel to let the old woman hear the child crying, but not provide the comfort she delivered to Rudolf and Gisela so adeptly in the years prior. Comfort feels like one of the few things still within her capacity to provide at this point, but Sisi refuses these bids, even from her husband.

The Archduchess Sophie has lived a life of strategy, and finally, that ruthlessness seems to have caught up to her. If this is the price, so be it. She had married a man she hoped might one day make her Empress, but had given up on that hope when she realized her husband would be an embarrassment on the throne. When her brother-in-law, the mentally ill Ferdinand, abdicated, it hadn't taken Sophie much effort to put pressure on her unambitious husband to step aside so that their son could become leader. Sophie would never be Empress, but behind her teenaged son, she could have the influence she desired on the future of the empire. The people had never been on her side. They called her the "only man at court," and though Sophie had always enjoyed that sobriquet, she knew it was never meant as a compliment. So be it. She did what she believed was best for the empire, and they needn't care for her personally if they thought favorably of the actions Franzl took at her suggestion.

When the young Sisi had shown up in Franzl's life,

she had initially been no threat at all to the power the Archduchess had come to inhabit so completely. The Archduchess mothered Franzl's children as though they were her own, set on ensuring the health of the line of inheritance by managing every detail herself. But Sisi had grown stronger over the years; on her more reflective days, the Archduchess could view the way that Sisi withheld Valerie from her as a sign that she was finally willful enough to be the Empress the empire needed. Raising her daughter with dedication showed greater maturity than wandering around to different health resorts and studying languages of inferior nations. Though the people of Austria had never favored the Archduchess (even if they didn't disagree with the agenda she set for her son), they loved Sisi, despite, or possibly because of, the fact that she rarely performed a single official action and was nearly impossible to even catch sight of. The Archduchess could see now that Sisi had no way of knowing that she would not interfere in Valerie's upbringing as she had with the other children, and so she did what she thought she needed to to protect her daughter as her one and only. Sad as she was, the Archduchess praised Sisi in her diary for her strength on this point.

Calling someone a villain is evidence of a limited view, and the Archduchess would never call Sisi a villain in her story, even now.

In Commemoration of a Foundation Being Laid

❈ ❈

A PLAN IN PLACE, the main block of Untersberg marble is laid as foundation for Neuschwanstein. A hollow in its interior holds the plans, some coins, and a miniature bronze of the King.

To celebrate, Ludwig asks Hornig to ride across the Marienbrücke that spans the deep Pöllat Gorge beside the castle.

"Your Majesty sentences me to death."

"Nonsense. You've proven your skill night after night tromping around the icy slopes behind my sleigh. This will be like nothing at all."

"But this is a suspension bridge," Hornig argues. "You realize it will sway when the heft of a horse so much as ambles across it."

"Oh, you will not amble and you will not trot. You will gallop. There and back. And when you return I will reward you for your faith in me."

Hornig does not want a reward. He wants to live to see his children grow, but he has not denied the King yet, and he cannot imagine another future for himself. Since his youth, taking over this position has been the only option presented to him, the only occupation he has been trained for. To decline the King's request would be to fail not only himself, but his wife and children and the futures that lie before them, a fate worse than plummeting to his death in the waterfall below.

Hornig mounts his horse Antigone and gulps from his canteen of whiskey. He looks at Ludwig, whose eyes have gone as wide as he's ever seen them. He wonders if the King wants him dead, if Ludwig's convinced he might squelch his desire if he takes away its source. But before he kicks his heels into the horse's flanks, he sees a look of regret on the King's face. It is too late.

Hornig and Antigone bound across the bridge and he feels less sturdy than he does on even the most blitzed of his night rides, but the drink has given him just enough courage to turn pure animal. He throws his body from one side to the other to counterbalance the range of the bridge's swing, and when the horse arrives on the solid ground of the other side, he hears the King's whoop of joy. Even if surviving the first leg of this journey has convinced Hornig of his ability, Antigone knows better than to take such a risk again. No matter what Hornig tries, the horse will not be ridden back across the bridge.

Hornig rides Antigone down the mountain slowly, and tries to wrap his mind around the fact of his situation. He is beholden to Ludwig's whims, but his family is well taken care of. He has an apartment in the Munich Residenz and a small home on the outskirts of town where his wife and children live. He is well-respected in the palace, and Ludwig is generous to him.

But he knows that the King wants more from him and feels more for him. Does Hornig feel more for the King?

Yes, he can answer that quickly in his uncensored thoughts, but if pressed to elaborate, he fumbles. He feels tenderly toward Ludwig, but romance does not seem like the correct word. Hornig can see that Ludwig is entirely himself and people often struggle to embrace him because of that, especially given the roster of responsibilities that are not well-matched to his nature. He feels duty toward his King, not in a grudging way. Instead he feels that serving the King, in every capacity, is a matter of allegiance to his country, and if his commitment to Ludwig is more personal than that, then so much the better. In any case, Ludwig has not asked anything of Hornig physically (aside from requesting that the stablemaster risk his life for his royal amusement). Hornig has been waiting for it to come to that, to see how he responds to an advance in the moment. He has not made any vows to himself, and, if it should come to placing these duties on either side of a scale, he sees his obligation to the kingdom as being superior to the bond of his marriage. When he is with Ludwig, he can feel a magnet drawing them together.

Back at Hohenschwangau at the bottom of the mountain, Ludwig is cheery, but he does not seem particularly impressed by Hornig's feat. After getting their horses settled, Hornig strips off his clothes and jumps into the Alpsee, wondering, as the icy water consumes him, if Ludwig is watching.

At the official premiere of *Die Meistersinger*, Wagner sits in the royal box with the King. The applause is so raucous that Ludwig bids the composer stand up and bow after the second and third acts. Ludwig tells him, "Fate called us to a great task. I owe everything, everything—to you. Hail German art!"

Wagner bows deeply to his King. "Savior and redeemer, I throw myself at your feet, speechless," he says, but, of course, their eyes remain level.

A Moment of Your Time

✳ ✳

IN SEPTEMBER, a pencil sketch arrives for Ludwig from Elisabet Ney, along with a note of praise. "I've attempted only to reproduce a general impression of your noble appearance, with Your Majesty's characteristic dignity and youthful perfection. I hope you'll forgive all of this hymning, but I find it useless to minimize the inspiration and dedication you elicit in my most artistic instincts, and I hope we might meet soon."

Ludwig is flattered by the sketch. It reflects how he sees himself on his most confident days: strength and passion embodied in his stance and expression. He writes back to admit her into the Residenz, under several conditions. She's not allowed to take measurements of him and she isn't to speak to him. Ludwig doesn't feel the need to explain, but he welcomes the opportunity to be silent and still for long stretches of time without anyone, especially the cabinet, bothering him, and he doesn't want that marred with chitchat.

Ney wonders if she should give up. How will she succeed in assisting Bismarck if she can't talk? She is certain she will find a way to convince him to let her speak eventually, and so she consents.

The sittings are postponed again and again, though. Christmas comes and goes and Ney has yet to gain audience with the King.

She writes Ludwig for what she promises herself will be the last time, telling him she is leaving for Italy soon, and won't be back until the following year. If he's interested in modeling, they must start immediately. She sends along the message contained in an envelope with a banknote for his aide-de-camp, and the aide makes sure Ludwig is handed the letter when he is in a good mood.

Ludwig finally sets a date.

More and More

❋ ❋

SLOWLY, SCAFFOLDING BEGINS TO PATTERN the Jugend Mountain that winter, clinging to the rock like so many spiderwebs. Neuschwanstein's redbrick gatehouse is finished quickly, but everything else takes much more time than Ludwig imagined. The three hundred workmen persist as ordered, despite the icy conditions. Dozens slip down the side of the mountain, returning to work tattered and bashed.

Impatient, Ludwig plans another palace, not twenty miles away. Pfistermeister tells him he should finish one before starting another, and Ludwig fires him. Or Pfistermeister quits. Maybe both.

Ludwig writes to Sisi, "Near the Linderhof, not far from Ettal, I am going to build a palace—a little mini-Versailles with tiered gardens. I need to make myself a po-etic place of refuge where I can forget for a little while the dreadful times in which we live."

Sisi wonders why his other palaces can't be "poetic places

of refuge," but she knows this brand of hope—that another place might hold the solution to one's disquiet.

A chain of architects takes charge of the projects, splitting their time between the palaces, but the newest one manages to pick up on an omission in both. "I see no bedrooms for a Queen, Your Majesty."

Ludwig says, "We can always renovate if necessary."

On the day of Ludwig's first sitting with Elisabet Ney, he hears her speaking sharply to his mother down the hall. "Women are fools to be bothered with housework. Look at me; I sleep in a hammock which requires no making up. I break an egg and sip it raw. I make lemonade in a glass, and then I rinse it, and my housework is done for the day." He flashes with joy at the thought of someone talking this way to his mother, but that positive impression quickly turns to intimidation. He works himself into a wretched state wondering why he struggles to be so bold.

When Ludwig enters the canvas-draped sitting room, Ney bows silently.

Ludwig notes her refusal to curtsy. "You are Fräulein Ney?"

She dips her chin.

"Are you the terror I heard reprimanding my mother earlier?"

She pauses and blinks.

"Did she steal your tongue? I have seen her do it before."

Ney realizes he has forgotten his command that she not speak. "Forgive me, Your Majesty."

"I heard nothing that needs forgiving. She needs to be challenged more often. Where would you like me?"

She shows him to the spot she has set up in the light and looks at him steadily, trying to take him in.

Ludwig's annoyance grows. "Well? Begin your work!" he shouts.

Ney is not a woman who accepts being ordered around, even by a King. "I will begin, Your Majesty, when I am ready," she says. His sulking causes his shoulders to slope. Ney knows she must pull him from this mood. "Your Majesty, I'd be honored if you'd allow me to read to you for a while before we begin. I've just started Goethe's *Iphigenie*, and I think it would set a perfect tone."

Ludwig perks up at this idea, and Ney reads the first act. Ludwig mouths along with his favorite lines: "And rescue me, you who rescued me from death, from this, the second death that I am living here."

Ney closes the book and suggests they get started, and when she looks at the King, she finds the strong, soulful figure she has dreamed of transferring to stone.

At the end of their session, as the light fades, Ludwig insists, "You must return tomorrow so we might read more of *Iphigenie*!" Ney bows deeply. Now that she knows she's allowed to speak, her job will be much easier.

On her next visit, Ludwig asks, "Is Garibaldi the genius we make him out to be?" He hopes he might uncover some gossip he can deliver to Sisi or Cosima.

"Genius?" Ney laughs. "Well, yes, I suppose at some

point he might have been, but when I found him, he was most concerned with feeding the flock of ducks on the estate where he lived. If one can be a genius at such a hobby, then he certainly was fast attaining that status. When I accompanied him on his walks, he announced himself, like a true leader, to the ducks. 'Canards, regardez votre Dieu!'" She smiles conspiratorially.

The King lets out a fit of giggles. "How is it your portrait of him is as dignified as it is, knowing what you do?"

Ney knows the King does not see that the same question could be asked of her desire to mold him. "All men have dignity, Your Majesty. It is the artist's job to eke it out."

"And Schopenhauer?"

"A lamb. He kept angling to see if I had fur upon my lip because he was so shocked a woman might behave the way I do."

Ludwig shivers and squeals.

Ney wonders how the King reconciles his hatred for Prussia with an artist who sculpted Bismarck and realizes it is a miracle she has been allowed in at all. Maybe Ludwig is more aware than he seems of the risk that accompanies her visits.

But Ludwig poses no such questions, and doesn't even appear to avoid them. He seems to Ney, simply, clueless. Perhaps she has succeeded in making herself seem innocent. Perhaps the duck story has done its job.

Ludwig notices Ney has dropped her hand. "If I'm no longer needed, I have much else to do."

When she snaps her eyes into focus on his face, she sees he has gone red. "My apologies, Your Majesty. I was trying to work out a technical issue in my mind. I won't dare waste another moment of your time. Would you like to take a break? Shall we read another scene from *Iphigenie*?" she says, and the King is soothed, like a baby pushed to a breast.

At midnight, after his lunch, Ludwig picks a spot on the map and calculates the distance there. He divides that by the circumference of the Royal Riding Pavilion and sets out. Again and again, as if on a carousel, the King circles the ring. At the completion of this distance, the King has a picnic set up for him to enjoy "at his destination."

Hornig could delegate the supervision of these night rides to another servant, but he talks himself into believing the King needs his sensitive companionship for this unusual habit. He shouts out the King's lap count each time he passes his post and then joins Ludwig for the picnic.

After a dozen of these nightly rides, Hornig ventures to ask the King why he prefers this simulation to a real journey.

Ludwig immediately blushes with embarrassment, and Hornig wonders if he's gone too far, but he responds, "In the forest and the mountains, there are far more dangers: the terrain and animals and marauders, and all of these threats are worse at night because you can't see them as easily."

Hornig hadn't expected Ludwig to have a reasonable answer. "I see your point, but why not ride during the day then? I can keep you safe from those threats. My eyes are good in the light." He jaunts his eyebrows about and Ludwig laughs.

"But during the day there are other threats that I fear

all the more. The ministers can find me, hunt me down, and burden me with work."

"But if we left early enough."

"Is there a reason you want to get me away from the palace?" Ludwig asks. He tries to flutter his eyebrows in the same way Hornig did, but fails.

Hornig has plenty of good reasons to argue for real rides—to break up the monotony, yes, but also to get back on a schedule that allows him to rest at all, rather than trying and failing to sleep during the day, when there is always more to be done. But he knows that that is not what Ludwig is asking, and he wonders if the time has come when he will be tested. "And if there is?"

Ludwig's whole body goes rigid. He stares at Hornig. "Is there something you'd like to show me out there?"

Hornig nods and leans in, and Ludwig falls the rest of the way forward, their lips pressing together, and everything in Hornig cries out and loosens and fills. When they pull apart, Hornig is the one who stares, and Ludwig hides his eyes. "I can't imagine anything more out there than we have right here," he mumbles shyly. He stands to re-mount his horse, and keeps up the ruse of riding all those laps "home," smiling at Hornig each time he passes.

Escape from Exile

❋ ❋

SISI IS INFORMED that she has a visitor, and she hisses, "Why would you even bother telling me, Ida? You know that I don't like to be disturbed while Valerie is napping."

"I think that the person who is here might be the one exception to your preference, though."

"No exceptions," Sisi says, hushing her lady.

"It is LV," Ida whispers, beginning to doubt herself.

Sisi turns from Valerie, her face alight. "Well, let him in! What a surprise! He can't be left in the sitting room! Someone might see him and shuttle him back to Salzburg!"

Sisi rises from her spot beside the bassinet and greets her long-lost brother-in-law. "Luziwuzi! You look so handsome!" she exclaims as she embraces him. Indeed he has grown into his expanse of forehead, and he now sports a full red beard to mask the long Hapsburg jaw. "But how are you here?!" Sisi cries, holding him at arm's length now, searching his face.

"Now that I see you, I can't imagine how I've stayed away as long as I have!" LV replies. "I heard you'd gone and had another one while I was missing, and I know now is never a good time for you, what with Mother always swiping the children out from under you. But you look happy! Explain."

"This one is mine, LV. Come look at her. She is perfect."

"Of course she is. But how did my brother convince you to go to the trouble again? He seems so gentle and then you see the havoc he wreaks. Me banished, Max dead, you pushing out more babies against your will."

"I traded this one for a Hungarian constitution, and because she is a girl, I get to keep her, too, so really it was a win-win for me."

"You have always been clever," LV says admiringly. "May I hold her?"

"You don't even like babies!" Sisi laughs.

"But a baby no one else can touch? If there's a time to make an exception, this is it."

Sisi retrieves the sleeping Valerie, who doesn't stir. LV accepts her like the rare treasure she is, and the two old friends settle in for a hushed chat.

"Salzburg is as provincial as you imagine, but there is at least art there. I tire of how obsessed everyone is with Mozart, but there is worse music to loiter in the backgrounds of one's days."

"But how are you here?" Sisi says, admiring the way LV looks so comfortable with Valerie in his arms.

"It's not that far, you know. What will one secret visit hurt anyone? It's not as though I'm asking to see Franzl while I'm here, just you and Mother. You could visit me, you know. I know you're always wandering around. A stop in Salzburg along the way would not delay you more than a day."

He is right, but Sisi has kept herself away from him because of the guilt. Perhaps if she had pushed harder, LV might have been allowed to stay in Vienna. "Of course. I will make sure of it the next time I must escape this place."

"I wish I could believe you, but I will not take it personally when you don't come. I know you must do what pleases you."

"Why must you do that?" Sisi says, smarting at the attention drawn to her false promise.

LV laughs. "Everyone needs one person willing to disagree with their nonsense; wouldn't you agree? I think that's why you've always liked me so much; I'm not afraid of offending you."

Sisi nods, suddenly sad.

"Don't cry! Good God. It's good I came when I did. Quick! Tell me what gossip I've been missing. Any news on our little cousin, Ludwig the King? How is Sophie faring? I warned you against trying to push her on another *warmer Bruder*."

"I hope you're right about him, because I could have murdered him for the way he strung Sophie along. You at least canceled once and called it a day. With the King, he just kept putting it off. Mother and Father were not happy."

"I should pay him a visit sometime soon."

"I don't think you should. He's even more private than me, and you and he don't have the history we have with one another. He's not well. I worry about him."

"You worry about someone! My God, you are going soft."

"Oh, stop," Sisi says, and she notices Valerie stirring. "Here, I'll take her."

LV hands over his niece and bids Sisi adieu. "Let

Mother see the little one once in a while," he says, aware he's breaching a boundary.

"She's gotten to you, too? Very well, for you, I might consider it," Sisi says, kissing him on the cheek. "Take care, Luziwuzi. Be ready when I show up unannounced."

LV smiles. "I will not be ready because I won't expect it, but I will be overjoyed all the same."

Sisi swats him on his way.

The Gold's Bright Eye

✳ ✳

LUDWIG WRITES WAGNER: "I would love for *Das Rhein-gold* to be performed at the Court Theater this summer. I'm so eager to see the whole cycle, but my heart might be sated by a portion for the time being."

Wagner receives the letter, and stews. As much as he wants to delay the production of any of the sections until the entire cycle is complete, he sees that to keep Ludwig happy (and thus his pockets full) it might no longer be under his control.

Bülow has resigned as conductor, increasingly unable to ignore the fact of Cosima and Wagner's affair. A team of characters visits Wagner in Switzerland over the summer to plan the production: performers, musicians, costume and set designers. The machinists draft solution after solution for the technical trickery they'll need to pull off transforming Alberich into a serpent and then a toad, constructing a rainbow bridge from the mountaintop to Valhalla, lighting Loge's fire, and making the audience believe that the Rhine-maidens are swimming through the river. A minor task: staging a show beyond Ludwig's wildest dreams.

Unsolicited Advice

※ ※

WITH EACH VISIT Elisabet Ney becomes bolder in her suggestions to the King. She tells him he should visit the Bavarian Parliament, rather than avoiding it, so that he might better protect his people. She has identified that Ludwig responds best to flattery. "Your Majesty embodies the spirit of modern times. You must impress upon Parliament that you expect them to live up to the confidence with which your people have entrusted them, to act as men of progress, and to cooperate with their King. I'll not mention any of this discussion to anyone, but my soul impels me to recommend you take action. To me, there is no other answer than for Bavaria to join the North German Confederation. If you are to protect the people, then Bavaria must become a state within that alliance. If you don't take action, someone else will make a decision for you, and it is surely better to go now willingly."

"But they'll think I'm weak."

"Who will?"

"Everyone!"

"A leader who takes action is not weak. A leader who waits for someone else to take action in his stead is pathetic." Ney swears she sees tears in the King's eyes. She packs up her supplies for the day.

"You have helped me," he whispers before he exits the room.

When Ney arrives for their next sitting, she is informed that she is not being granted further audience at this time.

In February, Ney writes to the King, "If you're now indisposed to further sittings, then I see no reason to delay my trip to Italy again."

After waiting a week and receiving no response, Ney sets sail.

In July, she writes to Ludwig to tell him she's been working on his statue in Seravezza. "I apologize for the delay, but successful portraiture demands time of both the subject and the artist. Our time together having been cut short draws out the work I must do on my own."

Ney wonders if the lack of response means some sort of punishment is on its way. No word has arrived about Ludwig joining the Confederation. Ney fluctuates between serious nerves and convincing herself she's overthinking it. She only voiced her opinions to the King. No one can fault her for that. If Ludwig takes action, it will be his own choice.

Instead

NEY HAS OVERESTIMATED LUDWIG in thinking that he'd be receptive to taking her recommendations so seriously and following her instructions so directly. Though he might eventually consider her recommendations about joining Prussia, far more urgent matters occupy Ludwig's mind.

King Ludwig attends the final rehearsal for the first installment of the *Ring* cycle. The Rhinemaidens can barely squeak out their notes lying on their stomachs across the iron ribs of the cradles that hoist them above the stage. The rainbow bridge looks like what it is: cheap wood covered in a single layer of thin paint. Wagner, embarrassed at the unimpressive spectacle, asks Ludwig if they might mount a different show instead, but it is too late. Ludwig will not let Wagner weasel out of another agreement.

By the time the show opens, Wagner is in Switzerland, unwilling to face the disappointment of a compromised masterpiece, and silence again falls between the Great Friends.

Over a month later, Ludwig writes to Wagner for the first time since seeing *Das Rheingold*. "If I may say so," he writes, "I think you imagine my position to be easier than it is. To be so completely absolutely alone in this bleak, cheerless world, misunderstood, mistrusted, this is no small thing."

Wagner waits a week to write back. He demands the King apologize for forcing him to mount the show before it was ready.

Ludwig replies, "I will admit frankly that it was *my* fault and that I am penitent . . . Your ideals are my ideals; to serve you is my mission in life. Nobody can hurt me, but when *you* are angry with me it kills me. Forgive your Friend! I have become the victim of utter despair; I am not far from thoughts of suicide . . ."

Wagner writes back asking that the King accept that the *Ring* cycle cannot be performed again until complete. Ludwig does not respond. It would be easier to give up his life than to promise to wait for Wagner to complete his work.

Ludwig has found a distraction, though. If the operas he previously relied on as an outlet for his passions are falling short and the palaces are taking too long, then a real human is a decent enough consolation.

While the midnight laps around the pasture persist, Hornig can occasionally tempt Ludwig into going for a walk just after he's woken up at twilight or just before he goes to sleep, as the rays of the new sun seep through the trees.

In the forests surrounding Hohenschwangau and Berg,

the pair are sure no one can see them exchange passions. With Hornig, Ludwig is entirely safe. Hornig's arms around him feel like armor and his mouth tastes like home.

Hornig does not question his actions. He knows the risks are great were anyone to find out, but he also knows that this is the right thing for his country. Better with himself than with anyone else, he reasons, because, with him, the King's secret is safe. These are the ways in which Hornig protects himself from the truth of his feelings for the King.

Letters from Sisi arrive, full of health tips, and Ludwig skims them. He passes them to his barber so he can mix new slurries for his hair and balms for his face. He wants every piece of exercise equipment installed that Sisi has, but once a salon is converted into an exercise room, he avoids that wing of the palace. No sets, no reps. Intention is only one-tenth of a health regimen and all that. Ludwig yawns.

He wishes he could write Sisi a letter about Hornig, how something finally feels right, but he knows he must keep this information to himself. Even Sisi—who has promised him that eventually he will find what it is he wants—would not understand this desire, or at least he is so convinced. So many of the love stories Ludwig cherishes come with conditions: secrets withheld and forbidden knowledge and hidden motives. He tries to find some magic in the way that—provided it is kept secret—his connection with Hornig belongs to them alone. But everything in Ludwig wants to share what he's experiencing. If he tells someone, it might feel more real. Or if he reveals the truth to someone, he might be exorcised, the craving cast out of him via his confession. The uncertainty is too great, though. If Sisi had admitted that that man she described so precisely, the Hungarian former revolutionary, was the object of her desire—even then—Ludwig would be so much further out on his limb. There is no hope of someone offering him something equivalent in exchange for his covert feelings, and so Sisi's letters go unanswered.

Instead, Ludwig begins a secret diary. He records his love of Louis XIV and his motto, "A match for the whole world!" He writes of the thrill he feels when he traces his hands through the sign of the cross. He records that he has fallen from grace because of the physical contacts he's had, venturing to specify on a folded page the number of times he's placed his lips upon Richard Hornig's. He cannot confess any of this even to his priest. Instead, he prays in this diary that he offers up to the altar in his bedroom each night for help in overcoming his desires. As he thinks of the words for his prayers, he idly intertwines *R*'s and *L*'s in the margins, and then scribbles them out before saying, "Amen."

This Mad Carnival of Loving

❋　❋

SISI RENTS FELDAFING, her brother's castle on the Würmsee, for the summer, and, while staying there, she remodels the interior.

When Franzl hears, he writes, "Sisi, you can't spend all this money on a home that isn't even yours. Come to Ischl and you can redecorate all you like. I miss you."

But Sisi is having a grand time being so close to her family. She is only a few minutes' ride away from Possi, where the rest of her siblings stay with their children and her parents. She sends an invitation to Ludwig to join them, but he claims to be too busy. Sisi is unsure what he could possibly mean, being that all the news arriving to her ears speaks of negligence and distraction.

She hires circus performers to put on a show at Possi for all of the children. Bears dance in dresses on the lawn. Zither players pluck away on the terrace. Out at the stables, women in flounces of crinoline and sparkling bustiers brush their ponies' manes, getting ready to race across the grounds. A trapeze is slung up between two linden trees and one very nervous servant shows the strong man around the house, searching for heavy, precious things that he can lift without the threat of being crushed with the debt that would be incurred if he dropped the bust or chandelier or enormous Meissenware bird.

The family gathers on the terrace and a rhythm develops, looping awed silence, laughter, and applause, until an elephant in a little hat is led out to the center of the lawn. The ringmaster overturns a metal tub and the elephant climbs onto the tiny surface and rises onto his hind legs, a picture more than a reality. In lieu of cameras, each one takes a picture in their mind that they will pull out again and again when thinking of "good times."

On the same visit, Sisi tries to communicate her situation to her sister. She needs to feel that *someone* understands. "Imagine you're a caged animal," Sisi tells Nene, "but your keeper is very well-mannered. Your keeper tells you how pretty you are and how charming. When you ask for an apple instead of an orange, though, the keeper refuses. When you birth a baby in your cage, the keeper takes it from you. When you birth another, you ignore it so that it won't hurt as much when the keeper comes to retrieve it, and then you're reprimanded for not caring. Finally, you convince the keeper that you don't need to be in the cage, and so the keeper opens the door, but even when you leave the pen, all of the apples have been hidden from you. You step outside, only to find yourself in a second, larger enclosure."

Nene wishes she could have all the comforts afforded Sisi in this life, but she can also understand the way her once-wild sister has become trapped. "You always have Valerie's hand in yours, though. I was surprised you gave her up for a moment so we could have tea."

"It's true, I finally get to shower one of the children with all the love I have to give. Valerie isn't any use to the empire. In Gisela, they have their Princess to fawn over, and in Rudolf, their future Emperor. Valerie is mine." Sisi's expression holds sorrow at this, though. Instead of the joy of having this child to herself, Nene can see that Sisi is focused on the grief she feels at the children she has lost.

Nene searches her mind for a way to cheer her sister—with something money and power can't buy, something that can be had only out of view of her watchers. "I've found a cave. Will you let me show it to you?"

Sisi perks up. "Where?"

"On the trail along the lake," Nene tells her, proud she has something Sisi does not, but just as happy to share it.

"It's impossible. We spent our lives on that trail," Sisi hisses.

"The entrance is small, overgrown by ivy and moss," Nene replies, already rising from their spot on the veranda.

They practically run down the hill, Nene tracking their progress by their view across the water. "Over here!" she calls. The sisters are girls again, permitted to do anything they like, feral. Nene runs her hands over the stone, pushing for the opening that she'd been careful to cover up, but she can't find it.

Sisi shoves her shoulder hard. "You had me! I can't believe I trusted you. You are a scoundrel and an imp."

Nene will not give up the search, though. She is dumbfounded at where the cave could have gone. "I wasn't making it up. It must be farther up the trail. I swear." She lifts a large smooth stone. "I put this here to mark it," she tells Sisi.

Sisi bends to pick up a pine cone. "Ah, yes, and I once

placed this here for the same reason." She throws the cone at Nene, who ducks. "In any case, you've diverted my mind from my troubles. I will give you that." Sisi turns back to the house and Nene follows, with one more glance to the wall, looking for proof of the story she believed to be true.

Andrássy visits Sisi at Feldafing on his way to Munich, and Sisi asks to be left alone with him in her salon. Upon seeing him, everything that had fallen dormant during her pregnancy and the early days of this newest motherhood has been reawakened in her. "I am so especially happy to see you, for my pleasure at being home here on the Würmsee is second only to being in Budapest." Sisi senses, though, a distance between them now. She teases him about being so formal, but his affect doesn't change for the length of their visit. There is no returning to their status quo after the separation forced on them while Sisi was pregnant. Andrássy has stopped thinking about Sisi constantly. He remains grateful to her and admiring of her commitment to their cause and entertained by her, but the passion and intrigue that used to fire between them no longer reaches the same level of fever.

When Andrássy leaves, Sisi's niece Marie finds her crying in the garden. "What's wrong, Auntie?" the little girl asks.

"Oh, I miss someone, that's all," Sisi says, trying to compose herself. Children, in her experience, can either be adept at keeping secrets or blabbermouths, but it is never easy to predict which.

When Sisi returns home, her brother sends her a bill for the work being done to revert his home to its former state, and so Franzl pays for Sisi's redecorating whim twice.

In November, Franzl tells Sisi, "We'll need to go to Egypt for the opening of the canal." His comment registers no reaction on her face. "Andrássy is going, too," he adds, sure this will convince Sisi to accompany him, but Sisi's face sours.

"I don't think I can make such a trip. My cough, it seems, is acting up again," she says, and she sputters out her weak *het-het-het*.

Franzl doesn't push. Andrássy had been his trump card, but maybe their affinity for one another has finally muted.

After Franzl departs for Port Said, Sisi takes the children to Hungary. She writes Franzl a letter every day, hoping he might mention their correspondence to Andrássy.

Franzl writes back to tell Sisi that she has really missed out on seeing Sultan Abdulaziz's stables in Constantinople: close to a thousand horses and exotic animals. "You would have been in heaven."

Andrássy addresses his letters to Vienna to Ida. "I've been wandering the streets of Constantinople, so romantic and fragrant. I think you might like the air. It hugs you tightly. It's strange to be back here and allowed the freedom to explore without the weight of exile on me. It is a much different city than I remember, or perhaps I am a much-changed man. I can see the beauty of the mosques now, the charm of the vacant gardens, half-dead and half-overgrown. That is always the way, isn't it? Something is always dying off and something always growing unruly.

On our pilgrimage to the Holy Land, I was the only one of all of us to walk into the River Jordan. It wouldn't have been proper to strip down, and the others were worried about sullying their clothes, but I could not resist such an opportunity. It was cold, as you can imagine, but some icy water is no trouble if the trade-off is that I might be granted the power to perform miracles."

Ida does not know how far things have gone between the Empress and the Hungarian prime minister, and she doesn't want to know. Recently, Ida has realized that her job is done. When she came into the Empress's service her goal was to pump the Empress's love of Hungary and make introductions to those who had the vision and diplomacy to actually make change. Yes, she will continue to affirm Sisi's interest in the Hungarian cause, but such nudging has proven increasingly unnecessary. She hands the letter to Sisi. "This is clearly not meant for me."

Sisi responds only to the man who addresses her directly. "Franzl, I do long to see Constantinople, and the Sultan's menagerie sounds divine. Perhaps you'll bring me something special as a reward—something impossible—for which I kiss you over and over again in anticipation."

Without Andrássy, without Franzl, without Ludwig, Sisi has only Ida to entertain her and to confide in, but what has Sisi to confide? She searches her mind for some secret to give up to her lady. Together they imagine Valerie's future—the way in which she will be allowed a freedom not granted the other children. She might travel farther and choose the way in which she develops her mind. Sisi realizes they must find a way to ensure that whomever Valerie decides to marry will not disconnect her from the support of the royal family. If Valerie chooses a cobbler to be her husband, then so be it. Valerie must be allowed to marry for love, and she mustn't be punished for it.

They take turns holding the baby and rocking her, staring into her eyes, willing her to know her power and to feel their love and commitment to her.

When Sisi's other secrets come to her lips to share with Ida, though, she pulls them back. Sisi knows that Ida pays attention, but to name her private transgressions would be going too far. To know a truth is different than to speak it aloud.

Ida knows this, too, and never asks Sisi to confess, and, for this, Sisi is grateful.

Franzl arrives home with a wooden trunk full of souvenirs, and Sisi waits for the lid to be crowed off. Her face falls when she sees the carved emerald from the Sultan's treasury and a host of carefully packed relics.

"What more could you want?" he asks. "That is the crown of none other than John the Baptist's skull!"

"Oh, but Ludwig already has the crown of John the Baptist's skull. It can't be real."

"That is the hand of Mary Magdalene!"

"Yes, yes. So it is." Sisi turns back to reading her book of poems.

Franzl knows that, if he were to ask Sisi what it was she wanted, she would not be able to answer. She knows only that none of these things is it.

Everything Has Its Price

※　※

EISENHART, PFISTERMEISTER'S REPLACEMENT as cabinet secretary, reads a letter to the cabinet that the King has dictated: "No one should speak of politics anymore, unless His Majesty asks a question." Every set of eyes widens, every head cocks ever so slightly, every nose takes in a little more air. The politesse is quickly followed by indignant refusal.

Ludwig pressures Wagner to stage the second piece in the *Ring* cycle, *Die Walküre*. If Wagner won't direct it himself, Ludwig will find someone else.

While he waits, he remodels the Winter Garden on the roof of the Munich Residenz. Ludwig purchases swans to swim in the pond and adds a cascade. He borrows a pair of gazelles and a baby elephant from the zoo. The building is five hundred years old, and every alteration tests the limits of the structure. Ludwig asks the stage designer Jank to paint vast backdrops that he might change regularly: an Indian palace, the Himalayan Mountains, tribal huts, a medieval castle, and lastly a night sky, before which they will suspend an enormous, illuminated moon.

Lilla von Bulyowsky has one more year in her contract at the Court Theater. She has given up hope of ever winning Ludwig's love, but she continues to receive flowers from him for her artful performances, and she has heard about this new Winter Garden that no one has seen except the King. She writes asking if she might pay a visit to perform a selection of his favorite monologues alone for him. Of course, this sounds ideal to the King. When she arrives she talks him into rowing her onto the lake in his tiny boat so she might make her presentation on the water, and Ludwig is charmed by the romanticism of the idea. Lilla grows too animated in her performance of *Emilia Galotti*'s seduction monologue, though, and the boat topples over, capsizing the both of them. The water is not very deep, but Lilla cannot swim, and panics. Rather than helping her to shore himself, Ludwig calls for a servant. Lilla swallows water, but Ludwig waits. "Someone! Servant! Lilla has fallen into the lake."

When a butler arrives, Ludwig orders him, "Well, go on! Fish her out!"

The butler removes his topcoat and shoes, and wades into the murky water to drag Lilla back to shore. Safely recovered, she clutches at her rescuer, opening her eyes to find herself in the arms of the butler, not Ludwig. She removes herself carefully and pats at her sopping dress. Ludwig has already left the garden, and the butler escorts Lilla out, trailing drips through the halls. This is the final visit between Lilla and her patron.

Within a month, with the murals hung over the Winter Garden windows, the plants don't get the light they need, and the garden goes brown and slimy. The baby elephant dies. The giant plaster moon falls from the sky and causes the lake to overflow. The cook, in his sleeping quarters below the garden, rigs an umbrella canopy over his bed so he can get at least a few hours of sleep without being woken by the drip-drip of the leaking ceiling. They take down the painted canvases, and Ludwig must face the fact that he is in Munich and nowhere else.

In July of 1870, tensions mount between France and Prussia. Ludwig behaves as though he doesn't know. War again? There must be some mistake. He plans to visit the site where his Linderhof Palace will be built, but his court secretary, Dufflipp, out of breath and frantic, catches him just in time and impresses upon Ludwig the importance of staying closer to home.

Ludwig journeys instead to nearby Berg and paces in his Balcony Room, windows and doors flung open to the summer night, candles unlit. When he sees Eisenhart, he throws himself into a chair to lament his predicament. Ludwig poses the same question again and again: "Is there no possibility of avoiding war?"

"There is no other way," Eisenhart says, already resolving to sleep on a bench outside this room to prevent Ludwig from escaping in the night. "Get some rest. Tomorrow will be a busy day."

Ludwig sleeps fitfully, worrying that if he takes this action, his friendship with Sisi will be ended for good. If he allies himself with Prussia, he is turning away from Bavarian independence, abandoning his family history and its Austrian connections. He has no choice, though. Eisenhart has made this clear. Or is Eisenhart just telling him he has no choice because Ludwig has opted *not* to choose in the past? He is too deeply embedded in this pattern to reason his way out, to find a loophole in this plan, to determine what is true and what his cabinet wants him to believe is true. He wakes in the dark hours between late night and early morning and, in a tantrum of futility, he orders the troops' mobilization on the side of Prussia, honoring the agreement he made at the end of the Austro-Prussian War. "Bis dat qui cito dat," he says. "He who gives quickly, gives doubly." Ludwig feels immediate relief, as though the hardest part is over with.

On July 19th, waiting for word that the war has officially begun, a crowd gathers outside the Residenz. Ludwig is nervous about how agitated his people are, but he escapes to the inner rooms to avoid the rustling in the square below.

Dufflipp finds the King to tell him that, while the people are nervous, they have not turned against him. He believes Ludwig might feel better if he sees for himself. Ludwig steps into the window and the crowd erupts in cheers. The national anthem rises up and Ludwig bows deeply to his people.

That evening, feeling unusually accountable, Ludwig tells Dufflipp, "I think I will skip the performance of *Die Walküre*. There is work to be done." He toils until two in the morning with his ministers, determining next steps, and everyone wonders how long this might last.

Ludwig's cousin the Prussian Crown Prince, Friedrich, arrives to take command of the army. The citizens of

Munich see the blue-and-white Bavarian flag fly alongside the red and white of the North German Confederation for the first time. They trust their King, though. At this point, even the Italians believe Germany is in the right, and so when Ludwig sides with the Confederation, the public believes that Ludwig has made the obvious choice. Their romantic, idealized King seems to be proving his political smarts.

As his ministers expected, Ludwig's enthusiasm for matters of state does not last long. A Bavarian delegation decamps to Versailles to negotiate with Bismarck the form of the new empire. Ludwig does not attend.

The delegation suggests Bavaria share the imperial crown with Prussia. While the Prussian King would hold the title of Emperor, the empire would be represented jointly by both countries. Bismarck thinks this suggestion ridiculous, especially considering Ludwig's lack of interest in actually *ruling*. Eager to stay on Bavaria's good side, however, he pretends this is a possibility. There's a good chance Prussia's position will continue to improve, and there's no need to lose the assistance of the Bavarian military now.

On his twenty-fifth birthday, Ludwig receives word that Wagner and Cosima are being married. Wagner has denied their relationship to the King all this time. Though offended at the secret's having been kept from him, Ludwig sends a telegram of congratulations all the same.

Ludwig pities himself that he has only Otto with whom to celebrate. If only Otto were more fit to rule. Lately, though, Otto is either depressed and completely nonverbal or babbling manically even when alone. For the past eight weeks, he has refused to take off his boots, even wearing them into the bath. When Ludwig returns from the lavatory to continue their game of darts, he finds Otto has extinguished all the lamps and is sitting in the dark. Ludwig wonders if his brother has organized some surprise for him. "Otto? I am here. What's the meaning of this? Can someone light a lamp?" A servant complies and Ludwig sees only the dim image of Otto's face pulling from grin to grimace and then into a silent scream. Tears fill Ludwig's eyes. "Pack up the darts to be sure he doesn't hurt himself, and put him to bed." Ludwig retreats to his room to spend the last hour of his birthday alone, wondering whether if he performed the same antics himself, he might free himself of the crown.

Autumn storms roll in, reflecting Ludwig's moods. Baden, Hessen, and Württemberg all agree to unify with the north on November 19th. By consenting now, they maintain a great portion of their liberties, and are promised the return of the land already seized from them.

Four days later, the Bavarian delegation signs the same agreement without consulting Ludwig. But there is one more step that needs to take place. Repeatedly, Bismarck invites Ludwig to come to Versailles so they can talk through this final measure. Ludwig needs to be the one to invite King Wilhelm to assume the role of German Emperor, but for Ludwig, this is one step too far.

Ludwig cannot reconcile the fact that, despite not wanting the responsibility, he feels he *deserves* the imperial crown, if anyone does. He sends his old friend Holn-

stein, who had joined him in the broken marriage pact, to see if he stands a chance in his fight.

When Holnstein appears at Versailles, everyone assumes he has been sent as messenger. They search him for a letter signed by Ludwig, but he is empty-handed. He asks to talk to Bismarck privately. The Bavarian delegation wonders what Holnstein is trying to keep from them.

Alone, just the two of them, Bismarck asks, "The King has sent an aide to represent him?"

"No need to be rude. I am also one of the King's closest confidants. I see the inevitable future before us. King Ludwig has sent me to argue on behalf of his imperial sovereignty, but I know he is fighting a losing battle. I believe his greatest desire is to be left alone, and so I suggest you write the letter you'd like signed by Ludwig's hand. If I bring him the ready-made document and tell him I've reviewed its sentiment, he will be extremely likely to comply. Let's not make this task more difficult than it needs to be. If you could compensate me for the risk I take here in betraying the King, then I promise to be all the more persuasive in my efforts. If you promise to compensate His Majesty for his concession, I think the deal may be called done."

Bismarck eyes Holnstein, wondering if he can be trusted, but the aide doesn't blink. Bismarck sets to work drafting what he will call the Kaiserbrief.

Holnstein dashes back through the rain to Hohenschwangau with the letter to find Ludwig in bed with a toothache. His room stinks of chloroform.

Holnstein reads the letter to Ludwig. "All you need

do is re-pen this letter in your own hand and your troubles will be over."

"But my tooth will still ache," Ludwig whines. It is not about the tooth. He knows he is cornered.

"Your Majesty, I need to leave for Versailles tonight with your answer. If we miss this opportunity, Bavaria could lose the few rights it retains."

Ludwig looks away. "I haven't the proper paper."

Holnstein jumps up. "Tell me where to get it!"

Ludwig points to his desk drawer.

Holnstein helps the King out of bed. Ludwig copies the draft of the Kaiserbrief, adding some additional language expressing the importance of the role of the Princes of the individual states of the Reich.

Back at Versailles, Holnstein hands the letter to Bismarck with a smile. They've done it.

Alone in his bedroom at Hohenschwangau, staring up at the construction on the mountain outside his window, Ludwig realizes he's made a mistake.

Payments from Bismarck's Reptile Fund are deposited in the accounts of both Holnstein and the King.

Tickets, Please

✳ ✳

A PAYMENT ARRIVES to Elisabet Ney, too, and she books her passage to America. Bismarck has given Ney at least some credit for Bavaria's capitulation.

Ney writes Ludwig a note to let him know she's leaving, to be delivered with his completed statue. She does not tell him that only an ocean of separation can make her feel safe from the repercussions of her efforts contributing to German unification.

Ney packs only what she needs for the journey and leaves behind a studio full of works in progress, plaster casts, and finished scuptures to be retrieved later. For now she must travel light.

No Hard Feelings

❋　❋

ON JANUARY 18TH, 1871, the birth of the new empire is proclaimed. Ludwig, embarrassed to represent the Bavaria he's sacrificed, sends Otto in his stead, but upon his return, the cabinet members make a move to prevent such a bait and switch from happening again.

Otto's doctor informs Ludwig that his brother is no longer safe to look after himself. Ludwig, pained, tells Otto that he agrees with the doctor's diagnosis. "You'll take up residence at Nymphenburg. You'll have your usual suite and the company of Dr. Brattler. Nothing else will change." Ludwig tries to believe his own words.

But within days, Otto writes to Ludwig to complain that the doctor ties him down to put shoes on him—torture considering the boils he says cover his feet.

Ludwig responds, "There's nothing there, Otto." Not that Ludwig can see, at least, but he knows such phantoms have a firm place in the family line. He thinks of the piano inside his aunt. He thinks of the beast inside Otto. He envisions the castle inside himself.

———

Ludwig requests that a group of men be assembled for a boys' night to distract himself. Footmen go out into the town to gather foresters and peasants. Ludwig lines them up in the Hall of Mirrors and picks out the ones he likes best to accompany him to a tent set up in the woods far behind the palace.

That evening, the men feast and drink. When Ludwig commands they wrestle, they take off their shirts and comply. When he asks Hornig for a piggyback ride, Hornig kneels down so the King might mount him. As dawn breaks over the mountain, the men are delivered home.

Ludwig writes in his diary: "Vivat Rex et Ricardus in aeternum."

In May, Ludwig demands that the Court Theater stage *The Countess du Barry* for only him in the auditorium in the Residenz. The company mounts the production in a single day and performs the next afternoon for the King. The performers gripe about the anticlimax of acting for an audience of one, but when their paychecks arrive, they mute their complaints.

On the 12th, Ludwig summons an actor to his room in the middle of the night. For days since the performance, he's felt a swollen droning in the back of his mind. The man who played Louis XV acted with such a vicious sensuality, Ludwig has permitted his body a swift release every evening after, but with each night, the desire to have the actor there in person has grown stronger.

Ludwig does not ask the actor's name. It will be easier

this way. The king sees dark roots peeking from the white-gray powder applied to Louis's curls. "You should touch that up," Ludwig says, first of all.

The actor had no idea what to expect, but this was not it.

Ludwig's criticism is the equivalent of a little boy pulling a braid, though. He feels his lust metastasize and lashes out defensively. In all the years of visits with Lilla, he never permitted his lips to touch hers. With Louis, though, the pull is too strong. A tight acid rises in his throat. Flames dilate in his stomach. He feels a clench in his groin and a dissolving pressure in his anus. He grazes Louis's jaw with his thumb. Ludwig smears some of the oily white makeup onto his finger and plants a print on the side of his own neck, dragging his finger to leave a mark. He repeats the gesture on the other side and then places a smudge on his lips.

Louis understands what is happening without *really* understanding. The sun is arousing the sky outside the window. He feels his own appetites awaken, against any will he has before experienced. The King, he thinks without words, is a desperate figure, but one with a clot of power, and the presence of such power causes Louis to thicken in a way he does not expect.

Truth spills from Ludwig's eyes. Fear claws through him.

Louis steps closer. Ludwig can smell him, the serrated scent of his body, the purple bloom of something musky on top of it.

Neither says a word. Neither has a name for this moment.

Louis leans in and places a kiss on the first mark on Ludwig's neck. He hears the soft pull of a sigh, and knows he can produce a mirrored effect on the other side. When his eyes list back to Ludwig's lips, the King tilts forward, pressing hard on Louis's mouth. He feels his insides go glassy with relief and excitement both, and drops to his knees. When he unfastens Louis's pants, he sees his desire reciprocated and shows the young man what he wants. Louis returns the favor.

When they are finished, it is Hornig who is awoken to prepare a carriage to take Louis home. Hornig is not surprised, but he does worry about the young man's discretion. He tries to convince himself that this is a good thing; maybe it releases Hornig from his obligations so that he might be home with his family more. He avoids the question that keeps prodding his mind: What more could Ludwig want than what *he* can offer?

Louis expects to be called back into the King's company, but, instead, he is dismissed from the company at Ludwig's request.

A Time for Humility

❋ ❋

IN MAY 1872, the Archduchess catches a chill and the doctors come up short on hope of recovery.

Sisi, in Meran with Ida, hears the news and returns to Vienna right away. "The Archduchess has always been the true Empress. I've served only as a pretty face to put on coins. I worry about the burden that awaits me once the Archduchess is no longer in charge."

"Now that the children are grown, except for your Valerie, I should think that you are in the clear. Anything the Archduchess was still doing will surely be cast off as old-fashioned without her here to insist on the tradition." Ida does her best to reassure Sisi, but she doesn't pay the Empress false compliments. Such sycophantism would only sour Sisi on her. Ida knows her purpose, and it is a boon that she can serve that purpose without having to pretend. Sisi keeps Ida around so that she can be reminded of how glamorous her life is. Ida gasps at Sisi's slightest indiscretions, but never criticizes. She calms Sisi's nerves by minimizing any concerns, never trying to tell Sisi that she is capable of more.

"Is it horrible of me to think of myself before worrying about my husband's grief?"

"Of course not. It is very practical of you." Ida knows that if she continues on with her needlework, Sisi will believe her. If Ida stopped and paused, inviting more discussion on the matter, it might seem like there was something to discuss. "I hope only that you'll be allowed a bit more freedom, one less thumb pinning you down."

"Now, Ida, let's not be too jolly about it," Sisi replies, picking up her own embroidery hoop.

This is another of Ida's purposes. Sisi can chastise Ida as a way of absolving herself. "Forgive me, Your Majesty," Ida says.

"Forgiven."

As the days pass, and the Archduchess grows weaker, Sisi avoids her ailing mother-in-law at all costs by going for longer and longer walks.

On May 22nd the doctors say the Archduchess might be gone within hours, and Sisi finally attends her bedside. She expresses contrition and love for the first time. She apologizes for not having treated her better, for not understanding how hard it would have been for the Archduchess to give up control. The Archduchess cannot reply, but that is probably for the best.

One by one, the rest of the family bid the Archduchess goodbye. Sisi doesn't leave the Archduchess's room as six days rattle by. Ida awaits Sisi in the antechamber, excusing herself only to retire to her bed each night, a luxury Sisi does not afford herself. Chatting with Andrássy in the cramped room, Ida asks, "Why shouldn't great people be allowed to die in peace, in the same holy quietness as beggars?"

A priest passes through the antechamber, carrying Empress Maria Theresa's cross and rosary, and the crowd in the tiny room knows the end must be near.

Franzl sobs like a baby through the last rites and Sisi clutches the hand of her father-in-law, a retiring man whom it is easy to forget about. Sisi blinks back her own tears, feeling it is not her place to mourn a woman with whom she battled so regularly, but, moments later, when the Archduchess is confirmed dead, Sisi leaves the room instead of staying to comfort Franzl. She doesn't have it in her. She cannot believe how overcome she is by grief. She can think of only their one truly happy moment together, hiding together and laughing with Rudolf behind the coffer on that Christmas Eve. Sisi, uncommonly, says a prayer for her mother-in-law's soul.

Sisi wants to write Ludwig. She wants to tell him she is free from the Archduchess's control, but she does not feel as triumphant as she had hoped. She does not want to hear any of the cruel words that Ludwig might lob at the dead woman in solidarity with her exasperation. Sisi feels a hint of sympathy for the woman now that she is gone.

And besides, Sisi has been trying to follow Franzl's requests to abstain from contact with her cousin. Bavaria remains firmly within Prussia's conglomerate and Austria is stranded out on its own and alone. Well, not alone, there is always Hungary, though Sisi has been pushing for more and more self-government. Sisi has confused herself. She cannot tell what is better: Unity or independence. Mutual aid or self-sufficiency. Safety or freedom. She turns these ideas over in her head and struggles to think her way outside of these simple opposites.

By the Pure and Holy Sign of the Royal Lilies on the Invulnerable Balustrade Enclosing the Royal Bed
❋ ❋

ON NEW YEAR'S DAY, 1873, Ludwig thinks of his night with Louis and writes in his diary: "I swear and solemnly vow that I will bravely resist every temptation, and never yield in acts or in words or even in thoughts . . ."

Ludwig had expected Hornig to be cold to him after his tryst with Louis, but Hornig is a consummate professional. When Ludwig asks him to warm his hands at a midnight picnic, Hornig does just that, rubbing them between his own, before tucking them beneath his arms. In this position, the King cannot resist kissing Hornig and apologizing. Hornig asks the King what he might be apologizing for, and the King cannot bring himself to admit his mistake.

On February 13th, he writes, "Never again and otherwise as little as possible . . . Even kissing must be avoided." Melting ice makes for slippery terrain.

———

The barber suggests a mustache and pointed goatee to add contour to Ludwig's broadening face. As his teeth loosen, the dentist pulls them, one by one.

As the once-admired King loses his looks, he searches for other ways to associate himself with beauty. Ludwig hears about a threat to cut down the luscious woods covering an island in the middle of a lake east of Munich, the Herreninsel. To prevent this from happening, he buys the island, and begins dreaming up yet another palace.

Season of Bright Sadness

FRANZL ASKS THAT SISI REMAIN in Vienna for Lent. Sisi agrees, but asks that, in return, Ludwig be allowed to visit. He is family, and this political grudge must not continue. Franzl resignedly allows it.

When Ludwig is admitted into her salon, he flinches at the door shutting behind him. Sisi goes to embrace him and he seems not to know where to put his hands. He avoids her eyes. "Cousin, what is the matter? Has my Parsifal exhausted himself in search of his Grail?"

This phrasing lights the dimmest fire in Ludwig. "So you are not angry at me?"

"It was out of your control, Ludwig. I see that your position has taken its toll on you, though. Is it so different to rule over Bavaria within Prussia than it was from without?" She motions to a settee so he might have a seat.

"It is somehow more trouble. I am in control of far less, and yet somehow I am bothered with even more questions and requests. It is such a lonely endeavor, governance."

"Well, which is it? Are you constantly surrounded or are you alone?"

Ludwig scowls at the way she picks apart his words, but realizes: "Both. I feel as though I am never by myself and yet there is no one who sees me. They see only how they can use me to get what they want."

"Yes, I often feel the same. But you must be grateful for all you have: Wagner's devoted creations for you and your building projects and—may I remind you—*me*."

Ludwig says nothing in response. He is thinking of Hornig and of Louis and of Paul in his tights and of the lumberjack he saw on the mountain and of his William Tell figurine. Without his explaining, Sisi will never understand. He begins to tear up.

"What is it?" Sisi sits beside him. She rubs his back and her tenderness only makes him cry harder. She gives him a handkerchief; Ludwig stares at the beautifully embroidered *E* topped with an imperial crown, and only this forces him to soothe himself. He cannot mar such a beautiful piece of fabric with his tears and the kohl he smudges around his eyes.

"I have an idea," Sisi says. "Every day of Lent I have been going to a hospital or an orphanage to try to lift the spirits of the sickly. Will you come with me?"

Ludwig moans at the thought.

"I think it might help you to see some people who are truly unfortunate. It will distract you from yourself."

Ludwig makes excuses, but in the end, Sisi convinces him to come along.

The orphanage puts Ludwig in a nostalgic mood, recalling the Christmas visits of his childhood in which he handed out gifts to the children. Sisi and Ludwig read stories and even perform an abbreviated version of *Lohengrin*.

Ludwig can't hit the right notes and Sisi needs prompting to remember what Elsa is supposed to do at different points, but the children's laughter goads them on.

Ludwig is in such a good mood that he agrees to visit the asylum with Sisi, too—a dire mistake. The asylum is far bleaker than the children's home, even with Sisi's bright light illuminating the men's faces. In them, Ludwig sees ricochets of the plights that plague Otto. Worse, many of the people seem entirely untroubled. Sisi tries to encourage him to talk to some of the men, but Ludwig begs to leave. He cannot take their gaze on him. It is not like when he goes to the country and he is embraced and celebrated. In the eyes of these men, he feels resentment and anger.

On their way back to the Hofburg, Sisi, frustrated at having had to leave without doing her usual rounds, sighs. "There but for the grace of God go we."

The truth of this statement sends an ache through every nerve of Ludwig's body.

On Holy Thursday, Sisi and Franzl are asked to wash the feet of twelve old men and women from the almshouses. Franzl worries that Sisi will refuse out of disgust, but she takes time gently scrubbing the people's skin.

Back at Gödöllő after Easter, the foxes whine in their cages until they're released so Sisi can chase after them each morning.

Sisi invites Andrássy out on the course. "Of course, the terrain is difficult and one has to ride devilish well," Sisi says, teasing, but Andrássy tells her he has too much to do.

In helping him get the position he deserves, she has lost her riding companion.

Sisi smarts.

Ida, happy with Andrássy's current role, offers to go out riding with Sisi instead. The last thing she wants is for Sisi to tell Franzl that Andrássy should be removed from his post because he is unavailable to her.

"Ida, that's very sweet of you, but you know you're no fun to ride with. I'd lose you before we even reached the edge of the forest."

"I will try to keep up this time! I've been improving!" Ida figures a white lie will at least get Sisi out of her head and onto her horse.

Sisi laughs at Ida's pretending this will go well.

"Please," Ida begs.

"Fine! It's your funeral, sweet woman," Sisi replies.

Ida tries her best, but in less than a minute, Sisi is out of sight and Ida knows she will never catch up. She turns back to have a quiet afternoon alone, but Sisi's sadness at the loss of Andrássy's interest has Ida remembering the old boyfriend she left behind in Hungary. She thinks of the way they kept up writing for some time until his replies slowed to a stop. Sisi never offers consolation because Ida never talks about how heartbroken she is, but everything is practical about how the correspondence had ended. Ida cannot argue with the fact that, now, Sisi is all she has.

When the Empress arrives home, flushed, hours later, she is in a much-improved mood, just as Ida had expected.

At sixteen years old, Gisela becomes engaged. Sisi has managed to ignore her middle daughter for most of her life. She was born a disappointment because of her gender, resented because she outlived her older sister, and easily usurped by little Valerie. "Can't we wait until the spring, when she is seventeen, for the wedding?" Sisi asks Franzl. "Sixteen is so very young an age to begin living life. I would know."

"And you have regrets?" Franzl asks.

Sisi saves herself. "Of course not, but I was exceptionally smart."

"Fine, the spring and then we'll have to admit we are old."

Sisi focuses her attentions on five-year-old Valerie instead. This child is the guarantee of Sisi's youth. Sisi knows, and is grateful, that Valerie is her last, and so she babies her, trying to keep her young and innocent and dependent for as long as possible. Valerie is the only one who never became shaped by or dependent on the Archduchess's strict instructions. Sisi assumes that, given the choice, everyone would opt for the life *she* has always dreamed of—the one she sees as unlived, different only in the way she must ask permission to do as she pleases rather than proceeding of her own accord. Sisi wants a life for Valerie in which she might skip this step.

That Will Be All

※ ※

Ludwig invites Hornig to private performances with him, and they take meals together in the Winter Garden. Ludwig wants to convince Hornig that the tryst with Louis was nothing. Ludwig promises Hornig, "In your company, I exist in the highest heights of ether. Your letters and words are more precious to me than all my possessions, castles, and pictures, and the memories in my soul connected with you and the hours I have spent with you are the most wonderful of my present life. I do not say this as *your* King, because, in fact, you are *mine*."

Hornig keeps his composure. "My sincerest gratitude, Your Majesty. Who should be so lucky as to be offered the admiration of someone so great as you? I appreciate you most highly in a spiritual way."

"And why do you emphasize that aspect in particular?"

Hornig, still stinging, wondering if there will be other dalliances, holds back. "I struggle to put my feelings into words."

Ludwig realizes he must be patient, but patience is not one of his talents.

———

Ludwig reads to Hornig late one night and looks up to find he has fallen asleep. The King pulls a gun out of his desk and points it at Hornig. "Wake up!"

Hornig startles at the sound and then again at the sight of the gun.

"You are dismissed. If I bore you so much, then it's impossible you should count me as your friend. You can remain on as stablemaster and that is all."

Hornig feels a rush of emotion that he cannot distinguish: it is relief and heartbreak in one. He had been anticipating the disappointment of another affair, or even the catastrophe of their relationship being made known and publicly condemned, and now he can stop worrying. It is no longer his concern. He doesn't pause to protest. He rides home and crawls into bed with his wife, who stirs, surprised he is home so early.

Ludwig shuts his diary and does not reopen it for a year.

Culture and Education

✻　✻

ALL SUMMER Sisi and Franzl must host royalty at the Hofburg because of the World's Fair. As soon as one king and queen leave, another pair shows up, and Sisi moans, "Couldn't they all come at once and keep each other company?"

At night, when Sisi's clothing is uncinched from her body, her form expands ever so slightly; the whalebone stays etch sores under her arms. The fabrics' rich dyes leave her pale skin looking bruised.

Sisi takes a liking to the Shah of Persia. He enters the Hofburg on his favorite horse, its mane dyed bright pink, and Sisi delights in a ruler with a knack for spectacle.

When Franzl tells the Shah he'll be staying at Laxenburg, the Shah complains that he heard Schönbrunn is the prettier of the palaces. "We believe you'll like the island on which the Franzenberg is situated. It's unlike anything else," Franzl assures him.

That afternoon, the Shah and his coterie of soothsayers

and astrologers descend on Sisi. They ask her when she was born and gasp. "Your life will end sharply."

"Sharply? You mean suddenly?" she asks.

"Sharply, sharply," they insist, and then one of them tells the Shah they must return to Laxenburg for the evening because the planets have shifted, and it is no longer a fruitful time to be in the company of other royalty.

At dinner that night, when the heavens have aligned again, the Shah insists on his grand vizier standing behind him at the dinner table.

"Give him the night off," Franzl suggests. "We haven't need for our seconds tonight."

But the Shah gives a spoonful of each dish to the grand vizier to test before he takes a bite. The grand vizier tries some of a veal dish and shakes his head.

"I assure you it's not poisoned," Franzl says, trying to mask the offense he's taking.

"He knows what I like and what I don't."

"Can we get you something else?"

"No need. My cooks are preparing me a meal back in Kleine Laxenburg."

"I should get myself a grand vizier, and then I wouldn't be obligated to eat this food, either," says Sisi.

The Shah laughs and raises his stein of beer to her.

Sisi, tickled, asks, "May I visit you tomorrow? I'd love to see that pink horse again."

He smiles. "For you, I will ensure all of the horses are dyed pink."

After all the royals have made their visits to the Exposition, Sisi removes herself to Gödöllő.

She invites Franz's companion Prince Nicolas Esterházy to hunt with her. Esterházy is too busy to bother with court life, but he will find time to avoid it in the country. Sisi knows the truth of Esterházy's situation. He has just been forced to sell his family's collection of paintings to Franzl to cover the debts of his father and grandfather.

"You ride well for a woman," he tells her at the end of their first day.

"I *ride well*. Full stop," Sisi clarifies. Sisi likes the way Nicolas is a little too rude to her. She absorbs his barbs, while both admiring his dark brooding *and* quietly pitying him. She can flirt with him and claim she's making an effort to involve herself in Franzl's inner circle. Esterházy seems to have no problem mirroring her conduct.

Despite all their hard work to help Austria recover with a successful Exposition, though, the event is an utter failure. Every contractor overcharges. Cholera runs rampant. The spring is wet, causing the commoners to postpone their visits until the crops are too high to take a break from harvest. Despite the seven million visitors, Austria's debt for the endeavor approaches fifteen million gulden.

The fiasco produces a gradually mounting body count. The shoe shiners who'd bought themselves new mahogany stands hang from the rafters of their front porches. The financiers take out their finest shotguns and imbue in them unshakable associations. Boats sailing down the Danube keep a tarp on deck with which to cover up the bodies they pull out of the water.

It is easier to blame Franzl than it is to blame weather and disease. Franzl had hoped the Exposition would be a success, but everyone else bet on it.

It seems Austria cannot catch a break.

Settling

✳ ✳

WAGNER REALIZES THAT, after the construction of his house in Bayreuth, the money he has left is only enough to complete the outer walls of the theater. He'll need to take out a loan and he'll need a guarantor. He writes Ludwig praying he'll agree.

A response arrives not from Ludwig, but from Dufflipp. "The King maintains that the twenty-five thousand thalers he's given you is the most he can contribute."

Wagner despairs and writes back to Ludwig that he'll need to ask the Kaiser himself for money then, but this is enough to prompt a response directly from Ludwig. He ekes out a hundred thousand thalers more to send to the Great Friend so that he might hold his place as primary patron. "I know you will repay me when you are able," Ludwig writes, a statement both know to be false, but he remains sure that the Festspielhaus will satisfy some unquenchable thirst in him. If seeing Wagner's works performed has already activated so many aspects of his being, then what will be the experience of seeing the next performance—the greatest accomplishment of his hero—staged in a structure built to maximize the effects of the opera? Ludwig is always hoping for more, sure that there is something that will fill him up so he never needs to feel the emptiness that always overcomes him. When he was younger, Ludwig thought of himself as a barrel with a slow leak, but these days he feels as though the entire bottom has fallen out. Joy is only available to him in the precise moment of the present.

Party Crashers

✳   ✳

THIS IS ELISABETH MARIE," Gisela tells her mother, trying to hand her the baby, hoping she might be won over by the name, but even this doesn't do the trick

"Don't start calling her Sisi, whatever you do. We needn't draw more attention to the fact that I'm old enough to have a grandchild," the thirty-six-year-old Sisi responds.

Sisi writes to sixteen-year-old Rudolf, "The baby is extraordinarily ugly, but very lively, like Gisela."

Sisi waits for King Ludwig in the dim audience chamber on a visit to Berg. She is confused by the shape and stature of the human she sees enter the room.

"Sisi!" the person says in her cousin's voice.

"Ludwig!" Sisi, consumed by appearances, cannot help but wonder how Ludwig has allowed himself to deteriorate in this way, but she is genteel enough to withhold this thought, and beyond that, she is so happy to see the cousin who made her laugh so hard she peed her petticoats at the orphanage. "Tell me how I can help! Shall I do a jig to cheer you?"

"You might as well, but it will make no difference. It's more of the same. I hate to bore you."

"A burden does not get lighter the longer you carry it," Sisi says. "We should go for a ride and you might scatter your troubles behind you on the fields!"

Ludwig shakes his head at her gravely. "I don't ride anymore. I've grown afraid. I don't trust myself."

Sisi's brows knit together. This is not like him. "A walk then. Nature will do you good."

"Sit here with me for a moment."

A servant enters with a platter. "Cake?"

Sisi, though, does not eat cake. "Maybe a thimbleful of orange juice."

"Of course, whatever you like," Ludwig says, nodding at the servant.

A pitcher, freshly squeezed, is brought out, but Sisi drinks only the tiniest sip.

"Don't you like it?" Ludwig asks.

"Delicious," she says.

Sisi sees that Ludwig cannot sit still. He paces the room but declines every invitation to move themselves outdoors. He rambles on about his worries, and Sisi watches his to-ing and fro-ing for hours. Finally she manages to say, "Ludwig, I must visit your mother today, as well. Perhaps you'd like to accompany me?"

"There's nothing I'd like less," he says. "I just saw Mother days ago, and I haven't recovered. Steel yourself. She is a banshee."

Sisi hugs her cousin and makes him promise that he will write. "And get some air. Full lungs, clear mind," she says.

Ludwig nods, miserable.

She watches him scratch at a scab on his hand and places her fingers on his. "Let it heal."

Queen Marie greets Sisi amiably before they settle in to catch up. "What else will you do while you're in Munich?" she asks her niece.

"I was at the cholera hospital yesterday, and I hope to visit . . . the asylum tomorrow." Sisi pauses, worrying she might upset the Queen given the state of Otto.

The Queen, having noticed the hitch in her niece's voice, asks if she might join her.

"Oh, you needn't do that," Sisi says, trying to give the Queen an out.

Queen Marie's face grows somber. "No, I'd be interested to see what it's like inside such a place."

"Very well. We'll pick you up."

At the asylum, Sisi listens intently to each of the men, while the Queen sits in a chair at the edge of the room, chatting with the director. "Some of these people seem almost normal." She waits to be contradicted, but she is not.

On the carriage ride back, the Queen asks Sisi what she's after in making such visits.

"What I'm after? Why, I'm after nothing at all beyond providing an understanding ear."

"And why the men's asylums?" the Queen asks.

Sisi has not allowed herself to dwell on this question for very long, but she knows the answer. If she attends the women's asylums, she will see more of the people being kept for reasons with which she is personally all too familiar: women paralyzed with grief at having lost a child, women stumbling under the pressures laid on them, women broken by the violence done to them. Sisi knows those troubles all too well. Instead she says, "I have always gotten along with men better than women."

"Nonsense," the Queen responds.

When Sisi wants to misbehave, she asks Ida's opinion. When she wants to be talked out of bad behavior she asks anyone else. "Ida, officially, I have stated that I am not well enough to attend Carnivale, but really, I just can't bear for my hand to be kissed by a thousand germy mouths," she says, shivering. "*But!* If I sneak out while everyone else is at the celebrations, that might be fun."

It's possible that what Sisi has always seen as Ida's agreeability has actually been indifference to any cause except that of Hungary. But now that the Hungarian matter is mostly settled, Ida must find a new reason to go on. If the Empress remains as well-behaved as is expected of her, Ida's life will be dull and uneventful. If she goes along with Sisi's schemes, then at least there will be some excitement in her life. Ida has abandoned the idea that anyone will find her marriageable at the advanced age of thirty-five, and so what is there to do but cause a bit of trouble? Ida agrees that smuggling themselves into Carnivale is a splendid plan.

Sisi has heard of the fragrant doughnuts and chestnuts sold in stalls, the colored paper strung between the trees of the avenue leading to the Wurstelprater, the puppet shows satirizing the chilly romance between Emperor and Empress, the way the guises allow the common people to mix with the pedigreed. She ties her mask tight around her eyes and drapes the hood of the domino cape she's borrowed from Ida so that only her tight-lipped mouth is visible.

On Shrove Tuesday, she and Ida sneak out to the Musikverein ball.

Sisi spots her riding companion, Nicolas Esterházy, talking with a woman she doesn't know, and jealousy floods her. She has the urge to seek revenge for a fidelity Nicolas is unaware of having betrayed. "Ida, find me a suitor." Sisi sends Ida away so she can approach Nicolas alone.

Esterházy clears his throat. *"Fräulein . . ."* he says, smirking at the pleasure of addressing Her Majesty with such familiarity.

Sisi completes his thought: *"Hildegarde."*

"Of Bingen, no doubt, with such music in your voice." Esterházy's date excuses herself: usurped, offended.

Her goal accomplished, Sisi doesn't linger. "If you'll excuse me, I believe I'm about to have a vision." She spies Ida talking to a dark and stormy young man on the other side of the room, and proceeds to the arcade outside the ballroom, leaving Esterházy speechless.

Ida must grasp Fritz Pacher's arm to keep him from running away. "Sir, I beg your pardon. I don't seek your attentions for myself, but for a beautiful friend of mine who is too shy to approach you on her own." Fritz doesn't move, silently consenting to hear more of what this little fairy godmother has to say. "She's out in the gallery."

"I'm not a member of court. I have no pedigree," Herr Pacher says.

"All the better," Ida replies. "Neither does my lady. She is beautiful, but of simple origin."

Ida leads Fritz to Sisi, standing just out of the direct light.

"A pleasure to make your acquaintance," Fritz says, speaking formally because he can tell—by the way that her mask has been made, by the pale smoothness of her jawline, by her delicate gloves—that she is a woman of nobility, playing at being common.

"My name is Gabrielle," Sisi says. He notes the way her mouth barely moves.

"An angel." He watches the tiniest smile play on her lips. "I am Fritz."

"I will call you Fritzl."

The way she commands this, without asking, causes Fritz to examine her more closely.

"I wonder if the Empress is at the ball tonight," Sisi says, playing with danger.

"What would she be doing here with us?" Fritzl replies, believing he has cracked a code.

"She might have wanted to escape the confines of her duties, to feel the thrill everyone else does on a night like tonight." Sisi speaks so softly that Fritzl is happy he must lean in.

Ida stands at the door, watching so that no one else comes in.

"Doesn't the Empress experience thrills all her own?" Fritzl brushes Sisi's wrist.

"I think she must be watched so closely, it is hard for her to take risks."

Fritzl sighs his understanding and runs his hand up to her shoulder.

"What do you think of the Empress?" Sisi asks.

Fritzl wishes that they might change the subject, but

Sisi seems insistent on walking this fine line. "Her Majesty is gloriously beautiful, but it is sad she is so averse to the public."

"She must have good reasons," Sisi says.

Fritzl hears a defensiveness in her voice. He almost calls her "Your Majesty," but stops himself. "My lady, you've pulled me away from the party. I suspect that permits me to ask a favor. May I remove one of your gloves so that I might kiss your hand before I say goodbye?"

"Why must you say goodbye?" Sisi asks.

"I think we both know it is best if I leave your company now," Fritzl says.

"Follow me," Sisi replies, and casts a look at Ida, commanding her to stay where she is.

Ida frets when she realizes Fritzl has identified the Empress. It is much easier to *decide* to become adventurous than it is to actually *become* adventurous. Ida, though, remains in place, as lookout.

The Empress leads Fritzl by the hand back into the ballroom, and now that Fritzl knows whose arm is tucked in his, he can't help but expect the faces of the crowd to recognize her. The glide of her step, the way her head inclines, all scream that this is a woman they've seen before, even at a distance. But no one notices.

In the ballroom, they join a circle of people watching some mummers perform their battle. Sisi smiles, lips clamped to her teeth, and, against the quiet of the crowd, he can hear a sound deep in her throat that he recognizes as laughter.

When the show is over, Sisi asks Fritzl where he lives.

"Why? Are you going to drop in for a visit?" he asks.

"One never knows," she says.

"And where might I find you?" he asks, putting her on the spot.

"I'm always somewhere else," she says slyly.

"So I'm unlikely to see you again."

"It's possible we might arrange to meet in Stuttgart or even Munich."

"But not here," he says.

"But not here." Sisi looks away, as disappointed as Fritzl is in this response, and catches the eye of Nicolas Esterházy. His glare guarantees that he has seen her little performance, and after this night, he no longer responds to her invitations to go riding.

Ida tugs the Empress's sleeve. "Your . . . *Gabrielle*, I believe it is best we leave."

"I'll walk you out," Fritzl says, scanning for one of the royal carriages, but Ida has hired an unmarked fiacre for the ride home. Fritzl moves to slide Sisi's hood down. If he sees the long plaits of hair winding around the crown of her head, he will be sure.

The tension bottled up inside Ida is shaken, though, and she flings herself between them. She tugs the hood back into place on Sisi's head. "We really must be going."

"Farewell," Sisi says.

"Farewell, fair maid," Fritzl says, and shuts the door.

The driver signals the horses into motion.

Sisi squeals.

Ida sobs.

Victorian England

✳ ✳

Up at 4:00 a.m. from his iron bed, bathed in a tub by a servant who shnockers himself into staying awake all night rather than waking up so early, fed by 5:00 a.m., at his desk soon after, audiences starting at 8:00 a.m.—often over a hundred people a day, each ended by an incline of his head, lunch at noon at his desk, more meetings until dinner. In bed by 9:00 p.m.

Sisi wishes for a sharp instrument each time she thinks of Franzl's schedule. A note from her sister Sophie inviting Sisi to vacation with her in England proves a welcome break.

Sisi sends a troupe of attendants on ahead: a chaplain, a smattering of governesses and nurses for Valerie, Sisi's hairdresser and her masseuse, chefs, fitness coaches, grooms, and a florist. The horde arrives at Steephill Castle and prepares it for the Empress.

A day later, dressed plainly, posing as a family of sisters, using the pseudonym "the Countesses Hohenembs," Sisi, Valerie, and Ida arrive at the castle undetected.

Sisi makes the rounds: Bathrooms have been remodeled. The enormous billiards table has been moved out of the billiard room to make space for her exercise equipment: trapezes hung from the ceiling, a vault placed with a springboard on one side and soft mattresses on the other for easy landings.

When Sisi says she is thirsty, her servants know this is a test. They set before her a glass of oxblood-and-chicken broth. Sisi smiles and tastes it, feigning her thirst quenched. "And what has been done with the steaks from which the blood was pressed?"

"Discarded," the maid confirms, but in the kitchen a pot of stew boils to feed the servants.

It doesn't take long for the town of Ventnor on the Isle of Wight to catch on that the Austrian Empress is in their midst. The tourists on the cliff above the castle spy through binoculars, trying to pick out the Empress from the clan of people bathing in the ocean.

"I have a solution," the Empress says. She asks for a bathing cap for herself and a wig for a servant. "You'll go out into the water accompanied by the guards. I'll follow soon after alone. They'll assume you are me. They won't be able to tell our bodies apart from such a distance. You're not so much fatter than me," Sisi says, and the servant accepts this statement with grace. In the water, the weight of the wig almost pulls the servant under. The hairdresser grimaces at the seaweed trapped in the yard-long locks of the dummy wig she must comb each day.

Sisi walks Valerie around the garden and points to the sprays of pollen-tipped starbursts. "Myrtle," Sisi says.

"Myrtle," the child repeats.

Sisi indicates the blousy white blossoms, shadowed in pink: "Magnolia."

"Magnolia."

She aims a finger at the baroquely petaled camellias, and Valerie knows this one on her own. "Camellia." Sisi lifts her child to assault her with kisses. She believes Valerie to be so much cleverer than any of her other children. It's not true, but Sisi never got to know the others like this, at this age.

After a stultifying visit with Queen Victoria, Sisi spends twenty-four hours in London, where she falls in love with a Dalmatian-spotted leopard Appaloosa and tells the breeder to hold him for her until she receives Franzl's permission. "The one I like costs twenty-five thousand gulden, so it is naturally out of the question," Sisi writes.

"Buy whatever you like," Franzl writes back.

Sisi returns to the island with her new horse, affectionately christened "Errand Boy," before she has even received the reply. In his company are Avolo, a Welsh pony, and Bravo, a Hungarian Leutstetten. It is the time of year to start hunting the fox cubs, and Sisi rises at dawn and stays out all day, testing the endurance of her male companions.

"I do like it here," Sisi says to Ida, "but great caution is necessary, for the English are clever people—intelligent and rich, but no one knows exactly where they come from."

————

In June 1875, the former Emperor Ferdinand dies, leaving Franzl his fortune after having handed him the throne twenty-seven years prior. The only change Franzl makes is to triple Sisi's allowance. Sisi uses it to build a new state asylum.

Confession

✳ ✳

AFTER A YEAR OF CELIBACY, Ludwig befriends Count Alfred von Dürckheim-Montmartin, an army officer acting as aide to Prince Otto. A beefcake with a ruddy complexion, Dürckheim flirts with the King, and Ludwig can't resist the flattery.

Despite remaining officially committed to Otto's service, Dürckheim travels with Ludwig to Linderhof, still under construction, where they stay in the Schachen hunting lodge.

At night, in the lodge, they can pretend that every time is the first time. Dürckheim can happen upon Ludwig undressing. Ludwig can ask Dürckheim to inspect a scrape on his back. Ludwig's skin bears no flaw, but Dürckheim can place the flat of his hand on his skin, letting his fingers crawl forward, looking for what Ludwig refers to. They purposely neglect the fire, because only in the dark is Ludwig able to permit himself what he truly wants. Dürckheim urges the King to act sooner, struggling to restrain himself, but Ludwig pretends he doesn't understand to what the aide refers. When the embers of the fire are dim enough, Dürckheim takes the King roughly, as punishment for his hesitancy. In the morning, being served breakfast, Dürckheim flirts with one of the maids, and Ludwig's ego blisters.

In the western parterre of the gardens, Fama, the goddess of fame and gossip, blows her trumpet. Dürckheim and the King sit on a bench, looking up at her bright gilded form. The aide turns to Ludwig and asks if he might be transferred into the King's service.

Ludwig clasps Dürckheim's shoulder. "I am pleased by your wish and yet I feel obliged to tell you: you lose your temper very easily, as is also the case with me. I am easily moved to strong anger. It is a painful thought to me that, if we were in frequent contact with each other, anger might arise between us and separate us forever."

Dürckheim goes to take the King's hand, but Ludwig draws it away.

After their trip, Ludwig writes, "The day you left, I was so melancholy that I could not find peace, even at the Höllental, where we spent such 'lively' hours."

And then the King cuts off contact. As soon as Ludwig admits his own feelings to himself, as soon as he acknowledges the truth of his actions, the old Catholic guilt gets the better of him. There was something about Hornig that felt moral, marital, but with anyone else, he feels unclean and is quick to detach himself.

When he invites Hornig out for a midnight ride, his old friend obliges.

Sisi writes to Ludwig on her birthday, a message that couldn't possibly serve to lift his spirits. "Nothing could be more terrible than to feel the hand of time laid on one's body, to watch the skin wrinkling, to wake and fear morning light and know that one is no longer desirable. Life without beauty would be worthless to me. I am grateful only that I can move from place to place, which keeps me young and active. If I remained imprisoned in the Hofburg, I would be an old woman in a year. I know you feel the same about the Residenz."

Ludwig does. He writes back to Sisi saying as much, and he goes out on a limb. He tells Sisi he's had an affair. He goes to great lengths to avoid mentioning the gender of his lover. He describes their passion as powerful, but tempestuous. He expresses his wish for a love that is more subdued, but fears that there is not someone whom the public will accept that might adequately fill this role. His heart chugs and halts. Ludwig keeps standing up and stepping away from the letter. He wonders if she will pick up on the code that he is locking into his words. He wants her to see it only if she can receive it with compassion. Admitting that he wants companionship is perhaps the hardest thing he has ever had to do: more difficult than kissing Hornig that first time, tougher than signing Bavaria over to Prussia, more complicated than making the decision to commit Otto to a doctor's care. He saturates himself with wine before sealing the letter and handing it off to the messenger.

A return letter arrives quickly: "My Eagle, I love you and I know how challenging it can be to love, and to feel that the only people available to you to love are not the ones you want. You have my sympathy. I am here for you, and I wish you peace. Love, Your Seagull."

Ludwig breaks down in tears. He can see in the careful way that Sisi has chosen her words that she must understand. It is remarkable to feel seen, but, somewhere in his heart, he must have hoped that she might offer a solution. In the absence of such advice, Ludwig knows there is no way around the fact that love will never be easy for him. He will always be cornered by his desire.

Ludwig asks that a table be installed on a dumbwaiter in Linderhof so that his dinner might be served from the kitchen below, rather than by having burdensome servants there in the room with him. Over the table a Meissenware chandelier hangs, like a frosted candy. Ludwig commands that the molds for the chandelier be destroyed so that the work can never be copied.

When the bust of Marie Antoinette is delivered for the rose cabinet room, Ludwig removes his hat each time he passes. On quiet afternoons, he goes to stroke her cheek and murmur compliments. Ludwig tells himself it's a superstition, not a compulsion.

The servants, of course, gossip. "Reverence for a Queen I can understand," says one particularly catty maid, "but each day, as I'm clearing his breakfast dishes away at three p.m., he kisses a column on the way out of the dining room, and I must follow quickly after him to wipe off the smudge. It shall need to be repainted. The grime is beginning to leave a mark."

The King summons the butler when a servant forgets to bow as he backs out of a room. "Have his head roughly banged against the wall. For three days, whenever he comes into my presence he must kneel with his head on the floor . . .

and he must remain kneeling until I give him permission to rise. For three hours of each day, you must yourself tie his hands in order to bring him into submission."

In the kitchen the butler informs the servant he's being transferred to groundskeeping duties. "If you're asked, I've bound you every day this week as punishment. Got it?"

The servant nods and goes to join his new crew. Weeks later, the King wanders by as he is clipping a bush. The servant bows deeply, nervously, and the King asks, "You've missed a branch. Are you new here? Tell your superior you're to be flogged."

A servant brings Ludwig tea that is too hot. He demands she be skinned alive.

A footman shuts the coach door on the tail of the King's jacket. "Off with his head!" he shouts.

Ludwig fumbles for any bit of control he might still possess. He has given Bavaria to Prussia. Wagner can't write new material fast enough, and he's not allowed in Munich anyway. The King has pushed Dürckheim and Hornig away. The construction of his castles has slowed down instead of speeding up. There are too many projects now. Even Sisi's letters are fewer and farther between of late. Mistreating the servants has been a way of releasing tension since his childhood, and he falls back into the bad habit.

Risk

✳   ✳

FRANZL RETURNS HOME from a visit to Dalmatia, and Sisi's first words after greeting him are to share the news that Valerie has been prescribed sea baths.

While Franzl was never sure if Sisi was feigning illness or using her periods of convalescence to her advantage, it seems to Franzl that Sisi has now transferred her ills to Valerie by proxy. He tries to slap the thought away.

"We're to go to the coast of Normandy."

"Sisi, you cannot go to France. The country runs rampant with anarchists who hate Austria."

"But who would want to hurt *me*?" Sisi asks, naïve to the fact that, in many ways, despite her best attempts, she is the most visible figurehead of Austria because of her beauty and the love the people have for her. Harm done to Sisi would surely be a bolder statement than harm done to the Emperor.

"I don't recommend it, but you'll do as you please," Franzl says.

As if in punishment, nobility of every stripe show up at the door of the Château de Sassetot-le-Mauconduit soon after Sisi and Valerie's arrival. The Empress, thinking it might encourage some of them to leave, sends her sheepdogs to greet the guests ahead of her, and so each visitor has their finest clothes covered in paw prints—put in their place before they've even bowed.

Ida warns Sisi about her riding master. "He takes too many risks."

"That's precisely why I like him!" Sisi says.

"Well, I won't ride with you anymore. I care too much for my well-being," Ida replies, happy to have a reason to spend some time alone while someone else entertains the Empress.

Sisi laughs at her friend and leaves her to trot around the garden in a tight circle.

The master suggests Sisi take a new horse, Innocent, promising that, despite the fact that he's not quite broken in, he'll be a great jumper on the course.

In the garden, Ida hears a cry, and rushes over. The Empress lies unconscious beside a hurdle, and the horse races around, shaken. In Sisi's hand, she grips the pommel of the saddle, torn off from the force of the fall, evidence that the error was not Sisi's but a failure of the equipment.

Sisi comes to quickly and, blinking Ida's face into doubled focus, says, "Why are you crying?"

"Oh, thank God!" Ida says, hugging her lady tightly. It is not as though Ida has been anything less than loyal to Sisi before, but the thought of losing her has magnified her devotion.

"Why am I on the ground?" Sisi asks.

"Your horse had a fall. Call the doctor!" Ida calls to the riding master, who has not even bothered to dismount. "Quickly! Do you want a dead Empress on your conscience?"

Sisi complains of knife-blade slashes of pain in her head. No amount of morphine or cocaine helps.

"If she doesn't feel relief soon, we'll have to cut off her hair," the doctor tells Ida. "The weight of it is impeding the healing process."

"You can't. If the injury from the fall doesn't kill her, losing her hair surely would."

When Sisi awakens the next day, her vision solidified into a single image, she asks if Franzl has arrived.

Ida tells the Empress, "He wants to come, more than anything, but we told him to wait so we could assess your condition. As you know, if he came here, there could be very serious repercussions. He has sent a telegram, though."

Sisi's head starts to pound again. She unfolds the telegram: "I cannot rid myself of the thought of what might have happened. What would I have done without my angel?"

Sisi turns to Ida. "He's going to try to use this as an excuse to keep me closer. He'll want me to quit riding," she says. "Send a telegram back: 'I am sorry to have given you such a fright. I am quite well now, but the doctor is terribly strict. I don't know when I'll be allowed to return.'"

Too Far

✷ ✷

OCTOBER FINDS SISI BACK at Gödöllő, receiving her brother, his actress wife, and their sixteen-year-old daughter, Marie, the little girl who had comforted Sisi in the garden all those years before when Andrássy had gone. Sisi finds herself totally charmed by the young woman Marie has grown into. Sisi makes a suggestion to her brother and sister-in-law: "Why don't you leave Marie here and go on vacation?"

The couple agrees, warning Sisi that Marie can be a troublemaker.

"It turns out I can, too," Sisi says with a wink to Marie.

In the early days of her visit, Marie sings and plays the guitar and piano for Sisi, taking requests, inviting the Empress to sing along, laughing when she makes a mistake. Marie rides almost as well as her aunt, and is unafraid of any challenge.

Ida is surprised to find herself jealous of the girl. She is young and beautiful and able, all things Ida knows the Empress prizes, and Ida has only recently admitted her fealty to Sisi above all. She watches as Marie flirts with Rudolf, and wonders what she is after.

Indeed, Rudolf is a catch. His tutors are relieved they don't need to lie about his academic talents, though they do conspire to think of excuses for his short temper and his exacting judgments when generosity would better serve. On most days Rudolf is a kind, rosy youth, but on the odd day, he spits the sharpest barbs.

Sisi writes to Ludwig with an idea. "If I send Rudolf to you, would you take him under your wing? Expose him to some culture. Take him to an opera, let him tour your building projects. I think it would do him good to have a role model who is more invested in the arts. Lord knows all he learns here is economic models and military maneuvers." Her hope is that, if Ludwig knows he's being observed as a role model, he will be on his best behavior and perhaps get himself out of his funk. There are so many wonderful aspects of her cousin's personality, and with a bit of puffing up, he might yet prove himself an exemplary ruler.

Ludwig, who doesn't want to see anyone ever, it seems, responds quickly. Anything for Sisi.

Meanwhile, Sisi organizes treasure hunts and themed parties for Valerie at Gödöllő. She tries to stay put, despite her misery. After the festivities, though, Valerie is happy to retreat to her room to study her language books, write poems, and paint. She can entertain herself happily, but Sisi hovers nearby to praise everything her daughter does. The surveillance, the praise—Valerie stops inventing and starts doing what she knows is right. Sisi, who had wanted Valerie to feel a freedom the other children never did, has managed to step directly into the shoes of the Archduchess. She thinks she is helping to make her daughter confident enough to be independent, but Valerie is instead learning to perform for others' praise.

Finally, Franzl tells Sisi to go to England. "Hunt. There's not much time left in the season," he tells her, and she swears that's the sweetest thing he's ever said to her. "It's like trying to keep a cork in a champagne bottle," he tells his aide.

A letter is sent to Captain George "Bay" Middleton asking if he might guide the Empress through the end of the hunting season after the calamity of the last captain. "What is an Empress to me?" Middleton writes back. "I see no benefit." He believes he's being lied to when he's told of Sisi's riding prowess, but he accepts in the hopes of getting at least one good story along with the endorsement.

Middleton is no more convinced of his luck when he sees the number of carriages required to hold all of Sisi's trunks as she arrives. "She will be a thorn in my side."

The next morning, though, Sisi is saddled and waiting. "Don't go easy on me," she warns him.

Middleton leads her through gentle terrain to gauge her reaction.

"I told you not to condescend," she says.

He leads her through a wooded area, up a sharp incline.

"Can't we have some fun?" Sisi asks.

He reaches a small creek and urges his horse to leap across it, seeing if she'll follow, and she does.

"Now, that was at least *something*," she says, taking a big breath of air.

Middleton laughs and doesn't look back.

———

At Easton Neston, Sisi can hunt with a different club every day.

On Mondays she can go out with the Pytchley pack. On Tuesday, Grafton. Wednesday, Bicester, and Thursday, Cottesmore. Only then might she take a day off before cycling through the rotation again.

Sisi discovers she enjoys talking to Bay almost as much as she does riding with him.

Bay admires the way the flames of Sisi's beauty smolder over the candlelit dinner table. She lets down her hair, tucks a flower behind her ear, lays a long string of pearls around her bared neck.

Like an immature boy, he seeks her attention with pranks, sneaking off to short-sheet the beds. Later, when everyone is ready to go to sleep, they know there is only one person to blame.

When another rider ribs the captain, saying that the old "apple-pie bed" joke is a bit old, Middleton stands from his seat. He comes up behind the young man and asks him to get up. The young man laughs, game for a comedic come-uppance. Middleton takes hold of the tails of the young man's coat and rips it from bottom to top, straight to the collar. The room laughs and laughs. The young man protests, "That was a bit much."

"Oh, come on. You wanted something more inventive, and you got it. Take a joke," Middleton says.

"If you'll excuse me," the young man says, backing out of the room.

Ida wonders if the captain has gone too far, but Sisi has always been up for a bit of nastiness, and can't stop her fit of giggles. "Bay, you are a phenomenon."

At the stables, getting ready to set off one morning, Middleton says, "I've been meaning to ask: How is it you connect your top half to your bottom half? There's not room for a waist inside that dress. Is it the belt that holds you together?"

"I don't fall to pieces. You should know that by now," Sisi says, flying up into her saddle. "And as for the rest, a lady never tells." Sisi bats her leather riding fan at her face once, and sets off.

"Hoho!" Middleton cries, hoisting himself up onto his own horse to catch her, but after a few yards, his horse stumbles a landing and throws Bay off. Sisi cycles back to find Bay is badly bruised, but he brushes himself off, eager to hide his battered ego.

Role Modeling

✷ ✷

WHEN RUDOLF ARRIVES at the Munich Residenz, Ludwig's first scheduled activity is a private performance of *Lohengrin*. The two of them applaud from their box at curtain call, and the performers clap back to show appreciation for their King—and to help fill the pitifully quiet theater.

As the King and Crown Prince walk back to the apartments through the courtyards, Ludwig studies his cousin in the moonlight. "You have all the greatness of your great-great-great grandmother Maria Theresa, and the genius of Plato, I think," Ludwig says. "And, of course, your mother's good looks."

Rudolf nods, unsure how to take such a compliment.

Table upon table of sweets awaits them in the Winter Garden, on the shore of the faux lake. "Where is that music coming from?" Rudolf asks.

"It's magic," Ludwig replies, but later Rudolf spies the arm of a violinist emerging from behind a screen at the back of the trees.

"Rudolf, I fear you have a future ahead of you as bleak

as mine, if not worse, being that you will be not only a King, but an Emperor, too."

"Don't you get everything your heart desires?"

"I must *procure* for myself everything my heart desires," Ludwig amends. "Once you have everything, you must continually dream up new things to want. And all the same, I am hounded day and night to sign papers and take meetings that don't matter at all to me, and this is my fate until I die."

"That is why I'd like to die young," Rudolf replies. "When death arrives to take me, I will accompany him willingly."

"The genius of Socrates, then. If your mother is any indication, you will grow only more handsome as you get older, though. Age is nothing to fear for you," Ludwig says.

"Yes, but the responsibility. You must understand. I've spent my entire childhood and young adulthood being instructed on how to be great. Good is not enough. It makes me wish for the opportunity to be neither. I want to rebel, to take my life into my own hands. Mother has tried to do this and she has suffered because of it. She reminds us all the time. And it's much more difficult for a prince who is heir to the throne. There is no such thing as opting out. You are born into this life and you must find a way to tolerate it. Any option is an illusion. Every decision you make has already been decided by a committee. I am exhausted and I have not even had to do anything yet. Who cares if I'm beautiful?"

Ludwig, who feels himself lacking in both freedom and beauty, cares.

Rudolf tags along with Ludwig for the following week. They visit the Neuschwanstein site and the decorator updates Ludwig on the building's progress. Ludwig decides to flex a bit in front of Rudolf, and makes a request for a new feature. "Could we . . . have a waterfall tumble down one of the staircases? Like a normal staircase, but water would flow down in a gentle blanket, as if the upper level has flooded?"

The decorator nods. He has learned not to deny the King anything. "Let's consult the architect, shall we? I think this is a matter of construction rather than design."

The architect is not so delicate in refusing Ludwig's request, though, and Ludwig feels humiliated to be dealt this blow in Rudolf's company.

Rudolf struggles to adjust his sleeping schedule to match the King's, and dozes while out on the midnight carriage rides. Ludwig admonishes the boy, telling him he will need to fortify himself. Falling asleep while in the company of another is hardly regal behavior.

Rudolf returns home with even more hesitation about the future ahead of him. When Sisi asks him how his visit went, Rudolf tells her that he has much to forget before he becomes Emperor.

In May, Ludwig summons the court secretary, Dufflipp, to inform the cabinet secretary, Eisenhart, that he's being removed from his post and then to let Friedrich von Ziegler, a lawyer by training—as well as a painter and poet—know that he has been appointed as Eisenhart's replacement.

Ludwig is characteristically rude to Ziegler for their first afternoon together until Ziegler quotes a poem and Ludwig grasps him about the shoulders. "A Byron man? Why didn't you say so?" Ludwig is embarrassingly easy to predict. Ziegler keeps the King stocked in good reading material and, within weeks, Ludwig declares Ziegler the best cabinet secretary he's ever had.

A Derby

❉ ❉

BAY VISITS GÖDÖLLŐ, and Franzl finds the captain
funny and high-spirited. "That Bay Middleton is a real
treat. I see why you enjoy joining his pack," Franzl says.

Sisi smiles. "He really is something."

Nicolas Esterházy, also at Gödöllő, isn't so generous. If
both he and Middleton begin talking at the same time, Sisi
gives Bay her attention by default.

"With Captain Middleton here, I fear there's no need for
me as master of the hounds," Nicolas tells the Empress.

"Very well. A pity, but we'll find another dog boy all
the same," Sisi coolly replies.

To enact his revenge, Nicolas begins flirting with Sisi's
beloved niece. He proposes marriage within the week, and
Sisi calls Marie into her chamber.

"If you marry Nicolas, your life will be miserable, for
he is only trying to get back at me. I am a faithful woman,
but over and over again men mistakenly believe that I must
hold the same feelings for them that they possess for me. If
Nicolas proves true to you over time, it might be worth
discussing. For now, put him off."

Marie is disappointed, but feels privileged that the Empress has let her in on veiled gossip.

"Why not find someone else to flatter with your interest?" Sisi suggests.

Marie smiles. "Rudolf, then."

"My girl, I hate to remind you that you are only half Wittelsbach, and the other half nothing at all. You'd do well to widen your search."

Alone together on the course, Sisi asks Bay, "Do you like it here?"

"I like only one thing about this place," he says, "but you are like an animal locked in a cage. You are watched and fondled and instructed every minute of the day."

Sisi doesn't ask for clarification. "It is indeed a rigid life, but better here than at the Hofburg, if you can believe it."

"If I have to sit through another Feuersitzungen . . ."

"My God, I know," Sisi says. "It's all I can do not to weep at each one. Instead, I sit quietly and think of . . . other things."

"What *other things*?" Bay says.

"Oh, things that can't be mine," Sisi says, a crease forming between her brows.

"Anything can be yours," he says, pulling his horse closer to hers.

But Sisi loses her boldness. She kicks her spurs and turns back, eventually finding Marie, who is trapped in a ditch.

Denial

✳ ✳

THE BAYREUTH OPERA HOUSE is finally ready to open. After only a dozen more financial panics, often bailed out by the munificence of Ludwig's waning purse, Wagner's dream of a destination theater in which his audiences might dedicate days at a time to his work is realized.

Ludwig's desire to see the *Ring* cycle in its completion competes with his desire to stay away from crowds, and he asks, instead, to see four consecutive rehearsals instead of the opening performances. Wagner agrees. Ludwig sends notes to both Sisi and Rudolf asking if they'd like to attend, but both reply with regrets. Sisi is off hunting and Rudolf has "something else." Ludwig chafes at the vagueness of the Prince's response. Perhaps Rudolf did not have as nice a time as Ludwig did on their previous visit together.

On August 4th, 1876, Ludwig's train arrives to an elaborately decorated station, full of royal subjects ready to greet the King they so rarely see, but he instructs the conductor to push on to the next stop, where the Great Friend waits.

Both of the men are startled by the appearance of the

other. Wagner finds the once lithe and vibrant Ludwig now bulky, sallow. The King's eyes search for the Great Friend from too deep in their sockets. Similarly, Ludwig cannot believe how old Wagner has grown. His hair has grayed, his physique has shrunk. The exhaustion of preparing the performances shows on his face.

Both men tear up, feeling the sadness of having been out of each other's company for eight years. Had they been visiting regularly, the minute daily changes might have deceived them into believing they remained mostly the same. Each wants to embrace the other, knowing all they've endured, but Wagner bows instead.

At the rehearsal of *Das Rheingold*, the echoing of the empty hall strikes Ludwig as a bit canned, and so he tells Wagner to allow people into the following three performances, hoping that the acoustics of the new theater will be aided by the warm bodies.

Returning to his chalet from the performance of *Die Walküre*, Ludwig goes for a walk alone. The servants light Bengal flares to illuminate the way and Ludwig can't help but wish he'd brought along a horse to ride while humming the infectious "Ritt der Walküren."

By the time Ludwig is seated for *Siegfried* he is informed that the dragon he has been so eagerly awaiting has been cut. When the construction shipped from London, in three pieces, the head and body arrived safely in Bayreuth, but the neck showed up in Beirut instead.

Despite this, Ludwig is impressed by the voice of soprano Josefine Scheffsky, playing the role of Sieglinde in *Die Walküre*, but is distracted by her size. He sends his congratulations to Josefine, but asks Wagner if it might be possible for the singer's body to be concealed behind a bank of plants onstage so he needn't look at her.

Wagner receives the note and refuses. He will not change the performance because of some hypocritical hang-up of Ludwig's.

Luckily, if Josefine is offended, she keeps her feelings hidden. She tells Wagner, "My body is my instrument. If the King wants to listen to a voice like mine, then he must face the form that produces such sound. This is what resonance looks like."

Ludwig leaves town without giving his congratulations to Wagner in person. Back at Hohenschwangau, he writes: "I came with great expectations, and, high though they were, they were far exceeded. I was so deeply moved that I might well have seemed taciturn to you . . . Ah, now I recognize again the beautiful world from which I have held aloof; the sky smiles down on me again, the meadows are resplendent with color, the spring enters my soul with a thousand sweet sounds . . . You are the true artist, by God's grace, who cannot fail and cannot err!"

On August 26th, when he has been thirty-one for only a day, Ludwig gathers the courage to return to Bayreuth for the final performance of the *Ring* cycle. When the last notes sound, he joins the applause. Wagner addresses the audience, telling them that the festival had been embarked upon out of trust in the German spirit and completed for the glory of the King of Bavaria, who had been not only a benefactor and a protector of, but also a cocreator of the work. Wagner knows that despite the festival's success, he will need to ask the King for more money soon.

The audience cheers as it turns to face Ludwig, and, for once, he revels in the attention. This is the last time he will appear before a crowd.

Manners

✳ ✳

FRANZL, OVERWORKED because of the threats on the Dardanelles, agrees to Sisi's request that she be permitted to go to Northamptonshire again after Christmas. "Take Rudolf with you."

Sisi doesn't love this idea, but she has no choice. Perhaps she'll be able to scare some courage into her son.

On the night after Sisi's departure, Valerie reads beside Franzl's desk as he finishes his work. He relishes her pleasant company. "I'm sorry. I know you will miss your mother terribly in this time, but she will be back soon."

"I hope she never returns," Valerie says.

"Valerie, you mustn't say such a thing. You will break her heart."

"Yes, I know, Papa. It's just that she is a child. And she smothers me, trying to cajole me into participating in her antics."

"She wants the best for you."

"I know she thinks she does. But I look to you as the

model for my own behavior. You are so practical yet sweet."

"You are a darling girl, and you will succeed at whatever you set your heart to. I hope that obliging some of your mother's love for you is among those endeavors."

Valerie stands and shuts her book. She kisses the bald pate of her father's head. "Of course. Good night, Papa."

In London, Rudolf is surprised that he sees less of his mother here than he does at home.

"Surely, you prefer to amuse yourself," Sisi says.

A week later, Rudolf realizes his mother has gone on to the country without him. When he arrives, he finds Sisi and Bay catching up over a glass of Scotch. Sisi doesn't hide her surprise. "Tired of the city already?"

Rudolf says, "Mama, I was hoping I might join you on the course tomorrow."

"You're getting a little old for this 'Mama' business, are you not, Rudolf?"

Rudolf inhales sharply and eyes the finger of liquor in their glasses, and then the decanter, to try to determine how many fingers have come before it.

"My darling Rudolf, do you know my reputation as a rider?"

"I have heard you are an Amazon."

Sisi beams. "And what about your father?"

"One of the best riders in Europe, but rulers are often flattered in this way," he says.

"It is no flattery, Rudolf. We are quite accomplished. I would venture I am even better than your father because

I'm doing everything with my legs arranged jauntily on one side. How would you classify your own ability?"

"I'm good," Rudolf says.

"No, you are not. And you won't persuade anyone of the opposite. Some loophole in our inheritance has allowed you to lack all accomplishment in this way, and for that I am sorry."

Rudolf turns a deep red. Sisi is clearly performing for her companion, completely without conscience in the takedown of her son. "I'll stay only the night then."

"Nonsense," Sisi says, smiling. "I'm sure you can be taken back today."

"As you wish, *Mama*," Rudolf says, and Sisi forces a smile.

Queen Victoria invites Rudolf to visit Osborne. He charms her with jokes, and the Queen wonders how Rudolf and Sisi could be cut from the same cloth.

Afterward, the Queen's son, Edward, Prince of Wales, teases Rudolf. "You put on quite a show. You know Mother doesn't really like anyone. I've never seen her flirt. Rather alarming."

Rudolf looks away, embarrassed to be called out in this way.

"There's no need to be shy about it. It's funny is all," he tells Rudolf. "Come, I'll introduce you around court."

Rudolf accepts but pays little attention to Edward, choosing instead to focus on the countless beautiful women populating the salon. He flirts with every single one.

"I see you already know what you're doing," Edward

says. "You put on such a show of being innocent for Mama, but at this rate, you're bound to earn a reputation in no time. I know some women who will remain discreet."

"I think I know to whom you refer, and to that I say: I refuse to pay for what I can get for free." Rudolf possesses some measure of his father's thriftiness.

"But *discretion* comes at a price." Edward leads the way to a different part of town.

Sisi sends a note to Franzl. "Some of the best riders were left behind yesterday, tired out by the heavy going, though it was almost all grass. But your good Bravo simply flew and was full of fire. Captain Middleton was delighted."

Ida takes the dictation faithfully, but can't help but interrupt. "Bay's engaged, you know."

"Ida," Sisi says simply.

"I mean only to ask if the fact that you're allowing an engaged man to stay in your home might bother the Emperor," Ida says. It was one thing when Sisi sustained her flirtations with Andrássy, but Ida does not see what there is to be gained through a romance with a common horseman.

Sisi sighs. "We know good and well that what the Emperor does not know will not hurt him." Her look implies that she expects Ida to apply the same moral code to Bay that she had to the Hungarian prime minister. Ida sees she has no choice.

The next night, Rudolf finds Sisi clutching Bay's arm at Prince Edward's party.

Sisi ignores her son, but Bay calls out to him. "Prince Rudolf! A pleasure to run into you. Your mother sprained her ankle yesterday and I'm afraid I have the task of being her crutch."

"Clearly," Rudolf replies, turning away.

Enter a Nefarious Figure

✳ ✳

ON JULY 28TH, Ludwig writes in his diary, "1877, year of redemption!—The Royal Lily triumphs and makes any relapse quite impossible!"

But on September 13th, Dürckheim pays the King an unprompted visit. Ludwig refuses him entry at first, but when Ludwig's aide informs him that Dürckheim will not leave without seeing the King, Ludwig's resistance breaks down. Upon seeing his old paramour for the first time in years, he begins to weep with pent-up desire. Dürckheim's eyes are harder, more gemlike than Ludwig remembers them. Ludwig feels seen. So often, even as he is being hunted by his cabinet, as the people's eyes search palace windows for his form, he feels entirely invisible, but Dürckheim's gaze sings a perfect tenor aria directly to him, a song that only the King can hear. Ludwig's blood roars through his veins and his mouth dries. He fights not to lick his lips.

When Dürckheim lunges at him, Ludwig tries to push him off, but he has grown weak. Dürckheim clings to him and plants an irreversible kiss on Ludwig's forehead. Ludwig, long-starved, first goes rigid as a stalk, and then, with a wild docility, his body unfurls against Dürckheim. Their tongues braid together with familiarity. Ludwig feels a confusing sense of safety layered over rusty compulsions. Dürckheim's hand goes to the King's sovereignty, before Ludwig again becomes a clumsy knight, straightening himself and pulling away with more commitment this time. "Guards!" Ludwig calls, and the doors open immediately.

"Your Majesty," Dürckheim responds, as the guards each take an elbow.

"Never again. Be gone," Ludwig replies. "I will not give you what you want and you cannot take it."

In the diary: "Au Roy. In this letter is given the *order* and with it also the necessity and possibility of fully abstaining from kisses, *anathema* in *aeternum*! Therefore conquered at the age of 32 and not quite 3 weeks, the last misfortune. Terribly near the brink of a complete fall last night."

While Ludwig is preoccupied with managing his various passions, Otto's health has been slowly deteriorating. Having escaped the loose confines of his Nymphenburg apartment one too many times, he is now secured within Fürstenried Castle. Bars are installed on the windows and extra locks on the doors. The man declaring such a transition necessary is a distinguished alienist—Dr. Bernhard von Gudden.

Ludwig goes to Linderhof so he might see the finished Venus Grotto. He climbs to a clearing in the mountainside and presses a secret latch on a stone slab. Inside, a waterfall fills a lake several hundred feet long. The sculpted concrete covering the iron girders makes the alcove look as though it's natural stone. A small boat waits at the entrance, shaped like a shell floating among the live swans. A pump relays artificial waves as a sequence of lighting cues transforms the mood, until a rainbow blooms. "This is the total theatre of which I dreamed." He sighs, relishing the lonely echo of his deep voice. He wishes he had someone to experience this with him, but even the thought of actual company sends shivers of anxiety coursing through him. To have someone to share things with would mean sharing things with others, and that is something it feels increasingly impossible to do.

Ludwig pays his servant Alfonso to hunt down and acquire a book of poetry by Numa Numantius. "Don't read it, Alfonso. Just bring it to me."

But by the time Alfonso has acquired a copy, he's figured out what it is Ludwig is trying so desperately to hide.

When the volume arrives under brown paper, Ludwig does not emerge from his room for days. Ludwig can't believe a book like this actually exists: men pining after other men. He can't turn away. He ponders the term "warmer Bruder" and thinks of the countless steel baths he's been dunked into, trying to cool and quiet his nerves. After the initial elation, though, he grows despondent. Love like this feels impossible for him. The poems are mere fantasy, and so he throws them into the fire, turning the pages to ash, but doing little to extinguish his desire or his fear.

———

The vivid descriptions within the book haunt Ludwig's imagination, and he begins inviting Hornig on his night rides again.

They sit together in the back of the carriage, hiding their activity beneath a fur lap blanket. The fear of being caught and the genuine desire hammer a syncopation at Hornig's heart again. He takes rotten swigs from his flask to distract himself, rather than enjoying the moment, and when he arrives home, his wife wonders if he is telling the truth about having been on duty or if he might be having an affair or feeding a gambling problem. She does not, however, imagine that it's all three.

Ludwig offers Hornig a title for his trouble, but Hornig refuses. When Ludwig gives him a house, complete with opulent grounds, on the Würmsee, though, he accepts. The gift, however, comes with a condition—Hornig must host the King for dinners at his home.

Frau Hornig is grateful to the King for his generosity to their family, if still confused. She tries to make only the dishes Ludwig likes, a menu that narrows with each visit. She delights when he brings presents for the children, but the children cry and scream when he leaves, and her nerves frizzle. With the children in bed and the house quiet, Hornig sits at his wife's feet and thanks her.

She is his best friend and he wishes he could tell her about the feelings he has for Ludwig. The warmth and attraction he feels for the King, complicated by the repulsion at his sinful actions. He has never felt this way about any other man, or he has never let himself feel this way about any other man. He used to talk himself into believing that his passion was driven by his allegiance to Bavaria, but he knows now that that is only the tiniest part. Yes, he likes the power the King holds. Even if Ludwig often avoids his obligations, Hornig finds His Majesty's presence magnetic. The people long to see their King and hear from him more, and Hornig has near unlimited access to the object of their curiosity. He would be lying not to admit that the way Ludwig has wooed other men has also made him jealous. Nothing makes one want something more than the risk of it being taken away, petty as that truth might be.

Hornig's wife strokes his head. "He is a strange man, but he cares deeply," she says.

Hornig releases an unexpected sob that startles his wife.

"You must be so tired. I have not seen you sleep in days," his wife says gently. "Come, I will tuck you in." Hornig feels guilt flood his body; he doesn't deserve his wife's kindness at all, let alone in this moment, but he accepts it all the same.

Misery Loves Company

✻　✻

AFTER ANOTHER SUMMER of riding in England, Sisi returns to Bavaria for her parents' fiftieth anniversary.

She listens to her sisters' and brothers' tiresome stories about the many nieces and nephews she seldom sees. She hears a man behind her say, "I'm not sure what it is we're here to celebrate. Everyone knows they haven't spoken to each other in years. It's a miracle they agreed to appear in the same room."

Sisi turns to find her own son. She blushes, embarrassed at not having recognized his voice. Rudolf smiles, having known she was there all along.

When Sisi returns to her sisters, they gesture discreetly. "Is that one?" Nene says.

"Of course," Sophie replies. "You can tell by the thin bridge of his nose."

"I saw a young woman over by the fountain. Not Father's best work," Sisi adds. "I've met quite a few of them now. They say he has them to Possi all the time."

"And I barely see him," Sophie says.

"Well, I assume you have a few more obligations than

the bastards do," Sisi says. "They're probably grateful for a warm meal."

Nene eyes Sisi. "I know someone else who could stand some comfort food. What are you on now? Lamb's blood and grapefruit rinds?"

"Don't be rude," Sisi says, taking pleasure in giving her sister a shove.

In the fall, Rudolf shoots himself through the hand. Sisi sighs and asks Ida if he's okay. "What happened?"

"Well, I guess he was cleaning one of those miniature pistols he has about."

"Cleaning, yes. Nice work trying to save him dignity. This is the kind of thing that happens when one is taught no other pastime. Such men become possessed by a *toy*," Sisi says. "The boy doesn't know what to do with himself, but to dream of how he might use his own life to end another's. Would that he might turn the gun on him—"

"Your Majesty!" Ida exclaims.

"I don't mean it, of course, but he does cause me such *concern*. Franzl, at least, stalks wild game. He thrills at the chase more than the kill. Rudolf, on the other hand, has a servant round up animals up in the preserve and picks them off one by one. I've seen Rudolf aim his gun at a closed window to try to shoot a sparrow."

Later, Sisi finds her son in bed, miserable, his hand hidden beneath a thick bandage. "Does he have some sort of infection?" she asks the doctor.

"No, no infection," he says, trying to be respectful.

"When can he take the bandage off?"

"I've already told him he can."

"Don't worry. I was not trying to take my life. If I were to do such a thing, I'd be sure not to fail," Rudolf tells his mother, as though he'd heard her conversation earlier.

Sisi resents the bid for attention she sees in this comment, and returns his cool affect. "Yes, I know you are adept at getting your way."

Despite his sorry state, or maybe because of it, Sisi is charmed by her invalid son. She waits on him in a way she was never allowed to when he was a child, and Rudolf allows himself, for once, to accept her love.

In April 1880, while Queen Victoria visits with Sisi at the Hofburg, a messenger enters and bows before the Empress. He whispers to her and she nods once before dismissing him.

The Queen says, "Good news, I hope."

"Bad news, but not the worst. My son is engaged to Princess Stephanie of Belgium."

Victoria harrumphs. "That's not good?"

Sisi replies, "It's likely to be a disaster, but time will tell."

A month later, when Sisi arrives to Brussels to meet her in-laws, Stephanie's family waits on the platform.

Sisi looks for her daughter-in-law, but her eyes land only on a chilblained giant with a round face and frizzy blond hair. Her traveling costume is too short and her chin too weak.

Sisi kisses Stephanie's cheeks. "You shall bring a new look to the family line."

Stephanie's self-satisfied expression fades to a saccha-rine grimace.

Sisi, bored with all the sitting around and chatting, returns to Vienna early. She finds Franzl working in his office. "Postpone the wedding a year," she says. "What's the rush?"

"You can't do this again. The wedding should happen as soon as possible. What if I were to fall ill? Better to have Rudolf squared away."

Sisi takes a deep breath and makes up a lie. "The girl hasn't even menstruated yet. Surely you can't have Rudolf consummating his marriage with a child."

Franzl studies Sisi's face. He wonders how she might know such a thing. "You know Rudolf will get into all sorts of trouble in the meantime."

"He seems quite devoted to her," Sisi lies. "A year will do."

The Emperor gives the Empress what she wants.

Unspoken

✳ ✳

IN NOVEMBER 1880, Bavaria celebrates the seven hundredth anniversary of the Wittelsbach dynasty, and Wagner attends a private performance of *Lohengrin* with the King. Ludwig has become so taciturn that he can barely muster a friendly greeting when he finds Wagner waiting for him in the royal box. The performance ends and the two men part wordlessly. They will never see one another again. This friendship—this arrangement—this constant flux between overblown ceremony and casual neglect and selfish insult—will continue only remotely.

Ludwig's habit of pulling people to him and then pushing them away has become evident to everyone in his life except himself. Hornig relishes the times that the King does not require his company, even as he longs for the time when he will be summoned again. Hornig has come to realize that humans override self-protection for a sense of closeness and attachment. He sees it in his children and the way they huddle into their mother for comfort even after she has slapped their behinds for misbehaving. Hornig tries to have faith that, if Ludwig has abandoned him before, then he will return to him again, too.

Ludwig, though, continues to search for less complicated passion. He resents having to contend with Hornig's wife and children.

A young man named Josef Kainz arrives in Munich to join the Court Theater. Despite Kainz's clippings saying that he is ugly and untalented, his nose misshapen and his calves lacking definition, the director sees in Kainz's eyes just the beauté de diable that might allure the King. The young man debuts as Didier, an optimist of humble origins, in a private performance of Victor Hugo's *Marion de Lorme*. Ludwig orders that all the court roses be cut and sent to Kainz for his brilliant performance. He tacks on a diamond and sapphire ring to the delivery. He requests a repeat performance and then another.

The thought of meeting Kainz is too much for Ludwig, though. Ludwig has vowed too many times to cease this behavior, so he arranges for Kainz to sit as far as possible from him at a private concert in the Court Theater. Ludwig can feel Kainz's presence buzz though the empty space.

The Royal Cycle of Disappointment

✴ ✴

SISI ARRIVES at Combermere Abbey. She thinks of writing to Bay to ask if he will join her, but she has never begged before, and she will not start now. She knows he has married since they last saw one another, and that seems like a natural ending for their time together.

But in the morning, Sisi finds Bay waiting for her at the stables. Her heart doesn't thrill in the way she expected it would. Instead, she feels angry at the way he made her wish for him.

They head out to the fields in a large cohort. Sisi follows close to Bay. When the fox is caught she looks around and finds that only a couple of other riders remain.

On the trot back to Combermere, Bay asks her, "What did you think?"

"A rather easy day, if you ask me."

"What a scamp you are."

Sisi can tell that Bay has settled for friendship, and Sisi is convinced she has no need of friends.

That night Sisi asks that a plate of raw veal and crushed strawberries be brought to her room.

She lies back on her chaise, patting the raw veal over her eyes and mouth and smearing the strawberries on her cheeks and forehead. The juices drip, running down onto the ugly fabric of the couch. She wonders what else her life might be. Is there a way to be happy? Is there a way she could be better using her time to feel satisfied and accomplished and contented? What doesn't occur to her is that she could find a way to be happy with what she has, that instead of changing her life, she might change her mind. She falls asleep there, and, in the morning she thinks she might be blind. She wonders why her head is so heavy. She can hardly breathe. When she sits up, the food falls from her face.

Before her bath, she weighs herself, and thinks she might have absorbed some of the calories through her skin. When asked what she'd like for breakfast she replies, "Nothing. And oranges for dinner tonight." She looks at the tub that's been prepared for her and dips in a finger, holds it to her tongue. "This isn't seawater."

The servant shakes her head.

"When you have a seawater bath prepared, let me know."

A note arrives from Bay asking when she'll be ready to depart on the hunt, and Sisi sends back no response, preventing everyone else from going riding that day. It is not until early afternoon that a tank arrives from the coast of Wales. "Did you bring only this much? I'd get another load on its way so I needn't wait next time."

The servant washes her hair, and when it is dry, hours

later, Sisi goes to dinner, where the hunting party waits, bored, their food cold on their plates. Sisi makes no apologies and slides a single wedge of orange between her lips.

Sisi returns to Schönbrunn in the first days of May to prepare for Rudolf's wedding. She discovers her son slumped in the main sitting room, beside himself with misery. He won't even lift his head from his arms.

She has a soft spot for his moods, and so she has arranged a treat for him. "Well, would you look at that?" she says, glancing out the window. "They've brought a wildcat from the Tiergarten."

Rudolf looks up. He runs to the window, and when he sees the handlers below, he waves to them and lets himself onto the terrace, where a shotgun rests on a bench. Rudolf gives a call of readiness, and the handlers open the cage and rush back into the cab of a carriage. Hard to tell what they fear more: the tiger or Rudolf's poor aim. The cat bounds out of its confines and Rudolf lifts his rifle. He shoots three times, and only the third shot hits the animal. It takes three more rounds for Rudolf to kill the beast, and the excruciating sounds of the animal dying linger in their ears.

"Rudolf! Why would you do such a thing?" Sisi feigns, but this had been her plan all along. Sisi relishes the rare feeling of bringing her son joy.

"Will you visit Stephanie before the ceremony?" Ida asks.

Sisi feels her back arch before she is able to identify the reaction she feels in response to this question. She thinks back to when she was Franzl's bride, of how nervous she was, of how they made her feel as though it wasn't her they wanted, but some hollow version of her they could fill up with their duties and customs. But none of that makes a difference. "I won't," Sisi says.

On the morning of May 10th, 1881, before the wedding, Ida delivers a note to Rudolf from Sisi. "Don't go away in such a hurry!" he says as she turns to leave.

Ida wonders if he could possibly be talking to her, but he grasps her hand.

The young man looks positively drained of joy. "I am so glad we can still meet as our old selves," he says.

Unnerved, Ida replies, "Your mother is expecting me," though she has nowhere to be.

"I, on the contrary, have all the time in the world."

Ida tenses as she sees what she believes might be a tear in his eye.

"In the name of Heaven, say something nice to me."

Ida freezes. "God bless you, Rudolf, and good luck to you." She can see the disappointment on his face.

The audience of the royal wedding in the Church of the Augustinians gasps as the flawless Sisi walks down the aisle, but when Princess Stephanie emerges—face lumpier than usual from her nervous weeping—the audience's breathing evens out. Even Rudolf, barely present behind his pale eyes, does not register that this—*this*—is his *bride*.

———

When Rudolf and Stephanie's coach pulls up to Laxenburg for their honeymoon, a fresh dusting of snow veils the spring grass, a poor omen that goes unacknowledged.

The sun rises the next morning, and Stephanie finds her fully underwhelming inheritance. She pens a note to her mother. "No one has taken the trouble to provide those little attentions, which do not seem to mean much, but which warm the heart. There are no plants, no flowers, to celebrate my arrival, no carpets, no dressing table, no bathroom—nothing but a washstand." The Princess dresses, making do with the poorly appointed toiletries available to her. She meets a hungover Rudolf for breakfast and asks if he would like to go for a walk with her on the grounds, but he begs off.

Stephanie goes out for about an hour and covers the entirety of the grounds. She pauses on a bench, looking out over the still water and trying to find some peace or perspective, but fails. On her way back to the palace, she thinks of what she might compliment about the sights she's taken in on her stroll, but at the doorway she realizes no one will ask.

Habits

✻　✻

OVER A MONTH AFTER he first sees Kainz perform,
Ludwig has the confused young actor pulled from a
rehearsal to spend three days at Linderhof with him.

At 2:00 a.m. he arrives and is hurried to the Grotto.
The King waits on the "shore" of the cave with supper laid
out for them. Kainz is not hungry. He's cold and tired. For
two hours the King looks at him expectantly, but Kainz
hasn't the slightest idea what it is Ludwig wants. Kainz is
nervous, referring to Ludwig with all the honorifics: Aller-
durchlauchtigst and Allergnädigst and Alleruntertänigst
and Allerhuldvollst. Ludwig, never consistent in how he'd
like to be addressed by whom, tells Kainz to speak plainly.

At 4:00 a.m. the two finally emerge. Ludwig tells the
aide to take Kainz back to Munich, but the servant convinces the King to let the young man rest first.

On their walk to his sleeping quarters, the aide tells
Kainz, "If you could play the role of Didier on your visit,
the King might be most pleased. I'm afraid he wasn't particularly charmed by you this morning."

Kainz's eyes widen. "I wasn't allowed to sleep!"

The aide nods. "Yes, I think it might help to imagine your visit to be a performance. Your true feelings are not in the least important while you're here."

In the afternoon Kainz wakes to a note reminding him he is not himself. At breakfast he leads with strength. Each time the King lobs a question his way, he pauses to consider how Didier might answer. Ludwig's interest is clearly piqued.

The King invites Kainz out for a tour of the grounds. They arrive at Hunding's Hut and Kainz marvels at the tree erupting through the center of the building. He removes his jacket and climbs the trunk, reciting lines from the play to Ludwig below. If Ludwig's life could be made up of only moments like this, he . . . would probably still find a way to be unhappy.

On their last evening together, as they bid one another good night, Ludwig seems close to asking for something more, but then suddenly it is as though he flips a switch inside himself, and he rushes away.

After only a week back in Munich, Ludwig writes a note to the director, excusing Kainz from performances so he might accompany Ludwig to Switzerland to see the sites of William Tell's legend. All of Kainz's acting chops are not enough to feign the enthusiasm Ludwig requires of him, though. As punishment, Ludwig sends Kainz off alone to make one of Tell's more difficult mountain climbs over the Jochpass, but after twelve hours of tromping through ice and snow and a frigid night in a tent, Kainz gives up, incensing Ludwig further.

Despite all this, later that week, the King asks if Kainz will join him when he has his portrait taken. Kainz, pouting, sits beside the King, but there is no hope of salvaging anything that was or wasn't there between them, and the photo commemorates only the ill feeling of what can hardly be called a breakup.

When Hornig next sees Ludwig, he can't help but comment. "I saw the photo of you and your young colt. Very fit choice, Your Majesty."

"Are you sore because I didn't ask to have a photo taken with *you*? In any case, I have already put him out of his misery. There is nothing to be jealous of."

Hornig replies, "Who would want a photo of an old man like me? I understand only too well."

The court secretary brings the King a translated paragraph of Mark Twain's new book, *A Tramp Abroad*. "It seems Your Majesty's reputation has gotten round to America," the secretary says.

Ludwig reads the paragraph aloud: "In the enormous Opera House in Munich there is some sort of machinery which in case of fire can call an immense water power into play. This could, we are told, place the entire stage under water. On one occasion when the King was the sole audience a curious scene took place. In the piece a great storm is introduced; the theatre thunder rolled, the theatre wind blew, the noise of rain falling began. The King grew more and more excited; he was carried out of himself. He called from his box in a loud voice, 'Good, very good! Excellent! But I wish to have real rain! Turn on the water!' The manager ventured to remonstrate: he spoke of the ruin to the decorations, the silk and velvet hangings, etc., but the King would not listen. 'Never mind, never mind! I wish to have real rain: turn on the cocks!' So it was done. The water deluged the stage, it streamed over the painted flowers and the painted hedges and the summer-houses; the singers in their fine costumes were wet from head to foot, but they tried to ignore the situation, and being born and bred actors, succeeded. They stood on bravely. The King was in the seventh heaven; he clapped his hands and cried, 'Bravo! More thunder! More lightning! Make it rain harder! Let all the pipes loose! More! More! I will hang anyone who dares to put up an umbrella!'"

Ludwig keeps pausing to laugh. He loves it. The secretary feels relief. It seemed equally as likely that Ludwig might declare that Twain should be assassinated for defamation of character. "His exaggeration is brilliant!" He laughs. "Truly inspired! Twain should write a whole book about this character."

Wagner writes up the formal thoughts he has on cultivating a Horde of superior humans. The newspaper expresses concern over the sentiments conveyed in the article, but Wagner assures the paper he has the King's support. The secretary delivers Wagner's article about a master race to Ludwig, though, and the King is none too pleased. Ludwig writes to warn Wagner against carrying on with his talk of a master race. "I am glad, dear Friend, that in connection with the production of your great and holy work you make no distinction between Christian and Jew. There is nothing so nauseous, so unedifying, as disputes of this sort: deep down all men are brothers, whatever their confessional differences."

Wagner believes he will bring the King around to his point of view eventually.

She Cares / She Doesn't
❋ ❋

SISI FINDS LUDWIG in his tattered Swan Prince costume at Berg with a bandage wrapped around his jaw. Behind the smell of the clove oil applied to his gums she detects the aggressive scent of the rest of his body. "What's all this I hear about you not going to Bayreuth for *Parsifal*?"

"I can't face all those people," Ludwig mumbles.

"I'm sure you could arrange a private performance," she says. "Would you like me to go with you?"

"I can't. Even seeing the people on the stage would be too much," he says.

"Have you been jilted by one of the performers?" she asks.

Ludwig sneers at the implication. "No, it is the entire world that rejects the love I have to offer," he replies.

Sisi is at her best when people are wounded and suffering. As with Rudolf after a bullet passed through his hand, and the people in the asylums and orphanages and hospitals, Sisi is able to conjure feeling for those who have lost an advantage. For close to a week, she stays with Ludwig. He has little to say, and begs her to leave, embarrassed at the way his pristine cousin is seeing him, but Sisi can see that his greatest fear is to be alone. She pets him and reads him poetry and does not push him to go outside when he declines. She applies masks to his face and curls his hair and even eats some cake with him. By the end of the week, Sisi is convinced that Ludwig might turn his mood around, but as soon as she departs his temperament plunges again, lonesome and forlorn.

And even despite all this, Sisi cannot see that she suffers the same destructive urge for solitude, and attempts to excuse herself from the Carnivale Ball yet again. Franzl admonishes her. "Sisi, you haven't been seen in court for ages. The people must have *some* access to their Empress."

Sisi has been sitting in front of the mirror for hours, tugging the skin on her face about, smoothing the fine lines, powdering her freckles. "These spots used to fade in the winter months."

"You're as beautiful as you've always been," Franzl attempts, but Sisi is wise to the truth.

Beneath the chandeliers, lit with thousands of candles, Sisi bears no instinct to stick close to her family, but neither does she have an interest in socializing. She accepts compliments, but offers no praise in return. The women notice that Sisi's outfit is old-fashioned, but still, at forty-five, even with a dress broadly patterned in huge flowers and leaves, she is stick thin and uncommonly tall. The warm glow of her embarrassment hides the freckles, and Sisi takes care not to smile. At best, she conjures mischief and tolerance with an amused smirk. Only Andrássy risks asking her to dance, and Sisi accepts, made passive and indifferent by the pressures of the overstimulating ballroom.

With Sisi in his arms, Andrássy steals glances at Valerie talking to a huddle of young women beside the dance floor. He, too, has wondered if it's possible she might be his own, if somehow the passion between him and the Empress might have immaculately conceived some human effect, but he can tell that her eyes are those of her mother and her mouth that of her father, and so, in her, he sees all that never came of his love for Sisi, all that was denied him.

Sisi is distracted by the sight of Rudolf, sag-shouldered at the other end of the hall with Stephanie. Despite the fact that he clearly toted a great deal of preexisting misery into the marriage, Sisi knows Stephanie adds to her son's gloom. With an heir firmly implanted in the Princess's womb, though, there is no end in sight.

Mourning—Chaos—Comfort—Detachment

✻ ✻

IN FEBRUARY 1883, Ludwig receives a telegram from Venice. Wagner is dead.

Ludwig weeps all night and demands that black crepe shroud the pianos. "There will be no music while we honor the Great Friend."

Ludwig sends a letter to Venice saying, "Wagner's corpse belongs to me," but his body has already been loaded onto a train back to Bayreuth. It stops briefly in Munich, where crowds of people have gathered to pay tribute, but Ludwig is not among them.

At Wahnfried, Wagner's Bayreuth home named to mark the place where his delusions were meant to find peace, as the casket is closed for the final time, Cosima presents gardening shears to her teenaged daughters. They accept them with horror, worried at what will be asked of them, but Cosima asks only that they cut her waist-length tresses. Isolde struggles with the dull blades while Eva takes firm hold of the hank, and Cosima screams the whole time, as though she can feel each strand cut. They place the fistful of hair in Wagner's hand before pounding the nails into the coffin lid. Cosima collapses in agony. "I am ashamed that his absence has not killed me!" she wails. "The Lord knows he would not have survived *my* death." Their daughters stand by, their grief waiting its turn.

The loss of Wagner ticks Ludwig's eccentricity up a notch.

Aware that there will be no new operas in the future, Ludwig thinks he needs to find a replacement to fill his time. He purchases the ruins of Falkenstein in the Bavarian Alps. He plans to build there a Gothic version of Neuschwanstein. He works again with the stage designer Jank to draw up the plans. This castle will cling even more perilously to the rocks, tall and spindly, as though it has dripped from the heavens.

A wild chamois bursts into the mirror room at Linderhof, smashing its hooves against the glass and bucking wildly.

Hearing the commotion, Ludwig makes his way over to marvel at the raucous reflections bouncing about. A servant tries to chase the animal out to stop the destruction, but Ludwig bids him stop. "Let him find his own way out, shall we? At least he doesn't tell lies!"

Later that week, walking from the dining room to his bedroom, Ludwig hears footsteps and whispers behind him. He glances back, but his eyes find nothing. *I'm to come to the same fate as Otto*, he thinks. "I can hear you!" he shouts, to be safe.

In the summer, taking waters at Kissingen, Bismarck finds his chalet filled with flowers, all courtesy of Ludwig.

Bismarck tells his treasurer that he can discontinue the payments to Ludwig from the Reptile Fund. "If he has the money to fill a room with flowers for no reason, then he doesn't need the help of the Prussian purse." Ludwig had meant this gesture as a thank-you for the chancellor's *continued* support, and will sorely miss that financial assistance.

Other Elisabeths

✿　✿

IN SEPTEMBER 1883 a baby girl is born to Prince Rudolf and Princess Stephanie. Sisi knows the disappointment of not having produced a rightful heir. When she hears they've named the child Elisabeth after her, she replies, "It grows tiresome, all my grandchildren having my name. We'll call this one Erzsi." Stephanie had been hoping for "Liza," but she doesn't dare smudge this moment with her own opinion.

Days later, at breakfast with Sisi and Valerie, Franzl says, "I've been told it's unlikely Stephanie will be able to bear more children. It was a difficult birth and certain measures were necessary to save both her and the baby."

"Perhaps better if they hadn't gone to the trouble," Sisi mumbles.

Franzl sets down his cutlery to stare at his wife.

"I mean only that it shall be a shame if no heir is produced," Sisi replies.

"We are grateful that the two of them are healthy," Franzl says, supplying the words Sisi is to repeat to others.

"Yes, yes, very good. All I know is I have suffered my

own ailments a long time, and I often wonder if it's worth it. I, myself, have considered more drastic options to relieve myself of the pressures placed upon me." Sisi wants a reaction, but she keeps her eyes trained on her juice.

Franzl coughs. "You would go to hell."

"What does it matter when one already has hell on earth?" Sisi asks.

Valerie keeps her gaze on her porridge, waiting for her father's response, but when she looks at him, she finds tears in his eyes as he scans his pages of policy. He has given her mother everything and Sisi wants even more.

Within a month, Rudolf's fondness for the baby has faded. Stephanie lets herself into the Emperor's apartment. "You must do something about your son! He is a father now and he continues to stay out all night. He comes home ragged, smelling of other women. Who knows the disease he drags back with him, let alone the damage to the family's reputation."

"Stephanie, he is a grown man and your husband. He is not my charge any longer," Franzl responds. "All I can do is urge you to remember he is responsible for himself. A husband is not a wife's underling."

Sisi invites Queen Elisabeth of Romania to Băile Herculane in the Carpathians with her. Sisi has heard that the Queen writes under the pen name Carmen Sylva, and Sisi is certain her own poems must be superior. The pair of women make a day of traipsing the town to see each of the statues of Hercules, and then they soak their flesh in the hot sulfur springs.

In the shade of the still snowy peaks, the Queen, having listened to the Empress complain all day, tells Sisi, "You, Your Imperial Majesty, are a fairy being crushed by the cruel pressure of circumstance."

"I appreciate that," Sisi says, but she fails to open her eyes or compliment the Queen's choice of words. She breathes deeply, grateful to be free of her corset. Sisi has been surprised to find the Queen clearly ordinary. *There's no hiding stupid thoughts with pretty words*, she thinks.

Carmen notices Sisi's smirk and asks what she is thinking.

"I just passed gas," Sisi says, to shut Carmen up.

Sisi moves toward the source of the spring. Carmen doesn't bother to warn her about the heat. She realizes the Empress knows precisely what she is doing.

"I've been thinking of publishing *my* writing!" Sisi calls, a challenge.

"You should! Doing so has breathed life into my every second. It has changed the way I peer out from my soul, knowing I will translate what I see into language."

"The problem is that my poems are collaborations."

"Is that so?"

"Yes," Sisi replies, "with Heinrich Heine."

Carmen coos. "I also think of my inspirations as a kind of coauthor."

"He's not only an inspiration. It is a very symbiotic exchange. His hand drives my own and his words fill my mind. The world will be only too excited to hear that there is new work from this master."

"I see," the Queen says, though it is impossible that she does. She has read the Empress's poems, and if those are Heine's words, then his abilities have deteriorated as his body has broken down in the grave.

Finally

✻　✻

THE CYCLE OF ARCHITECTS CONTINUES, each quitting as soon as they learn that the King hasn't the money to continue building as he wishes. Ludwig, at this point, has borrowed so much from future payments to those on his civil list that his debts tally over eight million marks.

Progress halts on all projects. The workers at Herrenchiemsee strike. Thirty-five women have been working day in and day out for seven years on the linens for Ludwig's bed, and now it seems the wages they are owed might not be paid to them at all.

Worried that the properties might be confiscated from him, Ludwig moves into the unfinished Neuschwanstein, two decades in the making, in 1884. Ludwig should feel the deep satisfaction of finally inhabiting the architectural wonder that has obsessed his imagination since he was a teenager, but instead he is scared and disappointed. His toothaches and headaches hold his skull in a vise. Not a minute in the castle can be enjoyed because the threat that it might be seized is so all-consuming. If he doesn't find a way to pay off at least a minimal amount on his debt, then this masterpiece might be taken apart for scrap. He wishes he were able to show off this wonder before it disappears, but everyone he might share it with has been taken from him: they have died or given up on his impossibility or he has pushed them away, certain that the punishment for his love would be more severe than the misery of being alone. Even Hornig visits only to talk about practicalities. Ludwig, who has lived his life in his imagination, cannot conceive a way to make his dream of everlasting love a sustainable reality. He sees the failure as his own.

In the gilded Throne Room that lacks a throne, Ludwig sits on the steps of the dais and asks the decorative kings circling the domed apse above for guidance. This place was supposed to be a way for him to reveal himself, a way to show the world all of the beauty pent up inside of him. Yes, it would be a fortress in which he could be kept safe, but, more than that, it was to be a way for him to be honest with the world, to allow honesty to take a different form. For all of his life, Ludwig has felt not only separate—different in some irreconcilable way—but also scattered even within himself. He felt as though he was not whole, and every endeavor was an attempt to find that wholeness. Now, here, in Neuschwanstein, even unfinished as it is, Ludwig can see that this castle will not be the thing that glues him together. Words have always failed him, though he loves the attempt to find the right ones, loves to marvel at the poets and lyricists who are able to come the closest. But what Ludwig wants is a world in which he might be understood without words, in which connection is mutual and needs no explanation. He looks at the plants and animals paved into the marble floor—his subjects—and realizes that if God won't guide him, then there is no hope of his guiding the people. Even the King of Kings, Jesus Christ, has abandoned him. He will need to find another way.

He cannot sleep in the ornate bed it's taken so many years to carve to his specifications. He has made the bedroom feel too much like a church: the bed too close to a confessional, the altar within sight. He suffers through the night, avoiding his thoughts, and takes a blanket and pillow into the Grotto off the bedroom, falling asleep more easily on the uncomfortable stone.

In the morning, the current court secretary, Gresser, taps out the Morse code of his greeting through the closed door of the study on the other side of the Grotto. Even the muffled sound of a human voice is too much for the King to bear these days.

Gresser deciphers the oft-repeated rhythms of the King's response: "Vermin, vagabonds, rabble."

In the small cave Ludwig is free of distraction, imagining himself into a more simple and beautiful time where ideas can shine more brightly against the dim rock. He taps out his orders on the artificial dripstone.

The secretary is sure he misunderstands, but when he taps back his confirmation, Ludwig raps his approval.

The King wants servants to go ask other kings and rulers across Europe and down to Persia and Turkey for loans. He asks Gresser to send a request to Bismarck for a lump sum. Gresser complies, hopeless though the endeavor seems.

Of course, most of the requests come to nothing, but Bismarck takes the bid seriously. His adviser warns against granting the request.

"If Ludwig wastes this as he has wasted everything else, his creditors could sue the Prussian treasury. Perhaps you can grant him a loan through some third party."

Bismarck sees the minister's point and works with a consortium of banks to procure Ludwig 7.5 million marks. With this, Ludwig's debts would be not so much cleared as consolidated, but Ludwig does not see it this way. He blinds himself to the facts and resumes building.

Please

✻   ✻

IN AN ATTEMPT TO KEEP SISI CLOSER to home, Franzl orders a palace constructed in the nearby Lainzer Tiergarten. He asks Sisi what they should call it and Sisi thinks of the way she feels that Heine communicates with her through his poems. She picks the name "Hermes Villa," after the messenger of the gods.

When it is time to place the finishing touches, Sisi tours the house with Franzl. "I like how far away it is, tucked so deep into the park. Only people who know we are here shall find us," Sisi says.

Sisi stays a few weeks to supervise the placement of the furnishings for the rest of the house. She writes to Ludwig, inviting him to come see her new summer palace, but Ludwig declines. He is not comfortable traveling so far. He asks for a detailed description, though, and Sisi obliges, illustrating the style of the house in her purplest prose. And then, with the house ready to be comfortably occupied, she leaves.

A Friend for Dinner

❋ ❋

IN LESS THAN A YEAR, Ludwig has doubled his debt: fourteen million marks' worth. His minister of finance declines his request to seek out another loan. "We're a laughingstock as it is. The only option is to pay down the debt that already exists."

"I suppose I'll be looking for a new minister of finance, then."

The other ministers refuse to recommend a replacement, threatening to resign. Ludwig wonders where all of his authority has gone. It's possible he doesn't realize that the greatest power he had was in ignoring his lack of control, and that no longer seems to be an option.

The King's uncle (his father's brother), Prince Luitpold, calls Prime Minister Lutz for a meeting. Seeing an opportunity to finish out his career in style, he wants to suggest the idea of ousting Ludwig from the throne. If Ludwig is declared unfit to rule, reign would pass over Otto—already incapacitated—and straight into Luitpold's hands. The uncle views himself as the practical head of the family, the only one capable of restoring true nobility to the Wittels-bach line.

"I'm not sure we have a case," Lutz replies. "Clearly, his finances are a mess, but where else can we strike a blow?" Lutz wants to hear what else the Prince knows.

"Well, he's not completing any of his public duties," Luitpold offers. "When was the last time he was in Munich? I can tell his signatures are forged. My grandfather always said, 'A function that remains unexercised is soon lost altogether.' I feel no guilt. Ludwig has done this to himself."

"You would be doing Bavaria a service in calling for a reckoning." Lutz pauses, delicately choosing his words. "I hope you'll forgive an honest question. Do you believe Ludwig to be in his right mind?"

Luitpold hadn't been prepared to make the suggestion himself, but the thought has occurred to him, too. "I couldn't guarantee it," he says.

Lutz nods. "If he's not, we may have a case for a regency."

Lutz thinks it best to check in with Bismarck. "We have reason to believe Ludwig's sanity may not be intact and are planning to take action preventing further damages. Do you have any objection?"

Bismarck takes their meaning. "I will not interfere."

Lutz calls in a cluster of servants he knows to be discreet. He requests they report back anything they observe in the King they might classify as out of the ordinary. "I'll reward the keenest eyes," the prime minister tells them, and their imaginations set to work.

One servant responds immediately. "His Majesty loses control of his limbs at times, dancing a kind of dislocated jig, ghastly to see." One thousand marks arrive the next day.

Ludwig requests his valet accompany him on a walk. "Fetch my overcoat."

The valet informs the King it's over a hundred degrees outside and sunny.

Ludwig replies, "What of it? Grab my umbrella, too." He wants these props only to shroud his body from the view of nosy onlookers. The gymnastics of privacy grow more pliant. Sanity begins to look insane and the servants dutifully send their reports to Lutz.

In September 1885, Herrenchiemsee is far enough along that the King can stay there for what will be the one and only time. Ludwig arrives after a leisurely boat ride. He refuses the coach offered to him in favor of a slow walk from the dock on which the palace might slowly come into view.

The state apartments closely mirror their Versailles counterparts. In his bedroom, Ludwig compliments the enormous candelabra next to the bed. "The man who made this armleuchter is certainly no armleuchter himself!" He looks around for his laugh. "You know, the maker of this poor light is no dimwit? Eh?" The valet nods politely.

The Hall of Mirrors is an extra 50 percent longer than Louis XIV's. In the morning the sun reflects off the glass so brightly that servants walk the long way around to avoid the glare.

Ludwig taps his walking stick on a crowned lion figure at the base of the main staircase, and it crumbles. He smashes his stick into its twin, as well. "What is the meaning of this?" The servants avoid eye contact. As money ran low, the plaster models remained rather than being replaced with marble. "Everything is false!" He orders that the person responsible for retaining the plaster be brought to him, and the servants choose the lowliest among them to serve as an effigy. Ludwig knows no different; he places a hot plop of wax on the valet's forehead and presses his seal into it. "You will wear this mark until it falls off on its own."

The only friend he feels safe enough to invite to dinner is his favorite horse, Cosa Rara. How whimsical such an evening will be, he thinks. Cosa Rara is the gentlest being, and to share a meal together in the grandeur of the dining room seems something out of a fairy tale Ludwig has yet to read.

Reality, though, is never as uncomplicated as Ludwig's visions. The servants tell Ludwig that they think it best if they call the evening off—the horse is agitated by the unfamiliarity of the palace. Ludwig, though, insists. He has asked that he and Cosa Rara be served the same meal, and a plate of schnitzel does nothing to calm the steed. "The strudel then!" Ludwig calls down through the floor as the servants load the magical table from the kitchen below. Ludwig has remembered the way his beloved horse swallows apples whole. When the table descends to receive the strudel, though, the horse rears up and crashes down, destroying the chandelier and chairs. The sound startles it even more, and it falls through the open floor. Ludwig excuses himself to mourn Cosa Rara, one more casualty of his skewed passion.

Lutz is the first to receive word of the ruckus.

Nothing a Little Mercury Can't Help

❋ ❋

SISI RETURNS FROM HOLIDAY in Norfolk to find Rudolf departing for a cure of his own.

"Nothing that can't be helped by a warmer climate . . . an affliction similar to your own?"

Sisi studies Rudolf's face for clues that he understands what he's implying. She has heard that her son has not allowed marriage or fatherhood to assuage his more hedonistic habits.

"Take care," is the most she can manage in response.

In her absence, Franzl has taken to attending regular theatre productions. "Finally allowing yourself to relax a bit, I see," Sisi says. "I'll go with you tonight." Sisi thinks she might see a pale blush in Franzl's cheeks.

That night, from their center box, Sisi can feel Franzl perk up when a young actress named Katharina Schratt takes the stage. She is no dramatic genius, but there is *something* about her that Sisi can identify as beguiling.

After the performance, Sisi ventures, "That Mademoiselle Schratt is quite something, wouldn't you say?"

Franzl doesn't pause. "*Madame* Schratt. She's married to a Hungarian. You don't remember her from the dinner we had with Tsar Alexander in Kremsier? It was such an embarrassment—the Tsar and Prince Bismarck telling those crude stories."

The memory dawns bright in Sisi. There are so many tedious dinners to keep track of, but that one had become lively. "Was she the one the Tsar was after?"

"Yes, she warded him off," Franz responds. "Such an appalling lack of politesse."

"Maybe you should invite her to dinner again," Sisi recommends.

Sisi's willingness to allow her husband a mistress is an inexplicable turn. She never asks for details of their time together. She is glad to find Franzl markedly happier. "They're soul mates is all," she tells Ida. "Peas in a pod. No threat."

Ida can't believe Sisi's insouciance. "Aren't you worried she might damage your image?"

Sisi says, "So long as she's also a friend to me, no one will suspect anything. For Franzl's Christmas gift, I've asked Heinrich von Angeli if he'll paint a portrait of Frau Schratt."

"That is very sweet, but where will the Emperor display such a gift?"

"In his bedroom beside my own portrait, of course," Sisi replies.

Valerie, ever more confused at her mother's behavior, asks if she can possibly be serious when she suggests Valerie fill an album with photos of Schratt for her father as a gift.

"I think it would be quite thoughtful," Sisi says.

"You don't think he might treasure more an album full of pictures of his children instead? That that might not be a more appropriate gift for a daughter to give a father?"

"It was only an idea," Sisi says, eager to change the subject. "Don't be mad, pet."

"You're obsessed. You think that woman is your ticket to freedom."

"Don't be silly. You know I love only you. If you left me, my life would end, for one can only love like this once in one's life, and I can't help that you are that for me, rather than your brother or sister, or your father."

Valerie's stomach turns. She thinks of Count Andrássy and Bay Middleton. "Yes, I can feel the weight of that love every day! It's suffocating. What will happen when I desire to marry? I worry you won't allow it!"

Sisi lies. "I wouldn't flinch if you fell in love with a shoemaker or a stable boy. I want only to be sure that *you* choose who you will marry."

"And how can I do that if I never meet anyone? You're rotting my chances of finding a worthy suitor."

Sisi stares at her girl and wonders how they can be both so similar and so different.

When Rudolf returns home from his convalescence in time for Christmas, Ida tells Sisi, "He seems even more agitated than usual."

"I haven't noticed a thing," Sisi says.

Knives, Poison, a Diagnosis
✳ ✳

TWO SERVANTS WRITE LUTZ on behalf of Ludwig's sanity. One: "I could observe no signs of the alleged mental illness of the King. Nor could I perceive any abnormal changes. I dressed him and served him. He often talked to me. Never did the King show any sign of instability."

The other: "I am in the King's personal service and I can only say that he is a good and just master. Although he sometimes scolds and storms when someone has done something wrong, his anger usually blows over quickly. I am impressed with how calm and composed the King is considering the way people have turned against him."

Of course Lutz ignores anything that doesn't match the evidence he needs.

Ludwig tells his valet: "If Linderhof and Herrenchiemsee are confiscated, I shall either kill myself or else leave this accursed land forever."

The valet has heard how gossip has paid off for the other servants and sends a note to Lutz.

———

Ludwig dispatches a group of servants to rob the Rothschild bank in Frankfurt. The servants visit the bank, but none even considers the prospect of a robbery. Upon their return to Munich, they report that a police car was stationed outside the bank every day so they couldn't carry out the plan.

Ludwig orders that they be transported to America, but they are instead transferred to the Residenz in Munich, a place where Ludwig will surely never see them.

In April 1886, the company that provides the castles with water and gas sues Ludwig for nonpayment. Ludwig secludes himself further, not leaving his room in Neuschwanstein. He stands in front of his mirror in the mornings, pulling the flesh of his face into strength and joy and concern, calling up the affect of emotions that feel so far away.

The cabinet insists that Ludwig comply with a list of demands. He's to return to the economical model of his father and cease additional building projects. Ludwig complies with none of the requests.

Ludwig's valet, Alfonso, enters the room to lay out the King's clothing for the next day, and the King commands him to put away the knife on his dresser. Alfonso looks at the bare surface, and says, "There's no knife on the dresser, Your Majesty."

Ludwig shakes his head, as if clearing out cobwebs. "But there should be one there. Where have you put it? Why have you put it away? Put it back immediately."

Alfonso reluctantly fetches one of the King's hunting knives from the cupboard, and lays it on the dresser. Ludwig looks back and finds the knife where he expected to see it. "Well, then, put it away!"

Alfonso returns the knife to the cabinet without another word.

On March 10th, the King pens a note to his mother: "In remembrance of the anniversary of Father's death, and because I am not in Munich, I feel urged to write you. I shall remain here, for I am unhappy and must wait until the reason for this bad temper disappears. I shall remember you in my prayers. In inmost love I kiss your hand, dear Mother. Your grateful son, Ludwig."

The Queen is unnerved by her son's uncharacteristic sweetness to her. She offers, again, to give him all of the money under her control so that he might continue construction, hoping that might cheer him.

Ludwig writes, "I feel urged to send you my warmest thanks for your charming offer, but I would like to ask you to allow me to decline. The Secretariat must succeed in adjusting the matter." Ludwig hands the letter to Dürckheim and crumples into tears. Dürckheim pities the man he once so desired. "Perhaps death is the only way out," Ludwig opines. "Would you be able to obtain some arsenic? Or belladonna? Whichever is the least painful." Ludwig doesn't know that his cousin Sisi also went hunting for lethal remedies decades before when her daughter died, but even if he did he would scoff, saying her pain was temporary and his is chronic.

Dürckheim excuses himself without making a promise.

The King makes the same request to his aide Hesselschwerdt, and Hesselschwerdt seriously considers.

When the King asks Dürckheim the following day if he's brought him anything, Dürckheim shakes his head, pouring apology from his eyes alongside resoluteness.

"No matter," the King says, trying to egg Dürckheim on. "Hesselschwerdt will comply."

Dürckheim, mistrustful of Hesselschwerdt already, corners the quartermaster. "Did you find what the King asked you for?"

Hesselschwerdt wrinkles his brow with a smile. "What do you mean?"

"You know what I mean," Dürckheim says, gripping his collar.

"Do you mean the young men he asks be delivered to him in the night?"

"I don't want the King to hurt himself. Do you?"

"Oh, of course not. No. I would never."

Dürckheim holds him there, searching Hesselschwerdt's eyes for a lie, but he does not falter. Dürckheim releases his neck, but does not back away. "If I hear of you asking around for poison, it's your heart that will stop. Understood?"

Hesselschwerdt shrugs, adjusting his jacket. "No need to be beastly about it."

On March 23rd, Lutz meets with Dr. Bernhard von Gudden, the director of the General Lunatic Asylum of Upper Bavaria, who'd diagnosed Otto. When they sit down, Lutz passes a list to Dr. von Gudden of the evidence he's compiled.

Gudden reads, and then composes his official report: "The mental powers of His Majesty are disrupted to such an extent that all judgment is lacking, and his thinking is in total contradiction with reality . . . Gripped by the illusion that he holds absolute power in abundance and made lonely by self-isolation, he stands like a blind man without a guide at the edge of the abyss. His Majesty is in a very advanced stage of mental disorder, a form of insanity known to brain specialists by the name 'Paranoia,' or 'Primary Madness.' He has a pathologically false conception of the relationship of himself to his environment. Healthy perception is impaired to a high degree. As this form of brain trouble has a slow but progressive development of many years' duration, His Majesty must be regarded as incurable, a still further decline of the mental powers being the natural development of this disease. Suffering from such a disorder, His Majesty is declared incapable of ruling, which incapacity will be not only for a year's duration but for the length of His Majesty's life." When he sees the smile on Lutz's face, Gudden wonders if he's done the right thing.

"Will there be any issue with your not having examined the King in person?"

"I will have three other professionals sign, and that should serve as all the support we need," he replies.

That night, Hornig visits Ludwig. Hornig has been visiting Ludwig almost daily to check on the King and relay messages for him, but for months they have been strictly professional, talking only about what orders need to be carried out. Tonight, though, Hornig arrives already half a bottle of arrack in. Ludwig knows why. Hornig must see that the end is near. Ludwig has, of course, known, too, but Hornig coming to him like this forces the King to face the truth.

Hornig leads Ludwig to the Grotto. No words are spoken. They both understand. Hornig traces Ludwig's face lightly with his fingers, as if he's confirming the details he already knows so well. He takes Ludwig's hands and kisses both of the palms, and then slips Ludwig's thumb in his mouth. The King lets out a groan, tears in his eyes. He slides his thumb out and holds Hornig's jaw in his hand. Hornig tries to lean in to kiss Ludwig, but the King has some strength left in him and grips Hornig's face more tightly, holding him back. He turns Hornig's head away and bites his earlobe before pressing his lips into the hollow right above the hinge of Hornig's jaw. When Ludwig pulls away, Hornig stares into his eyes with such a sadness. He opens his mouth to speak, but nothing comes out. Ludwig wants to hear Hornig say it so badly, but Hornig's lips shut, unable.

Instead, he unbuttons Ludwig's jacket with ceremony. He pulls Ludwig's shirt off over his head. A valet does this for Ludwig every day, but Hornig is so attentive in his actions, the tenderness makes Ludwig feel cared for. *Why?* he thinks. Ludwig cannot understand why he responds in the way he does. When Hornig is done undressing the King, he undresses himself, and Ludwig watches.

It is rare that the two of them can see all of each other like this. Usually they must be quick, hidden in the woods outside Berg or in the stable late at night or beneath the blanket of the carriages. There is never the time or safety to undress completely. The Grotto, though, reminds Hornig of the cave they found hidden in the hillside of the Berg woods, beneath the heavy vines, just large enough for the two of them. Hornig stops for a moment and looks around him, realizing that the room around him is *exactly like* their cave. "Did you build this for us?" he asks.

Ludwig avoids the question by hugging Hornig to him, his chin tucking over his shoulder. Hornig can feel the quickness of the King's breathing and rubs his back, gently at first, trying to soothe him, and then more firmly, massaging Ludwig's shoulders and then kissing him and clutching him, their groins pressing against one another. Hornig turns and bends Ludwig, pulling his legs apart and kneeling down behind the King. He places the flat of his tongue against Ludwig to ready him, and lets the saliva build up. He can feel the King relax and stands. When he enters Ludwig, they both gasp. The King is so warm and soft, and Hornig's strong arms wrapped so firmly around Ludwig feel so satisfying. It is the one moment when the King feels whole, complete. When all he does is want, and there is no shame associated with the desire because it's clear that someone else wants the same thing. He is not alone.

Ludwig feels everything, joy and ecstasy and gratitude, and then those feelings start to fade and the sadness and grief and guilt begin to slip in. After he finishes, Hornig goes to retrieve the washbasin and a towel from the bedroom. He dips the cloth in the water and softly cleans the King. He wipes Ludwig's tears and slips him into his nightdress. Ludwig doesn't tell Hornig that he can't sleep in the bed here. He allows his lover to tuck him in and slip away without a goodbye.

"On this the first of June, two months and three weeks before my 41st birthday, from henceforth never! From henceforth never!!! Sworn in the name of the Great King, now invoking the puissant aid of the Redeemer. (Also, from kisses strictly to abstain, I swear it in the name of the King of Kings.)"

Ludwig signs his name and asks that his valet, Alfonso, sign as well, as witness. He seals this note with the royal cipher and crown and tucks it into the tabernacle of the altar in his bedroom.

While he sleeps that day, Alfonso removes the letter and delivers it to the commission. He has been waiting for this day since he read the Numa Numantius poems he'd acquired for the King all those years ago.

Bismarck is shown the doctor's report and he calls it mere "raking from the King's wastepaper basket and cupboards." He points out all the parts that make no sense, that need more evidence. He says he won't have anything to do with it until these items are addressed, but his notes go ignored.

The armies are warned that Luitpold is about to take power. Any uprisings must be squashed.

A session of Parliament is set for June 15th, but only the cynical ones, the ones who have been paying attention, have a hunch as to why.

On the 8th, Ludwig wakes at 2:00 p.m. in his room at Neuschwanstein. He lies in bed, staring up at the frame it took a team of fifteen artisans four years to carve. His servants, going about their business, are surprised to see him awake so early. They ask if he's feeling all right.

"A bit restless, to be honest," he replies. He smashes the

busts he's had made of his favorite valets and aides-de-camp. He leaves only the bust of Wagner intact. The marble history of his friendships lies in pieces on the ground. The servants sweep up the shards, and Ludwig goes back to bed.

At midnight the commission arrives at Hohenschwangau, just down the mountain from Ludwig. They eat seven full courses of supper and talk through their plan. "I feel the message from Luitpold stands the best chance of convincing Ludwig that our actions have authority," Holnstein recommends. It is appropriate that Holnstein is involved in this; after all, he swindled from Ludwig when he orchestrated the signing of the Kaiserbrief.

"Yes," Gudden agrees. "After you read him the note, Dr. Müller and I will tell him we are there to help him. I've an excellent manner in breaking such news. I'm very gentle."

"Hopefully, he comes peacefully. I'm sure he'd prefer to be with Otto at Fürstenried, rather than alone."

Gudden interrupts. "I disagree. First, I think it might be an insult to the King to suggest that he is as bad off as Otto, but second, if placed together they might feed one another's delusions."

Prince Luitpold's adviser Crailsheim speaks up. "Berg would be best. It's small and close to Munich."

The group works up their gumption with forty quarts of beer and ten bottles of champagne.

The Meaning of Asylum

❋ ❋

A T ONE O'CLOCK, the commission sends Holnstein up to the stable to tell Ludwig's coachman not to harness the horses for one of the King's night rides. Holnstein tells him to put the horses back in the stall.

The man refuses. "That would contradict the King's orders. I'll do no such thing."

Holnstein tells him, "The King is no longer in command. Prince Luitpold has taken power."

The coachman apologizes to Holnstein and puts the horses away. He finds Ludwig in the Singers' Hall reciting Schiller at the top of his lungs.

"Yourmajesty . . ." The honorific comes out in one choked word. "They'retryingtodepose . . . you."

Ludwig replies, "You know I don't like to be interrupted. Lie on the floor and explain."

The coachman assumes his usual position flat on his stomach and turns his head to get the words out. "Holnstein . . . he just . . . came to the coach house . . . and told me . . . Prince Luitpold . . . is my new master . . . I think . . . they're coming for you . . . soon."

"Impossible!" Ludwig exclaims.

"No, really . . . we need . . . to get you out of here!"

"Hesselschwerdt would have warned me of any threat," Ludwig says.

"I don't think he knows. Please, Your Majesty."

The coachman's voice is so plaintive that Ludwig's heart drops. "Bar the entrance to the castle."

The coachman scrambles to his feet and back down the mountain.

At four o'clock in the morning, the commissioners finally drive up the road to Neuschwanstein. Cold rain blows horizontally. Dawn peeks around the edge of the sparsely wooded path and the commissioners see the castle outlined against the gray-pink sky. The gate is already crowded with a reinforcement of guards who refuse to let them in. "Another step, and we fire!" cries the sergeant. "These are the King's orders and we obey them."

The Baroness Spera von Truchsess, a Füssen socialite, wields her parasol like a sword.

Dr. von Gudden knows the Baroness well. He's treated her in his asylum on numerous occasions. He knows the stories of the flashy parties she throws, always inviting the King despite his never once accepting. He knows how she books a room at the front of the Alpenrose Inn, so that she can sit at her window and watch Hohenschwangau, ready to dart out if the King emerges.

The Baroness hollers treason. "Your children will be ashamed of you! Are you not ashamed of betraying your King? Think of the legacy you'll leave!"

At 5:30 a.m., the commissioners give up. They ride back down to Hohenschwangau, exhausted and embarrassed.

After they shed their sopping clothes, the Füssen police arrive with orders from Ludwig to arrest them all.

The police march the men up to Neuschwanstein in their underclothes at bayonet point. People now line the streets.

The town jeers cruelly. One woman says, "Take a good look at them! When you grow up you will be able to say that you once saw traitors."

The police lock the commissioners in the gatehouse. The head of the guards enters to tell them, "The King has ordered that those guilty of treason be chained and beaten. We're to starve you for two weeks and then skin you alive. You'll have your eyes put out, and if you're not dead by then, you're to be left to decay in your own filth." The delegates have heard Ludwig's empty threats before, but still they worry.

In a couple of hours' time, though, the commissioners are released without explanation.

Dürckheim tells Ludwig to go to Munich. "The people will show their support. It is the safest place for you now. You can assert yourself as King and prove the commission wrong!"

Ludwig shakes his head sadly. "The air in Munich does not suit me."

Dürckheim explodes. "You're about to be dragged from the throne. You need to get out. Now. We could go across the border to the Austrian Tyrol if you'd prefer. Certainly Emperor Franz Joseph will grant us asylum. Sisi will insist on it." But Ludwig refuses this idea, too.

Dürckheim begs Ludwig to write an appeal to the Bavarian people, and Ludwig tries. "I, Ludwig II, King of Bavaria, am under the necessity of addressing this appeal to my Faithful and beloved people, as well as to the whole German Nation. My uncle, Prince Luitpold, designs, without My consent, to have himself proclaimed as Regent of My Kingdom, and My former Ministry has, by means of false reports, rendered itself guilty of High Treason. I enjoy perfect health, and my Mind is as sound as that of any other Monarch, but the contemplated High Treason is so sudden and astounding that I have not had time to take the necessary measures to meet it, or to frustrate the criminal designs of my former Ministers. I enjoin every Bavarian Citizen, true to his King, to fight against Prince Luitpold and the Ministry as against dangerous traitors. I have confidence in My People and feel sure they will not desert Me in the Hour of My Need."

Dürckheim has ten thousand copies printed, but most never make it out of Füssen.

Ludwig is relieved when he sees an armed contingent arrive from the capital, until he is informed the group is there to prevent his escape.

Dürckheim receives a message from the War Ministry that he must return to Munich immediately, but Ludwig insists he stay. "You're the only one I can still trust!"

Dürckheim writes the commission back saying he will not go.

This time the response comes from Luitpold. "You'll be tried for high treason if you don't follow orders, Dürckheim."

Dürckheim reads the telegram to the King, and Ludwig recommends he ignore it. The aide waits out one more threat, and when it arrives, Ludwig tells him, "Go. If you can get through this unscathed, you might be able to help me again down the road. But before you go, fetch me that poison I asked for, just in case."

Dürckheim apologizes and refuses, ad infinitum.

The phone lines and power to the castle are cut, but Ludwig demands the castle be lit up. Servants rush around lighting every candle and lamp. The chimneys billow smoke. Ludwig imagines the palace as a beacon for Lohengrin to come to his rescue.

Below, in Füssen, the townspeople see the dark castle begin to glow, and wonder if the King has decided to burn the place down.

On June 10th, a proclamation announces Luitpold as regent, signed by all of the heads of government except Ludwig.

When Dürckheim arrives in Munich, he is arrested. "For what?" Dürckheim exclaims.

"For helping to write this counter-proclamation," Lutz says, waving a document.

Dürckheim seizes it from his hands. "This isn't Ludwig's signature!"

Lutz grabs the forgery back. "Of course it is. You're both guilty of treason."

The police disperse from the castle grounds. The servants slip away one by one. Ludwig, so agitated and isolated, hardly notices that he is more and more alone. "If the barber comes tomorrow he will find my head in the Pöllat Gorge," Ludwig jokes to Alfonso, but the barber has already fled.

Ludwig wanders the castle saying his goodbyes. He knows, if he is taken into custody, Neuschwanstein will be sold off immediately. He asks that the best bottles of wine be brought up from the cellar and sets to drinking them one by one. He asks Alfonso for the key to the great tower, but the servant knows why the King is asking and says the key has been lost.

Ludwig calls Alfonso to his chamber. "Do you believe in the immortality of the soul?"

The young man nods.

"So do I," replies the King. "They hurl me from the highest summit down into nothingness, they destroy my life; while I live they call me dead, and that I cannot endure. Had they deprived me of my crown, *that* I could have survived. But to deprive me of my reason, take my freedom from me, and treat me as they treat my brother—no, that is intolerable. From that fate I will escape. Drowning is a fine death: there is no mutilation. But to jump from a height . . ." The King leaves the room and returns with twelve hundred marks and a brooch for Alfonso. "You deserve it; you've been the most loyal one."

Alfonso refuses, knowing the way he has betrayed the King again and again. "We are not on your deathbed, Your Majesty," he says.

"I believe we may be," Ludwig replies. He hands Alfonso his prayer book. "Pray for me."

At 12:30 a.m., Ludwig repeatedly declares he's ready to die.

A second commission arrives from Munich. Alfonso meets them near the gatehouse and tells them to hurry. He'd rather the King be taken into custody than take his own life.

Dr. Müller feels a particular excitement run through him. He has never seen Ludwig in person.

Alfonso enters the King's bedroom. "Your Majesty, I've found the key to the tower."

Ludwig kisses the valet on the mouth and grabs the key. He rushes to the stairwell, but Gudden waits there.

"Do you remember we've met before? I helped diagnose your brother Otto."

The King nods. Since having Otto committed all those years ago, he has been waiting for some sort of punishment, and today it has arrived. "How is he?"

Dr. von Gudden is surprised that Ludwig thinks to inquire about his brother in this moment. Or is it that Ludwig doesn't see how dire the situation is? Perhaps his concern for his brother's well-being is more evidence of his madness. "We've helped find a way to reduce his agitation," Dr. von Gudden replies, hoping this might be a comfort to Ludwig, "but I come with a purpose, the saddest task of my life. Your Majesty's case has been appraised by four alienists and, following their pronouncement, Prince Luitpold has assumed the regency. I have the order to accompany Your Majesty to Berg tonight. If it pleases Your Majesty, the carriage will depart at four o'clock."

The King lets out a siren of a wail. The orderlies each take an arm and Ludwig's bulky body twists in their grasp. They carry the King, his feet dragging, back to his bedroom. The smell of arrack overwhelms them, and they realize the King must be very drunk.

"How can you declare me insane when you have not examined me?" Ludwig asks.

This stings the doctor, for he can acknowledge, privately, that his actions have not been entirely ethical. Out loud, though, he tells the King that an examination was unnecessary because of the evidence provided by his servants.

Ludwig's face contorts with disgust. "Those paid lackeys that I have raised from nothing! If Prince Luitpold had told me he wanted to occupy the throne so badly, I would have happily stepped down." Ludwig hears his speech slur. "How long will it take to 'cure' me? If I'm so sick, when do you believe I'll be well again?"

Dr. von Gudden hedges. "That depends on Your Majesty. It will be necessary for you to submit to my instructions. If you're dedicated, the process will take at least a year."

Ludwig slumps. "Take my life instead. It would be easier and no less moral."

"I won't respond to that," Gudden says. "Pack your things. We leave at four o'clock."

———

The doctors, the King, the orderlies, the policemen: all descend to the forecourt to board three carriages in the rain. The King rides alone in the middle carriage, dreaming of jumping out and being trampled by horses and striated by wooden wheels. When he tries the door handles, though, he realizes they've been rigged to open only from the outside. The villagers lining the roads raise their hats.

On June 12th, after an eight-hour journey, the carriages arrive to Berg. It is high noon but dark as evening as the rain pours down.

Ludwig steps out of his carriage and sees his most heimlich home through a new lens. In the past, it had been a place of joy and refuge for him, but now the building looms.

Inside, Ludwig cannot escape the sound of workmen hammering iron bars onto all the windows. Peepholes have been installed in every door. Ludwig's skin crawls with the thought of being spied on at all times. He lies down on his bed and tries to silence his mind, but the pounding persists. When finally it is quiet, Ludwig asks a guard to please wake him at midnight, but the guard informs him that he's to keep "normal" hours now that he's under medical supervision. Ludwig snorts. "What could be *normal* about this?"

Ludwig wakes at 3:00 a.m. He asks the guard if he's to serve as valet. The guard shakes his head, and Ludwig responds. "Very well. Who's to fetch my clothes then?"

The guard says, "Your clothes have been taken away. You must go back to sleep."

Ludwig paces, slapping the walls, until he sees how his behavior might be construed. He waits until 6:00 a.m., when orderlies arrive. "I'd like to attend mass, please."

The orderlies inform Ludwig that he can't leave the castle grounds.

"But it's Whitsunday. Are you telling me I can no longer honor my faith?"

The orderlies don't have any answers.

Nothing to Be Done

✳   ✳

SISI, VISITING POSSENHOFEN, hears of Ludwig's arrest. She asks to go to him, but she is told it would be too dangerous. Instead, she goes out for a walk on the paths along the lake, trying to dream up a way to help her cousin.

She telegrams Franzl to ask him to intervene, but her husband sides with the commission. Ludwig has not behaved responsibly in a long while. He might not technically be deranged, but if Ludwig will not abdicate the throne and let someone more capable of the duties take over, then a show of force is the last resort.

Sisi writes Ludwig a letter, but she fears rightly that it won't be delivered. "If you need someone to vouch for you, if you need asylum, if you need a show of force, give some signal. I will come to you. I will house you. I will be *your* eagle for once." But poetry and art, which have saved Ludwig many times over, are not enough this time. Metaphors reveal themselves as the empty promises they are.

The King Is Dead
❋ ❋

L UDWIG SPENDS HIS MORNING TALKING to the doctors. "I'll do anything you ask," Ludwig says, "provided I'm treated with respect."

Dr. von Gudden tells the King he'll need to lead a life of moderation. Ludwig must keep diurnal hours and follow the diet and exercise regimens the doctors have designed.

Ludwig thinks of his dinners with imaginary guests and his rides through the starlit skies. "Fine, but might I have my books? I'll need some entertainment."

Dr. von Gudden replies, "Some of the fantasies you read are, no doubt, contributing to your illness, Your Majesty. We will consider books on an individual basis."

After their morning meeting, Dr. Müller makes an inquiry of his colleague. "Is it possible the King is sane? He seems very cognizant. I am having second thoughts."

Dr. von Gudden knows if they back down on their diagnosis, their careers will be ruined. "If you are not committed to our decision, then you may leave. The King's condition is, as stated on record, permanent and incurable."

Gudden sends a telegram to Prime Minister Lutz: "So far, everything here has gone marvelously."

At 11:30 a.m., Dr. von Gudden enters the King's room. "A walk by the lake, Your Majesty?"

Ludwig likes this idea. He admires the newly clear skies and the calm water until he realizes a man walks about a hundred feet behind them.

Ludwig leans into the doctor. "Gudden, don't look, but we're being followed. I worry he might be an assassin."

Gudden laughs. "Your Majesty, that is an orderly."

Ludwig sighs, feeling relief for a moment before the sadness returns.

Ludwig peers out the window all afternoon. Through the eye of his telescope, he can see the Roseninsel in the distance, so close to where he knows Sisi is vacationing now. An unusual number of boats glide across the Würmsee, and Ludwig wonders if they're villagers trying to catch a glimpse of him. Perhaps tomorrow the water will be quieter and he can swim to Sisi. Ludwig pens a note to his cousin with this possibility and asks an orderly to have it delivered. "How many guards are on duty on the castle grounds?" he asks as casually as he can.

The orderly, without thinking, responds, "Maybe six or eight."

"Are they armed?" Ludwig asks, but the orderly shakes his head.

Ludwig smiles. "Could you summon Müller for me?"

The orderly nods. Gudden makes Müller promise not

to let the King sway him. "He might be out of his mind, but he is the darling of the people for a reason. Be wary."

The King batters Müller with questions. "What is your medical training exactly? How good is your eyesight? Do you get to read much?"

Müller answers all of these inquiries to Ludwig's liking.

"Very well," the King says. "I must tell you: I do not trust Gudden. I don't believe he knows what he's doing. To be honest, I worry he might take my life."

Müller assures the King that they have his best interests at heart, but Ludwig remains unsoothed.

At 4:30 p.m., Ludwig eats a late lunch alone. He drinks a glass of beer, but then asks to switch to wine instead. The servants fill his glass seven times.

An orderly informs the King his evening walk has been canceled because of rain. The King asks Dr. von Gudden, "Please, might we still go out? It needn't be long, but I'll lose my mind if I'm made to stay in this place hour upon hour."

The doctor bites his tongue and agrees, asking that their overcoats be fetched. At 6:45 p.m., they head out to the lake with hats and umbrellas to walk the same path they had earlier. Dr. von Gudden sees Ludwig notice the orderly behind them again and decides to do the King a service. He shouts back to dismiss the servant.

The policeman on duty, Lauterbach, sees the orderly and asks him why he's returning so quickly. "Gudden told me they'd be back by eight." Lauterbach is skeptical. When he sees a policeman named Klier returning to the castle by an upper path, he jogs to meet him. "Please resume your post," Lauterbach says. "The King and the doctor are still out walking."

At 7:15 p.m., Klier returns to Lauterbach. "I can't locate them."

"What do you mean? They must be out there. Go out and have another look."

At 8:30 p.m., Klier returns shaking his head. "Still no sign."

At 9:00 p.m., Dr. Müller begins to worry. "Maybe they've decided to wait out the rain." Guards and orderlies set out. Each man takes a lantern and they divide up. An observant guard notes that the King's friend Hornig lives in a villa at the end of the lake path, and the pair proceed there, hoping for the best, but when the doctor and his aide ask Hornig if he is hiding the King, Hornig blanches. "I wish we were."

"You wish you were committing a crime?"

"If he is not with us here, then I fear the worst," Hornig says, and joins their search.

For over an hour, the hunt turns up nothing.

Klier notices some carriage tracks outside the gates pointed toward Munich, but all of the horses are accounted for.

Dr. Müller panics. He suggests they hunt the lake, as well.

Not long after, a footman shouts, "His hat! His hat! I've found the King's hat!"

The search party convenes near the water's edge, about a half mile from the castle. The men wade into the water and find Gudden's coat. One feels something uneven beneath his foot and discovers Gudden's hat, too, half buried in the mud.

Soon after that, they find the King's coat on the shore. "It seems this was taken off in a hurry. The jacket is still inside and the sleeves are turned inside out."

"They're drenched, though. He must have gone into the water and *then* taken the coat off? That doesn't make sense."

"But it was raining."

"Not hard, though."

Another guard shouts from a bench nearby. "There's an umbrella here!"

Some servants have dragged a rowboat into the water, and Dr. Müller and a guard climb in. Almost immediately they see a shadowy figure floating in the reeds and row closer. They fumble to flip the body over, their eyes trained on the face.

What they see, before the body slips from their grasp, are the whites of Ludwig's eyes, his mouth stretched into a howl.

The men struggle to haul the King into the boat, his feet stuck in the stones lining the shallow water.

Another orderly calls out. Nearby, fixed in a seated position, his back underwater, but his vacant eyes gazing up at the stars, is Dr. von Gudden.

"What does his watch say?" Müller calls.

The orderly lifts Gudden's wrist and shouts, "Eight p.m."

Müller tries to work through what the time could mean, but he can't focus as the gravity of the event washes over him.

They lay the bodies of the King and his doctor side by side on the shore. The orderlies work to revive the men, but their efforts show no results. At midnight, Müller formally pronounces the King and his doctor dead.

In the lamplight of the main hall, the examiners can see that Gudden's face shows several scratches and a sizable bruise over his right eye. A deep gash on his forehead weeps a gluey scarlet. Dr. Müller scans slowly down the body looking for evidence of what might have happened. When he arrives at Gudden's right hand, he finds a nail nearly torn off.

On Ludwig, though, he finds no clues whatsoever. The King's body is unmarred. The pocket watch in Ludwig's waistcoat pocket reads 6:54, an hour earlier than Gudden's.

Müller fills out the death certificates. On Gudden's he writes that the doctor drowned. On the King's, he leaves the cause of death blank. A death mask and a cast of the King's hands are made before they lay him out in his bedroom.

Insult to Injury

✳ ✳

S ISI'S OLDER DAUGHTER, Gisela, arrives to breakfast. Her usually sunny face is bloated. Sisi's stomach drops. Valerie sets down her fork.

"I must see you alone, Mama," Gisela says.

"Ludwig is dead," Sisi replies. There is no other reason for Gisela to be there. "Your father-in-law inherits the throne then. Luitpold? And your Leopold is then heir apparent. You'll be a queen after all. Are you crying tears of happiness?"

Gisela collapses into a chair, heaving.

Only Sisi could manage such coldness in this moment.

A Shadow

✳   ✳

A CARRIAGE TRANSPORTS LUDWIG'S BODY to Munich. As it moves through town, the people of Berg toss flowers and wreaths in its path as tribute. Their shoulders ache from having spent the day before rowing around the lake, trying to make sure that their King wasn't being mistreated, ready to risk everything and whisk him away to their cottages, if that's what he asked of them.

The carriage passes Fürstenried, where Otto watches from a window.

He has been informed of his brother's death and of the way his rule has been passed onto Luitpold, but neither piece of news appears to have any effect on him.

On the evening of Whitmonday, Ludwig's heart is removed and sent to the Chapel of the Miraculous Image in Altötting, the "heart of Bavaria," where it's placed in a silver vase alongside twenty-seven other urns containing Wittelsbach hearts. His body is dressed in his most formal uniform: the costume of the Knights of Saint Hubertus. He is laid into a casket for viewing in the Old Chapel, housed in the Residenz. His left hand is placed on the handle of his sword. A bouquet of jasmine from Sisi is nestled into his right. The casket lies on a frame covered in lush ermine robes. Servants drape the chapel walls in black as they did the pianos when Wagner died, just three years before.

The visitors lean in to get a look at their King as they say their goodbyes. One man says to another, "He doesn't look like any drowned man I've ever seen."

Another: "Time has made the King nearly unrecognizable."

Flags fly at half-mast. Church bells toll, reminding people to pray for Ludwig's soul.

On Saturday, June 19th, eight white horses pull Ludwig's hearse through the sunny streets. People flock the route to the church as Ludwig's favorite horse follows close behind, outfitted in its own mourning costume. Behind the horse walks Prince Luitpold, anxious and unwelcome.

The service at St. Michael's is brief. Monks carry the casket down the stone stairs to the crypt below the nave.

The Queen has a wooden cross installed in the lake to mark the spot where Ludwig breathed his last.

A week after Ludwig's death, 250,000 marks are mysteriously withdrawn from Bismarck's Reptile Fund.

Familiar Phantoms Rise Again

✳ ✳

Sisi tells her niece Marie that Ludwig visited her in the night. "The moonlight made the room bright as day. I watched as the door slowly opened and Ludwig came in. His clothes were heavy with water, dripping little pools on the parquet floor. His wet hair was plastered round his white face, but it was clearly Ludwig, just as he had looked when he was alive. We stared at one another in silence and then the King said, 'Are you afraid of me, Sisi?'

"'No, Ludwig, I'm not afraid.'

"He sighed. 'Death has brought me no rest, Sisi.'

"'How am I to know that I am not dreaming?' I asked him.

"Ludwig approached my bed, and the coldness of the grave gave a chill to the air. 'Give me your hand,' he said.

"I stretched out my hand and his wet fingers enclosed it. At that moment, I cried, 'Oh, Ludwig, pray with me that you shall have your peace.' But while I was speaking the figure disappeared."

Marie tries to comfort Sisi, but after this, the same dream haunts Marie's sleep, too.

Or...

❋ ❋

FOR EVERY PERSON ACQUAINTED WITH LUDWIG there exists a theory as to the cause of his death.

Holnstein believed it must have been Bismarck who had Ludwig assassinated, fearful that the King might reveal the payments he'd received to sign the Kaiserbrief.

The servant Alfonso wondered if Lutz might have done it, to prevent a civil uprising by those insisting that Ludwig was in his right mind.

The police chief examined the diagram he made of the footsteps beside the lake again. He believed Ludwig entered the lake first, followed by Gudden. Gudden must have collapsed in the struggle, perhaps from a heart attack or a strong blow to the head, the one that caused that deep bruise above his eye. Then the King must have attempted to swim out across the lake, but the water grew too deep too fast. Both men drowned and their bodies washed toward shore, their shoes leaving trails in the mud. He convinced himself that it made sense that they would both wash up in the same shallows.

Dürckheim believed the carriage tracks outside the front gate must have been someone trying to rescue the King.

Hesselschwerdt believed the tracks were those of an assassin, hired to kill Ludwig, and forced to kill Gudden, too.

Sisi believed Gudden must have carried a rag soaked with chloroform. Ludwig made a break for the water and Gudden tried to force him into submission. The exertion of dragging Ludwig back to shore was too great for the old doctor.

Dr. Müller couldn't believe that Gudden would be party to regicide. Murder had never come up in their discussions.

Lutz believed Ludwig must have bashed Gudden on the head with the umbrella and drowned him, and then drowned himself shortly after.

One of the searchers that night told friends that he saw Ludwig dive into the water and start swimming for a boat before his body seized up and stopped moving. He turned in this statement to the police, but nothing came of it. When he returned to the station months later, the officers pretended they didn't know what he was talking about. They told him the night was far too dark and stormy for him to have seen what he claimed he saw.

The doctor who had assisted in Ludwig's autopsy, unable to bear it any longer, confesses to his priest that the officials insisted he report Ludwig drowned, but the doctor had seen a bullet hole in the King's back.

Warning Signs

✳   ✳

SISI CANNOT BEAR TO REMAIN on the Würmsee and spends the rest of the year in Vienna. The mystery of her cousin's death is enough to keep her close. Despite his ghost having visited her, despite her having a theory about how he must have died, she remains uncertain as to whether he is actually dead. She believes it might still be possible that he finds her and knocks on her door, asking that she hide him from the world.

Sisi writes letters to him in the form of poems, hoping she might draw him back to his earthly life. She asks for Heine's guidance in formulating the strongest spells, but Ludwig does not return again.

Later that year, another one of Sisi's fears comes true: Franzl informs her that Valerie has broached the idea of marrying her cousin Franz Salvator.

"It's best I didn't hear this news from her. The older Valerie gets, the more I see that she is, in love and consequence, stupid, and I'd certainly tell her as much." Sisi knows she cannot be the one to delay the marriage of another one of her children, but that doesn't mean she needs to be happy about it.

For Franzl's fifty-seventh birthday at Ischl, Sisi allows Franz Salvator to sit between her and the skeptical Valerie. Surely this is too good to be true. Sisi must be up to something.

As they are seated, Sisi says to her daughter's love interest, "If I were to die today, my mind would be perfectly at rest at the thought of leaving Valerie to you, but there is no denying that you are a robber to have stolen her heart so easily." Sisi doesn't smile.

Valerie takes his hand below the table, to reassure him that this qualifies as a compliment from her mother.

"Have you any journeys planned?" he asks Sisi, knowing that this and horses are two of the only topics that might genuinely engage her.

"I'm going to Greece on a tour that follows the path of *The Odyssey*. It is my hope that I'll find a place to retire in my old age."

"That sounds lovely for you and the Emperor," Franz Salvator says, but Valerie squeezes his hand tighter and shakes her head.

Sisi returns from Greece before Christmas, having found what she had been looking for on Corfu: a villa, perched high on a hill above the coast, perfect for taking in the watercolor sunsets. But this is her secret for now.

At the dinner table, Sisi sees all of her brothers and sisters. She should be happy, she realizes. She should appreciate all of them having made the trip, but instead she focuses on the way even her youngest siblings have faded with age. All of the people whom Sisi loves are here—the ones who have managed to stay alive this long, at least—laughing together, and trying to tease out the stories of her recent travels, but Sisi feels the most alone she's ever been.

Franzl is distracted by a letter that's gone unanswered by Katharina Schratt. He'd written her saying they should stop their affair, hoping she might argue against the decision, but no response has arrived.

Queen Victoria has just bestowed upon Rudolf the Order of the Garter at her Golden Jubilee, but no one in the family seems to care. With no reward for good behavior, he refills his glass of arrack to wash down another tablet of morphine.

At the next ball, Sisi's niece Marie Larisch wears the Worth dress she's accepted as a bribe to put in a good word about Baroness Vetsera's daughter with the families of the upper echelon of eligible bachelors. Marie is looking to cause a bit of trouble, though, and, gossiping with Rudolf, out of earshot of Stephanie, Marie points to Mary Vetsera, a curvaceous girl with heavy-lidded eyes and a knowing smirk. "I hear she's interested in coming to *know* you."

Rudolf lifts his sleepy eyebrows and excuses himself to approach the young woman.

Before long, Stephanie again knocks on the door of the Emperor, who admits her, but warns her that he only has a minute in the midst of the constant barrage of his appointments. He is accustomed to Stephanie's disturbances, and he is tired of the interruption, always for the least little things, which seem of the utmost importance to her.

"I am married to your son, and my allegiances, of course, lie with him, but I have concern for his well-being, as well as for my own at this point, and you are the only one to whom I would betray his trust."

Franzl deigns to set down his pen.

"Last night, as he has each night for over a week, Rudolf begged me to join him in a suicide pact. He has asked that we pick an evening in which we will both take our lives, so that we might be joined together in death as we are in life."

Franzl pauses, sees the tears forming in Stephanie's eyes, but he picks up his pen again. "Don't give way to your fancies, girl."

"Please do something," Stephanie begs.

"There is nothing wrong with Rudolf, and even if this story you tell is true, he will never act on such a suggestion. He is merely bidding for your attention, which you owe him. If he has a problem it is that he goes out too much, and that is a result of your not doing a good job making home a place he'd like to stay. Do your work and he will calm himself." The Emperor judges most harshly in others what it is he doesn't like about himself.

The Emperor and Empress spend the end of the summer of 1888 in Ischl. The Emperor works in the day and they visit with one another in the evenings. All in all, they are surprised that they enjoy this time together for once.

Despite the comfortable summer they spend together, Sisi tells Franzl she still plans to go to Corfu in the fall.

Franz accepts that his wife will never change. "I hope you will think often of your boundlessly loving, sad, and lonely little one." He tries to take her hand, but Sisi pulls back.

"You know I don't enjoy when you make yourself so pitiable."

The Villa Braila is small and quaint. Sisi studies Greek with a local professor. She sails now, instead of riding, going out in even the roughest weather.

King George of Greece orders a road constructed to her villa so he might visit, but when Sisi is informed the King has arrived, she declines to grant him an audience.

In November, word arrives that Sisi's father has died. Her companions are shocked to see her express sorrow. "I neglected him, Ida. It's unpardonable the way I failed to cherish such an unusual and charming man, responsible for so much that I hold dear."

Ida thinks that the Duke's charm had been mostly based in his irresponsibility, but she doesn't mention this.

For once Sisi attends a funeral.

At Christmas, Franzl, Sisi, Rudolf and Stephanie, Gisela and Leopold, Valerie and her new fiancé, Franz Salvator, and all of the grandchildren go around the table asking questions: What is your earliest memory? Would you rather lose the ability to see or hear? If you had to choose between strudel and pretzels, which would it be?

When the turn comes around to Rudolf, he looks into his lap for a moment, as he mumbles, "How would you like to die?"

The family sucks in air and Stephanie laughs. "Darling, what a funny joke! You've such a dark sense of humor. I've got one," and she poses a different question as Rudolf excuses himself.

Back in his apartment, Rudolf fondles his miniature pistol, spinning it about his finger, considering whether he is truly as ready to move on from this life as he keeps telling himself he is.

Instead he walks to the home of a young woman named Mitzi, one of the few he likes enough to visit more than once. She is returning from a celebration with friends. He grabs her arm and forces her inside, desperate.

"I can't die alone," he tells her. Her apartment is small and dirty. Though she no longer dances, it still smells of sweaty petticoats and camphor.

"You won't. You have Stephanie," she says, confused. "And besides, you're not dying."

"But I am. I am so close to death, it's terrifying."

At this moment, Mitzi's confusion changes to fear. "Rudolf—"

"Mitzi, I need you by my side when I fire this gun." He pulls the tiny pistol from his pocket, and the young woman tries to wrest herself free.

"Rudolf, I'm flattered, but I can't. It's Christmas. Sing a carol with me." She guides him to the tiny sprig of a fir tree propped in the corner of her room, and sits them down as she begins a chorus of "O Tannenbaum" through her shaky breath. Her voice lulls Rudolf, who lays his head on her breast and falls asleep, and in this way, Mitzi sits all night wide awake with her attempted murderer in her lap, this outcome the only gift she wants this year.

After Rudolf leaves, Mitzi tidies herself and goes to the

police station. The policemen are used to such claims. They have a form already drawn up for her to guarantee she will not spread the story.

Stephanie confronts Marie, trying to gain insight into her husband, but Rudolf's cousin defends herself. "Your Highness, your husband and I exchange only the friendliest of gestures, a passing flirtation, for which I do apologize, but it is the Crown Prince who initiates such endearments and I respond in suit only to be polite," Marie says. She's careful to speak in the present. No need to return to the past. "I do think you should keep your eye on Mary Vetsera, though. She is a girl with plans."

"Mary Vetsera?" Stephanie asks. "You mean the girl with all the jewels?"

"Ha! Everything at once, right? All that glare helps to hide the fact that her face is not much to remark on."

"How did Rudolf get mixed up with her?"

Marie Larisch won't admit that she introduced them, of course. "Hanging out with the wrong crowd, I suppose."

On January 29th, 1889, the Prince attends a party at the embassy with Stephanie. Mary Vetsera is in attendance, too, sticking close by the side of her mother, who has forbidden Mary from further fawning over the Prince. "He is not eligible, Mary. The more you consort with him, the less marriageable you are. Your brother and sister will suffer the consequences of your ill-guided actions, too."

But Mary feels something real between herself and Rudolf. She knows Rudolf's marriage will never be dissolved, and so she stands no chance of marrying him. She must prove her devotion in another way.

Marie Larisch corners Mary in the bathroom. There is something alive in Mary tonight that wasn't there before. "What is it? Have you some good news?" Marie's mind clicks into horrified focus. "You're going to do it, aren't you?" she asks.

Mary only smiles.

"A spot in history as a dunce isn't worth your life."

When the guests line up to bow and curtsy their good-byes to the Prince and Princess, Mary looks Stephanie defiantly in the eye.

At noon the following day, Sisi's Greek lesson is interrupted. Ida can hardly control her tears, but she knows she must. "Rudolf's been found dead at Mayerling."

Sisi remains silent, waiting for more.

Ida forces the next part. "He was not alone."

"Why would Stephanie not call someone for help?"

"I mean that there was another *body*. Mary Vetsera."

Sisi recoils. "The tramp poisoned him. I knew his bad taste would catch up with him."

Ida can't summon the will to contradict the Empress. "The Emperor isn't aware yet, and we believe the news should come from you."

Sisi has yet to shed a tear, a champion of nerves only in moments of crisis. "Of course. Shall I go now?"

"He is coming here." They hear his footsteps approaching.

"Let the Emperor in and may God help me now."

Ida closes the door behind Franzl. Only a single cry of

refusal is heard in the hall and the rest muffles itself in grief.

When the door opens, the Emperor stumbles down to his office, an empty shell.

Sisi summons Valerie. Upon seeing her mother's face, Valerie asks, "Rudolf has killed himself?"

"What on earth are you talking about?" Sisi asks. "He was poisoned by that little tart he was bopping around with."

"You haven't talked to Stephanie, then."

"What do you mean?" Sisi asks. "She hasn't been informed yet."

"Good God, Mother," Valerie replies.

When Stephanie is summoned, even she remains composed, though. "Rudolf?"

Sisi's face screws up in confusion. "Yes."

"Has he killed himself?"

Sisi bangs her fist against the table. "Why does everyone keep asking that?"

"I tried to warn the Emperor, but he wouldn't hear it. Rudolf was obsessed with the idea. He asked me if I might join him. I'm surprised he had the courage to do it alone."

Valerie chokes on her tea. "He didn't, I'm afraid."

This is what causes the tears to well in Stephanie's eyes. "Who?"

Valerie chokes out, "Mary Vetsera."

Stephanie excuses herself.

When the court physician arrives to Mayerling to inspect the scene, he notices first the revolver on the floor. The pair lie on the bed, blood bloomed behind their heads.

Mary's long tresses cover her breasts and a rose has been placed on her pubis.

"Rudolf most certainly took his own life, and judging by the temperature of their bodies, and the condition of their blood loss, he a good seven to eight hours after her."

"Disgusting. Sitting here with her body, trying to summon his courage to join her. A coward," the detective replies coldly.

Five letters are found, none addressed to the Emperor. Franzl reads Sisi's letter instead. "I know quite well I am not worthy of being the Emperor's son." Franzl is devastated that this is a thought his son took to the grave.

In the Heart

✳   ✳

For two days, the body of Mary Vetsera sits in an unused storage room at the local police station, an afterthought while the Prince's body is tended to.

Late that Thursday night, Mary's two uncles arrive and dress her in a fur coat and hat. They prop her in the carriage beside them, and begin the journey to a monastery. Her uncles have had to do some bribing to find a place that will agree to bury a mistress dead by suicide.

On the rocky, frozen road the two uncles retch, surprised at the failure of their constitutions, as the body bounces between their shoulders, pitching forward. Her hat falls off, revealing the oozing wound. Mary, once so diabolical, now seems an innocent worm of a person. They pity her and themselves.

The priest who meets them at the door leads them to the rough coffin. They try to place her as delicately as possible, but the shape of the box is not intended for a woman so short and curvy, and so they must bunch the fur coat around her waist to accommodate her generous hips. She looks scrunched, and these men have no talent for the arrangement of the dead. They don't bother to close her single open eye before placing the lid on the casket.

The priest muddles through a well-memorized sermon. He reveals that there is no groundskeeper on staff, that the other brothers of the monastery have dug the hole in the frozen ground, so the uncles lower the coffin down, but a strap breaks, and the box wedges itself in the plot askew. One tries to kick at it to get it to fall the rest of the way, but eventually they give up and shovel the dirt on top of the casket as is.

In Rudolf's postmortem, the doctor makes a generous revision. "His Imperial Highness shot himself in a moment of mental derangement."

This note is enough to ensure the Prince a Christian burial.

Franzl responds to the countless condolences himself. "I can find no words warm enough to express how much I owe to my dearly beloved wife during these sad days, and what a great support she has been to me." The Emperor knows Sisi is not viewed as the most compassionate or supportive woman, but all the years of her detachment are made up for in this time of trouble. Sisi does not mention that she recognizes in Rudolf's actions echoes of her own instincts to escape. She doesn't speculate on the fact that both she and Franzl contain the Wittelsbach blood, of how the dose they delivered their son was an exponent of their own. Instead she consoles Franzl, who, considering the iron constitution with which he has ruled, has always felt more deeply and displayed his emotions more plainly than his wife.

———

The only family members to attend the funeral are Franzl and Gisela. Sisi waits five days, and then—after the rest of the house has gone to bed—she dresses herself in the simplest mourning attire: a gown she can button herself and a veil. She slips out a side door and walks to the Capuchin monastery.

When the prior answers the bell, he is shocked at who he finds on the other side of the door. "I don't recommend visiting alone, Your Majesty. It is cold and dark in the crypt."

Sisi insists.

The prior wakes several of the other monks so they might light the torches. The scent of the flowers leads the way to the vault.

The prior waits at the entrance so he might later see the Empress out, listening to her call her son's name between sobs.

When Sisi retraces her steps, following the dimming torches, she nods to the prior. "My apologies for any sleep you have lost tonight."

"It is an honor to serve you," the prior says. "Allow one of the brothers to escort you home."

"No, I have time enough to walk before the sun rises," she replies, and the prior watches her lightning-fast steps carry her away.

Sisi, Franzl, and Valerie travel to Budapest to escape the rumors about Rudolf. Gyula Andrássy, despite his body's being racked with cancer, makes the trip to deliver his condolences in person. "Your Imperial Majesty, there is no woman like you on earth. The thing that grieves me is that so few people know you for what you are. It is a boon that they love you so devotedly, but they love their version of you, and if they knew the real you, they should love you all the more, as such a rare personality deserves. But I console myself with the thought that I am one of the fortunate few who do. My sympathies, you know, are with you now more than ever." He bows, taking her hand, uncertain he will have the strength to right himself again, but he does, for her.

In July of 1890, Valerie marries Franz Salvator. At the back of the church, Sisi tells her daughter, "I cannot understand how people can look forward to marriage so much and expect so much good to result from it. Really, your marrying today is just the latest in this long parade of deaths of those I love."

Valerie wouldn't expect any less of her mother on her wedding day.

Valerie invites Sisi to see her at her new home in Lichtenegg. Sisi knows no way to refuse, and so promises a short visit. She is surprised to find an atmosphere that resembles her childhood at Possenhofen. Valerie can see how comfortable and at ease her mother is, and, generously, asks if she'd like to stay, perhaps indefinitely, but Sisi refuses. "It is because I feel so happy here that I have to go, for a seagull is out of place in a swallow's nest. You will need to come visit me on Corfu."

Valerie and Franz Salvator do just that, but Sisi is self-conscious about the newly finished Achilleon, and she can't help but critique her house as she shows them around. "You know, I picked the motif, but now I wonder if it was in the best of taste," she says, sighing. Porpoises appear on the new porcelain, napkins, hand-printed wallpaper; they're stamped on the handles of the silverware.

Valerie is grateful to have Franz Salvator's hand to squeeze. "It is a *lot* of dolphins."

Sisi agrees with a wince, stung by her daughter's willingness to be honest.

Valerie changes the subject. "Stephanie said that you've declined to visit with Erzsi. She is still your granddaughter, you know."

Sisi absorbs this second knock to her spirits more easily. "The girl reminds me too much of Rudolf. I can't bear to be with her."

"But she is all we have left of Rudolf. We should love her all the more," Valerie argues.

Sisi closes her eyes and touches her forehead. "I hope you'll forgive me if I depart to lie down for a while. A tremendous headache has come on all of a sudden."

"Of course, Mother," Valerie replies.

But the following years show that Sisi's lack of interest in her grandchildren has a broader base than her grief over Rudolf. When she is invited to attend the birth of Valerie's firstborn in 1892, she cannot summon enthusiasm even for her favorite child. In her regrets, she writes, "The birth of another being always seems to me a misfortune. I feel the burden of life so heavily that it is often like a physical pain.

I would rather be dead." The child is named Elisabeth, like all the others. Sisi becomes a great-grandmother twice over in 1895, but she visits neither of the children in their infancy.

Sisi is done with births. She is done with weddings. No more funerals, though she was never very good about attending those. That doesn't mean, though, that people stop dying. She loses her mother. Bay Middleton dies jumping his horse over a fence. After being reunited with her remaining sisters—Sophie, Marie, and Mathilde—on a trip to Paris, exchanging gossip like girls again, Sisi receives word that Sophie has perished in a fire at a charity bazaar, after refusing to leave the blazing stall until all the servants were evacuated. Each time, Sisi is barraged again with "symptoms," and goes to Corfu. It is no wonder that she tires of the Achilleon so quickly. It becomes a mourning house for her—a place to think about all she has lost.

Sisi wanders farther and farther away, to Spain and then to Egypt. She finds new companions and tutors who can keep up with her still athletic pace. Ida accompanies her only on mild, more domestic journeys now. As Sisi's children have grown, and she has increasingly pulled away from her imperial obligations, the Empress has found a way to come closer to the life she imagined for herself. When she is away from Vienna, she feels almost like a regular person, rather than an underperforming deity.

Sisi accompanies Franz to Budapest in the summer of 1896 to celebrate the city's thousand-year anniversary. She writes to Valerie, "To appear again amid all the pomp and splendor of the opening ceremony, exactly the same as the last time I was here with Rudolf, was very sad indeed."

When Sisi wakes the next morning, with a rash on her face, she wonders if she's no longer suited to the climate at this advanced age. She hides in her apartment for the rest of her visit, and the people of Budapest wonder what happened to their formerly doting Queen.

When plans for the Emperor's Golden Jubilee begin to take shape in 1898, Sisi procures a prescription to go farther away for further recovery. Franzl kisses her goodbye, unsurprised that he'll celebrate his fiftieth year as Emperor alone.

In Nauheim, the dust invades Sisi's lungs and the flies swarm her eyes, but even this is preferable to greeting all those people at the Jubilee, to being *seen*. She writes her well-wishes to Franzl, making him promise to visit her in Switzerland at the end of the summer.

In September, Sisi walks along with Ida in the woods outside Caux, Switzerland. Ida reads to Sisi as beggars and peddlers bid to break their concentration. One young Italian man follows closely, and Ida speaks up. "Give us some space, young man."

"Isn't it a ruler's duty to care for those who can't care for themselves?"

"She is not your Empress," Ida counters, and the young man hisses and retreats.

———

The Empress feels well enough to accept the invitation of friends in Geneva, but opts to book passage on a steamer and travel under the old pseudonym the Countess Hohenembs. Sisi stays the night with Ida at the Hotel Beau-Rivage. A telegram from Franzl asks that she notify the police of her presence so that they might keep an eye on her. He has heard that revolutionary activity in Geneva is reaching a peak, but Sisi won't risk blowing her cover. She consents only to allow along her private secretary for protection.

On board the steamer, a little boy who reminds Sisi very much of Rudolf sits on a deck chair beside her, and she produces from her basket cakes and fruits, which he gladly accepts.

When they arrive in Geneva, Sisi actually deigns to try every dish her hostess lays before her. On the menu, she underlines the Timbale de Volaille and the crème glacée à l'Hongroise, and asks that the card be sent to Franzl as proof of her good spirits.

In her corner room, she refuses to close the shutters or curtains, and lies awake, lit bright by the moon, sleepless, reveling, for once, in a feeling of gratitude.

On the morning of the 10th, Sisi leaves the hotel early to pick up some last-minute souvenirs: chocolate for the children and a pocket watch for Franzl.

She sends the secretary ahead of her to hold the boat.

By the time Sisi and Ida get to the quay, it is empty, all

the passengers having boarded and the rest of the town having tucked themselves inside for lunch.

A young man approaches from the other direction. Sisi swears she knows him from somewhere.

"Is that the man who confronted us in the woods at Caux?" Ida asks, but before Sisi can answer, the young man collides violently with her. Sisi drops her parasol and falls backward, her head hitting the dock. Ida screams and the man runs off. A hotel porter from across the street rushes over to lift Sisi to her feet. "Shall we call an ambulance, Madame?" he asks.

"No, no, I'm fine. Only frightened," Sisi says. "Come, we'll miss the boat!" On the other side of the gangway, though, her color fades as her balance gives way. The deckhand grabs her, but Sisi has already lost consciousness.

A panic blooms inside Ida.

The captain arrives to the gangway to tell Ida to take her friend back ashore, so that she might receive medical attention.

"This is the Empress of Austria!" she gasps.

The captain looks at her as though she has lost her mind. "Come again?"

"We are traveling undercover. This is Empress Elisabeth of Austria and she has been attacked."

The captain realizes the woman does bear a resemblance to the faces on the coins he's saved from his travels. He offers his cabin to Ida and the Empress, and Sisi's secretary arrives with a nurse who tells them it would be better to keep Sisi in the open air. The hands carry her back outside onto the deck, as the captain pulls away from the dock.

They splash water on her face, rub alcohol-soaked sugar on her lips, and wave smelling salts beneath her nose, but she opens her eyes for only a moment to ask, "What is it?" A smile plays on her lips before she loses consciousness again.

When the fabric of Sisi's bodice is loosened, they see the stain spreading at her ribs. The nurse knows there is no hope and cannot restrain herself. "The Empress has been murdered!" she cries, the premature declaration drowned out by the noise of the engines. The captain reverses back into the dock and orders Sisi removed.

On a chaise-turned-cot, in a private room off the lobby of the hotel across the street, a doctor hears the rattle in Sisi's breath. Upon inspecting the tiny puncture wound directly into her heart, he tells Ida the only reason Sisi has lived as long as she has was because of the cinch of her bodice.

Ida thinks of the man's face. The *rebel's* face. Yes, he must have been. It is the only answer. Ida had never imagined she would outlive Sisi. For almost thirty-five years, Ida has served in the company of the Empress, and for the most recent two decades, she has had no ulterior motive, dedicated solely to Sisi's well-being. Ida hasn't the slightest idea of what shape the future might now take. She clutches Sisi, mourning what she had made of her life: a single friend.

A priest arrives to administer the sacraments, and if Sisi has a last thought it's that her prayers have been answered. The world will not watch her beauty fade any further.

Franzl is writing Sisi a letter when the messenger arrives. "It is bad news. Your Majesty will not be able to leave this evening, for there is a telegram from Geneva saying that the Empress has been seriously injured."

Franzl assumes Sisi has gotten up to her old riding tricks again, but another messenger enters, with a stunned look on his face.

Franzl takes the letter out of his hand and reads what he already knows to be true: "Her Majesty, the Empress, has just passed away."

The Emperor falls to his chair. "Is nothing to be spared me on this earth?"

Franzl does not even think to ask the cause. He is certain that his wife must have suffered the same fate as their son. She had warned them so many times that she would be the one to decide when she could no longer bear her life.

But within the hour more information arrives to prove Franzl wrong. A disgruntled Italian anarchist confessed, boasting that he had acted alone, and was taken into custody.

Franzl thinks about all of the times he pledged he would die to protect Austria, but in the end it is Sisi who lost her life for the empire. Shame rings behind the drone of grief in Franzl's head as he waits for Sisi's body to be returned to Vienna. At the palace, the window installed in the tripled coffin is slid back so he can see Sisi's face one last time. Engraved on the casket is the title "Elisabeth Empress of Austria" and Franzl requests, immediately, that "and Queen of Hungary" be added beneath. If the Hungarians felt they'd been overlooked after all of Sisi's devoted service, they might risk another revolution. Sisi's tomb is laid in the Capuchin crypt, reunited with Rudolf and little Sophie.

The assassin, meanwhile, is disappointed that Geneva outlawed the death penalty. He writes a letter asking that he be tried under Lucerne law, signing his letter, "Luigi Lucheni, anarchist—and one of the most dangerous." He is denied all the fame and glory he seeks, though, tried as a common murderer instead of a political criminal, condemned to life instead of death. He devotes the next dozen years of his life to writing his memoirs, but when a guard destroys them, Lucheni fixes his belt to the pipe above his bed, giving himself the sentence he believes he rightfully deserves.

On Christmas Eve, Franzl and the children gather. They are accustomed to celebrating Sisi's birthday without her, but they are surprised to find themselves feeling a lightness in each other's company. Sisi always hated her birthday, and now, they can think of her fondly without the complications of her melancholy. They can focus instead on the holiday's joy.

In attendance: Gisela and her husband Leopold, with their sons Georg and Konrad. Her daughters with their husbands, and three grandchildren between them. Valerie and Franz Salvator and four of the ten children they'll eventually produce in a joyful whirl. Even Erzsi is there, Franzl having taken over her guardianship, but Stephanie is nowhere to be seen: always around, but rarely present.

The family decorates their tree with candles and sweets. Parents hoist children to light the flames on the highest branches.

They eat fried carp and Linzer torte. The adults toast with schnaps and the children sip hot chocolate.

Finally, before the children are put to bed, they sing "Silent Night" together, and no one can help but think about Sisi, as they always do, hands joined, but with an open spot left for their matriarch. This year Franzl takes the hand of Valerie, though, and the circle is closed once more.

A Meditation

✳   ✳

WHAT IS LONELINESS? Telling one's story, when no one will listen. Not sharing one's truth out of fear. Letting others dictate one's narrative, none of the versions just right. Attaching oneself to those tales so that one becomes distant even from oneself. Maybe a truly lonely person doesn't even believe they have a story to tell. Loneliness is keenest in the company of others, when comparisons suggest that everyone else is relating to and forming bonds with one another. To lose a friend is to lose an identity—the self defined only by one's relation to that singular person.

To make a connection requires risking rejection. To share a story requires an audience trustworthy enough to receive it. The longer a person remains isolated, the more sensitive they become to potential threats. The longer a story goes untold, the harder it gets to tell.

Long Live the King

❋　❋

ONLY RICHARD HORNIG KNEW Ludwig's truth.
Which was that the King was: nowhere.

Ludwig was a figment. A body in struggle against mind and against society. He was an amalgam, an inconsistency, an illusion when the people made an attempt to reconcile all that they wanted him to be. He was a knot that couldn't be untied. And then he was gone.

But not in the way they thought.

Like the servants sent to scout new kingdoms or rob banks or beg imaginary shahs for money, Ludwig had sent Hornig, too, on a mission. Ludwig instructed Hornig to dress in his tatters and venture to the sheep fields, the villages, the public houses. "Find another Ludwig," the King said, one afternoon in his study.

Hornig hedged. He knew Ludwig was at his wits' end, unreasonable in his desperation about a future he couldn't imagine in any satisfactory shape. The order was not just silly, it was impossible. "No one will be fooled by a doppelgänger, Your Majesty."

"*Your Majesty?* Richard, no need to be snippy. It will work if we do it just right."

"You know I will not leave my wife and children behind," Hornig said with a stern regret. Ludwig's face didn't change. His body didn't falter. Still, Hornig could sense the King's disappointment in the millisecond delay of his response.

"I suggested no such thing."

"Of course. You know my habit of presumption. My apologies. What is it you intend to do should I find this twin?"

"*When* you find the twin," Ludwig corrected. "I think it best I not reveal my intentions to you, for they might stand in your way."

"I mean only: Once I find him, I assume you want me to bring him to you?"

"Yes, preferably alive. I'm sure if you impress on him that he's to receive some honor from the King, he'll come along willingly. Maybe you can pretend to faint or choke and he might save you, and then you will promise a King's reward for his good deed? You'll think of something."

"*Preferably alive.*"

Ludwig stared at the love of his short and tortured life. "I'd get started now. The more faces you look at, the more likely I am to turn up among them." And with that Ludwig departed Hornig's company to take a nap.

The search began in 1885. It took almost a year, but a man who bore a resemblance did turn up. His hair was the wrong color and he was not fat enough. His name was Dumple, and he had a wife and three children. Hornig considered keeping his discovery from the King. Perhaps there was time to find a bachelor who met the necessary requirements. But, in the end, his allegiance to Ludwig was too strong.

Ludwig made it Hornig's job to cultivate the man: convince him he'd look better with black hair that contrasted with his pale skin. Feed him full of schnitzel and beer at the pub. Ludwig said he'd cut back his own intake so they might meet in the middle, but Hornig knew better than to trust the King's willpower and asked for an ample budget to pay for these evenings of camaraderie and rearing.

Hornig grew fond of the man, crude and insufferable as he seemed at first. He knew this would make it harder to separate the man from his family, but this was the job he was tasked to complete and so he pressed on. Hornig talked of matters of the palace. He spoke of Wagner's operas and the construction sites underway, hopeful that anything the man could hold in his head might eventually be useful in convincing the rest of the world that Dumple was the King.

Hornig, keener than Ludwig to the threats being bandied about the cabinet and the court, could sense that the day Dumple would be needed was nearing. He told the King he must know the plan.

"I told you I don't think that's a good idea," Ludwig replied. "You will become less diligent."

"Your Majesty, I believe I have shown you my commitment in my search and enculturation of our subject. I want only to help you when that aid is necessitated, and so"—he actually knelt—"I sincerely beg you to allow me to be your confidant. You cannot bear this burden alone."

Ludwig took Hornig's hand and pulled him up. The King mumbled, wanting to hide his sin in the obscurity of his closemouthed talk, but Hornig urged him to speak up, and the King obliged. "The man, my twin, will not survive this transition of power. It pains me to sacrifice another, but I need time to repent, and it is impossible for me to do so with these stressors and temptations surrounding me. I need to go somewhere where I might cleanse myself of my impurity."

"How will you do it?"

"I will go on one of my night carriage rides. With only the driver. I will tell you where to find us and you will bring . . . the man . . . there—I can't say his name. It is too horrid."

Hornig tried to maintain his decorum, but he could not. A tear dropped from his eye.

Ludwig continued. "You will need to shoot the driver. And then my double. We will dress the body in my clothes and I will put on his. Or maybe you could bring a clean set of your own for me, for, now that I think of it, I would be too haunted by the clothing of a dead man."

Hornig's eyes coursed, but Ludwig would not look at him.

"You will take me away and then I will disappear and the two bodies will be found and I will be absolved of my earthly responsibilities so that I might tend to my heavenly ablutions. You'll never see me again, which will be my greatest regret, but we have always known there was no way for an eternal communion between us, except in our hearts."

Hornig wished Ludwig would look at him, but the King knew too well what he would see. Hornig couldn't stand the coldness of Ludwig's demeanor, the way he had thought this through so evenly and reasonably. "I will shoot Dumple in the face. That way there will be no question," Hornig suggested. Even then, knowing everything, he was hopeful for the King's approval.

"That does seem best." Ludwig nodded.

"When?"

"I will let you know, or you will be able to tell yourself based on circumstance. You have always had a sharp intuition. That is why I love you."

Hornig cracked clear through at these words. They had never said them directly. Despite every action and synonym that had made the feeling plain, this clarity elevated this moment to the sublime.

And then, as always, Ludwig dismissed him.

When Hornig heard that Ludwig had been taken into custody, when he was moved to Berg, down the path from Hornig's own home, Seeleiten, Hornig knew it was time.

He met Dumple at the pub and faked choking on some wurst. He grasped for Dumple's arm, and the doppelgänger hammered on his back until Hornig spat the sausage tidily onto his plate. He promised a reward from the King and then muddled the story by asking Dumple to help him rescue Ludwig from the impudent men trying to steal the throne. Dumple, patriot that he was, didn't hesitate to follow Hornig's lead.

All day and into the evening, Hornig and Dumple rowed paces up and down the coast of the Würmsee along the path, looking for Ludwig. Hornig planned to stage the gambit that he and Ludwig had worked out, but with some minor variations. Hornig knew he might have to kill a few more men, but he had made a promise to Ludwig, and, despite his eccentricities, the charge that Ludwig was not of his right mind was too extreme. The regency was traitorous, plain and simple. Hornig's allegiance was clear.

At last, in the evening, Hornig and Dumple saw the King and his doctor through a small opening in the reeds along the shore. Hornig told Dumple to row as fast as he could and shot the doctor, with Dumple cheering him on. They pulled the boat up to shore and jumped out, just long enough for Ludwig to see his own face staring back at him. "In the back," he said to Hornig, unwilling to watch this mirror image implode, and then Dumple was dead. They redressed Dumple, giving up with the coat and leaving it on shore, and then they dragged the two men into the water, no small task, accidentally scratching and bruising the men's tender, lifeless bodies. The chill of the May lake reminded Ludwig of the ice baths of his youth, and he thought of the way he was never able to shiver off all that they tried to rid him of. Ludwig climbed into the boat with Hornig, and they rowed back to Seeleiten.

When Hornig docked and helped the King out, he pulled the King's face to his own and kissed him and tried to say everything he had always wanted to with the gesture. Ludwig opened his mouth and allowed Hornig in and the two men held one another until, finally, Ludwig turned himself away, and asked if he could have a horse, an apt request from the Stallmeister. It had been years since he had ridden, but Hornig helped to hoist him up, and with that, Ludwig disappeared.

✻   ✻   ✻   ✻   ✻   ✻

To be dissipated on the air,
among the floods of the voluptuous sea,
in the resonance of the aerial waves,
in the universal breath of the All,
drowned, and absorbed;
oh, oblivion, supreme joy.

—Richard Wagner, *Tristan und Isolde*

Acknowledgments

※　※

This book is based on real individuals and events, but it is very much a work of fiction. Many details have been invented. Figures and their actions have been reimagined, consolidated, and manipulated.

I owe a great debt to the writers and researchers who have written about these figures before me, and to the subjects themselves for often leaving records in the form of letters and diaries. That said, many of the figures written about here are well-known for exaggerating and embellishing the facts of their own lives, and so, in a way, this book could be seen as a fiction based on many personal fictions. What follows is an incomplete list of texts consulted in the construction of this book.

Adorno, Theodor. *In Search of Wagner.* Translated by Rodney Livingstone. Verso, 1981.

Blunt, Wilfrid. *The Dream King: Ludwig II of Bavaria.* Penguin Books, 1978.

Braun, Susan Barnett. *Not So Happily Ever After: The Tale of King Ludwig II.* Self-published, 2012.

Bülow, Hans von. *Letters of Hans von Bülow.* Edited by Richard Count du Moulin Eckart. Translated by Hannah Waller. Vienna House, 1972.

Chapman-Huston, Desmond. *Ludwig II: The Mad King of Bavaria.* Dorset Press, 1990.

Cutrer, Emily Fourmy. *The Art of the Woman: The Life and Work of Elisabet Ney.* University of Nebraska Press, 1988.

Francke, Kuno. "The True Germany." *Atlantic Monthly* magazine, Jan. 1, 1915.

Geck, Martin. *Richard Wagner: A Life in Music.* Translated by Stewart Spencer. University of Chicago Press, 2013.

Haasen, Gisela. *Hohenschwangau Castle.* Wittelsbacher Ausgleichsfonds Munich, 2013.

Hall, Gertrude. *The Wagnerian Romances.* John Lane Company, 1907.

Hamann, Brigitte. *The Reluctant Empress: A Biography of Empress Elisabeth of Austria.* Translated by Ruth Hein. Alfred A. Knopf, 1982.

Haslinger, Ingrid, Olivia Lichtscheidl, and Michael Wohlfart. *The Vienna Hofburg: Imperial Apartments, Sisi Museum, Imperial Silver Collection.* Schloss Schönbrunn Kultur- und Betriebsgesellschaft, 2000.

Haslip, Joan. *The Lonely Empress: Elisabeth of Austria.* Phoenix Press, 2000.

Hausler, Wolfgang. *Laxenburg: Franzensburg Castle.* Schnell & Steiner, 2006.

Heine, Heinrich. *Heinrich Heine: Lyric Poems and Ballads.* Translated by Ernst Feise. University of Pittsburgh Press, 1968.

Hill, Thomas C. *Hill's Manual of Social and Business Forms.* Hill Standard Book Co., 1881.

Hilmes, Oliver. *Cosima Wagner: The Lady of Bayreuth.* Translated by Stewart Spencer. Yale University Press, 2010.

Hojker, Gerhard. *King Ludwig I's Gallery of Beauties.* Schnell & Steiner, 2015.

Iby, Elfriede. *Schönbrunn Palace: Guide to the Palace.* Translated by Sophie Kidd. Schloss Schönbrunn Kultur- und Betriebsgesellschaft, 2014.

Ildikó, Faludi. *The Royal Palace of Gödöllő.* Gödöllő Királyi Kastély, 2012.

Koestenbaum, Wayne. *The Queen's Throat: Opera, Homosexuality, and the Mystery of Desire.* Poseidon Press, 1993.

McIntosh, Christopher. *The Swan King: Ludwig II of Bavaria.* Tauris Parke Paperbacks, 2003.

Millington, Barry. *The Sorcerer of Bayreuth: Richard Wagner, His Work and His World.* Oxford University Press, 2012.

Montez, Lola. *Lectures of Lola Montez (Countess of Landsfeld): Including Her Autobiography.* Gilbert, 1858.

Nietzsche, Friedrich. *The Birth of Tragedy and The Case of Wagner.* Translated by Walter Kaufmann. Vintage Books, 1967.

Pfarl, Peter. *The Hapsburgs in the Salzkammergut.* Bonechi Verlag Styria, 1994.

Program for Wagner's *Das Rheingold* at Lyric Opera of Chicago. Performance Media, 2016.

Program for Wagner's *Die Walküre* at Lyric Opera of Chicago. Performance Media, 2017.

Program for Wagner's *Siegfried* at Lyric Opera of Chicago. Performance Media, 2018.

Program for Wagner's *Tannhäuser* at Lyric Opera of Chicago. Performance Media, 2015.

Ross, Alex. *Wagnerism: Art and Politics in the Shadow of Music.* Farrar, Straus and Giroux, 2020.

Rutland, J. W., editor. *Sursum!: Elisabet Ney in Texas.* Self-published, 1977.

Schmid, Elmar D., and Gerhard Hojer, editors. *Linderhof Palace: Official Guide.* Bayerische Schlössverwaltung, 2006.

Schmid, Elmar D., and Kerstin Knirr, editors. *Herrenchiemsee: Museum in the Augustinian Monastery, Royal Palace, King Ludwig II Museum.* Bayerische Schlössverwaltung, 2007.

Seymour, Bruce. *Lola Montez: A Life.* Yale University Press, 1996.

Shaw, George Bernard. *The Perfect Wagnerite: A Commentary on the Nibelung's Ring.* Dover Publications, 1967.

Smith, Matthew Wilson. *The Total Work of Art: From Bayreuth to Cyberspace.* Routledge, 2007.

Steinberg, Jonathan. *Bismarck: A Life.* Oxford University Press, 2011.

Stephens, I. K. *The Hermit Philosopher of Liendo.* Southern Methodist University Press, 1951.

Taylor, Bride Neill. *Elisabet Ney, Sculptor.* The Devin-Adair Company, 1916.

Till, Wolfgang. *Ludwig II, King of Bavaria: Myth and Truth.* Translated by Justin Morris. Brandstätter, 2010.

Unterreiner, Katrin. *Sisi: Myth and Truth.* Brandstätter, 2015.

The Victrola Book of the Opera. 6th ed. Victor Talking Machine Company, 1921.

Von Wallersee-Larisch, Marie Louise. *Her Majesty Elisabeth of Austria Hungary: The Beautiful, Tragic Empress of Europe's Most Brilliant Court.* Doubleday, Doran & Company, 1934.

——. *My Past: Reminiscences of the Courts of Austria and Bavaria; Together with the True Story of the Events Leading Up to the Tragic Death of Rudolph, Crown Prince of Austria.* G. P. Putnam's Sons, 1913.

Wagner, Richard. *The Art Work of the Future and Other Works.* Translated by W. Ashton Ellis. Bison Books, 1993.

Whobrey, William, editor and translator. *The Nibelungenlied with The Klage.* Hackett Publishing Company, 2018.

Wrba, Ernst, and Michael Kühler. *The Castles of King Ludwig II.* Translated by Ruth Chitty. Stürtz, 2013.

I am sincerely thankful to the people who have championed this book throughout its gestation: First, to my agent, Claudia Ballard, for believing in the project when it was the messiest of ideas pretending to be a draft. Next, to its first editor, Emily Bell, who gave it a home in which to grow and strengthen. Finally, to the dynamic and attentive editorial team of Daphne Durham and Lydia Zoells, who patiently read many versions and helped to shape and sharpen the work in major ways.

I also owe great thanks to Amanda Goldblatt and Amelia Gray for reading drafts and helping me to see more clearly what I was making.

Much of the work for this book was done in the supportive environments of artist residencies, and I am thankful for the time and community of those spaces: the Thicket Residency, the Vermont Studio Center, the Virginia Center for the Creative Arts, HALD: the Danish Center for Writers and Translators, the Oberpfälzer Künstlerhaus, and the Ragdale Foundation. I am grateful to St. Lawrence University and the University of California San Diego, among other schools, for providing me employment around which I could make this work.

Thank you also to the rest of the team at FSG. Gratitude to Claire Tobin for her support in helping the book find its audience and to Brianna Fairman for ushering the book through the final stretch of its creation. Thanks to Greg Villepique, Chandra Wohleber, Andrea Monagle, and Bri Panzica for helping to clarify and correct this text in its final stages. And thanks to the countless others who have provided additional support. I want to express my immense gratitude also to independent booksellers and librarians for keeping literature alive.

I feel very lucky to have an incredible community of supportive family and friends, too numerous to name, but special thanks are due to Rich and Cheryl Jemc; Jenny Mierisch and family; the Larson and Vrooman families, especially Judy and Kate; Lauren Haas; Cindy Hill and Bob Jemc and family. There are countless others who deserve thanks here, but will go unnamed, and I hope I might be forgiven for that.

My greatest debt of gratitude is to Jared Larson, who listens to me and encourages me and makes me laugh and gives me unlimited space and time. I love you and thank you.

A Note About the Author

Jac Jemc is the author of *The Grip of It*, *My Only Wife*, *A Different Bed Every Time*, and the story collection *False Bingo*, which won the Chicago Review of Books Award for fiction, was a Lambda Literary Award finalist, and was long-listed for the Story Prize. She teaches creative writing at the University of California San Diego.